GRUESOME DISCOVERY

Paul stepped into the narrow divide between the trees. A scratch of a trail descended, and leafless branches threatened to claw his face. The footpath wound down further, then opened into a large dell encloaked by trees. Paul noticed steam. . . .

He couldn't see much, but he could see enough. A faint stench drifted up in the biting cold air. *Bags,* he realized.

A pit had been dug out of the dell, and the pit was full of large, stuffed, plastic garbage bags. And the two bags nearest the top wafted steam.

Paul climbed down.

His fingers, like cold prongs of stone, tore open the uppermost bag.

Paul gazed down. Focused. Then gasped.

His feet took him briskly back up the narrow, tree-lined trail. His heart raced, and his eyes, even if he closed them, refused to release the image.

The bag he'd torn open had been full of steaming human body parts.

THE CHOSEN

Edward Lee

PINNACLE BOOKS
Kensington Publishing Corp.
http://www.pinnaclebooks.com

For Jasmine Sailing

The author, though in debt to many, would like to particularly thank the following cool people: Adele Leone; John Scognamiglio; Doug Clegg; Jack Ketchum; and Chara Mattingly (for all the great names!).

PROLOGUE

Zyra withdrew the ice pick from the man's throat. Her big eyes widened, sparkling. She loved to watch them bleed out.

"Ooo, lover," she whispered. "That's sweet."

The naked body thrashed between her legs. Zyra leaned over and pinned him down, to watch his death throes more closely. Each raving beat of his heart emitted a thin jet of blood from the puncture, most of which shot up onto her breasts. She'd timed it just right—she liked irony: the points of three matrixes all touching at the same precise moment. It seemed to give the deed more meaning. It seemed to give it truth.

"Come on, baby," she'd said earlier when they'd come in. *A dump,* she thought, glancing around. Lamplight blazed to reveal smudges on the walls; the room smelled of grease and old fried food. From a dark velvet portrait, Elvis sneered.

The redneck burped, fascinated as he pawed her impeccable physique. Zyra kicked out of her jeans, peeled off her top, and then hauled his pants off. She felt excited and hot. She straddled him right there on the tacky do-it-yourself carpet tiles.

"That's right, baby. You just lay back and let Zyra make you feel *real good.*"

He beer-burped again, struggling under her to get out of his flannel shirt. Crooked teeth showed through his grin as he looked up. "You shore got yourself one hell of a killer bod, hon."

Killer bod, she reflected. She could've laughed.

"Oh, yeah . . . yeah," the guy began blabbering; Zyra promptly reached around and inserted him into herself. *Not very big,* she lamented. In her line of work, of course, she was used to much bigger, but he'd do. This was business, after all.

Her spread buttocks slid down, deepening the meager penetration. She thought of riding motorcycles as she leaned forward and ran her hands over his hairy, fat-layered chest.

"Good gawd, hon." His eyes bulged in ludicrous ecstacy. A ball of lint filled his navel. "You shore's shit feel good. Ain't had me a scrap like this in a coon's age."

A coon's age? She massaged his fatty pectorals as though they were breasts, while her own breasts swayed before his stupid, cross-eyed, redneck face. *Poor little lover,* she thought. He wouldn't last long; they never did with Zyra. "That's it, baby, that's it," she cooed.

His big rough fingers fiddled with her nipples. They plucked and pinched. His hips began to tremor; his face looked like a twisted balloon. *Not yet,* she commanded herself. He began to groan. Then—

Now.

Zyra's climax released in a burst of vivid, hot spasms, when she felt the redneck's own climax unleash. *Ooooooo,* she thought.

That's when she jammed the ice pick into his throat.

He attempted to scream but succeeded only in gargling. Zyra smiled and held him down—she was a strong woman. He bucked beneath her like a just-gelded mule. From the tiny puncture, the streams of blood emitted

8

with a considerable velocity—it reminded her of a squirt gun. *Squirt, squirt, squirt,* on and on. This bizarre synchronicity fascinated her: his ejaculation exiting in time with his blood . . .

"Ready for my surprise?" she whispered. This was not a reference to the ice pick—as if that weren't surprise enough!—but just another aspect of her demented lust. Weren't writers always writing about sex and death? Zyra viewed this as a . . . literary pursuit . . . to further her orgasms as uniquely as possible—during the final convulsions of his life.

It seemed thrillingly perverse!

When she was done, she whispered, "Hope it was as good for you as it was for me."

She leaned up. Blood dripped off her nipples. On a silly impulse she placed both hands in the center of the redneck's chest and pushed down once very hard. A thread-thin stream of blood launched out of his throat and shot across the room. *Wow!* Zyra thought. The blood drew a high line along the wall and hit Elvis in the eye.

"I'd love to stay and chat, baby, but I'm afraid it's bye-bye time for you." She jammed the ice pick deep into the base of his skull and jiggled it around. The redneck stiffened once, gurgled a final objection, then died.

Muffled thumps beat from the bedroom. Zyra smiled when she heard the stifled shrieks. Lemi was in there taking care of the redneck's little girlfriend. They'd come onto them at the bar, some frowzy hole called the Crossroads. Peanut shells carpeted the sticky floor; a country and western band ineptly twanged chords from the stage. "We all's swingers," the redneck had offered after the second pitcher of Carling. "How 'bout yawl? Think ya might like ta come back ta our place fer a little partyin'?"

"Sounds good to me," Zyra had said. "Sure," Lemi had said.

9

"And it was plumb one rat nass party," Zyra now mocked. She was always talking to herself, or to dead people. "Thank ya much, yawl." She sauntered nude into the bedroom. Lemi's muscles tensed as he wrapped duct tape around the girl's mouth. He'd already tied her hands behind her back. "Christ, Zy. You sure made a mess of yourself. Get cleaned up, will you? We've got to pop this blow stand."

Zyra shook her head. "It's *blow* this *pop* stand, Lemi. Get your quips right."

He glanced up from the girl's shagged head. "What's a quip?"

So stupid, Zyra concluded. All men were. Her pretty bare feet left scarlet footprints to the bathroom. She showered quickly, turning her face and breasts into the cool spray. "Blub, blub, blub—bye," she gestured, and watched the redneck's blood swirl down the crusty drain.

She put her clothes back on as Lemi inspected the girl, who he'd lain out on the bed. He appraised her meticulously, like a housewife fussing over which melon was the ripest at the Safeway. "Hmm," he considered. He rubbed some of her mousy lank blond hair between his fingers. "What a rat's nest. We're gonna have to do something with this." Then he patted her buttocks. "And I've seen better asses, that's for damn sure."

"Quit complaining," Zyra scolded, buttoning her fancy inlaid blouse. "We're lucky to have her at all."

"And look how skinny she is—Christ!" Lemi turned her over, frowning. "Practically just skin and bones."

"We'll get some meat on her."

"Hope so." He gave one of her breasts a squeeze, and seemed more satisfied. "Decent pair of tits, though, for such a lightweight. Firm" He patted her pubis. "Nice bush, too."

"She'll do just fine, Lemi," Zyra exasperated. "How was she? You tried her out, didn't you?"

" 'Course I tried her out. Not bad. Tight."

Zyra rolled her eyes. "Shit, Lemi, an elephant'd be tight, as hung as you are."

Lemi chuckled. "She was pretty fiesty at first. But once old Lemi boy got in there with the rig—that took the fight out of her and fast. Not a half-bad tumble, as far as girls around here go."

Zyra shook her head again. Men could be such pompous assholes, like having a big dick made them special. Zyra figured Lemi had more brains in his glans than his skull. She took a moment to look down at the girl. Zyra tried to feel sorry for her, but why should she? It wasn't her fault it was a cruel world, was it?

The girl's eyes bulged in terror, her thin chest heaved. She whined beneath the duct-tape gag as Lemi lashed her ankles and rolled her up in the sheets. "Get the stiff," he said. "We gotta . . . blow . . . this . . . pop stand." He scratched his head. "What a dumb quip."

He carried the girl out to the van. Zyra went back into the living room. That was pretty dumb too. Living room? *Dying room,* she thought, smiling. She could still feel a tingle between her long, firm legs.

The redneck looked pallid as jack cheese, now that most of his blood had drained out of him. Zyra picked him up by his ankles, and dragged him like a big bag of leaves out of the bungalow.

The air had some nip to it; winter grew close. An errant breeze braced her, whistling through the trees. Zyra rolled the corpse into the back of the van alongside the girl. Then she slammed the doors shut.

"Start her up." Lemi shivered in his flannel shirt. "I'll take care of the joint."

Hurry up! It's cold! She gunned the van's engine, cranked on some heat. A few minutes later, the secluded little bungalow burst quietly into flames, flooding the grove with wavering orange light and heat. Lemi jogged back out and climbed in. "Let's googie, Zy."

'*Boogie,* Lemi. Let's *boogie—*"

"Googie, boogie, I don't give a shit. Let's go home."

Zyra wheeled the van down the long gravel drive. The flaming house shrank in the rearview, crackling.

Yeah, let's go home. The main road took them toward the mountainside, into darkness, while the darkness took Zyra's thoughts away into a silent, inexplicable joy. *Every end is a new beginning,* she pondered. It made her feel ageless.

"You know," Lemi remarked, "I really like your hair that way. Glazed."

"Not *glazed,* you idiot. *Frosted.*" All she could do was shake her head and smile. It was hard to believe that men, however uniformly stupid, ruled the world.

"I can't wait till things get started again," he said, and relaxed back in the van seat.

Neither can I. The gagged girl in back shrieked in her throat. Zyra paid it no mind. It was a sound, among many others, that she'd long grown accustomed to. As she drove on, she got lost in more personal wonderings. It was a beautiful night. Crisp. Clear as crystal. The stars looked like a smear of luminous, cosmic spillage. There was beauty everywhere, if one looked closely enough. . . .

Every end is a new beginning.

Indeed, this was their lot. They were always ending, and always beginning again.

The moon disappeared beyond the ridge when she turned up the narrow mountain road, toward home.

the offer

Chapter One

The kitchen was a madhouse.

Busboys fought with waitresses over racks of hot silverware. The hostess double-timed, coming in for water glasses and bottles of Evian, while full garbage cans were quickly dragged away and replaced with empty ones. "Get me some clean broil pans sometime this year!" one prep cook yelled. "Eat me!" the beer-bellied dishwasher yelled back. Cute waitresses bustled in and out, lost in the deep concentration of wine-list memory, the specials of the day, and the perpetual balancing act of carrying six entrees on one tray one-handed. "These salads have been up for five minutes!" the cold-line cook yelled. "Get 'em out of here before I start throwing them!" More preps shucked oysters, made hollandaise from scratch, and butchered lettuce heads to bits simultaneously. The swingdoors banged open and closed with equal simultaneousness, flushing the kitchen's hot confines with periodic wafts of cool, reviving air.

It's a madhouse, all right, Vera Abbot thought. She stood at the end of the hot line in a three hundred dollar vermilion evening dress. *But it's my madhouse.*

In a sense it was. The Emerald Room was the best restaurant in town, and Vera Abbot was its queen. A year ago they were lucky to do twenty dinners on a

15

weeknight, now they were doing a hundred plus. It was more than good fortune—Vera had used her foresight, her management skills, and good hiring sense to turn the place inside out. She'd also worked her ass off. The kitchen was like a multipart machine where the failure of one component would shut down the entire works. It was Vera who kept the machine properly tuned. If you wanted the best restaurant in town, you had to find the best people, bring in the best food, and offer the best facility. Vera had done all of that, and had transformed The Emerald Room from a glorified steakhouse to a state-of-the-art dining room.

She walked down the hot line, minding her high heels over the black slipmats. "Ready for the good news?" she asked the bulky figure at their dual Jenn-Aire ranges.

Dan B. jerked his gaze up from a pan of sauteed soft crabs, his tall white chef's hat jiggling. He had every burner going with a different entree, not to mention the prime rib and the duck in the ovens. He smirked at her with a look that said *Maybe it hasn't occurred to you, but I'm kind of busy right now.*

"The governor's liaison just called," Vera announced. "He's bringing in a party of ten in twenty minutes."

"Tell him to go to Burger King!" Dan B. close to yelled. "I'm running eighteen dinners per half hour since seven o'clock, and now he's bringing in his stuck-up cronies? Christ, those guys eat like pigs! Last time they ordered two entrees each!"

"You can handle it, Dan B.," Vera assured him. "You have my absolute and unhesitant faith."

"I don't want your faith," the big chef sputtered. "I could use a raise, though, and while you're at it how about getting me some secondary so I don't have to do the jobs of three men six nights a week. And how about . . ."

16

Vera traipsed off, smiling. A good chef was never happy unless he was complaining. Dan B. was the best chef she'd ever known. No matter how well Vera ran the place, it didn't amount to much unless the orders were superlative every time.

"Hey, gang!" he yelled. "Governor and his fat pals'll be here in twenty! Get ready to bust your humps!"

The entire kitchen released a wave of moans.

Good staff worked best under pressure. The line preps didn't even look up as she passed—they were too busy. Successful staff management involved the maintenance of respect and acknowledgement. Vera had pulled off both. Her employees respected her without fearing her, and they knew that good work would be properly acknowledged. They also knew that bad work would be properly acknowledged too, with a prompt invitation to take their skills elsewhere. Vera had honed The Emerald Room into a model of excellence, and in doing so, its reputation only attracted the most serious to its payroll.

"Would you please get me some clean broil pans!" the hot prep whined again. "You want me to start cooking the fucking fish under my Zippo?"

"You can cook it on my fat ass," yelled back Lee, the dishwasher. His long hair swung in wet strings at his shoulders as he slammed full racks into the machine one after another. Then he rushed to the conveyor exit, madly unloaded the clean dishware, stacked it, and carried it to the shelves. Lee's long hair and tremendous beer gut made him look like Meat Loaf on the skids. Vera dismissed his shortcomings: he drank on duty, griped to no end, waged nightly wars with the cooks—but he was a great dishwasher. Vera pretended she didn't see the carafe of Wild Goose Lager that he'd secreted behind the machine.

"Like I don't have enough to do," he complained to

himself. "You dumb fuckers make all the money and I do all the work. One day I'll put my foot up all of your a—" He paused as if shocked, only then noticing Vera standing by the rack stand. "Oh, uh, hi, Vera. I, uh, I didn't see you there."

"Hello, Lee. Happy at work?"

"Oh, yes ma'am," he stammered, then slipped away to carry more broil pans to the hot prep. Vera could easily put up with his manner. Any guy who would wash dishes all night, steam-clean grease-laden floors, and wade waist-deep in dumpsters—all for six dollars an hour—was worth putting up with.

She passed the coffee station. The kitchen's din faded behind her. Going from the kitchen to the dining room was liken to going from one world to another. Humid heat traded places with cool calm, the racket of the dinner rush gave over to quiet conversation and light Vivaldi from hidden speakers. The maitre d' was expertly pouring Perrier-Jouet for a table of state legislators. A troup of bussers prepared a large banquet table in back for the governor's party. A smug critic from the *Post* meticulously sampled an assortment of appetizers: Oysters Chesapeake, grilled Muscovy duck, Crab Meat Flan, and a tuned-up variation of antipasto. He did not look displeased.

Even this late—9 P.M.—every station was full or close to it. The dining room, in three wings, was well appointed, leaning toward more of a social club ambience; Vera had seen to a complete face-lift when she'd taken over as R.M. Rich gray paneled walls rose to a high, raftered ceiling from which hung a great octagonal chandelier. Tapers flickered from inset cherrywood sconces; well-framed nautical artwork adorned the back walls. Vera had made sure to replace the old steakhouse furniture with real armchairs and oak dining tables. The east windows offered a spacious view of the lit city dock and the bay.

My baby, she metaphored. She stood by the service bar, gazing out into the quiet robotic activity of her employees. This used to be the place where diners came as a last resort, because downtown was booked. Now their weekend reservations extended a month in advance. Since the changeover, The Emerald Room had yet to receive a negative or even mediocre review. Whenever celebrities were in town, this was where they came to eat.

"Vera, you want to hear something strange?"

Glasses clinked. Vera peeked into the service bar. Donna, the night barmaid, talked as she automatically washed, scrubbed, and rinsed a flank of #8 glasses in the triple sink. She'd been hired as a big favor to Dan B. Donna was his wife. Donna was also a reformed alcoholic. Vera took her on with a condition: that she get on the wagon and stay there. "One fall, and you're out," she was informed. That had been six months ago, and Donna hadn't had a drop since. Her return to sobriety had changed the telltale dark circles and pastiness into a fresh vitality. She was midthirties, sort of short and full-bodied. Twin short blond ponytails wagged as she vigorously bent to clean the bar glasses.

"Sure, Donna," Vera answered. "I'd love to hear something strange."

Donna stood up and faced her. Her eyes gleamed. "Someone's been asking about you."

"Let me guess. The county liquor board? The health department? Oh, I know, the feds, right? I knew I should've declared that sixty-cent tip I got last week when we were a waitress short."

"You know that guy Chip, the manager at The Ram?"

"Well, I've known him for about five years, so I guess that means I know him."

"Well, I was talking to him today, and he says this weird guy came in for lunch yesterday afternoon."

"A weird guy. That's not strange in this town."

"So the guy asks Chip what's the best restaurant in town, and naturally Chip says The Emerald Room."

"Naturally," Vera concurred.,

"So then the guy asks Chip who's the best restaurant *manager* in town, and naturally Chip says—"

"Me?" Vera asked.

"That's right. You."

This was obscurely flattering—being touted as the best R.M. in town to "weird guys." But what was the point?

Donna rambled on, "And a couple of hours ago we ran out of ice, so I drove down to McGuffy's to get some, and Doug Harris tells me the *same thing*. The same weird guy went in there for a drink and asked who's the best R.M. in town."

Vera's brow lowered. "What did he say?"

"Same thing Chip said. You."

At least I've got a good rep. Vera asked the next logical question. "Anybody know who this weird guy is?"

"No, no one's ever seen him before. But Doug got his name. It's Feldspar. Ever hear of him?"

"Feldspar? No."

"Doug watched him leave; he parked in front of the Market House." Donna paused for dramatic effect. "He was driving a brand-new red Lamborghini. Doug said it probably cost two hundred grand."

Now Vera felt curious to the point of aggravation. *Lamborghinis? Weird guy?* What was this all about?

Donna raised a soapy finger. She had a way of making a short story long. "But that's not the best part."

Vera tapped her foot, waiting.

"Fifteen minutes ago, a nine-thirty reservation comes in. Want to guess what the name was?"

"Feldspar," Vera ventured.

"Exactly. And he said he wanted an 'interview' with the manager."

Vera understood none of this. "What do you mean? A *job* interview?"

Donna laughed. "Vera, I doubt that a guy who drives a new Lamborghini is going to be looking for work as a busser. He said he wanted an interview, of the 'utmost exigency.' Those were his exact words. I took the call myself."

Utmost exigency. No, he probably doesn't want a job as a busser. "Nine-thirty, you said?"

"That's right," Donna verified. "You've got about ten minutes. Isn't it mysterious?"

"Thanks, Donna." Vera scurried off to the ladies room. Yes, it was mysterious, and she enjoyed mysteries. Was Feldspar an eccentric critic? The Emerald Room got them all the time, but even the most renowned critics didn't drive two hundred thousand dollar cars. Then—

A buyer? she considered. *An investor?*

She hurried to freshen up. She checked her liner, powdered her nose, checked her coiffed, jet-black hair. *Not looking too shabby tonight,* she considered to the mirror. She adjusted the bustline of the low-cut evening dress; its vermilion chiffon gave off a warm, silky luster. Against her bosom glittered a brightly polished amethyst on a gold chain, a Valentine's gift from an old boyfriend. The boyfriend hadn't been worth a shit, but at least the necklace was nice. The stone's crisp deep purple sparkled just right with her gold and sapphire earrings. But when she raised her hand to pat her hair back, a greater sparkle flashed in the mirror. Vera smiled automatically. Her engagement ring was beautiful—Paul had given it to her just last week. It reminded her of something more than what it was: the ring was a covenant, a piece of the future. She held it up, turned it in the bright light and watched it flash like

21

a starburst. Yes, for a moment she knew she could see the future in its sharp-cut facets. The ring, and the bright likeness of herself which faced her in the mirror, reminded her how wonderful life could be, and how blessed.

The valets scrambled. The red Lamborghini purred up into the entry court and stopped. The driver's door didn't open, it *raised*. Then a figure stepped out.

Vera, Donna, Dan B., and Lee watched discreetly from the double doors, peeking through the great front window into the court. "The valets are in the way!" Donna whispered. "I can't see him!" Nor could Vera; she squinted between heads to catch a glimpse but only caught some vague dark shape. Just as vaguely, then, the shape claimed the valet stub and made for the entrance.

"Here he comes!" Donna whispered excitedly.

Lee scratched his beer belly. "Looks kinda short, don't he?"

"And what's that?" Dan B. squinted. "He gotta beard?"

"Come on, gang," Vera complained. "It's no big deal, it's just some rich guy coming to dinner. Let's get back to work."

The group disbanded. Vera remained in the kitchen cove, watching through the swingdoor window. She didn't want to seem presumptuous; Feldspar knew that *she* knew he wanted to see her. Vera figured it was more professional to let the hostess seat him. When time came for this "interview" of "utmost exigency," he would simply have to ask for her.

The hostess led him through the front dining room; Vera could only see his back. Dark suit, an unusual cut. Jewelry seemed to glitter on his hand. And Lee was right: Feldspar seemed short, as well as awkward. He slowly followed the hostess's sleek shape as if walking with some equivocal caution.

No big deal, huh? Vera smiled to herself. *If it's no big deal, how come you're standing here with your face glued to the window?* Once again, the sense of mystery embraced her—it even titillated her. *Who is this guy? What's he want with me?*

The hostess seated him at their best four-top in the window wing. Now Vera could only see him sideways from the rear. Stubby hands opened the menu. Feldspar seemed to study the entree list as if studying technical writing.

Was he disappointed? Let down?

Stop being silly, Vera suggested to herself. She went back to the hot line. Orders sizzled, tempting aromas sifted through the air. Vera looked off as the chef expertly pan-blackened two more orders of aged prime rib on the industrial eleven-inch burners.

"Relax, will you?" Dan B. Said. He spoke as he put an order of baby lamb chops up to go out. "You're turning yourself into knots. Didn't I just hear you say it was no big deal?"

Yeah, Vera thought. "I just hate being curious. What does he want? Why did he ask to see me?"

"He's probably a wine distributor or something. Gonna drop a big check to impress you, then try to cut you a deal on whatever he's peddling."

Maybe. That sort of thing happened all the time; The Emerald Room's wine list was coveted by every wine distributor in the county. Yet, for some reason, Vera felt certain that this was something else.

I'm sure that it is. But what?

She'd kept tabs on him constantly, via the waitress. Feldspar had ordered the Flan and Calamari Italiano for appetizers, the smoked scallops salad, and Veal Chesapeake. He'd also ordered two snifters of Remy Martin Louis XIII, which cost seventy dollars a shot. The waitress had squealed when she'd come back to the kitchen.

"You look like you just won the lottery," Vera remarked.

The waitress giggled. "Almost. His check came to one-eighty. He left me a hundred dollar tip!"

"I must be on the wrong end of this business."

"And Vera. He wants to talk to you now."

"Go get him, killer," Dan B. chuckled.

Lee guffawed behind the dishwash conveyor. "Maybe he's a pimp, Vera. Wants some new stuff for his stable."

Assholes, she thought. Dan B. and Lee's laughter followed her through the kitchen swingdoors. She felt foolish yet enthused. Outside, dinner was winding down. A Corelli violin sonata whispered beneath subtle dining room chatter and clinking coffee cups. In the window wing, a bulky shadow rose in silence.

"Ms. Abbot?" The voice was darkly genteel. A thick hand extended in greeting.

Vera smiled curtly, shook his hand. "You must be—"

"Feldspar," Feldspar verified. "Please. Join me."

Vera took a seat across from him. The table was clear now; a cup of coffee steamed between them. The candlelight seemed to blur her guest's face.

"I apologize for the inconvenience," the figure said. "I realize the hour, and how short time must be for you as the manager of this fine establishment. You *are* the manager, correct?"

"That's right, Mr. Feldspar." Behind him she could see the city's late-night glitter through the window. Moonlight floated shardlike on the bay. It distracted her, making her avert her eyes from the man across the table.

Some manager, she caught herself. Managers were at

least supposed to be interested in the satisfaction of their patrons. "How was your meal?" she asked.

"Preeminent."

Now Vera could see him. He looked . . . *odd,* she evaluated. He seemed wide without being fat. He wore a black pinstripe suit—which looked like very good material—and a black silk shirt. No tie. The large pale face defied calculation as to age; he was old and young at once. His hair, as black as Vera's, appeared oddly pulled back; an eloquently trimmed black goatee rimmed his mouth.

"Indeed," he continued to compliment. "The finest meal I've had in some time."

"That's very nice of you to say. I'm glad you liked it. Would you like anything else? We have a wonderful assortment of homemade desserts."

"Oh, no. No thank you. I'm not much of a sweets person."

The moment held in check. Suddenly Vera felt childlike, looking at him in some kind of canted wonder.

"There's something I'd like to discuss with you," he finally went on. "A matter of—"

"Utmost exigency."

"Yes, yes. A . . . business proposition."

Maybe Lee's right, she wanted to laugh. *Maybe he is a pimp.* Several big rings glittered on his squab hands. A gold cuff link glittered F in tiny diamonds, and about his wrist she unmistakably noted the Rolex.

He must have sensed her distraction. "Forgive me. Of course, this must be a bad time for you. What time are you off?"

Vera fought not to stare at him. She felt certain he hadn't come here to make a play for her. They were strangers. *A business proposition,* she reminded herself, yet still she shivered against the distraction.

What did he say? "I, uh . . . I'm off at midnight."

25

"Fine. Would you care to meet elsewhere, then?" His hooded eyes seemed to recede in some of their gleam. "Or perhaps you'd prefer not to meet at all."

"Oh, no, I'd be happy to," she agreed too quickly. But why had she said that? Why hadn't she first asked what exactly it was he wanted? The thought never occurred to her.

Feldspar nodded. "At your convenience, but of course. I'm afraid, though, that I'm quite unfamiliar with this city. Where would you care to meet? I'll need directions."

She couldn't keep her eyes off the sparkling jewelry on his hands. Her consciousness felt like a split thread, twisting as it unwound. The confusion made her tipsy.

"How lovely," Feldspar remarked.

"Pardon me?"

"Your amethyst." His eyes gestured her necklace. "I've always found it to be the most attractive stone, regardless of price. True beauty must never have a price." Then he turned his hand and showed his own amethyst set into a large gold pinky ring. "Your engagement stone is quite beautiful too."

Now she knew beyond doubt that he wasn't putting moves on her. If this was merely some sexual interest, why acknowledge her engagement?

"Thank you," she eventually muttered. She had to visibly blink to get her mind back on track. What could it be about Feldspar that distracted her so?

"There's a little tavern a block down the street," she said. "The Undercroft. It's quiet and quite nice."

"Excellent. The Undercroft it is." Feldspar rose and strayly straightened a lapel. "I'll see you there at midnight. And thank you very much for giving me the opportunity to talk to you."

Vera didn't think to rise herself. She remained sitting

there, looking up at this finely dressed, and strange, man.

She squinted. "But what exactly is it you want to talk to me about, Mr. Feldspar?"

"A job," he said. "I'd like to offer you a job."

Chapter Two

Research, Paul thought. *Yeah, that's what this is.*
I'm simply an observer.

It wasn't that Paul didn't trust himself—he was just bothered by conventions, by *ideas*. He knew he wasn't going to do anything he shouldn't do, but that did not fully legitimize the fact that he was an engaged man sitting in a singles bar.

Paul was a freelance journalist. Thus far he'd done over two hundred pieces for the area papers. Both the *Sun* and the *Capital* had offered him staff jobs, but Paul had turned them down. He liked to write about what *he* wanted, not some editor. It had been tough at first, real tough—when you were freelance, you were a man without a country. Yet, now, after five years, good writing and good ideas had made not only a name for himself but also a decent living. He liked social pieces, with a twist to give them some zing, some uniqueness. Apparently the papers liked them too; Paul hadn't had anything rejected in several years. In fact, now they were actually paying him before his articles were finished, which was rare in freelance. It was an equally rare complacency: Paul Kirby had beaten the odds and was *making it.*

The Singles Scene: An Existential View. Paul liked the

title. There'd been plenty of pieces on the area singles scene, but they were all fluff. The *Sun* had answered his query by commissioning it as a four-week series. Paul would investigate all of the local singles bars, describe each one, and then make a sociological comment. He didn't just want to see the face, he wanted to look *behind* the face of this notorious chess match between the sexes.

So far he was not impressed.

Maybe he was too philosophical. Was he trying to philosophize something that was really barren of philosophy? *Or maybe I'm too cynical,* he considered. Before his involvement with Vera, he'd dated regularly, but never like this. If you were looking for love, a bar seemed the least likely place to find it. It was like trying to find health food at McDonald's. Paul wanted to catagorize the difference in perceptions—between single men and single women. Here, the men all seemed phony, and the women oblivious. It was a show of veneers of false faces and lust. It depressed him.

Kaggie's, the place was called. It was starting to fill up. Big place. Two long bars, front and back, snazzy decor. The huge sunken dance floor stretched before a giant projection video screen. Above the pit the obligatory glitterball spun slowly, darting lancets of multicolored light. The air beat with music—some technopop bit by New Order, upbeat yet bleak if you listened to the lyrics. Paul felt buried in light, sound, and the motion of busy bodies.

This dump must've cost millions, he reflected. He ordered a Heineken but the keep brought him a Corona out of habit. Paul preferred not to drink beer that had the same name as the end of a penis. *Subliminal advertising?* he wondered and laughed. This place wasn't selling beer—it was selling sex.

Lines: he jotted in his notepad. He'd heard some

doozies already tonight. "Excuse me," a glittery-dressed brunette had asked some tall guy with a black whitewall. "What's a stuck-up, stone-faced asshole like you doing in a place like this?" "Looking to get laid," the guy'd answered without a flinch. Paul had seen them leaving together after a few dances. Here were a few other winners: "Pardon me, but haven't we *never* met before?" And, "Hey, baby, what's the difference between a blow job and a Big Mac?" "What?" "Go out to dinner with me and you'll find out." And the best one of the night—a guy in a blue suit had walked up cold to a girl at the bar: "Hi, my name's Dan Quayle. Can my father buy you a drink?"

But levity aside, Paul felt glum in disillusionment. These places were packed every night; plus, he'd seen many of the same people in a lot of the bars he scouted already. It seemed a way of life for them. How could anyone expect to find a true relationship in one of these dance catacombs?

Now the dj put on The Cure, a song called "Give Me It," which about said it all. The crowd danced happily under the shroud of grim lyrics. Paul considered the dichotomy.

Then he considered himself.

I'm free of all this.

He was. It seemed an absolving realization. What made him more complete than anything else was Vera; his love for her was the last piece of his life fit firmly into place. He looked around him in this den of falsehoods, this den of lies, and knew how lucky he was. Paul had something real; these people didn't.

I'm in love, he thought.

This realization, too, dazzled him. It seemed to purge him of mankind's flaws. Love. Real love. Could there be any greater or more complete truth? He proposed to her only a week ago; she'd said yes immediately. It had

30

been murder waiting, though: they'd been involved for two years but Paul knew in the first week that she was the one. Sometimes you just *knew.* You knew at a glance, you knew in a heartbeat—the essence of real love. It made him feel very grateful, to God, or fate, or whatever.

No relationship was perfect; too often couples failed because one side was left holding the bag of responsibility—one person making all the effort, the other making none. But Paul and Vera had grown *into* each other. They'd each made the effort to overcome life's obstacles. It was almost too easy. That was how he knew it was real—the manner in which their bond had developed. Sometimes he could melt just thinking about her, seeing her in his mind: her beauty, her kindness, her ideals. He could not imagine being with anyone else in the world.

Paul's love made him feel exalted.

"Excuse me. Aren't you Paul Kirby? The writer?"

Paul glanced up. Two women stood to his right, a redhead and a blonde. "That's right," he said. "How did you know?"

"I saw your picture in the *Capital* once," explained the redhead. "I've read a lot of your stuff."

Paul felt distantly flattered; he was not used to being picked out of a crowd, especially in a *bar crowd*. He tried to think of an erudite reply, but some distraction pecked at him. Dots of light from the glitterball roved the redhead's bare shoulders. She wore a short strapless black dress with a sash, black nylons, black heels. A knockout. The blonde looked less formal: a shiny blue blouse and designer jeans. She was slim, wan. Straight white-blond hair had been cut straight just below the bottom of her earlobes. She smiled meekly and said, "The *City Paper* said you were doing some articles on singles bars."

"And that you'd be here tonight," the redhead finished.

"Ah, so you girls came here just to meet me," Paul joked.

"Maybe," the blonde replied.

That was it. That was his distraction. Guilt. Single guy. Singles bar. Two single girls. Subconsciously he felt in violation. *I'm an observer,* he reminded himself, not that he needed to. He knew he wouldn't cheat on Vera under any circumstance—he had no desire for anyone else. It was just the ideal that haunted him. But this was a good thing. He could talk to these girls, try to analyze them for their perceptions. It would make the article better.

"Actually, my name's Dan Quayle," Paul said. "Can my father buy you two a drink?"

The girls laughed and sat down on either side. He ordered them each White Russians, a Heineken for himself, and rolled his eyes when the suspendered barkeep brought him a Corona.

Then the redhead leaned forward, eyes alight, and said, "So, Paul, tell us about your article."

At precisely the same moment, Vera Abbot strode through the entrance of another bar, a small brick-and-mortar tavern called The Undercroft. "The 'Croft," as it was known to regulars, existed quite apart from the downtown hangouts and dance clubs. It was a bar with brains which attracted a specific patronage: beer connoisseurs, artists, writers, academicians, etc., not drunks, floozies, and sex predators. Ceiling rafters sported hundreds of imported beer coasters. Pennants decorated the front walls, from breweries as obscure as George Gale, Mitchell's, and Ayinger. The long polished bar accommodated ten taps, and their inventory boasted over a hundred beers from all over the world. The 'Croft was not a place where one came to drink Bud.

Winter now had its teeth firmly set; Vera nearly shuddered in relief when she entered the 'Croft's warm confines. Here everybody was everybody's friend—almost everyone in the place, staff too, greeted her as she hung up her overcoat. Being here suddenly reminded her of the other less admirable bars in the area, and that reminded her of Paul, and the series of articles he was writing about local singles bars. Part of her didn't like the idea of her fiancé surveying such places on his own, but that was selfish. Jealousy was one of many negative emotions that had never shown its face to their relationship. He was a professional writer; he'd been commissioned to write the series, and he was therefore committed to do so as effectively as possible. His dedication to his work was just more proof of his love. Before, he'd endeavored to be a good writer for himself—now it was for Vera too, and for their future together. She'd never had such easy mutuality in a relationship before, nor such unselfishness. It made her feel very stable with Paul, a verifier of his love.

It made her very happy.

Feldspar, the name seemed to pop upright in her mind. She'd almost forgotten why she'd come. Feldspar. The job offer.

Vera scanned the modest crowd. Down the bar three guys proposed a toast with Windex shooters. A couple at a side table leaned forward to kiss, while two art students argued over who was the more important writer: William Faulkner or Kathy Acker. *Maybe Feldspar's not here*, Vera considered. Several friends who worked at the Radisson waved into her confusion. *Maybe he lost interest*. But what *was* his interest? Just what kind of job did Feldspar have in mind?

A smudge of darkness seemed to move, nearly glimmering; Vera sensed more than saw the squat figure rise. The back corner table by the fireplace, over which hung the 'Croft's famous painting—a classically depicted nude woman lying in the woods before a ram and a goat. Feldspar, in his black Italian suit, smiled subtlely at her and bid the table with his jeweled hand.

"I got out a little early," Vera hurried to explain. "I didn't want to keep you waiting."

"That's very thoughtful of you," Feldspar replied. "And again I'm grateful for your time. Please."

Vera took her seat. Feldspar seemed to sit himself with some difficulty, as if he had a trick knee or something. It was the diaphanous black material of his suit that gave his shape the elusive shimmer. "I realize your time is precious," he went on, finally settling himself. "But first, what would you like?"

Feldspar was drinking a Chimay Grand Reserve: Trappist ale in a huge bottle. He'd had several Courvoisier's at the restaurant, plus two Remy's, and now this. Yet he didn't appear fazed at all. If Vera had drunk all that, she'd be on the floor. *He's paying, so what the hell?* "A GM would be nice," she said.

"Fine." Feldspar signaled the tablehop and ordered. He wasted no more time with subtleties. "I work for an investment company of sorts, one department of which is involved in exclusive resort facilities. We're opening one in this propinquity."

Vera opened her mouth, then closed it. *He's something, all right.* "I hate to seem stupid, Mr. Feldspar, but I don't know what propinquity means."

He'd nearly flinched, as though the confession were absurd. "What I mean is, my superiors are opening a similar resort nearby. We'd like you to run it, or I should say, we'd like you to run the resort's restaurant."

Before she could make any response, the waiter

34

brought her Grand Marnier. She sipped from the large snifter, luxuriating in the sharp taste and aroma. "I need to know more—"

"Details, but of course." A thread of foam touched one side of his moustache when he sipped his ale. The ale looked murky, nearly crimson, with fine white sediment sifting in the glass like a snow orb. "We're a renowned chain, and an exclusive one. . . . Also a very private one. In other words, the name of my firm would be meaningless to you."

"Try me."

"Magwyth Enterprises," he said.

"You're right, I've never heard of it." He must be exaggerating. Vera read all the hotel journals and trade magazines; how "renowned" could this company be if she'd never even heard of it? She made a mental note. *Magwyth Enterprises. Look it up.*

Feldspar stroked his trimmed goatee. "And I must add, in all due appropriateness, that our resorts are extravagantly successful." He took another sip of his ale, held it in his mouth as if deliberating a fine wine. "To the extent that we have considerable capital at our disposal. We're prepared to spend it, without restraint, in order to facilitate the best exclusive resort hotel in the area."

Was Feldspar really a businessman, or a dreamer? Such endeavors, these days, cost multiple millions. This sounded like big talk to Vera, but then she reconsidered. Feldspar's jewelry glittered at her; he was probably wearing enough rocks to pay her rent for a year. And she remembered the Lamborghini.

"Most of the renovations are complete," he continued. "The restaurant is all that's left to be finished, just minor details, which we'll leave to you."

"What exactly are you renovating?"

"An old manor just north of here." He quickly

produced a slip of paper, squinting at it. "Waynesville—that's the name of the town."

Just north of here! Waynesville was north, all right—about a hundred miles north, right on the state line. Then . . . *Old manor* . . . *Waynesville* . . . She had read something now that she thought of it. "Not Wroxton Hall," she said.

"Yes," he beamed. "You *have* heard of it."

God! "Mr. Feldspar, Wroxton Hall is a dump, I've seen it—" And that she had, last year on a drive up to Eerie to visit some relatives. "Dump" was a compliment; the great Gothic mansion had been gutted, vacant for decades. And the location . . . "Why on earth did you choose Waynesville? It's so . . . ." She faltered; she mustn't insult him. *It's the sticks. It's the boondocks.* Vera couldn't think of a worse location for this sort of resort. This was mountain country, the northern ridge, and no major cities in a fifty mile radius at least. Just destitute little farm towns and some logging burgs. Fine dining would never make it up there. The whole idea was crazy.

"I know what you're thinking." Feldspar, again, produced that bewildering smilelike facial gesture. "And I understand your perplexity. As I've stated, our resorts are very private; a remote locale is an essential prerequisite for our patronage. You needn't worry about an insufficient following."

But how could she not? And that wasn't all Vera was worrying about. The locale was bad enough, but there was one thing even worse than that—

"You're aware that Wroxton Hall has quite a past, aren't you, Mr. Feldspar?" She twirled the pretty liquor around in her snifter. "In the twenties and thirties Wroxton Hall was a rather notorious—"

"Sanitarium," he finished for her. His next chuckle was the most genuine yet. "Yes, Ms. Abbot, I'm quite aware of that, and the things that supposedly went on. But that was over fifty years ago."

Vera wondered if that mattered. You could paint over a stain all day and the stain would still be there. "And you're also aware—"

Feldspar maintained his chuckle. "Yes, Ms. Abbot, I'm well aware of the stories. But, really. We're an enterprise, we're business people. We don't believe in ghosts."

Neither did Vera, but that was hardly the point. "I just don't think that anyone's going to cater to a resort with a history like that." Like . . . *what,* though? Vera didn't know all the details, but she got a fair gist from the little she read of Wroxton Hall's history. The hall had been leased by the health department as a convalescent domicile for the state's most hopeless mental patients, and evidently some things went on that probably wouldn't qualify as ethical health-care protocol. Questions arose as to exactly why the bodies of deceased patients wound up in military research labs, and still more questions arose as to exactly how these patients came to be deceased. There were also reports of the ward staff taking some considerable liberties with female patients. There was something about sadism, torture, pregnancies.

And, of course, something about ghosts. . . .

It didn't matter that this drivel had been fabricated by lore mongers and demented imaginations. Bad reputations had a way of lingering. Vera could see the ads now: *Escape to Waynesville's Romantic New Resort, Wroxton Hall, a Dreamy Little Getaway Complete with Torture Chambers and Luxury Suites in Which the Mentally Ill Were Raped and Murdered. Just the Place For You and that Special Someone to Get Away From it All and Mingle with a Delightful Coterie of Ghosts.*

Christ, Vera thought.

"What is your current salary?"

She struggled not to smirk. But as ludicrous as it seemed to her now, this was still business. Why not at least see what Feldspar had to offer?

"Twenty-eight," she said.

He stared back. "Well, I assure you, Ms. Abbot, we routinely pay our R.M.s many times more than that. More in the vicinity of a hundred thousand or so."

Now it was Vera's turn to stare. This was preposterous; no one paid R.M.s that much. "A *hundred thousand a year?* Are you serious?"

"Quite." He seemed to shrug. "In addition, there are many other benefits which, I should think, are rather standard."

"Such as?"

"Well, two weeks paid vacation, travel expenses included. Free health insurance, free life insurance. Free room and board—"

"You're kidding?" she questioned, astonished.

Again, Feldspar appeared as though nothing were amiss. "The inn has one hundred and sixty rooms. Some of them we're reserving for staff. As upper management, of course, you would be entitled to a suite of your choice. They're quite nice, I assure you. And there's always the company car, for which we assume all expenses—"

"Wait a minute, wait a minute," Vera interrupted. She could fathom none of this. She held her hands up, thinking, trying to assess this unassessible circumstance.

"If the money's insufficient," he added, "I'm sure we can come to a mutual agreement. Say, a hundred and . . . fifteen thousand?"

Vera flagged the tablehop for another drink. *This must be a sham,* she concluded. *It MUST be.*

"And, naturally, we will assume your moving expenses, plus a cash compensation." From the black jacket, Feldspar next produced a check, which he slid across the table.

Vera picked it up. Stared at it. Gulped. PAY TO THE ORDER OF *Vera Abbot* THE AMOUNT OF *Ten Thousand Dollars*—$10,000.00.

This was not a personal check; it was a precleared certified *bank check*. Unbouncable. *Start-up compensation and moving remittance*, it read on the FOR line. It was dated today.

"You're offering me all this?" Her breath felt short. "You don't even know me."

"Personally, no," he said. He poured more Chimay very steadily, careful to run the murky ale down the side of the glass to forestall a rise of head. "But as a manager myself, I know what I need to know about you with regard to my company's business interests. I've dined in every restaurant in the city. Yours is by far the finest. I've made extensive inquiries as to the most efficient restaurant manager in town. Your name came up more than any other. That is all the knowledge of you I need. You, Ms. Abbot, are the person we want to run our restaurant."

But Vera was still gaping at the check.

"And there's another consideration, isn't there?" Feldspar removed a black-and-gold cigarette case, then lit a Sobraine with a diamond-studded Cartier lighter. "I've been all over. I've been doing this for years. And I know that everyone has their dreams. What are your dreams, Ms. Abbot? I have yet to meet a restaurant manager whose ultimate long-term aspiration was not to one day own a restaurant of his or her own. With the money that we're paying you, if you're sensible financially, you would have sufficient funds to purchase your own establishment, most anywhere you like, in four or five years. Many of our R.M.s have gone on to do just that. Am I correct in my surmise?"

Vera could not dispute this; Feldspar was right. This *was* Vera's dream, to some day own a place of her own. . . .

And I could, she realized. At that salary, with all her major expenses paid by the company, she'd be able to save enough to buy her own place *in cash.* No assumed loans, no mortgages. If she invested the majority of her net, in four or five years she'd have more than enough.

But—

The image crumbled, a house of cards exposed to a sudden draft.

What are you thinking, you idiot? she asked herself.

"I'm engaged," she said.

"I foresee no problem in that regard," Feldspar promptly replied. "Your fiancé can move with you. The suites are not only well restored but quite large—"

"I'm engaged to a metropolitan journalist," she explained. "He writes about cities, not farm towns. There'd be nothing for him to write about in Waynesville. His career would fall apart."

"Then he can commute."

"Waynesville is a two and a half hour drive at least."

"Then he can remain here during his assignments, and be with you on weekends or some such. This is not an uncommon occurrence. Many upwardly mobile professionals maintain relationships around their separate careers."

Upwardly mobile professional. She stared glumly at her drink. *Is that what I am?*

It's your call, Vera, another voice seemed to trace across her mind. She could talk to Paul, but . . . it would never work. Driving nearly three hours each way every day? Or a weekend romance? Vera knew too many good couples whose bonds had snapped under such circumstances. This job offer was phenomenal. She'd be crazy to turn it down if she wasn't—

40

If I wasn't in love, she realized. *But I am. And that's more important to me than money.*

That simple truth made her smile. She was in love. Suddenly nothing else mattered, nothing else at all.

"I'm sorry, Mr. Feldspar," she said. "I appreciate your confidence in me, and I'm grateful for your generosity. But I'm afraid I can't accept your offer."

She handed the ten thousand dollar bank check back to him.

"Why not sleep on it?" the man suggested. "Think about it. Why not at least consider trying us out? We won't hold you to a contract. Come and work for us on a probationary basis. If you don't like it, or if, in fact, it does burden your relationship, then quit."

A fair proposal, and a logical one. Vera could not deny that the offer excited her. But she *knew.* Sleeping on it wouldn't change that, nor would trying the job out. She knew it would distance her from Paul. And she knew she would not risk that, not for anything.

"I'm sorry," she repeated.

"Your mind's made up, I can see." Feldspar didn't seem angry at all, nor disappointed. He'd made his pitch and he'd lost. He would simply have to find someone else. "It's regrettable, and I'm certain that you would do wonderful things for our restaurant, as our restaurant would do wonderful things for you. But your priorities are set, and I see that they're admirable. I must go now, Ms. Abbot—" Feldspar left a one hundred dollar bill on the table. "I thank you for your consideration, and I wish you luck in all your endeavors."

"I wish you luck in yours," she returned.

Feldspar awkwardly stood up, pushed his chair in. His jeweled hand glittered like tiny lights, particularly the amethyst in the gold pinky ring. In the odd man's eyes, Vera saw it all: no, not anger or disappointment. It was sadness.

Feldspar smiled. "I'm leaving tomorrow morning; I'll

41

be staying at the Radisson tonight. On the off chance that you should change your mind, please contact me.''

''I will, Mr. Feldspar.''

''Good night then. I'm happy to have made your acquaintance.''

He turned and left. Vera's eyes followed him out. It wasn't a limp he walked with but a slight slow-step. Vera felt sad herself, seeing him leave. In a moment the short, broad figure had wended through the standing crowd and disappeared.

Vera finished her Grand Marnier. Something seemed to struggle in her psyche, but the notion quelled. Her love was worth more than money. She knew she'd done the right thing.

It was time to go home now, back to her life and to her love.

Chapter Three

His mind seemed to disperse as though his skull had dissolved. Lights ran like smeared neon. *Where am I? Who am I?* He wasn't sure. Gradually all that was real to him transposed with a thousand unreal ecstacies. Shapes moved like intent chiffon blobs through the close space of wherever he was.

What's . . . happening?

He saw voices and heard tastes. Luxuriant scents touched him palpably as deft hands. From somewhere music played; he could see the notes floating from the speakers, a slow passacaglia by Bach. Each dark note seemed to approach him like an amorphous physical presence.

He felt skewered; he couldn't move. He felt cosmically heavy and light as air at the same time. He could hear the blood push through the arteries in his brain.

"Watch," a voice kneaded him.

He opened his eyes. The smeared lights dulled to pasty white, images congealing like lard, squirming.

When he realized what he was looking at, he screamed.

He was looking at his own body sprawled beneath him.

43

He felt his distant muscles seize, his tendons tighten. He watched his sweat-sheened chest heave in terror.

Wet, syrupy laughter launched about his head like a flock of great black birds.

The old Tercel coughed against the cold, then sputtered to start. Cracks had formed in the dash, the upholstery was peeling, and the brakes squealed as Vera pulled out of the lot and turned onto West Street. *Even a company car,* the thought drifted. *I wonder what kind? An Iroc? A Mustang GT? Maybe a Vette!* She knew she was being silly. Even a moped would be better than this clunker.

It was fun to think about, at least.

She knew she'd made the right decision. What other decision was there? To even consider taking Feldspar's offer was nothing more than a fantasy. Still, she wondered what Paul would say.

The Tercel puttered on, hitching through gears. The heater blared cold air. She rounded Church Circle and veered onto Duke of Glouchester. Spectral blue lights illuminated the great dome of the State House, below the bright moon. Icy street lamps shimmering through the winter air made the streets look frosted. More light weirdly assaulted her at the turn before the bridge: an ambulance roving slowly with its red lights throbbing but no siren.

Her mind strayed as she traversed the bridge. The bay chopped, treacherously black with squirming tails of moonlight. Beyond, myriad sailboats and yachts bobbed in their marina slips. *A hundred and fifteen thousand dollars a year,* she mused. A higher tax bracket, but so what? With the free car, plus no rent or food expenses, she'd be able to bank fifty a year probably. She'd—

Stop it! she commanded herself, half laughing. *A fantasy is all it'll ever be.*

She and Paul shared a decent two-bedroom apartment off Spa Road. It was nice, not too expensive, and all they needed. Paul used the second bedroom for an office, to write. They'd accepted the commonplace nuisances of apartment living—occasionaly squalling babies, footsteps on the ceiling, and the explosive wee-hour arguments from the neighbors—as part of the deal. Soon they'd move to a townhouse, or maybe even a small home when they'd banked enough money for a decent down payment. Like most else in life, a relationship could only proceed one step at a time.

Vera parked. The lot stretched on coldly with dark cars. It wasn't even midnight yet; she was home earlier than usual, which was a good thing, considering the crush of diners they'd had tonight. She felt seduced by the idea of a good night's sleep.

The moon rose so brightly she squinted; her high heels tapped along the frigid sidewalk. She whisked herself up the steps, fleeing the bitter cold like muggers, and sighed at the gush of heat when she let herself in.

The living room was dark. *Paul must be asleep.* Despite her fatigue, the excitement still ticked: she couldn't wait to tell Paul about the offer, but now it looked as if she'd have to wait till morning.

What will he say? she wondered again, more intensely this time. The question, now, seemed to shimmer, like the cold night, the moonlit bay, and Feldspar's squat, jeweled hand and silky suit. She stood, suddenly stiff in the dark living room. Why was she thinking these things now? Maybe Paul would *want* her to take the job. *Maybe he wants to move.* He often mentioned a desire to write books someday. *He could pretty much do that anywhere, couldn't he?* Vera's new salary, plus the free room and board, would give Paul all the time he needed to write.

Why didn't I think of that before?

Was she being selfish? Vera wanted the job—just not at the expense of her relationship. She was prejudging the situation. Perhaps Paul would be as enthusiastic about it as she was.

There was only one way to find out.

She went down the warm, dark hall, not even yet having taken off her coat. This was important, and the only way she'd know how he felt was to ask him. She'd wake him up and ask him.

But only a few steps showed her she wouldn't need to. The bedroom light glowed in the door's gap; he wasn't asleep after all. *Must still be up, reading.* Paul read a lot of books, lots of philosophical fiction like Kafka and Drieser and Seymore, and a lot of sociology texts. Vera's excitement carried her to the door, and when she opened it—

What the . . .

The scene divided her perceptions. *Wrong apartment!* she squealed at herself, forgetting that *her* key had unlocked the front door. She did not consider logic at this precise moment, she couldn't. She'd walked into the middle of an orgy.

Her hands fell limp at her sides. At once her senses collided with the lewdest scents, sounds, and glimpses. *Wrong apartment,* she thought again, only now it was the limpest thought that had ever occurred to her, and the palest lie.

This was not the wrong apartment. It was *her* apartment—hers and Paul's—*theirs.* This was their bedroom, their furniture, their carpet and their pictures on the wall.

This was their bed—

—on which now the most perverse scene unfolded.

Vera's eyelids felt held open by hooks. Three nude figures crowded the bed. A skinny lank-haired blonde, whose wrists had been lashed to the bedposts, lay on

46

her back with her legs splayed. Her eyes looked glazed; she was grinning stupidly. A man stood between her legs on hands and knees, his head lowered in steady cunnilingus. He looked like someone trying to push a peanut with his nose. Though his face was busily buried, Vera knew at once that the man was Paul.

A second woman, much more beautiful than the blonde, knelt aside. She grinned down fixedly, as if in supervision, stroking Paul's back. She had perfectly straight light-red hair which shimmered like satin, and large, erect breasts.

"Baby want some more?" she asked.

The skinny blonde wagged her head. On the night stand sat a small jar of some mauve powder. The redhead leaned across, stuck a tiny coke spook in the jar, then brought it to the blonde's nostril, into which the small amount of powder instantly disappeared. The blonde went limp against her wristbonds, her grin widening. "Aw, God," she moaned and lolled her head.

"That good, baby?"

"Aw, God . . ."

"How about you, Paulie?"

Paul's head raised between the blonde's canted thighs. He took the spoon, indulged himself of the whitish powder three or four times, then reburied his face into the blonde's great spread of tawny pubic hair.

Vera watched all this as if watching a traffic accident—in remote horror. They hadn't even noticed her standing there. The bright light felt raw in her eyes. Past the scene, on the dresser, sat a framed photograph of Paul and Vera arm in arm on the City Dock last Valentine's Day.

Vera couldn't even begin to speak. She felt encased in a block of concrete with only two holes through which to peer. Her impulse was to scream, to lunge forward—to *react*. But her body would not respond to the commands of her brain. All she could do was stand there, immobile as a post, and bear witness. . . .

The blonde looked pallid, the deep lines of her ribs highlighting her malnutrition. A tiny tatoo showed at the center of her throat, a diminutive southern cross. Her bare feet churned in the sheets; her hips subtlely rose and fell against the dutiful attentions of Paul's mouth. "I'm gonna come again, I'm gonna come again," she kept murmuring through her stupor. Her wrists strained against the stocking bonds, tendons flexing.

Next the redhead walked around the bed to fetch something. Midstep she stopped and turned. She grinned at Vera.

"Hey, gang. We have a guest."

The blonde glared. Her breasts looked like nippled pancakes. "Get lost, cunt, unless you want your face rearranged. Find your own blow—four's a crowd."

"Now, now," the redhead toyed. "We can be more polite than that, can't we? Besides, she's kind of cute, and I could go for some fresh pussy." Her blue eyes sparkled at Vera. "Come on, sweetheart. Get out of those clothes. Let's see how you taste."

Vera stared back in the sickest shock. Paul's head came up again, his mouth shiny. He looked at Vera for perhaps a second, seemed to make no recognition at all, then returned again to his oral duties. His tongue churned furiously.

"Don't be shy. We're all friends here, we're *good* friends. Paul picked us up at Kaggie's, he even paid for our drinks." The redhead traipsed to the night stand opposite, took something up in her pretty shiny-nailed hands. "Or maybe you'd just like to watch first. That's okay. I like to watch too, like to get real wet and boned up, you know?" Her breasts stuck out like skin-covered glass orbs. She looked healthy, robust; lean but very shapely. Paul continued to maneuver his tongue against

48

the blonde's unruly thatch. Vera's stomach roiled at the wet smacking sounds; it sounded like someone eating a sloppy meal, which, in a sense, it was. Vera dizzied at the zeal with which Paul devoured his seedy slat-ribbed companion. "Your boyfriend likes to be fucked," the redhead proclaimed. "Did you know that?"

The comment seemed cavernous, echoed down from a high, rocky palisade. What did the woman mean? The lewd noises went on, enlaced with the blonde's loud, slow moans. Then came a sliding, sucking sound, like opening a can of peanut butter, then an even worse slick clicking.

What . . . what is . . .

The redhead scooped something out of a big jar. She came around to the foot of the bed—

. . . what is she . . . doing?

Vera wanted to scream till her face turned red. *Your boyfriend likes to be fucked.* She saw now the lengths to which this obscenity would go. Her eyes erratically roved the redhead's robust physique: the sleek, pretty legs; the thimble-sized nipples; the trim waist and gorgeous hourglass figure. A hot breath snagged in the redhead's chest as she stickily applied something to herself.

Oh—my—God . . .

Regardless of the clearly feminine physical attributes, the redhead sported one feature that was not particular to her gender.

A penis.

Vera's stare melted like a paraffin mask.

She's got a . . . she's got a . . .

The redhead was a transexual. At least that's what Vera thought she must be, halfway through the procedure. This was a hideous parody, the near-perfect female physique made aberrant by male genitals. At first Vera thought it must be artificial, but a more intent inspection easily revealed its authenticity: the gorged purple glans, the veined shaft.

Also revealed was the label on the bigger jar: VASE-LINE.

The redhead hummed contently, slicking her hideous erection with the lubricant. It looked huge, gorged stiff and throbbing. The redhead stroked it a moment, leaning her head back with closed eyes. Testicles large as eggs constricted in the dangling scrotum.

"Sandwich time, Paulie. Guess who's the bologna." The redhead glided her greased hand up Paul's buttocks, then pushed him forward.

This is impossible, Vera tried to convince herself. *This . . . can't . . . be.*

But it was. Paul crawled up the bed, then slowly lowered his hips. The redhead guided Paul's penis into the moistened fissure of the blonde's sex. She let him pump awhile. The bed groaned along with the blonde, whose legs flexed beneath Paul's thrusts. Her bonds stretched against the brass bedposts. Paul plied her meager breasts and sucked red marks into her throat.

"That's it, Paulie, nice and slow and deep." The redhead continued to stroke herself. "Stick that cock in her right up to the balls." Then she kneed up onto the bed, leaned forward. She carefully parted Paul's rump and began to sodomize him.

Vera gulped as if swallowing a stone. Her bulged eyes strained against their sockets. The redhead, poised on her hands, paused a moment to grin at her. "Stick around, sweetheart. I'm gonna come up his ass so much it's gonna squirt out his ears."

Vera churned back, broke her paralysis, and tripped out of the room. Nearly mindless, she staggered down the dark hall, found the kitchen, and vomited into the sink.

Each eruption of vomit seemed to shake her heart

50

loose from the seats of her soul. Yes, that's what it felt like: emptying her soul as well as her stomach. Each spasm blinded her.

How long she remained bent over the sink she'd never know. The bedposts thumped the wall in the other room, squeals and chuckles fluttered behind stifled grunts. Vaguely she detected music—an organ work by Bach that she'd bought Paul for his birthday.

"Gimme more of that class A blow," she heard the blonde hotly request. "I'm gettin' ready to come again, and I wanna do a big toot while I'm gettin' off."

Vera walked numb out of the apartment. She let the front door close behind her. She walked down the stairs, out the lighted brick entrance, and into the cold night.

A single tear hitched down her cheek. She did not scream, she did not sob, she did not tirade.

All . . . gone.

She simply got into her car and drove away.

Chapter Four

Sunlight blared in her slitted eyes. Vera awoke shivering in the back of the parking lot at Mr. Donut. She'd slept in the car all night, in the bitter cold. Her lips felt like pieces of coral, her fingernails were blue. Frigid air circulated through the car: she'd left the motor running, to keep on the heat, but had run out of gas.

She stared into the sky.

No, she thought.

Several cars crawled by to the drive-in window. Faces peered at her. The sunlight felt like a mainline of memory, rekindling to her brain the disgusting scene she'd witnessed last night on her own bed.

No. No. No.

But it was no dream. It was all true, she knew it was. She could deny it forever and it would still be there. How many times had Paul promised his fidelity to her? How many times had he said *I love you?* None of that mattered now. Lies never mattered, did they? All his love, all that he'd said to her and promised her, was a lie. This truth terrified her: how you could love someone, *live* with someone that long, and then in a single, jagged moment realize that you never ever really knew that person at all?

Tears had dried to crust on her face. She leaned up.

How long had Paul been living this demented double life behind her back?

My God, she fully realized now. She brought her nearly frozen hands to her face, staring. How long had he been doing those things?

Drugs. Bondage. Transexuality.

He hadn't even been using condoms, nor had that hideous redheaded she-male. Double life aside, how could Paul have been so thoughtless as to engage in such practices, with such people, and not even consider the risk to Vera's health?

"Ma'am?"

Tap-tap-tap-tap.

"Ma'am?"

A face hovered in the glass—a city cop. It seemed to warp before her in the curved glass. He tapped his nightstick against the window incessantly as a bamboo drum.

"Are you all right?"

Vera got out of the car. She could imagine how she looked, nearly blue-lipped, shivering, and eyeliner streaked down her face. "I'm fine," she said.

"Are you sure?"

"Yes!"

She began to stomp away, toward West Street, her heels rapidly clicking against asphalt.

"Wait up, miss. You sure you're—"

"Yes!" she almost screamed at him. "Is it against the law to run out of gas in a fucking donut-store parking lot!"

She hurried off, leaving the cop to scowl. She didn't even know where she was going. Where *could* she go? She couldn't go home. *I don't have a home,* she said to herself. She couldn't even fathom returning to that apartment. A glance to her watch showed her the time: 10 A.M.

In an hour The Emerald Room would open for lunch.

53

Dan B., Donna. She'd make some arrangement to stay with them for a few days, until she could figure out what she wanted to do. The bank account was joint; after being caught, Paul was probably at the teller's now, cleaning it out. She'd just have to scrape by until payday, get a place, restart her life.

Then she stopped.

Her mouth opened. The cold wind burned her eyes.

Feldspar.

Vera ran, suddenly a sleek maniac in a Burberry over-coat and high heels. Feldspar had told her he was staying at the Radisson. Checkout time was eleven!

On the off chance that you should change your mind, please contact me.

She ran on, stopped again, hopping, took off her shoes, and continued. Pedestrians gaped after her. A Yellow screeched to a halt when she dashed through a DON'T WALK crossing. Her feet pounded the stone-cold sidewalk, the air whipped against her face. Just as she turned into the hotel court, the gleaming red Lamborghini idled up to the light, which then turned green.

"Wait!" she screamed.

The car turned away, accelerated down West Street.

"Oh, no, oh, shit, wait!"

She scampered through pedestrians. The bottoms of her stockings wore out as she shouldered through clusters of business suits on their way to work. The Lamborghini had stopped before the red light at Cathedral Street. Vera's lungs felt fit to explode:

"Wait!"

The light blinked green just as Vera trampled up. Feldspar's goateed face looked astonished in the window. He leaned over.

The passenger door raised.

"Ms. Abbot—what's wrong?"

"I—" Vera sunk into the plush leather seat. The door

lowered closed automatically, sealing in the heat "I wanted to catch you before you left."

Concern lined Feldspar's broad face. "Something's quite wrong, I can tell. What is it?"

Vera let the heat sink into her skin. How could she explain herself without sounding daft? The way she looked now, shivering, stocking-footed, must already have reduced her former credibility to the lowest ebb. So she would make no excuses.

"Mr. Feldspar, is that job still open?"

He turned around and drove straight back to the Radisson, booked another room, and took her up. "What changed your mind?" he asked, and opened the door.

He'd rented a conference room. Vera took off her overcoat, for the first time since last night. Feldspar set an alligator-skin briefcase on the meeting table.

"Your fiancé turned out to be open to the idea?" he ventured when she didn't answer.

He's open to ideas, all right. "No. I never discussed it with him. We're not together anymore."

"I'm sorry to hear that." Feldspar sat down, lit a Sobraine. "I do hope that it wasn't the job offer that caused your separation."

"It wasn't," Vera said. "It had nothing to do with it."

"Well, it's none of my business—your private life is your own. It's distressing to see you like this, though. You're obviously repressing a trauma."

Am I? Of course she was. How could he not sense that, how could anyone? "If it's all the same to you, sir, I'd rather not talk about that right now. Let's talk business instead."

"Ah, yes."

Vera felt ludicrous. She'd lost her shoes on a mad dash

through rush hour. Her vermilion dress was so crumpled it looked slept in, which in fact it was. Her lips were parched, and she could feel her makeup flaking on her face. Yet here she was, with a stoic business man, accepting a job for nearly four times her current salary.

First, Feldspar gave her back the bank check. Then he slipped her a sheet of paper. "This is our employment contract. It guarantees terms upon your signature. Before you sign, though, I must explain that the work won't be easy. Expect to put in ten to twelve hours a day, six days per week."

So what else is new? Vera signed the contract, the back copy of which Feldspar gave her to keep. "I'd like to elaborate now on some of the specifics," he went on. The sweet cigarette smoke dispersed before his face. "As I informed you last night, we're opening an exclusive resort; it's a country-inn type of establishment."

"Is the restaurant in the same building?"

"Oh, yes, and it's quite well done. I can't wait for you to see it."

Neither could she, though she wasn't sure if that was good or bad. "I'll need to know what kind of staff you're giving me."

"There is none yet. As the restaurant's manager, you will be expected to hire the restaurant's staff. And do it quickly—we'd like to open in two weeks."

"Two weeks?" That was no time at all. "And what about the menu, the wine list, who are your distributors, your delivery agencies?"

"That, too, will be up to you."

"Mr. Feldspar, I think it's great that you want a state-of-the-art restaurant, but that's dependent on a whole lot more than an R.M. I could be the best manager in the world, and the restaurant would fail if I don't have the right people. The first thing you absolutely must have is a great chef—"

56

"Hire one."

"A skilled chef doesn't come cheap. The guy we have at The Emerald Room gets paid forty thousand a year."

"Pay him eighty," Feldspar bluntly told her. "You know this business, Ms. Abbot; that's why we've hired you, and we know that good staff won't leave their current jobs for a pittance. Simply solicit the people you need. I should think that if you offer them twice their current salaries they'll be most willing, especially considering the free room and board."

Vera had forgotten about that. Feldspar had said he was reserving some of the hotel's rooms for staff. She could hire people here, and get them to move.

Feldspar passed her another bank check, but the amount space was blank. Next he gave her a thin stack of employment contracts. "Pay them each, say, a thousand dollars for moving expenses, and give them their first week's salary as a bonus. Waitresses and busboys might be a problem, since many are students and hence unable to leave the localities of their schools. Room service should be able to provide some people if that's the case. Keep it light at first, you can always hire more staff as business picks up. But a good chef is essential, and whomever else you feel necessary to start-up operations."

He just gave me a blank check, Vera realized in disbelief. *He's dead serious. These guys must have more money than King Tut.*

"All right, Mr. Feldspar. I can do that."

"And as far as distributors and inventory sources go, I'm sure you're familiar with all the proper channels. Make the arrangements."

That said it all. Feldspar wasn't fooling around. Here's the job. Don't bother me with details, just do it. Period.

Yeah, she thought. *I can do that.*

"When can you be at the estate?"

57

Waynesville, she remembered. *Staff.* "I'll need a few days to get the essential staff together."

"A few days, fine. But no more than that. We want things under way in—"

"Two weeks," she recalled. "No problem." Of course, it really *was* a problem, but she'd simply have to solve it. She realized the tremendous job ahead of her, yet in spite of that she felt anticipatory. She felt *excited.*

"What's the name of the inn, by the way?" she asked.

"We're simply going to call it The Inn."

Original, Vera thought. *It's his place, he can call it whatever he wants.* "How about the restaurant?"

Feldspar shrugged and crushed out his cigarette. "You choose the name. Something continental, I should think. Again, we'll leave it to you."

Vera joked to herself over the possibilities. *Vera's Hash House. Good Eats. The Boondocks Room.* "How does this sound?" She paused for effect. "The Carriage House."

Feldspar's eyes widened slightly in a sudden approval. "An excellent choice, I must say."

Easy to please, Vera thought. *But now that I've got the name, I better get on with the job.*

A knock tapped at the door. Feldspar let in a young and very beautiful blonde pushing a room service carriage. Truffles, Baci Chocolates, and Dniva Caviar. A bottle of Kruge sat wedged in a bucket of ice.

Feldspar poured two glasses of the fine champagne. He passed one to Vera, curtly smiling down. "A toast," he proposed.

Vera raised the sparkling glass.

"To The Carriage House."

Their glasses clinked.

* * *

Feldspar parked the Lamborghini in The Emerald Room's valet cul-de-sac. The large, cut amethyst on his pinky ring shined as he withdrew a final piece of paper. "Directions," he said.

"I'll see you in a few days," Vera promised.

An equal promise, at least in a way, seemed to highlight the otherwise dark voice. "I believe that wonderful things await us in this venture, and tremendous success. I'm looking very forward to working with you, Ms. Abbot."

"Likewise." Vera shook the stubby hand. She felt—what? She looked once more at Feldspar's features: the broad face, the goatee, the ink-black hair pulled back in a short ponytail—an absolute clash to the fine clothes and jewelry. Twelve hours ago, he was merely a weird-looking squat stranger; now he was her boss. She felt she could even consider him a friend. "Thank you for giving me this chance, Mr. Feldspar. I won't let you down."

"I'm quite certain that you won't. But before you go, might I make one very trifle suggestion?"

"Sure."

"Get some shoes. Soon."

Feldspar actually laughed as she got out of the sleek car. Vera laughed too, waving as he pulled onto West Street and drove away. Yes, she'd have to get some shoes—she'd have to get a lot of things. But far more important was what she already had—or in fact had been given: a chance at something big.

She stood before The Emerald Room, looking out into the busy thoroughfare. Passersby paused to gape at her, this tousled woman standing in freezing weather with no shoes and mussed hair. The wind slipped around her, but now she felt warm.

A second chance, she mused. That's what this was, really. She had a good job here but no longer a life to go with it. It hurt to think of Paul, and of love in general. Love was supposed to be ultimate emotion between two people, the ultimate truth. Where was her truth now? It was all gone, it was all a lie and always had been. How could she live with that?

I know.

Very slowly, her left hand raised in the cold. The big engagement ring gave a crisp glitter in the sun. She slipped the ring off her finger and threw it into the middle of West Street.

Eventually a mail truck ran it over.

Time to move on, she thought.

Chapter Five

"Hey, Jor! Split-tail at twelve o'clock!"

The Blazer slowed. It was one of those big four-runners, souped up, with Binno Mags, Bell Tech springs, and tires that looked about a yard high. All the rednecks drove them; it was status. Jorrie Slade's eyes thinned at his friend's announcement—or, to be more accurate, his *eye* thinned, since the left one was glass. He'd lost it one night when he and Mike-Man were rucking it up fierce with some Crick City fellas out behind Duffy's Pool Hall. Didn't matter all that much to Jorrie, though; the right eye worked just fine, and that back-woods peter-licker who'd poked out the left one had wound up losing a lot more than an eye. Try his ears, his lips, and his balls. Jorrie was good with a knife.

Mike-Man, Jorrie's best rucking pal, swigged on his can of Jax. "I say, ya see that, Jor?"

"I see it, all right, Mike-Man, my man. Looks like we'se gonna have our dogs in some decent poon after all. Shee-it."

The Blazer's high headlights and floods glared forward. A van sat stalled on the opposite shoulder, and stooping over the opened hood was one buxom full-tilt brick-shithouse blonde the likes of which neither Jorrie nor Mike-Man had ever laid eyes on—or *eye,* in Jorrie's particular case. Beautiful long blond hair swirled in the wind. Her tight, broad rump jutted as she bent over, diddling with wires.

"Now I say, a pair of gentlemanly types such as us could not never ignore such a woman in distress," Jorrie pointed out to his friend. "I mean, on a wicked night like this? Goodness, the poor thang could catch her death of cold, now couldn't she?"

"That she sure could," Mike-Man replied in full agreement, "and it just wouldn't be Christian-like for two strong young fellas such as ourselfs to allow sumpthin' like that to happen."

Jorrie and Mike-Man exchanged laughter. You could call these two boys unipolar sociopaths, or you could call them pure-ass crazy motherfuckers—it didn't much matter which. And as for this here foxy blonde stranded at the shoulder? No harm, really—not that they could see anyway. Hell, they was just two red-blooded American fellas out for a thrill. It wasn't like such things never happened out in these parts, what with them creekers up in the hills and all, and them damn white trash buggers north of the ridge. And it wasn't like they was fixing to kill her. They was just gonna poke her up a tad, give those fine womanly parts a working over, that's all. Probably be doing her a favor, they figured.

Mike-Man crossed the line and stopped on the shoulder. The Blazer rumbled, lighting up the front of the disabled van. That's when the blonde straightened up and faced them.

"My-my, I say, *my goodness!*" Mike-Man articulated.

"Well shee-it my drawers and my mama's to boot," Jorrie commented.

Her coat hung open, revealing breasts large enough to threaten to pop the buttons on her flannel blouse. She looked as if she'd been poured into them there jeans of hers, you know, those city-type jeans with the funny labels, like from Italy an' shit.

Jorrie slapped Mike-Man on the back. "Now thems there is what my daddy would call one dandy set of milkers, boy. Like that famous chick Dolly Carton on all them supermarket papers, you know?"

"Yes sir. And that kisser on her? Looks like Vanner White or sumpthin', or one of them prissy gals on *Cosmerpolitan.*"

Jorrie polished off the rest of his beer. He drank Red, White, & Blue, on account of he was classier than Mike-Man about what he drank. "Man, we'se lucked out better than a coupla egg-suck dogs throwed in the henhouse tonight, ain't we?"

"Yeah boy, that's some fine gandering that there, and I'll bet she's got herself a bush on her you could plant a fuckin' garden in."

"We'se gonna be plantin' more than gardens in that sweet stuff, just you watch, Mike-Man, my man. Don't look like one of them stinky creeker chicks like we bust up all the time, either, and she's sure's shit no road hog. Bet she's got one of them nice clean 'n purdy coozes on her, don't ya think?"

"Yeah boy," Mike-Man concurred, still staring excitedly at her in the Blazer's highs. "An' I'll bet she wears herself a lot of that nice city perfume like ya can buy in them fancy stores like Garfunkel's and Ward's and all."

Jorrie gave Mike-Man another comradly slap on the back. His glass eye glinted in the expectation. "Come on, buddy-bro. My dog's a barkin' already. Let's you and me put a little spark into this here little lady's girlyworks."

They climbed out of the Blazer. They left both doors open; they always did. That way it was easier to get to work on them. Just slide 'em in right across that big bench seat. Mike-Man'd hold 'em down with the knife from one side while Jorrie'd get them starkers from the other. It was a dandy system. They had it down pat.

"Hey there, purdy lady!" Jorrie greeted, and stepped up in his fine pointed shitkicker boots. A good point on your boots was always the ticket when you was gonna go out on a romp. For shakin' down guys for their green, just one good hard kick in their works would take the fight outa the biggest and gnarliest of fellas, yes sir, or you hop up on the hood real quick like and give 'em a good kick in the chin. Then there was that time Jorrie'd been rucking it up with this stinky creeker gal out by Croll's field, and Jorrie, see, he wasn't all too keen on putting his pride and joy into that dirty stuff, what with the AIDS and the herpes and all, 'specially after he'd gotten himself a look at it, so he thought he might like a little of what his daddy called "mouth-lovin'," but this dog-stinky creeker chick, you know what she said? She said, "You gawd-damn mama-fuckin' cracker piece of shit! You just try puttin' that in my mouth an' see if I don't bite it right off!" a comment which Jorrie, of course, did not take too kindly to, so what he did, he just gave that creeker gal one good swift kick in the spine, and that quelled her threatening protestations just as fast as shit through a city pigeon. Heard she was gettin' around in a chair these days, and he figured it served her just right for saying something so downright awful. A gal'd have to be plumb crazy! Biogenic amine imbalance and sociopathy aside, when a fella the likes of Jorrie Slade tells you to entreat his genitals of the mouth, well you just better bone up and do it, unless you wanna spend the rest of your days rollin' around in a chair, too, yes sir.

"I say, hey." Jorrie smiled his great big chumly warm-hearted smile as he approached this ravishing, brick-shithouse-with-tits-like-ta-knock-your-socks-off blonde. "Me and my buddy here, we'se seen ya pulled over an' all so we thought we'd stop and give you a hand."

"Oh, you're a godsend," the blonde said, a relieved hand to her chest. "The engine just stopped cold on me. I don't know what to do."

Mike-Man played the game, scratching his head as he peered into the little hood. "Lemme see what I can do here, yes sir . . ."

"I really appreciate this," she continued to gush. "It's so cold out tonight. I'd be in a hell of a spot if you two boys hadn't come by."

"Now just you don't worry yourself about that, sweetheart. Mike-Man here, he's an expert on these kind of problems."

"And you know what, Jor? I think I done found the problem already."

"Oh, that's wonderful!" the blonde exclaimed.

"Well, not really, at least not for you." Jorrie chuckled. "The problem, see, is we don't give a flyin' feedbag full of Berkshire hogshit about your busted van, don't ya know."

The blonde turned to him. "What do you m—"

"See, the problem is you're probably the hottest-lookin' piece of angel food cake to ever cross these here parts, and me an' Mike-Man here, we'se each got ourselfs a rock-hard dog that I think it would be a real good idea for you to take care of. *That,* sweetcakes, is the problem."

The blonde screamed high and hard as Mike-Man got his big meaty arm around her neck and was dragging her back. "Don't help none to scream," Jorrie pointed out. "Ain't no one around to hear ya. So just you go ahead and scream all ya like."

It wasn't more than a couple of seconds before Mike-Man had the blonde in the Blazer kicking up a storm across the big bench seat. "Ya hold still now," he thoughtfully advised. "I'd sure hate to have to kill ya, as fine a set of hooters as you got." She gagged, trying to scratch him, but went rigid when Mike-Man placed the blade of his pearl-handled Buck against that soft, smooth throat of hers.

"There now that's better, ain't it, sweetcakes?" Jorrie queried. "Let's see what we'se can do about gettin' you out of these here constrictin' garments, hmm?" He yanked her sassy fancy-labeled jeans right on off and tossed them in the road.

"Check out them purdy panties!" Mike-Man enthused. They were frilly and pink. "Bet she bought 'em at Garfunkel's!"

"Or maybe even Ward's," Jorrie ventured. He peeled them off likewise. Suddenly the cold moonlight reverted his ruddy face to a primordial mask. His glass eye stared. "And a shaved snatch, lookit that, Mike-Man! Don't that beat all?"

"Sure's hail does," Mike-Man was quick to agree. "That's damn sure the purdiest slab of pie I ever did see."

The blonde lay shivering. Terror pried her eyes open. Those big firm breasts of hers quivered like turgid Jell-O when Jorrie busted open that nice flannel blouse. "Best pair I've seen in quite a spell," he was cordial enough to compliment, and he didn't waste no time getting his hands on them. His erotomanic one-eyed gaze reveled in their shape: big as they were they didn't have no sag to 'em at all, not like a lot of these gals who sport an ample rack and wind up havin' 'em swinging to their bellybuttons once they get out of the bra. No sir, these didn't have no flop to 'em whatsoever, and Jorrie really took a fancy to that, just as he took a fancy to that pretty shaved box. He gave her breasts a good, thoughtful

66

kneading, then began to fiddle with her lower. "Ain't it cute?" he observed. "Bet if I squeeze it, it squeaks!"

Mike-Man chortled his companion on. "Yeah boy! Bet it squeaks like one of them rubber dog toys!"

"Please don't please don't please don't," the blonde whimpered over and over through gleaming, perfectly straight white teeth.

Jorrie made to unbuckle his pants. "Down boy! Down!" he joked, alluding to his current state of libidinal animation. "First I think I'll treat this purdy shaved pie to a good ole in and out, then I'll have me a good creaming on this dandy knockers, huh?"

"Yeah boy!" Mike-Man celebrated, keeping the knife in place.

Jorrie's good eye roved up and down the blonde's tremoring flesh. He jacked his trousers down his hips. His glass eye felt cold in his hot skull, and he was tremoring himself quite a bit now, so close to this hot dish. He climbed up between those long, lean, silky legs, but when he looked up again—

"What the—Hey!"

Mike-Man was gone.

Jorrie craned forward, straining his monocular vision past the open driver's door.

"Where the fuck's you gone!"

Then he heard a quick, slick, ever faint *crunch!*

And a groan from way down low in the gut.

Within the block of darkness beyond, Mike-Man fumbled back up into view, teetering and cross-eyed. Jorrie stared.

"Yeah boy," Mike-Man managed to croak. His eyeballs seemed to revolve. "I think, I say, I think we done picked the wrong gal to pull a romping on tonight . . ."

But what was wrong? Mike-Man's voice sounded really low and shaky like when you're sure-fire drunk and can't even say the words proper. Jorrie couldn't figure it until he took a closer look and realized the cause of his friend's newfound speech impediment.

"Holy Sheeeee-it!" Jorrie screamed.

Mike-Man's eyes rolled up, and he sidled over dead in the footwell. A long, shiny knitting needle had been stuck clear through his ears.

The blonde smiled up at him in the moonlight; she began to laugh. *A shakedown!* Jorrie realized. He flailed to crawl out over the blonde, but a hand reached in and snatched onto his hair. He was dragged out of the Blazer, spun around, and slammed back. "Howdy," a youthful voice greeted him. Jorrie's visions swirled—it was some young dude trying to take him down! Where'd he come from? *The van!* he realized. *We done been set up!* Jorrie maneuvered to defend himself. His fine, hard-pointed boots had never failed him in the past; he'd taken out a good many fellas a lot bigger than this dude. He reeled back, then lashed out to kick this fucker a good one right in the nut sack.

And missed.

The blonde was still laughing, leaning up on the bench seat to watch. Jorrie's throat was grabbed, and the back of his skull was slammed once, twice, three times good and hard against the inside edge of the door. On the fourth *whack!* his glass eye popped out of its socket and shattered on the road.

He collapsed as if crushed.

"Hey, Zy. I'll bet you thought I'd never get out here."

The blonde stepped over Jorrie, retrieved her designer jeans, and stepped back into them. "Actually I wish you would've waited a little longer. These two were a riot."

Jorrie's right eye dimmed; he could still see in blurred pieces. The dude was dragging Mike-Man toward the van, grabbing either side of the knitting needle as though it were a convenient carrying handle. The blonde was grinning down at Jorrie, buttoning up her jacket.

"Thanks for stopping to lend a hand. It was very charitable of you."

Jorrie couldn't move.

"Hey!" the dude said. "I *like* those boots."

The blonde shrugged. "Help yourself. It's not like this hayseed's going to be needing them anytime soon."

Jorrie felt his fine hard leather shitkicker boots pulled off his feet. The dude stepped into them. "Nice fit, fella. Thanks."

The blonde departed to start the van. The dude, whistling "Eighteen Wheels and a Dozen Roses," dragged Jorrie to the vehicle and threw him into the back.

His consciousness seemed adrift in a sea of dull pain. He felt heaped atop things. The van doors slammed shut. Jorrie's one eye moved against its nerves. Mike-Man's body lay limp upon several more bodies. One fella's head had been crushed. Another fella lacked a head altogether. On the other side, though, Jorrie felt movement. His eye darted. More bodies lay atop one another, only these were alive. Three of them at least, all girls who'd been tied up and gagged. They squirmed together in shared terror.

The dude climbed into the passenger side. "Not a bad night," he commented, taking a glance into the back.

'Sure." The blonde pulled onto the road. "But you're going to have to be more thorough in the future, Lemi. He's still alive."

"Huh?"

"The guy with the boots. He's still alive."

"Oh. Well I'll fix that splickety-lit."

"That's *lickety-split*, Lemi. Jesus."

"Whatever." This Lemi dude climbed into the back, ducking his head. He was still whistling. Jorrie gave a crushed grunt when he took the first kick in the middle of the spine. Suddenly his legs felt like dead meat. Next, the fine hard point of the boot rammed into his neck-bone, quite effectively fracturing the #2 and 3 cervicular vertebrae, hence transecting the spinal column.

Jorrie Slade's brain went out like a light.

Candles flickered behind him from sconces set into rock. The Factotum stepped forward to the nave. It was damp down here, and strangely warm. Seepage trickled. The stone floor bore the vaguest shapes: blood, no doubt, decades old. The blood of all the people who'd been murdered here. Did their ghosts linger as well?

Ghosts, the Factotum pondered. He could have laughed.

He wore a garment akin to a priest's black cassock, but the Factotum was no priest. He might be called a priest of sorts, yet only in the darkest connotation. The back of his bald head reflected the wavering candle-light—tongues of gentle flame squirming over skin. Beneath the cassock, his naked body felt purged, revitalized. He felt strong again. He felt *good.*

He breathed in the nave's damp vapor. Untainted, fresh. When he closed his eyes, a smile touched his lips, for he saw things—the most *wonderful* things. Things like exaltation, glory, reward. In the onyx-black shapes behind his eyes, he saw tenacity and the sheer, crystal promise of infinity.

Such a blessing, he thought. His heart felt afire.

Such a blessing to serve.

Chapter Six

"Carriage House, here we come!" Dan B. rejoiced.

"Hey, Vera?" Lee asked. "You think this Feldspar guy'll let me have beer on the house?"

"I can't wait to see this place!" Donna excitedly joined in. "I've seen pictures of it. It's like a big Gothic mansion!"

Vera smiled.

Dan B. drove—the big Plymouth wagon he and Donna owned—and Lee rode next to him, tracing the upstate maps. Vera sat in the back with Donna. They were all the essentials Vera would need right off; secondary help she could hire from Waynesville. A large MOVE-IT! truck, which Vera had contracted for them, followed the wagon up the narrow winding roads of the northernmost edge of the county.

None of them had hesitated at Vera's offer; Feldspar's perks, cash supplements, increased salaries, and guaranteed employment contracts were irresistible. "Why not?" Dan B. had remarked. "This city's getting old anyway. Besides, it'd be selfish for a chef of my extraordinary skills to deprive the rest of the world of his delights." "Free room and board in a renovated suite!" Donna had exclaimed. "I'm there already!" And Lee: "Did I hear you right, Vera? You're asking me if I'll

71

wash dishes for twelve bucks an hour instead of six? What do you think?''

The four of them quitting The Emerald Room without notice did not exactly elate the general manager, but there was no love lost there. He was an uncouth slob who frequently harassed the younger waitresses and had a propensity for leaving boogers on his office wall. Good riddance to him. The next day Vera had rented the truck and hired the movers. "What about your stuff?" Dan B. had asked when they were finished loading up. Vera hadn't answered; she wasn't ready to even talk about it much less actually return to the apartment and face Paul. *He probably wouldn't care anyway,* she suspected. *He'll probably be happy when he finds out I'm gone.* Instead, she'd bought some clothes and sundries with some of the money Feldspar had given her for coming on. She'd get her things from the apartment some other time, if at all. What did she really need, anyway? Her room would be furnished; the company was providing a car. Everything else she needed she could buy. Not ever seeing Paul again was fine with her; the few appliances they'd bought mutually he could have. And the old Tercel could sit in the Mr. Donut parking lot forever as far as Vera was concerned.

Talk about starting with a clean slate, she reflected.

The countryside was beautiful, plush, even in the grip of winter. Its openness seemed unreal, like a long-forgotten dream. The northern ridge rose as an endless expanse of pines, oaks, and firs. South, for miles and miles along State Route 154, farmland denuded of its fall harvest stretched on to an equal degree of endlessness. City life had smothered her; its smog and rush hour and asphalt and cement had veiled her memory of the countryside's spacious beauty and peace. R.M. at The Emerald Room had been a good job but, she realized now, it had entombed her. *There is life after the city*, she amused herself with the thought. *A better life.*

"Come on, man, get with the map," Dan B. complained at the wheel. "We almost there yet or what?"

"How about eating my shorts?" Lee returned, his lap full of a clutter of maps. "This thing says—"

"We're about an hour away, Dan B.," Vera verified. "It's pretty much a straight shot up the route. Would you relax?"

"I'm excited, I can't help it. I can't wait to see the place."

Neither can I, Vera wondered. If Feldspar was exaggerating, she'd know soon enough. A complete renovation of Wroxton Hall would cost millions. If Feldspar's company had that kind of money to pump into refurbishments, she couldn't imagine what kind of money he'd be able to sink into advertising and promotion.

"I don't quite understand it all," Dan B. queried. "This place is going to be like—"

"A country-styled bed and breakfast type of place," Vera answered. "With a separate restaurant to cater to locals. Feldspar wants to target upper-market businessmen and rich people—a weekend get-away-from-it-all sort of thing. But he also wants a full-time restaurant to cater to the better-off people in the area. That's where we come in. Feldspar says it's cost-no-object; we'll get to do pretty much what we want. He's more concerned with the hotel operations himself. He's entrusting the entire restaurant to me, or to us, I should say. The whole thing sounds really great, but what we have to remember is the only reason he's paying us all this money is because he doesn't want the headache. What he wants is a state-of-the-art dining room without having to worry about it himself."

"So if we fuck up," Lee remarked, "our shit's in the wind."

"I'd put it a little more eloquently than that, but yeah. Feldspar seems like a real nice guy, but you can bet he didn't get to where he is today by passing out second chances. If we don't turn The Carriage House into something that meets all of his expectations, he won't think twice about giving us our walking papers and finding someone else."

"What are we all worried about?" Donna proposed. "We did it at The Emerald Room. We'll do it here."

"Damn right," Vera said. "The Carriage House is going to blow Feldspar right out of his Guccis. I figure we'll run with a menu close to what we had at The Emerald, but with a lot more exotic specials—"

"Just show me the kitchen," Dan B. said.

"Feldspar's talking anything and everything good. He doesn't even care what the food invoices are. He just wants excellent food every night."

"I'll give him that," Dan B. promised. "I'll show him."

"And excellent service."

"I'll give him that," Donna said.

"And clean dishes, right?" Lee mocked.

"That's right, Lee. Clean dishes. And I don't want to see you sneaking carafes of beer into the back. This isn't going to be like The Emerald Room—it's going to be better. So I don't want any fooling around back there. And no drinking during your shift, okay?"

Lee shrugged, smirking. "For twelve bucks an hour, I can even do that."

Yeah, Vera thought. She felt proud. They were a team on their way to something new. *This just might work.*

She lounged back. Donna was reading. Dan B. and Lee continued to bicker back and forth over directions and exchange less than complimentary regards for one another, which was normal for a chef and a dishwasher. Vera took some time to just look around, let the vast countryside speed past her eyes. It was almost tranquilizing, the long open road, the encroaching ridge, and the fact that they hadn't passed another car for miles. She felt free now, released from the cement confines of the city and from a relationship that had been false for God knew how long.

"Only one thing bothers me," Donna suddenly said.

"What's that?" Lee inquired. "Dan B.'s crane won't rise anymore?"

"It rose just fine last night when I was at your mother's house," Dan B. informed him.

"Yeah, but what about your sister?"

"Would you two idiots shut up," Vera snapped. She couldn't imagine how Donna could put up with Dan B.'s profane sense of humor. "What were you saying, Donna?"

"The rep. It bothers me."

"What do you mean?"

"Who's going to want to spend big money staying at a country inn with such a reputation?"

Vera knew what she meant; she'd thought about that herself, and quickly came to the conclusion that they needn't worry. "Forget it, Donna. It's all a bunch of crap, and even if it isn't, that stuff supposedly went on fifty years ago."

"What stuff?" Lee turned around and asked.

Donna seemed enthused. "The Inn used to be a place called Wroxton Hall. It was a sanitarium."

"What's a sanitarium?"

"It's a place where you study sanitation, you dickbrain," Dan B. laughed. "Didn't they teach you anything in reform school?"

"They taught me how to lay pipe with your mom," Lee came back.

"Please, please, stop," Vera pleaded. "A sanitarium, for your information, Lee, at least in this case, is an

75

insane asylum. Not like the mental hospitals of today. Back then they pretty much just locked the mentally ill away instead of treating them. That's where they sent people who were schizophrenics and psychotics."

"And male virgins, too," Dan B. added. "So you better be careful."

"Oh, that's real funny," Lee said. "Almost as funny as your last special. Remember? We ran out of veal for the medallion soup, so you used pork."

"That's right, skillethead, and you didn't even know the difference, so blow me."

"I'd need tweezers and a magnifying glass to bl—"

"And what Donna is just itching to say," Vera interrupted, "is that this particular asylum ran into a few problems."

"What kind of problems?"

"Well," Vera hesitated. "Evidently, some people died there."

"They didn't just die," Donna augmented. "They were murdered."

Vera shook her head. "Donna, even if it's true, no one will remember it. It happened too long ago."

"Someone must remember it." Donna held up the book in her lap. *The Complete Compendium of Haunted American Mansions*, the title read in silly, dripping letters. "This book just came out a few weeks ago. And there's a whole chapter on Wroxton Hall."

"Wait a minute," Dan B. testily jumped in. "What's the big deal? Some people got murdered in an insane asylum—so what?"

"They were tortured to death," Donna said. "By the staff. And a lot of the local residents say they've seen ghosts walking around in the building at night."

"Ghosts?" Lee said. "You mean the place is haunted?"

"Aw, relax," Dan B. chuckled. "There's no ghosts.

76

It's just your mom with a sheet over her head, looking for some free peter.''

Vera rolled her eyes. *What am I going to do with these three nuts?* she wondered.

"You've got to be kidding me, Vera," Dan B. complained. "How much longer?"

"We're almost there. It's right up the ridge." At least she thought it was. The access road wound upward; cracks spiderwebbed the old asphalt. Skeletal branches seemed to reach out, trying to touch them. The tall forest blocked out the light.

They'd passed through Waynesville twenty minutes ago, a sleepy, rustic little town. It looked poor, rundown. A simple turn off, the route brought them into the face of the northern ridge. A haphazard sign signalled them: WROXTON HALL in hand-painted blue letters, and an arrow. *Get a new sign,* Vera thought, nearly groaning. And all this brush would need to be cut back, and the access road would have to be patched, and . . .

That was all Feldspar's problem. Again, she wondered about these "restorations"; The Inn would have to be more than merely impressive in order to attract patrons through this mess. Surely, Feldspar knew this.

"This can't be right." Dan B. whipped his head toward Lee. "If you'd get your hand out of your pants and watch the map, then maybe we'd know where we were going."

"Relax, Dumbo," Lee came back. "This is the right road. It says right here on the map, Wroxton Estates."

The moving truck rumbled behind them up the incline. Farther up, Vera felt some relief. A contractor's sign, RANDOLPH CARTER EXCAVATORS, INC., had been posted. They *were* fixing the road and cutting back the overgrowth. Soon, construction vehicles came

77

into view, refuse trucks, chipping machines, tree-trimming crews. At last, the winding, dark road opened into crisp winter daylight.

"Jesus Christ," Dan B. muttered.

Lee's face flattened in astonishment. "I don't believe what I'm seeing."

The car slowed around a vast, paved court. Vera and Donna gazed over the men's shoulders. Center of the court was a huge, heated fountain; Sappho in white marble poured twin gushes of water from her elegant hands. Great hedges had been trimmed to the meticulousness of sculpture. And just beyond loomed the immense edifice of Wroxton Hall.

"Somebody pinch me so I wake up," Donna said in wide-eyed wonder.

"Jesus Christ," Dan B. repeated.

Lee's rowdy voice hushed in awe. "This place is gonna kick . . . butt."

Vera could only stare. A single glance quelled all her doubts at once. *It's beautiful,* she thought.

Huge, high as a castle, Wroxton Hall had been restored to a Gothic masterpiece. Its old bricks had been sandblasted to a new earth-red luster. Sheets of ivy had actually been replanted in the new grout. The first-floor windows stood ten-feet tall, each opening to smooth, granite-edged verandas. The building rose in canted sections. Awninged balconies protruded from the second- and third-floor rooms; garret-suites, like ramparts against the sun, extended along the top floor. The roofs of each story had been laid in genuine slate, with polished stone friezes running the entire length of each. The building, in whole, looked nearly a hundred yards long.

Words occurred to Vera. *Magnificent. Gorgeous. Awesome.* But none seemed quite good enough to be applied to what stood before her. *Palatial.* There, that was it.

Wroxton Hall was far more than a restored mansion. It was a *palace.* Feldspar had retained the beauty of its age while rebuilding the place at the same time. *Extraordinary,* Vera thought. *Feldspar's a genius.*

The four of them got out but could only remain standing speechless in the court. Birds looked down on them from the roof's fine iron cresting. Each frieze bracket sported a gargoyle's face, and the corner boards shined in polished granite against the plush red brick outer walls. The new glass of each high, narrow window reflected back at them like mirrors.

Behind them the MOVE-IT! truck rumbled up and stopped, discharging two loutish hired hands. "Fuckin' *Dark Shadows,* man," the driver commented through a high gaze. "Some joint, huh?" the other one remarked. "Where's Trump and Marla?"

This was better than Vera could ever even have conceived. Feldspar was quite right; Wroxton Hall provided a resort of the utmost exclusivity. The remote locale meant nothing now. Once word got around in the trade magazines, people from all over the country would be coming here. People from all over the world.

Her excitement surged so intensely it seemed to arrest her will to move. She attempted to step forward, toward the front steps, but found she could only remain where she stood, her gaze scanning the building's incomparable exterior. When the reality of what she was seeing set in, her breath grew light, and she actually felt subtly dizzied.

Slate-topped red brick steps led to the double entry doors, sided by great polished-granite blocks which gave perch to lazing stone lions. More articulate friezework underlined the transom's gray-marble ledge and stained-glass fanlight. Wedged directly center was a small keystone of pure onyx in which was mounted a round, cut amethyst as big around as a silver dollar.

Great brass knockers decorated the high, walnut doors. More gorgeous stained glass filled the sidelights, set into ornate, carved sashes.

"We *live* here?" Lee mouthed in astonishment.

"Yes," Vera nearly croaked.

"Jesus Christ," Dan B. remarked yet again.

"Are we going to stand here all day like four dopes," Donna proposed, "or are we going to go in?"

A click resounded. Behind them, the heated fountain gushed. A black line formed in the elegant veneered walnut trim. Then the great front doors pulled slowly apart.

Feldspar stubbily stepped onto the wide stone stoop. He wore a fine heather-gray Italian suit, black shirt, and black silk tie. He let his eyes rove across their upturned faces, pausing. Then he smiled within the fastidiously trimmed goatee.

His voice loomed like the building: expansive, vast. "Welcome to Wroxton Hall," he greeted. His broad, short hands opened at his sides, as a minister's might, during the sermon. 'Or I should say, welcome, my friends . . . to The Inn.''

Chapter Seven

Vera's awe redoubled once she stepped past the inlaid foyer. Tall vases sprung with flowers stood at either side; Feldspar closed the front doors behind them. Dan B., Donna, and Lee all squinted off in different directions while Vera glanced upward at the great crystal chandelier. Its icelike shimmer seemed to hover.

"The atrium," Feldspar remarked, rather dully. "Satisfactory work, but I've seen better."

I haven't, Vera thought. If anything, The Inn's interior was more magnificent than its exterior. Paneled walls rose thirty feet, adorned by great framed oil paintings of Victorian theme. A sharp scent of newness hovered, like the chandelier's shimmer: newly cut wood, fresh shellac and stain, new carpet. Between the twin, curving staircases sat a beautifully veneered oak reception table; all of the atrium's tables, in fact, were obviously of the exceptional quality, and centered before fine, plushly upholstered armchairs. The atrium had a classy, quiet feel to it, all soft, dark hues and dark wood, more akin to an English men's club than a mere hotel entry. Statues in dark marble stood upon pedestals ensconced into the atrium's paneled walls.

"This way," Feldspar said.

They followed the odd man off to the right, to the

lower west wing. A long wall of wooden lattice filled with myriad small glass panes ended at opened French doors. Above the door, off a black iron rung, suspended the mahogany sign in etched letters:

THE CARRIAGE HOUSE

Vera's excitement strewed. Feldspar had spared no expense; this made The Emerald Room look like a rib shack. Fine, white linens over oak tables, quality wing chairs, plush, dark carpet. A long planter formed an aisle between the dining room and the kitchen entrance, full of a vast medley of fresh flowers. Tastefully framed rustic artwork, all original oils, embellished elegant, gray-paneled walls. Vera slowly wandered among the dining tables, and in rising awe she recognized the best of everything down to the most minute details. Le Perle silverware, Tiffany & Company saucers and cups, Homer Laughlin plates, Luminarc glasses, shakers, and table vases.

"You, of course, have final say on the serviceware inventory," Feldspar told her, "should this prove insufficient."

Insufficient? Vera could've fainted. She remembered her own inventory procurement when she'd taken over at The Emerald Room—a fortune, but *nothing* compared to this. If anything, Feldspar had spent more than he'd needed to.

"You gentlemen will want to inspect the kitchen facilities," he went on, addressing Dan B. and Lee, and to Donna, "and the service bar and waitress stations." Feldspar faintly smiled. "And I'm happy to say that, as of now, my affiliation with all technical aspects of the restaurant are at an end. In other words, should you find anything unsatisfactory about the facilities, voice your grievances not to me but to Ms. Abbot."

"Oh, we're quite used to that," Donna remarked and laughed.

"Come on, Curley," Dan B. said to Lee. "Let's check out our gig."

"Sure, Shemp," Lee replied as the three of them made for the swingdoors to the kitchen.

Vera still felt prickly in her excitement. Panning her gaze, she could scarcely believe that this beautiful restaurant was, for all intents and purposes, hers.

"Conclusions? Comments?" Feldspar bid. He seemed suddenly worried. Could he possibly fear that The Inn's refurbishment did not meet her approval?

"I'm still in shock," Vera replied. "I couldn't be more impressed. You've done an outstanding job."

"I'm happy to hear you say that."

"And we'll do an outstanding job for you."

Feldspar unconsciously diddled with his big amethyst pinky ring and the other bright jewelry which adorned his stubby hand. He was a complex man, and Vera could sense that complexity now very clearly. He was a man with a vast mission who, step by step, discharged each of his tasks like machinery. Vera paused to wonder about his direct conception of her. *Am I just another gear in his machine, or does he see me as an associate, a real person?* Probably the former at this point—this was business. Odd as he was, Feldspar was an extraordinary man, and she admired him. But she knew that she would have to prove her worth quite quickly in order for the admiration to be mutual. *You'll see, buddy,* she thought. *I'm gonna turn this pretty joint of yours into the best restaurant in the state.*

"You'll probably want to expend some time now on a closer examination of the facility. My office is in the west wing; let me know when you're done here, and I'll have someone show you your room."

Before Vera could reply, Feldspar was moving back toward the atrium—not walking, really, but sort of half-ambling in that peculiar, faltering gait of his. The sudden quiet of his departure focused Vera's speculations, even her dreams. She felt wistful and exuberant. With a little luck, a little advertising, and more than a little hard work, they would turn The Inn into a money machine.

Something clinked. Almost startled, she turned. A woman was pushing a wheeled cart full of crystal candle-holders down the aisle along the planter. Through colorful splays of fresh, potted bluebells and poinsettias, she stopped—as if startled herself—and looked right at Vera.

"Hello," Vera said. "I'm—"

How rude. The woman trundled away at once, more quickly. She must be one of the housekeeping staff. *She better not be one of my staff,* Vera thought. Not only was she rude, ignoring Vera's introduction, but she was . . .

Gross, Vera determined. Not ugly as much as simply unpleasant-looking. An unattractive bun had been made of her dark, frizzed hair. Though she didn't appear to be old, she seemed slightly bowed as she walked away, and short, husky. Vera glanced after the odd woman, frowning. *I'm upper management, honey. You better start being a lot more cordial than that.*

The cart's casters squealed across the atrium, and the woman briefly gazed back at Vera.

Vera nearly winced.

The woman's big, jowly face looked pasty as old wax. Large breasts sagged in the pale-blue staff uniform. And her eyes—her close-set and nearly rheumy brown eyes—gave off a very clear message of disdain, or even disgust.

"We're getting down to the wire on that first Kirby piece, boss," said Brice, the layout director.

Harold Tate glanced up from his desk, which was, appropriately, a mess. Newspaper editors were entitled to have cluttered desks; it was their trademark. Tate was the editor for the *City Sun,* and his quickened smirk showed the extent of his concern. He'd been in this business long enough to realize the unnecessity of shitting a brick every time a journalist was getting close to a deadline. "Don't worry about it," he muttered back to Brice. "Kirby's a pro, he'll have his copy in on time."

"What if he doesn't?"

Tate smirked doubly. "If he doesn't then I'll put my foot so far up his ass he'll be able to taste the dogshit I stepped in on West Street this morning. But don't worry about it, it ain't gonna happen. Kirby's never missed a deadline yet."

"That's what I mean, boss. He's usually a week early with each piece. If I don't have his copy by tomorrow noon, we're going to have to re-lay the entire section. That's a fifteen hundred word block, plus a three-by-four picture grid. It's not like we can fill it in with ads at the last minute."

"Maybe we can fill it in with prints of me kicking you in the ass for bothering me with bullshit," Tate proposed. "How many times I gotta say it? Don't worry about Kirby; his copy'll be in on time."

"It's just kind of weird—"

Tate glared. "You're still here?"

Brice took a hesitant step forward, a lamb straying into the lion's den. He was a worrywart but he was also a good layout man, so Tate tolerated him. The newspaper business was like any business—give and take. You want good people, you put up with their quirks. "I gave Kirby a call today," Brice finally said.

"You have a nice little chat?"

"He hung up on me."

Tate's smirk quickly dulled. "What do you mean he hung up on you?"

"I was just double-checking, you know. This is the

first time he hasn't had his material in early. I thought maybe he forgot about it or something."

"He better not have," Tate remarked. "I've already paid him for half the goddamn series. What did he say?"

Brice's eyes looked distant. "That's the weird part, boss. He sounded hungover or something, or like I'd just woken him up. Didn't even sound like he knew who I was."

"All right, so he was tired. Big deal."

"I reminded him of the deadline. . . . "

Tate tapped his blotter with a red pen. "And?"

"He hung up on me. Just like that."

Tate gave this some thought. God knew he'd met his share of pretentious journalists, people whose egos were bigger than the fucking Sears Tower. But this didn't sound like Kirby. Kirby was low key and very professional. He never caused a fuss and he didn't make waves. And he'd never been known to be rude.

"Don't worry about it," Tate repeated after a pause. "Go back to the dungeon and haunt your own office. You let me worry about Kirby."

"Just thought I'd let you know."

"Yeah, yeah . . ."

Brice left. Tate couldn't figure it. Maybe the kid was exaggerating. . . .

Tate thumbed through his Rolodex, to the Ks. KIRBY, PAUL, WEST WIND APARTMENTS. He dialed the number and waited.

Six rings, then: "Hello?"

"Kirby, this is Tate. One of my people says you're lollygagging on the singles piece. Is—"

"Who?" Kirby's voice drifted. "Who is this?"

Tate ground his teeth. "Tate, you know? Harold *Tate?* Editor and chief of the *City Fucking Sun?* The guy who just paid you three bills on a series for the *Weekender—*"

"Oh, yeah. Right." Kirby sounded drained, barely coherent. A pause lapsed across the line. "Don't worry, it'll be in."

"Well it goddamn better be, son, and if you don't mind my saying so, you sound like shit. You—"

Click.

The line went dead.

"How do you like that son of a bitch," Tate muttered to himself, and hung up. *Fucking writers,* he thought. *They're all a bunch of fucking weirdos.*

Chapter Eight

"This is unbelievable, Vera," Dan B. enthused.

Vera strolled down the shining hot line, gazing. The kitchen was huge, and it had been outfitted to the max. Groen industrial ovens and braisers, additional deck ovens, and twin South Bend ranges with ten burners each. And behind the line: Vulcan friers, Blodgett roasters, and Cleveland/ALCO professional steamers.

Dan B. looked dismayed. "And it's all brand-spanking-new. Feldspar could've saved himself forty or fifty percent buying used or rebuilt, but he didn't."

"I don't think that's Feldspar's style," Vera acknowledged. "He's not interested in cutting corners."

The cold line, too, was replete with the same: brand-new Bloomfield salad and soup stations, three Univex mixers, and Groen speed-drives, plus an array of shredders, slicers, graters, and grinders. The entire kitchen glimmered in stainless steel newness.

"Every chef's dream, right?" Vera suggested.

"You ain't kidding." Dan B. walked, nearly in a daze, behind the lines, glancing astonished at an entire wall of Dexter/Russell cutlery, Wearever pots and pans, and Wollrath prep gear. "Service bar's the same way," Dan B. went on. "Donna's in there having a baby rhino. And Lee . . ."

"Holy shit!" the voice exclaimed around the line.

Lee was running around like a kid under a Christmas tree. His chubby moon face bloomed in delight with each of his shocked glances to and fro. Then his belly jiggled when he stopped before a mammoth Hobart chain-washer, which could crank three hundred sixty racks per hour. Lee's eyes widened in something like veneration. "It's . . . it's beautiful," he stammered.

"Look at that," Dan B. laughed. "He's getting hard. It's not the Hustler Honey of the Month, it's just a dishwasher."

"No, no, it's more than that." Lee grinned at Dan B. "It's the best dishwasher in the world, and it's even more beautiful than . . . your mom."

Dan B. promptly gave Lee the finger. But Lee was right; the great machine was one of the best dishwashers in the world, and so was the three-stage glasswasher behind it. Vera realized that just the equipment in this kitchen probably cost upwards of half a million.

"Let's not embarrass him," Dan B. suggested. "Lee wants to make love to the dishwasher." He took Vera by the arm, getting serious. "Come here. I want to show you something."

Vera followed him to the end of the line, past a pair of five-hundred-gallon lobster tanks and customized Nor-Lake walk-ins.

"What's wrong?" Vera asked. "Aren't you happy about all of this?"

"Sure. But there's something . . . I don't know. Something's not right."

"Like what?"

"Like that Hobart machine, for one," Dan B. said. "That's a fifteen-thousand-dollar rig, it's something you use for a banquet house or a mess hall. You don't need a machine that elaborate for a country restaurant. And the same goes for all of this stuff—sure, it's all great stuff, but it's overkill. Feldspar's got to be out of his mind dropping this much cash for a restaurant in a questionable location."

Why are men always so skeptical? Vera wondered. "Don't complain. If we work our tails off, and get in some good advertising, we could fill this place every night."

"Come on, Vera. That's wishful thinking. You and I both know that the chances for *any* new restaurant, anywhere, are less than fifty-fifty."

"That's why Feldspar's going full-tilt, to up the chances."

"Maybe," Dan B. conceded. "But take a look at this."

He led her next to a stainless steel door at the back of the kitchen. He pulled it open. Vera stared in.

"Can you believe this?" Dan B. inquired.

Vera shrugged. Okay, maybe Feldspar was going a little crazy with the money. What she was looking at, past the door, was *another* kitchen, nearly identical to theirs.

"A second kitchen just for room service?" Dan B. questioned. "Feldspar thinks business is going to be so great that he needs a separate kitchen just for the hotel orders? It's ridiculous."

"No, it's not."

Vera and Dan B. turned at the remark.

A young man stood immediately to their rear: tall, trim, wavy longish light-brown hair. Vera found him instantly attractive in a lackadaisical sort of way. He wore tight, faded jeans, a white kitchen tunic halfway unbuttoned, and old clunky line boots. He smiled, almost cockily, and extended his hand to Vera.

"You're Ms. Abbot, right?"

"Vera," she said.

"I'm Kyle, the room-service manager. And you're . . . Don?"

"Dan B.," Dan B. corrected, and shook hands. "The chef."

"I heard what you were saying just now," Kyle went on, "and I can understand where you're coming from. I felt the same way when Mr. Feldspar first took me on. But I can tell you, Magwyth Enterprises has inns just like this all over the place, and not one of them has lost money yet. In fact they've all jumped into the black right off. So don't worry about the location, or the fact that Mr. Feldspar's spent so much money up front. The guy knows what he's doing."

"We didn't mean to imply that he didn't," Vera hastened to say. First day on the job she didn't need this guy running to Feldspar with negative implications. Immediately she viewed Kyle as her personal competition: room service would have an instant edge in gross receipts. *Make friends with him fast,* she warned herself. She'd been in the business too long to play hoity-toity.

"And I can tell you something else," Kyle added, and flipped a lock of hair back off his brow. "You do good work for Mr. Feldspar and the sky's the limit. But you have to prove yourself first. You have to show him what you're made of."

Vera repressed a sarcastic face. Kyle was showing his true colors right off the bat. It was the same as him saying: *I'm the one to beat around here, and I'm not going to give you an inch of slack.* "We appreciate the input, Kyle," Vera eventually said.

Kyle glanced to Dan B., nodding. "I hear you're pretty good behind the line. I'm looking forward to trying out some of your grub."

"My 'grub' will knock your socks off," Dan B. promised.

"Me, I do all the cooking for room service. I always

have a standing bet with the restaurant chef, quarterly evaluation. Whoever comes out on top takes a C-note from the loser. Interested?"

"Sure," Dan B. said. "I'll take your money, no problem."

Kyle laughed. "Okay, man, you're on. It'll be fun, you'll see. Mr. Feldspar wants me to show you to your rooms whenever you all are ready. I'll be over here in my gig."

"Thanks, Kyle," Vera said.

"See you all later."

Kyle went into the room-service kitchen and closed the door behind him.

"What an asshole," Dan B. concluded at once.

"Yeah, but at least he's a good-natured asshole," Vera said.

"And I didn't like the way he was scoping your rib-melons."

Vera squinted at him. "*Whating* my *whats?*"

"The way he was looking at your t— . . . your breasts."

Vera nearly blushed. "He was not—"

"Of course he was, Vera. Christ, I thought the guy's eyeballs were gonna pop out and land in your blouse. Talk about low-class. And how do you like that shit he was spouting about a quarterly evaluation? That snide punk probably can't even cook microwave tater-tots. I'll bet he thinks mahi-mahi is an island in Hawaii. If I ever lose a cook-off to him I'll turn in my gear and jack fries at Hardee's for the rest of my life. The *punk.*"

Chef rivalry, Vera realized. It was worse than the Redskins and the Cowboys. "Don't get your dander up," she advised. "Try and get along with him for now; we don't need any personality conflicts before we even open."

"And I'll tell you something else." Dan B. lowered

92

his voice, as if Kyle might hear him through the steel doors. "Me and Lee saw a couple of really freaky types wandering around the place earlier. Maids or something. Looked to us like they were stoned on 'ludes. We tried talking to them, but they just walked away."

"Yeah," Vera acknowledged. She remembered the odd woman she'd seen pushing the cart of vases back in the dining room. She hadn't spoken a word. "So what?" she allayed. "What do we care about the maintenance staff? They're probably people Feldspar grabbed from some other inns, foreigners probably. They don't talk to us because they probably can't even speak English. Ten to one a lot of them don't have green cards, so don't make a stink about it. If Feldspar wants to run illegal labor in the background, that's his business."

"Really ugly too," Dan B. articulated. "These two chicks looked like cave women in maid uniforms."

"Be nice," Vera scolded. "I don't know which one of you is more sexist and insolent, you or Lee."

"Me," Dan B. asserted.

"You're probably right. I'm going to check out my room now, and see what else this Kyle character has to say. Meantime, I want you, Donna, and Lee to go over every single piece of equipment in the kitchen. Make sure everything's hooked up and wired properly, and keep a list of anything that doesn't work. Also check out the dry stocks, see what Feldspar's already got. We don't want to find out on opening night that we don't have any salt."

"Got'cha."

Dan B. went back down the line. Vera opened the big room service door and found Kyle marking things off on a clipboard. He looked phony, like an act. Vera had the notion that he'd been waiting for her all along, and wanted to appear busy when she came through.

93

"I'm pretty much done for now," she announced. "Can you show me my room?"

"I'd be happy to." Kyle put down the clipboard and grinned. "I don't know about you, but I'm really excited. We're gonna *crank* in some business. Did Mr. Feldspar tell you? The Inn's already got its first four weekends booked in advance."

"You're kidding me."

"Nope. Hundred percent occupancy. All ninety rooms."

Vera doubted this. "He told me there were a hundred rooms."

"Total to let, sure. The other ten are for the local room reservations, the ones on the second floor. Those are the ones you're in charge of. Didn't Mr. Feldspar tell you?"

"He told me," Vera answered. *You run ninety rooms and I run ten, but I've still got the restaurant.* This was getting absurdly complicated. If Kyle was the room service manager, why shouldn't he be in charge of *all* the rooms? "How many of my rooms are booked in advance?"

"None," Kyle said.

Vera frowned.

She followed him to the opposite end of the RS kitchen. It infuriated her: if anything, Kyle's kitchen was even more elaborate than hers, with more walk-ins and equipment. She stopped cold at the next sight. "Hey," she said. "How come you've got four lobster tanks and I've only got two?"

Kyle held back a laugh. "Look, Ms. Abbot—Vera—don't get hot under the collar. Just because I have a bigger facility than you doesn't mean that Mr. Feldspar thinks I'm any better than you. It's business."

"Business?" Vera objected. "What's business got to do with you having two more lobster tanks than me?"

94

Now Kyle did laugh, openly. "I don't believe it. We're having an argument over lobster tanks. . . .

"And you've got more ranges, more ovens more convection steamers, more—"

"Stop and think a minute at what you're saying. You run the restaurant, I run room service. I've got *ninety rooms* to handle, all you've got to worry about are the separate dinner orders."

"Oh, and that instantly means you're going to be doing more business than me?"

"Of course it does."

"Back in the city I used to run a hundred and fifty dinners a night—that's a lot more than ninety."

"No it isn't, not really. I've got ninety *rooms,* sure, but the average room books two people, and that's three meals a day, not just one."

Vera paused. He had a point . . . sort of. Perhaps she was letting a petty jealousy cloud her ability to see facts. "Well," she attempted, "some of those people will be coming in to The Carriage House to eat."

"Maybe, but I doubt it," Kyle baldly told her. "Mr. Feldspar figures that most of your business will be from the locals."

"Is that so?" she huffed.

"Like it or not, the majority of The Inn's business will be from wealthy out-of-towners, a select clientele. That's why he needs me running the RS."

"Oh? And why is that? You're saying that my people aren't good enough to serve your 'select clientele'?"

"Hey, you said it, I didn't. I'm more experienced in this gig. I'm sure your man over there is a great chef, but there's a difference between a great chef and a great room-service chef. It's a different job."

All right, all right, Vera tried to settle herself down. She was falling right into Kyle's trap, fighting already for higher ground—and losing. "I see what you mean."

"We're a team, Ms. Abbot—Vera." His grin remained subtly sly. "Let's be friends. I'm not out to compete with you."

Bullshit, she thought for sure. She'd run into plenty of Kyles in her career, people who come on as nice guys, yet they're stabbing you in the back whenever they get the chance. Everything Kyle said made objective sense; nevertheless, she didn't trust him for a minute.

At least he's cute, she thought next. A moment later, though, when she considered the thought, she felt shocked. Vera was not a libidinous woman. Her sex life with Paul had been good, but that was over now. It didn't seem part of her character to suddenly acknowledge her attraction, however remote, to some kid she'd met fifteen minutes ago.

Be a good girl, Vera. Forget about this guy's tight ass and start acting like an adult.

"Come on," he prodded. "You're gonna love it. Mr. Feldspar says you have your choice of suites."

Nearing the end of the RS line, they passed two elevators. RS STAFF ONLY, one read, and ROOM SERVICE DELIVERY read the other. But suddenly he was taking her through a door which opened up behind the reception desk in the atrium, between the twin winding stairwells.

"I still can't believe how beautiful the atrium is," she commented. Once again, her gaze strayed out over the array of plush carpet and furniture, and the gorgeous artwork, statues, and flower arrangements. Kyle, however, seemed to take it all for granted, turning up the left stairs without a second glance.

"Let me grab my bags," Vera said. "I didn't bring much in the way of personal effects."

"Forget it." Kyle waved her up. "I'll have the dolts bring it up later."

"The *what?*"

"The dolts, you know. The housekeeping staff," Kyle designated. "That's what we call them. They're good workers but not much in the smarts department."

Vera's lip pursed. *Dolts,* she thought. "I don't know what school of management you come from, Kyle, but tagging your manual labor with derrogatory nicknames doesn't exactly do wonders for employee morale."

"Jesus, you're touchy. I hate to think what kind of nicknames they have for us."

Vera grabbed two of her suitcases, which the movers had left in the foyer. "At least let me take them," Kyle insisted.

"I can handle it," Vera replied.

Kyle grinned. "You're pissed off, aren't you?"

"No, Kyle, I'm not pissed off. I just think you've got a lot to learn about dealing with people."

Kyle laughed. "Hey, I'm a nice guy—I swear. I'll bet my next check you'll be calling them dolts a week from now. They're all immigrants from eastern Europe or something. Most of them can't understand a word you say."

"Oh, so that means they're stupid? That means they're *dolts?*"

"All right already, I'm sorry. Boy, you and me really are starting off on the wrong foot."

Vera sighed, following him up the stairs. "Do they have green cards?"

Now it was Kyle's lips that pursed. "That's the wrong kind of question to ask around here. Mr. Feldspar got them from one of the other inns."

"He's got inns in *eastern Europe?*"

"Sure. Eastern Europe's a boomtown now, are you kidding? Since the cold war ended, all kinds of U.S. investors are setting up shop over there. We've even got an inn in Russia."

"And it's making money?"

"Hand over fist."

Vera contemplated this as she stepped onto the landing. She'd read that the Radisson and some other major hotel chains were opening in eastern Europe, but they were for travelers and businessmen. But what kind of clientele could Feldspar possibly have attracted to Russia? She couldn't imagine such a business risk.

"They're cheap," Kyle was saying. "That's all that matters."

"What?"

"The dolts—er, excuse me. I mean the custodial engineers."

Vera ignored him. He began to lead her down a similarly plush, dark hallway. But then she stopped. "Wait a minute," she queried.

"What's wrong now?"

The stairs, she thought. *What the hell?*

The twin staircases led from the atrium to the second floor. And ended. But The Inn had four floors, didn't it?

"Why do the stairs end here? How do you—"

"Get to the third and fourth floors?" Kyle finished her question. "VIP entrance in back, by the parking lot and helipad."

Odd, she concluded. She understood the desire to separate the high-priced suites from the cheaper rooms. But separate *accesses?* It seemed an indulgent expense. She couldn't imagine the additional construction costs for such a nicety. On the other hand, though, rich people were often eccentric, and the more their eccentricities were pampered, she realized, the more frequently they'd come back and, of course, the more money they'd spend. When executed properly, it was a system that always worked in the long run.

It was the short run, however, that she worried about. How could such an expensive venture survive during

98

start-up? Just how extensive *was* Feldspar's marketing influence? And could she really believe that the first four weekends were already booked?

Worry about The Carriage House, Vera, she reminded herself. *One step at a time.*

Kyle opened the first door on the right, which, like all of the doors, was solid oak, and ornately trimmed. He stepped back to give her room. "Check it out."

Vera set her bags down and slowly rose. For a moment she lost her breath. What faced her past the entry was not a bedroom but a great chamber like an eighteenth-century French boudoir. Soft pastel papers covered the walls, with high pine skirtings. Dark, plush V'Soske throw rugs bedecked the rich hardwood floor. Most of the furniture was restored antique: a beige scroll couch, a cherrywood highboy, a walnut chiffonier and inlaid night stand. Heavy velvet drapes, a deep avocado hue, were tied back before the white vanity and mirror. The room itself seemed nearly as large as her entire former apartment back in the city. Best of all was the huge four-poster bed hung with quilted dust ruffles and white mesh trains.

"Pretty decent pad, huh?" Kyle observed.

"It's so beautiful," Vera slowly replied. "I've always wanted a room like this."

Kyle dawdled to the twin French doors and pulled them open, letting in the crisp winter air. "You'll have a great view once the trenchers are done."

Trenchers? Vera stepped out onto the high veranda, oblivious to the cold. The forest rose further up the ridge. Below, several one-story additions stretched. "Spas, pools, Jacuzzis, exercise rooms," Kyle explained. "We'll have tennis courts too, in the spring."

This was magnificent. To her left, though, several big yellow trenching machines idled beside a long deep ditch which disappeared around an outcropping of trees.

"What's all that?"

"We had to reroute the sewer and waterlines to the county junctures. The old lines are a hundred years old."

It was another thing that must have cost a fortune. "In the meantime," Kyle went on, "we're still on the old system. But everything'll be hooked up before we open."

"What about the plumbing in the building?" she asked.

"All brand-new and refitted.' "

They came back in and she closed the doors. "And the wiring?"

"The same. The building was gutted when Magwyth Enterprises bought it. Someone tried to burn it down years ago."

"Why?" Vera asked, and immediately regretted it. She had a feeling what he would say in response. *Ghosts* . . .

"I'd rather keep you in suspense. How about later you let me show you around the whole building—the grand tour." His cocky grin sharpened, and Vera remembered what Dan B. had observed. *Scoping my . . . rib melons?* She almost laughed. Dan B. had always been jealous; and it was like a brother's jealousy—guarded, and negative about any man who expressed an interest in her. He hadn't even liked Paul. Now she wished she'd listened to him. But was it her imagination, or was Kyle really leering at her?

"Sure, Kyle," she said. "I'd love for you to show me around." Perhaps she could turn his confidence game inside out, and use it on him. She could play games just as well as he could.

"Great. I'll drum you up about seven. Is that all right?"

"That's fine," she assured, and finished with the thought, *you phony tight-jeaned asshole.*

He made to leave, then, but stopped. "I almost forgot. You do have your *choice* of rooms. I can show you some of the others if you want."

She paused in the question, and looked around one more time. "No," she nearly whispered. "This is fine. . . . This is *home*."

Chapter Nine

Zyra pondered: *What a beautiful night.*

And it was: clear, starry, deep as heaven. The moon shone as a crisp, blazing rind of light. It summoned back many other, equally beautiful images, of blood and mayhem, of heads split apart like big ripe fruit, sharp blades sinking into random flesh, and chorales of screams—yes, such wondrous images, and many more, of times gone by. Zyra stood nude before the bedroom window. Her sex felt warm and tender in the denouement of her orgasms. Her appreciation for life felt as wide as her gaze.

What a beautiful night for murder, she thought.

She fancied the moonlight as a ghost's caress. She could feel it on her skin; it seemed to purify her. What had nutty Mr. Buluski said earlier—earlier, that is, as in before she'd strangled him with the lamp cord? "Oh, pristine siren in radiant light. I bid thee now—be mine tonight." What a nut. *Oh, I'll be yours, all right,* she'd thought. *I'll be yours forever.* At least this pair was interesting, and good for some laughs. She and Lemi had answered the personal ad they'd spotted in a magazine called *The East Coast Swingers Guide:* "LUNTVILLE: Attractive (and endowed!) quirky couple seek same for concupiscent interlude." Dumbass Lemi hadn't even known what concupiscent meant. "It means they like to get it on, Lemi," Zyra had had to explain. "And that's just what we're looking for."

"Come in, come in!" Mr. Buluski had invited when they'd knocked on the door to his remote rancher which sat miles from any other dwelling along Route 154. "Why, you two are even more delectable than your photos!"

Mr. Buluski had, by the way, answered the door naked.

He was skinny, bald up top, and looked about forty, with this nutty, kinky, torqued-up enthusiasm stamped onto his face. "I do hope you're all hungry," he commented. "I've prepared a wonderful dinner!" Next, he'd introduced Mrs. Buluski, who was also naked save for pepper-red high heels. She looked about ten years younger, with poshly curled dark hair, and she was kind of cute and fat, which was fine. They didn't all have to be high-fashion knockouts. Physical diversity was far more important. An additional point of note: her pubic hair had been quite expertly shaved into the configuration of a heart. "Please, friends, make yourselves more comfortable and join us in the dining room," she urged.

"When in Gnome, do as the Gnomans do," Lemi figured.

"That's *Romans,* Lemi," Zyra corrected.

Lemi shrugged. They both quickly stripped and took their seats at a long, maroon-linened table. "Oh, what beautiful young bodies," Mr. Buluski gushed. "Such sights make my heart just SING!"

"He gets carried away sometimes," Mrs. Buluski then informed them. "He's a dreamer, a visionary. And he's very, shall we say, deft of tongue." The woman promptly winked at Zyra, who doubted that she was referring to his eloquence.

Mr. Buluski had prepared a glazed roast duckling,

baby potatoes with bell peppers, and succulently steamed fresh asparagus stalks. The four of them then, as they dined, exchanged opinions upon such intense topics as the future of the Middle East, the difference in inflation rates during Republican and Democratic administrations, the ozone layer, and the possible psychological explanations for Michael Jackson's addiction to plastic surgery. All the while, Zyra, who was not especially inhibited, felt distinctly embarrassed. Even psychopathic murderesses were not accustomed to dinnerside chats in the nude. This new insight into herself at least struck her as interesting. Events, however, became a trifle more interesting when Mrs. Buluski, large bare breasts bobbling, promptly stood up, remarked "Let me get out of these hot things," kicked off her pepper-red high heels, placed her rather large derriere on the dining table, and began to masturbate with one of the larger stalks of asparagus. Mr. Buluski was then appropriate enough to comment: "You should see her when I serve corn on the cob."

What a world, Zyra thought. There were all kinds, that was for sure. At least these two loose-screws were more diverting than the usual acquisitions; rednecks, prostitutes, runaways. Zyra had seen her share of bizarre things in her time, but she could never recall witnessing a portly woman with heart-shaped pubic hair masturbate with asparagus. No, she'd never seen such a thing in her life. *Maybe I should try it someday,* she considered.

Lemi wasted no time in sampling this new preparation for vegetables. Meanwhile, Mr. Buluski rose and suggested to Zyra, "My dear, shall we adjourn to my parlor of passion?"

"Lead the way," Zyra said.

He took her down the hall to a black-and-white art deco bedroom. Her body felt levitated when she lay back on the slogging waterbed. She looked down at herself from a ceiling mirror; it was fun watching this eccentric, reedy man do things to her. She thought of astral projection, of doppelgangers. Mrs. Buluski wasn't kidding about her husband's prowess of tongue—Zyra watched her own eyes thin lewdly in the mirror, vising his cheeks with her thighs. Her orgasms issued as a steady, tender pulse of waves. Mr. Buluski seemed delighted. Through a variety of positions, then, he eloquently muttered lines from some of the century's greater poets: Stevens, Pound, Eliot, Seymour. Zyra's next orgasms pulsed deeper and more precisely; she felt something in herself letting go. . . .

This realm of release wasn't enough. Each abrupt, quivery climax left her groping for more.

It's never enough, she thought through a sheen of sweat.

She sensed the approach of his own release, as one often wakes undetermined minutes before the alarm clock. He seemed surprised by her strength, and the vitality of her resolve when she pushed his bony body off of her, lay him back, and let his orgasm spurt warmly down her throat and into her stomach.

Then she said: "I have a surprise for you. . . . "

And quite a surprise it was. Indeed, no, there was never enough, was there? That's what made Zyra who she was. Mr. Buluski's poetical quotes quickly changed over to high, wavering screams. He screamed long and hard through the delivery of her surprise. The screams provided a sweet icing for the finale of her desire, and she came yet again as she watched herself strangle Mr. Buluski in the overhead mirror.

Never enough, she pondered.

Mr. Buluski's face turned dark blue above the ligature of the lamp cord. As more time went by, the face began to swell, much like a balloon. For a moment she feared it might pop.

She dragged him back out by the ankles.

"Have a good time?" Lemi asked.

"Yeah." And she had, she always did. She dreamily redressed as Lemi finished tying up the chubby—and by now, the quite sated—Mrs. Buluski. "Me too," Lemi confessed. "She's a wild one."

They loaded dead husband and live wife into the white step van, then returned to the quiet house. Zyra turned on all the gas burners on the stove and blew out the pilots. Lemi set the timer.

"I like you better as a brunette," he said.

As they drove away, off into crystal darkness, the thought replayed in Zyra's mind.

What a beautiful night.

Chapter ten

"A touch of class," Lee remarked. He lit the candles on the bay table by the west window, which offered a long view of the forest. Vera had decided to combine their evening staff meeting with dinner. "Don't know what the hell we're going to eat, though," Lee went on. "Today me and Dan B. ran a stock check."

"How's it look?" Vera asked.

"Like we're gonna be starving till The Inn opens. Nothing but dry goods and condiments."

Vera hadn't considered this. They couldn't live on bread crumbs and salt. "We'll be getting some shipments in soon. Until then we'll have to rough it."

Donna poured iced tea that she'd prepared from the service bar. "There's no liquor inventory, either," she said. "We might have a hard time finding a decent distributor this far out in the sticks."

"Shit, you mean there's no beer in this joint?" Lee asked, glancing worriedly at his beer belly.

"I'm working on it," Vera said. "I think I got a deal with the company that services Waynesville. Their list looks pretty good." Start-ups were always a hassle. Many distributors were slow, and many unreliable. Trial and error was the only way you found out who was good.

"Dan B. to the rescue," the big chef announced. He lumbered out from the kitchen, bearing a large tray.

Lee smirked. "What are we having? Pine nuts and tomato paste?"

"Try eighteen-ounce Australian lobster tails," Dan B. answered, and set the tray before them. A delectable aroma rose.

Donna nearly squealed in delight. "I don't think we'll have any problem roughing it on these."

"I found ten cases of them in one of the walk-in freezers. A lot of langoustines and king crab back there too. There's also a hundred pounds of frozen Greenwich shrimp we can use for stock base and toppings."

Dan B. had thawed the tails, split them, and broiled them atop their shells with a pinch of spice. "Dig in, gang," Vera said. The tails were delicious, moist and tender despite their size. When they were finished, Vera got on with business. "What I need first is a gauge of everyone's impressions so far. Donna?"

"I don't anticipate any problems from my end. I'm still as excited about all this as ever."

"Good. Lee?"

"I could use a beer, but other than that I've never had it so good. All my gear in the back is quality stuff. I'll be able to handle rushes bigger than the ones we had at The Emerald Room without any backup. That Hobart dishwasher practically does all the work itself, and so does the glassware rig. They even have element driers in them."

"Same goes for my gear, Vera," Dan B. said, inserting another big dollop of lobster into his mouth. "Everything works great. Only thing I got to complain about is that Kyle motherfucker. He wants to start some shit, and I don't like it."

"I know," Vera said. "He wants to make us look bad and himself look good—brownie points. The best way we can counter that is to forget about it and just give everything our best. We can't let room service show us up, and we won't if we don't let Kyle get to us. I know his game. Let me handle him."

"And what about these funky-looking maids?" Lee observed. "Walking around here, giving us the eye, not talking. They're treating us like trespassers."

"In a way, we are trespassers," Vera commented. "To them, we're the newbies walking on their turf. Just stay on good terms with them, and they'll get used to us. And don't cause a stir; I think a lot of them are here without green cards."

They all concurred, however reluctantly. Then Dan B. continued, "And there's another funny thing. I was snooping around the room service side today after I inventoried our stock. I wanted to see what they had compared to us—"

"Let me guess," Vera ventured. "They had twice as much stock as us."

"That's just it, I don't know. All their pantries and walk-ins had padlocks on them."

Vera's brow rose. "What did Kyle say about that?"

"Nothing, he wasn't there. In fact, I haven't seen nimnose since earlier today when you and I first met him."

Neither have I, Vera realized. And she hadn't seen Feldspar either. After Kyle had shown her her room, she'd looked for Feldspar, needing the initial workman's compensation and F.I.C.A. forms for her staff payroll, but Feldspar was not to be found in his office or anywhere, though she'd spotted his Lamborghini out in the lot. Perhaps he and Kyle had gone out on the grounds to supervise the tree-trimmers or the excavator crew working out back. "I'll hunt him down later," she remarked. "He said he was going to give me the twenty-five-cent tour tonight."

Dan B.'s quick scowl made no secret of his emotions. "Better if you just stay away from the guy unless you're with one of us. He's got the hots for you fierce—"

"No, he doesn't," Vera dismissed.

"I don't know about that, Vera," Donna jumped in. "That guy's a womanizer if I ever saw one—"

Then Lee: "And you should've seen the way he was—"

"I know," Vera interrupted. "Gandering my rib melons. Dan B. was kind enough to point that out to me earlier, and if you want my opinion, I think you're all being silly. I'm an adult, remember? I know how to handle guys like Kyle."

She left them, then, to their objections, amused and mildly flattered. "I'm not kidding, Vera," Dan B. continued to rant after her. "You be careful around that guy."

Vera laughed and went out into the atrium. It was dark and quiet now; The Inn felt subdued. Someone had lit a fire in the huge stone fireplace. She could feel its heat crawl on one side of her face. The front offices occupied the lower east extension of the ground floor. Cool fluorescent lights buzzed down on her when she entered the short L-shaped hall. Again, Feldspar's office, done up like a London banker's, was empty. GENERAL MANAGER, the door's brass plaque read. It surprised Vera to find the office unlocked. There seemed to be many expensive curios about: Hummel ashtrays, a gold Mont Blanc pen set, and a beautiful gold-and-crystal carriage clock, not to mention a brand-new PC and Hewlett-Packard laser printer. She saw no harm in taking a quick peek into the top desk drawer. Rolls of stamps, clusters of keys, and an enameled cash box. *Jesus,* she thought. *This guy's not very security conscious.* The cash box, too, was unlocked. She flipped it open and noticed a few bands of one hundred and fifty dollar bills. *There must be ten or fifteen grand sitting here,* she realized, squinting. *Lucky for him I'm honest.* She was about to reclose the drawer when she noticed something else.

She touched it, slid it out. . . .

A gun.

Vera frowned. All right, it was legitimate for a general manager to have a gun, but that didn't mean she approved. The gun itself, a revolver, looked big, clunky, and old, like an antique. Perhaps Feldspar owned it as a collector, but if so this whole thing made even less sense. *Anybody could walk right in here and take all of this stuff,* she thought. It was good to know that Feldspar trusted his people, but this was just plain stupid. She locked the door behind her when she left.

Around the bend came another office. Unlike Feldspar's, it was locked. Vera frowned hard at its doorplate. ROOM SERVICE MANAGER. A third door read, simply, AC-COUNTING. This addled her. *Where's my office?* she complained to herself. *Fucking Kyle gets an office but I don't? Where do I do my work? The goddamn coffee station?* A petty complaint, she realized, but it still pissed her off.

"I know what you're thinking."

Vera turned, almost startled at the voice. "Hello, Kyle," she said when she recognized him. "I've been looking for you."

His grin flashed white, even teeth. "You're wondering where your office is, right?"

"Well . . . yeah."

"It's right here." Immediately he produced a Philips'-head screwdriver and removed the ACCOUNTING plate. Then he replaced it with a brand-new one. RESTAURANT MANAGER, V. ABBOT

That's better, she thought. "Where are you moving the accounting office?"

"You and me, baby," he jested. "We're it. But you won't have to worry about any of the auxiliary bills, like housekeeping and utilities. I'll be doing all that myself, since I'm more experienced."

You dick, Vera thought. "What makes you think you're more experienced at accounting than I am? I've got a degree in restaurant and hotel management."

Kyle shrugged. "A degree means nothing. I've been working for Mr. Feldspar for ten years. I know the ropes. Don't get hot about it."

Ten years, my ass. He couldn't be more than twenty-five. What, he'd been in the business since he was fifteen?

Kyle stood with his hip cocked and arms crossed, smiling derisively. "Best way to learn is to just jump in there and do it, you know? I started at the bottom and I worked my way up, learned everything. When Mr. Feldspar first took me on, I was peeling potatos and emptying garbage cans. Now I do the quarterly taxes and all the deduction schedules with my eyes closed."

Big man, Vera thought. This was not worth going on with. "It's getting late," she changed the subject. "How about showing me the rest of the place before I turn in."

"Sure."

They left the front offices and recrossed the atrium. Firelight jittered about the carpets and paneled walls, prismed through the great chandelier. A coved door to the left of the reception desk took them down a long wide corridor appointed in dark hues and deep-green carpet. "Banquet room," Kyle pointed through a set of double doors. Vera gaped at its size. "It'll seat five hundred easy," Kyle bragged on. "Got a couple smaller banquet rooms upstairs, on the third floor."

"Mr. Feldspar anticipates a lot of banquet receipts?"

Kyle laughed. "You kidding? Most of our other inns

haul in forty percent of gross receipts from banquets. You'll see."

"And I suppose you're the banquet manager too, copping the two-percent commission?" Vera couldn't resist asking.

Kyle chuckled. "Of course."

Asshole asshole asshole! she thought, following him on down the wide hallway. He cockily muttered a designation, pointing to each door they passed: "Weight rooms." "Saunas." "Jacuzzis." "Racquetball courts." "Locker rooms."

Vera was beginning to wonder if there was anything Feldspar hadn't considered. They even had mineral baths, rooms for mudpacks, and, though it wouldn't be completed till spring, a stable for horseback riding.

"Pool's in here," came Kyle's next revelation. Another set of high double doors led to the long, dark echoing room. "Nice set up, huh?" Kyle bid. "Quarter of a million gallons."

It was the biggest indoor pool Vera had ever seen. Heat seemed to float before her at once. Underwater lamps set into the sidewalls pulsed odd dark hues—blue, red, green—which melded under the lapping surface. It was an interesting effect; it seemed almost romantic. The pool itself had been built in a long tile-aproned T-shape, yet the dark underwater lights only illumined the straightaway; the extensions at the top of the T, in other words, were completely unlit. Vera could barely see the room's end.

"We keep it heated to eighty-six degrees," Kyle informed her. "You got any idea how much it costs to heat a pool this size?"

As she had probably a hundred times already today, Vera found herself considering costs. "A fortune," she slowly answered Kyle's question. And it must have cost several more fortunes to build.

"Let's go for a swim," Kyle said.

"What?"

"Come on." He began to unbutton his shirt. "We're upper management—we can do what we want."

I should've known, Vera thought. *Look at this guy.* He was taking off his shirt right in front of her! Eventually, she made the excuse, "Sorry, Kyle. I don't have a swimsuit."

He chuckled abruptly. "Wear your birthday suit, that's what I always wear. Or if you're bashful, wear your underwear."

Some tour this turned out to be. She would have liked to have seen the other facilities more closely, but Kyle had deliberately rushed by them to bring her here.

"You're not a very smooth operator, Kyle. You've got to be out of your mind if you think I'm going to go skinny dipping with a guy I just met."

"Hey, sorry." He passed it off with a shrug. "We're both adults. I just thought you might want to—"

"Well, I don't. I'm tired, and we've both got a big few weeks ahead of us."

"All the more reason for us to relax, have a good time, right?"

"Wrong, Kyle." Did he actually believe she would strip right in front of him? Good-looking men had a tendency to expect women to slaver at their feet. *Nice try, pal,* she thought. She couldn't help but notice, though, Kyle's attractive build. He was trim yet well muscled, with sturdy arms and a developed chest. Some sort of thin silver chain glittered about his neck.

"No biggie." He flung his shirt over his shoulder. Then he cast her a last, snide smile. "Maybe some other time . . . when you've got a swimsuit."

"Yeah, Kyle. Maybe." *Then again, maybe not.*

"See you in the morning." He walked out and turned down the hall. Vera frowned after him. *Dan B.'s right.*

114

But just a second later, Kyle quickly reappeared in the door way, his chest flexed as he grinned in at her. "Oh, and I just wanted to let you know, Vera. Don't let the stories get to you."

"Stories?"

"Yeah. The Inn's haunted."

Then he disappeared again. Vera wanted to laugh. Did he think he could freak her out? Perhaps he wanted to scare her for snubbing his skinny-dipping plans. *What an idiot,* she dismissed.

She smiled at her amusement. *The Inn's haunted.* Yet for some reason she remained standing there, looking down the long straight body of the pool. The merged light floated languidly atop the water. Then she heard—

What was that?

Her smile faded. She thinned her eyes toward the very end of the pool, the unlit area. She heard a quick rush, then an even quicker dripping sound, then—

A door?

No, it was ridiculous. It must be her imagination.

Vera thought, for a moment, that she'd heard someone climbing out of the dark end of the pool.

Chapter Eleven

His visions churned. His mind felt caught on the grapnel of a convulsive tilting nightmare.

He was watching himself. . . .

But it *was* a nightmare, wasn't it? He lay awake on the bed, the sunlight like a bar of white pain across his eyes.

A nightmare, he thought. *Yeah.* Hastily as it seemed, the conclusion helped him feel safe again.

It was a nightmare.

"Jesus Christ," Paul Kirby muttered. The clock's digital dial read 5:23 P.M. He'd slept the entire day away, which wasn't like him at all. He was a writer, sure, and generally writers slept late. But . . . *Five in the evening?* he questioned himself. *Must have picked up the flu or something.*

Vera wasn't here—of course not, she worked at two. Paul attempted to get out of bed, and an abrupt pressure in his head sent him right back down. *Hangover,* he realized, wincing. This was no flu. He'd been out drinking last night, hadn't he? And—*Holy shit!*—was he hungover.

Slower this time, he got up. A glance in the mirror made him groan: naked, pale, dark circles like charcoal under his eyes. He curiously raised a hand to his face,

116

and noted an excess of stubble. It felt like more than a day's growth.

He stared into the mirror, bloodshot eyes going wide. . . .

Vera, he thought. The thought turned to ice.

Nightmare.

He was watching himself . . . in the . . . nightmare. . . .

He mouth tasted like a cat had pissed in it. Some nameless crust seemed flaked around his mouth and across his stomach. Suddenly he sneezed. Pain quaked in his skull, and into his hand he'd sneezed . . . blood.

"What the hell?" he slowly asked himself.

BAM! BAM! BAM!

Paul nearly shrieked at the hard thuds. Someone was knocking on the door. Correction—they weren't knocking, they were *pounding*.

BAM! BAM BAM!

"Open up, Kirby!" hollered a sharp, muffled voice. "Your car's in the lot, I know you're in there!"

BAMBAMBAMBAMBAM!

"All right, already." The thuds made his head hurt worse. But who could it be? *I don't owe anybody money, do I?* He pulled on his robe—the blue monogramed one Vera had given him last Christmas—and straggled to the door.

"Open this fucking door, Kirby, before I kick it down!"

It was Tate, his editor at the *City Sun*. Paul opened the door and was almost bulled over by the big, beefy man.

"Where is it?" Tate demanded. Some mysterious rage pinked his face. His fists opened and closed at his sides.

"What are you so pissed off about?" Paul asked. "Take off your coat, have a seat—"

117

"I ain't got time to have a fucking seat. I got a news-paper to put out, remember? So hand it over!"

"Hand *what* over?"

"The first installment on the singles bar series. It was your bright idea, wonderboy, so where is it?"

"You'll get it. It's due Thursday noon."

"Yeah, and that was five and a half fucking hours ago!" Tate bellowed. "Don't tell me you don't have it, Kirby. I got the whole weekend section set to go, and a big blank fifteen-hundred-word block sitting there wait-ing for your shit! Do you have it or not?"

Paul's memory felt like a clogged artery. This was impossible. "It's . . . Thursday?"

"Yes, you moron, it's Thursday—that's Thursday as in the day we send *The Weekender* to fucking press." He thrust up his stout forearm—for a second, Paul thought he was going to hit him—and pointed to the date squares on his watch. THURS it displayed.

"And who the hell do you think you are hanging up on my men?" Tate continued with his wrath. "And hanging up on *me?* Let me tell you something, wonder-boy. No writer, and I mean *no fucking writer in this city* hangs up on *me!*"

"I didn't . . ." Paul faltered. Had he? Suddenly he recalled distant bells, distant voices. But they were part of the nightmare. They had to be. "I . . . hung up on you?"

"You're goddamn right you hung up on me! What the fuck's wrong with you, Kirby? You on drugs? You lose half your orbital lobe the last time you took a *shit?*"

Paul could only look back in unblinking turmoil. Blurred images began to sift through his memory, pieces of colors, slabs of sounds, and distantly unpleasant sen-sations. For one frightened second, he didn't even feel real.

"I—I've been sick, I guess," he stumbled. "The flu

118

or something." His memory struggled to disbirth the rest, but nothing came. He fitted together the few facts he had on hand. *I'm a metropolitan journalist. The very pissed off man standing in front of me is the editor in chief of the biggest paper in the city. I owe him a story, and the story was due over five hours ago. And I don't have it.*

"I don't have it," Paul said.

"I didn't think so," Tate replied. At once his voice tremored down, the prickling rage supplanted by low disgust. "I should've known you were a fuck up, Kirby. You're out. You're never getting published in my paper again. Period. And that advance I gave you? I want it back. If you don't give it back, I will sue you, and if I have to go to the trouble of suing you, hear this. I will devote my life to seeing that you never get published, anywhere, ever again."

Paul felt ablaze in shame. Nothing like this had ever happened before. Worst part was, he had no idea how any of it had come about. *What's wrong with me?* he pleaded with himself. *I don't even know what day it is.*

"I'm sorry," was all he could say. "I'll give you back your check. Give me a couple of hours, I'll have the piece for you. I'll even write the rest of the series for free. Give me a chance to make it up to you."

Tate's expression turned astonished. "I was born at night, Kirby, but not *last night*. What do you think I am, a fucking idiot? You think I'm *stupid*. I used to like you, you know that? I used to think you were one squared-away kick-ass journalist. But all I gotta do is take one look at you now to know what you really are. You're a fuckin' cokehead, Kirby, and if you ask me, there's nothing more disgusting in the fucking world. Drugs are for losers, Kirby, for assholes who don't give a shit about anything but their own cheap thrills. Don't you realize that the people you buy that shit from are the same evil motherfuckers who hook nine-year-olds on crack? Don't you understand that every single penny you give them only makes them stronger? You've let yourself become part of the same machine that's tearing this country up. Your talent, your career, all the great things you could've been you've thrown out the fucking window, and for what? For cheap thrills. And why? Because you don't give enough of a shit about yourself or anyone else to be strong enough to live right. So go on and feed your head, Kirby. I could care less. You make me sick.''

Tate's entire monolog left Paul standing rigid as a granite statue. What was he talking about? Paul had never used drugs in his life. "I'm not a cokehead," he eventually said, after the shock wore off. "I've never even used it once, and—"

"Don't hand me a load of shit," Tate cut him off. "You're making an ass of yourself. Take a good look in the mirror, sport. You say you got *the flu?* Don't insult me. You're sweating, and your eyes are all fucked up. You're shaking like you're standing on a live wire. You've got blood leaking out of your fucking nose, for God's sake.'' Tate paused to rein some of his disgust. "I'm leaving now, Kirby, and I'm gonna try real hard to pretend that I never knew you. In fact, I'm ashamed that I ever published you in my paper. It makes me want to puke knowing that the money I've paid you for your stories was used to buy drugs. It makes me sick to my fucking stomach that I used to think you were a good writer. You're not a writer, Kirby. You're just another shuck and jive, don't-give-a-shit, cocaine-snorting loser . . .''

Tate walked out of the apartment and slammed the door. Paul felt riddled in shock. He wiped his upper lip, and his hand came away red. And he *was* shaking, he *was* sweating. But there was one thing he knew without doubt. He was not a drug user. The entire confrontation was too impossible to even contemplate.

120

But his memory still hung before him like a black hole. He couldn't remember the last four days. *I better call Vera,* he realized. *Find out what the hell's going on.*

His joints ached when he went to the phone. He couldn't even remember The Emerald Room's number; he had to look it up.

"Vera Abbot, please," he said when the hostess picked up.

A long pause. "I'm sorry, sir, but she's . . . gone."

Paul frowned. "What do you mean gone?"

"She quit a few days ago, for some job in north county."

Quit her job? "That's impossible," Paul countered. "I—"

"Apparently," the hostess persisted in the rumor, "she caught her fiancé cheating on her, so she took another job the next day and left town. And she took three of our best people with her . . ."

Listening further would've been useless. Paul's senses blanked out. Something in his psyche snapped, like a bone cracking, and his eyes blurred. He dropped the phone.

Strange—and awful—visions showed him things. He stared ahead, at nothing. The small glass panes of the dining room cabinet reflected back his pallid, unshaven, and bloody-lipped face—

And in that face he saw the nightmare. Its whorls seemed to congeal above him.

"Oh my God," the reflection whispered.

Then the memory crashed down.

Lemi's blade gleamed like molten silver. He used it with a calm and lavish finesse. Organs slid wetly from the cadaver's sliced abdominal cavity; they landed on the

121

floor in a sloppy, sort of crinkly sound. The corpse's blood had long since gone dark.

The Factotum liked to watch Lemi work. He saw resolve in the young man's eyes, determination and an almost reverent placidity. *Faith,* the Factotum thought. It was faith, he knew—a doubtless, unvacillating, and even *radiant* faith in the promise behind their tasks. Zyra was the same way: incorruptible in her loyalty to the Factotum and their calling.

Zyra, her beautiful eyes set in placid determination, undraped the female, who lay prone in the stark light. Bound and gagged, her face looked similarly stark—drained of its color by dread. She was plump, ebon-haired, and her light blue eyes would have been alluring were it not for the pink circles of shock about them, and the muddy smudges of mascara. Her entire body faintly trembled.

"Don't be afraid," the Factotum consoled her, not that she could reply. "Wondrous things await you. But you must have faith!" And he thought of sacrifices, of warm hearts plucked from opened bosoms and held high to the eyes of gods. He thought of the flesh consumed, and the blood drunk fresh from newly sliced veins. *Time immemorial,* his pondering persisted. *All of history wears the same face. Good and evil are only masks which change like the seasons. The designs scarcely matter.* It was all the same in the end. Heaven or hell. Abstinence or pleasure.

Denial or truth.

The Factotum chose truth. It was his own god which beckoned him now, with providence, with truth.

What a wondrous acknowledgement!

"The balm," he instructed. "Calm her down; she's terrified."

Zyra knelt and opened the tiny hand-blown bottle. The bottle looked ancient. She dribbled several drops of the warm leahroot oil onto the gagged woman's bare abdomen, then gingerly massaged it into her skin. She did this with great care, caressing the slippery oil over the plush belly, breasts, and legs. A pleasant, cinnamony fragrance rose up with the woman's body heat. The fervid squirming began to wind down, then abated altogether when Zyra gently rubbed a few more drops between the abductee's legs. Now the strained face relaxed, and her eyes—previously pried open by sheer terror—narrowed against the seeping repose of the balm.

"There," the Factotum whispered. "That's better."

And it was. Everything was better. The Factotum felt becalmed in his surmise of the future. The silence, now, hung about his bald head like a halo, or a static tiara as he lent a final, smiling gaze to his acolytes. "Take the corpse up," he instructed Lemi, then, to Zyra, "And take her down." His gaze seemed radiant on them. He thought of them as his children.

"Soon," he added, "it will be time to begin."

Chapter Twelve

Vera slowly closed her bedroom door, noticing the unopened bottle of Grand Marnier on the antique night stand. Below it lay a one white rose, a snifter, and a little note:

Dear Ms. Abbot,
I hope that your first day at The Inn proved a rewarding one, and one of countless such days. I'm indebted to you for the expertise that you have so enthusiastically brought to this endeavor, and I'm delighted as well as proud to have you as one of my staff.
Sincerely,
Feldspar

What a lovely gesture, and how fitting. The day had been long and hard, and Vera knew that they would all be like that; a nightcap right now was what she needed. She uncorked the bottle and poured herself a drink, twirling the pretty liquor around in the wide glass to let it aerate. *But why the rose?* she wondered. It had been plucked of its thorns. She took it to the veranda doors with her drink. Certainly Feldspar was not making a romantic gesture—the rose was just an appreciative token. Still, she contemplated this, and herself. It seemed almost bizarre to her. Despite Feldspar's clipped, businesslike demeanor and squat looks, she felt remotely attracted to him. *Is he married?* she wondered. *Is he involved?* Somehow, she didn't think so; she couldn't picture it. *And why am I thinking about this anyway?* What did she foresee? A potential relationship with him? An affair? *Ridiculous,* she scoffed. Besides, she knew full well that the biggest mistake a manager can make was getting involved with people she works with. Still, the notion tickled her.

Maybe I'm just horny, she flightily considered. The day and all its work was over now. This fact cleared her head, and left her to ruminate her own life outside of work. What did Paul think of her leaving? What was he doing now? This she could only wonder about for a moment until the awful imagery returned, and the wretched scene she'd walked right into. Even the thought of his name gave her a quick shock. *I hope I never see that cheating, lying, demented son of a bitch ever again,* came the bitter words.

But it made her feel naive, embarrassed. How long had she been fooled by him? How many times had she come home from work to make love to him without a clue as to what he'd been up to earlier in the day? Drugs, bondage, kinky sex. The whole thing made her positively sick.

She let the sweet liquor buff the edge off her thoughts. At least it was all behind her now, and thank God she'd always used condoms with him. Who knew what kind of diseases people like that had? *Probably all of them,* she thought.

The French doors offered only a view of deep winter dark now, but it was warm in the bedroom, and cozy. Then another thought—an unbidden and crude thought— popped into her mind. *I wonder how long it'll be before*

I get laid again? It would require some adjusting to; she'd been sexually active with Paul for the last two years, but now, like a gavel striking its pad, the outlet was closed. *Well, Vera,* she joked, *if things get too high and dry, you can always take Kyle up on his swimming offer.* She wondered if he pulled the same come-on with other women. What a hound. *Sure, Kyle, I'll go swimming with you, but only if you wear a chain-mail jock strap with a lock on it.*

She poured another drink and ran a warm bath. Even the bathroom shocked her in its opulence: a lot of gorgeous, swirled marble, bright brass fixtures, mirrored walls. The sunken bath, encircled completely by stark black curtains, was as big as a hot tub. It even had jets. *Live it up, girl,* she thought. *Tomorrow's going to be a long day.*

She undressed and eased into the froth of bubbles. The warm, fragrant water cloaked her; she nearly drifted off to sleep. There was too much to think about; her mind felt desperate to decide, so instead she thought about nothing. That felt *much* better.

Yet inklings kept betraying her. Sexual inklings. She sipped the sweet liquor and began to wonder more about herself. *Am I attractive?* Sometimes she thought she was, sometimes not. The fact that Kyle had made a pass at her was no proof of desirability. Guys like Kyle made passes at watermelons if they could put holes in them. Attraction was not something she gave much thought to—she'd always believed that physicality was a veneer, and that veneers had no valid use in relationships. *But my relationship with Paul is over.* So, as a single, unattached, successful, and possibly attractive woman, where did that leave her?

Alone in a bathtub, well past midnight, a million miles away from everything, she answered herself. But that was good, for now at least. Prevaricating prick that he

126

was, Paul wouldn't be forgotten overnight. She'd spent two years with him, a block of her life. It wasn't something you could blink your eyes at and erase. Being so far away, however, would make it easier to deal with and, eventually, get over. She couldn't imagine how unpleasant it would be to still live in the city. She knew so many of his friends, and she'd be running into him all the time, at the Undercroft, downtown, at restaurants, etc. A grim consideration. Here, though, she'd never have to worry about that. She could devote her full energy to making The Carriage House work.

So why, suddenly, did she feel so concerned about her sexual desirability?

That's it, she thought.

She climbed quickly out of the tub, padded naked across the floor, and eyed herself in the full-mirror wall. She'd read that top-rate models were often convinced they were ugly. It was paranoia. *Am I paranoid?* she wondered, looking at herself. *Am I attractive or am I a bow-wow?*

The mirror replicated her image in bright, dripping crystal clarity. The bath water had layered her short black hair to wet points; her flesh shined in the glass. *Hmmm,* she contemplated. She stood 5′ 5″, and weighed 110 pounds the last time she stepped on a scale. Her trimness did not reduce her frame to boyishness; Vera's contours clearly came together femininely. Long legs, well-defined hips, delicate shoulders. Her lean waist offered a slightly inverted navel, which tickled insanely when nibbled, and though she'd not had a suntan in years—her profession's hours eluded the sun—her skin shined fresh, robust, and unblemished. Some of the more ribald girls at The Emerald, during girl-talk sessions, ranted endlessly over treatments of the pubic hair. They plucked, clipped, trimmed, waxed, electrolysized, etc., to no end. Vera saw little need for this—it seemed

127

vainly silly. She'd discussed it once with Paul—the prevaricating prick—and he'd urged her to leave it be, with
a sound observation. "It must be there for a reason,"
he'd stated, "though I can't imagine *what* reason. Mother
Nature must know what she's doing, you think?" It made
sense, at any rate. Therefore, Vera left the dark, black
plot alone, save for the occasional scissor-snip when
things got too unruly.

Next, her eyes focused on the mirror's cast of her
breasts. . . . *gandering your rib-melons,* she recalled
again, and laughed, but then concluded, *not much to
gander.* She supposed women were as concerned over
the size of their breasts and men were over the size of
their penises, and that this was an irrelevant concern.
Vera wore a 34B, not exactly Chesty Morgan, but the
breasts themselves were sufficiently erect and firm.
"They feel like tomatos!" one short-term lover from
college had once informed her during a sexual frolic,
which—she recalled now—included whipped cream,
strawberries, and Hershey's chocolate sauce. "I'm not a
dessert cart, you know," she'd pointed out. "We'll see
about that," he'd replied, shaking vigorously the big blue
can of Reddi Wip. *I wonder what happened to him?* she
thought now. *Probably weighs three hundred pounds.
God, those were the days. . . .*

Indeed they were, and they were gone now, tran-
scribed into a new reality. Vera could come to terms
with that. What she couldn't come to terms with was the
great big question mark of the future. Suddenly she felt
very irritated, and she didn't know why.

She dried off with a huge black terry towel, then encloaked herself in it. She took her drink back out to the
bedroom. The odd sexual anxieties continued to nip at
her; she felt antsy. *What is wrong with you?* she thought.
Eventually she finished her GM, turned out the light,
and lay back in bed.

She crawled nude under the covers but kicked them off moments later, feeling smothered. She tried to blank her mind, to sleep. Each time her eyes closed, however, they snapped back open. An image seemed afloat beyond the room's grainy darkness, and beyond her mind. Somewhere down the hall, a clock ticked almost inaudibly. She lay on her belly, hugging a pillow.

Go to sleep!

But the image continued to reform: two hands splayed, descending to touch her. The more fervently she tried to dissipate the vision, the sharper it grew in her mind. After many minutes of resisting it, she gave in to the truth. The fantasy hands belonged to Kyle. *All right,* she admitted. *So I'm attracted to Kyle. It's a primitive, purely physical, and silly attraction. So what?*

Yeah, so what? Her skin felt flushed, sweat broke on her back like hot beads, and her sex moistened. The only way to get rid of the image was to acknowledge it. At least then she could get some sleep. She squeezed her eyes shut. . . .

The hands formed arms. The arms extended to a body. It was a trim, young, muscular body. She concentrated on the image, let it focus in her mind, and suddenly she felt so anxious she was nearly whining. She put a face on the image: Kyle's face.

She felt ashamed thinking of this, she felt immature and slutty. Nevertheless, her thoughts bid the hands. . . .

Touch me.

She remained atop the sheets, on her belly. Her legs lay out behind her in a wide V.

Touch me right now. . . .

She let herself feel the fantasy. The hands opened around her ankles, then began to slide up her legs in excruciating slowness. They felt soft, intent, firmly clasped. Vera's feet flexed, her body went rigid. The hands proceeded in their slow journey up the smooth terrain of her legs, over the tightened calves, the insides of her knees, then widened, still slowly rising. . . .

Vera was biting into her pillow. Her nipples hardened to pebbles against the mattress, and her moisture welled. The next impulse could not be resisted. Her own hand squeezed between her belly and the sheets, working its way down. She gently stroked the apex of her sex as the hands of the fantasy rose ever steadily, tenderly squeezing her thighs, then rising still to caress the tensed orbs of her buttocks.

Soon she was gushing. The rapt ministration of her finger, along with the fantasy's sensation, had her panting on the verge of climax in minutes. But she didn't want to come that way—the fantasy must be more complete, more sustaining.

And as if on the command of her desire, the hands, now slick with her sweat, slid down her hips, joined at her prickling sex, and then lifted her buttocks up until she was on her knees.

GRAND OPENING

Chapter Thirteen

"Jesus," Vera muttered under her breath. She stood in wait at the hostess station, but there seemed little to wait for. Opening night was halfway over, and they'd served a grand total of nine dinners.

The Carriage House glimmered in candlelight. Beyond the east wing's opulent bay windows, the winter sky winked with stars and a high, bright moon. From hidden speakers, Beethoven's String Quartet No. 15 threatened to put her to sleep in its lilting, quiet strains.

Damn good thing Feldspar turned down my request for a waitress, she thought, looking around. Packing them in like this, Donna waited all the stations, ran the service bar, and still had time to stand around. Vera'd nearly thrown a fit when Feldspar had buried her suggestion of running an advertisement in the local newspaper, *The Waynesville Sentinel.* "Oh, I don't see any necessity in that," he'd told her. "We're booked solid." *No, The Inn's booked solid,* she'd wanted to counter. *But my goddamn restaurant's only got two reservations for the first weekend!*

The previous weeks had been hard and fast. Setting up deals with decent suppliers had been like pulling teeth, but eventually Vera had managed to stock a quality inventory. The liquor order had come in yesterday,

133

and half of their posted wine list remained to be seen. You don't post Kruge, Perrier-Jouet, Dom Perignon and then reveal to customers on opening night "I'm sorry, sir, our champagne shipment didn't come in, but we have a delightful, zesty little local wine called Squashed Grapes Red, and it's only $5.95 per bottle." No, seekers of fine dining did not want to hear that. Vera had had no choice but to pull all the wine lists.

The sleek, leather-bound menus looked good. She'd copied the biggest draws from The Emerald Room and used some of Dan B.'s own culinary inventions such as Crown Roast of Pork with Cajun Mustard and Sweet Potato Puree, Spiced Crepes Julienne, and Angel Hair Pasta Lobster Cakes in Lemon Butter. He was back there right now, probably leaning against a Cress-Cor prep rack, trading cuts with Lee and wondering when his next order was coming in.

"Don't look so discouraged," Donna prompted, stopping on her way to the only four-top they'd filled tonight. She was carrying smoked scallop salads and more drinks. "It's opening night. Nobody knows about us yet."

"I know," Vera replied. "I just hoped the turnout'd be a little better than this."

"Once word gets around, you'll see. And who knows, maybe we'll get a bunch of late diners from the room reservations. Mr. Feldspar told me all the rooms are filled."

"Yeah, but only the third and fourth floor suites. None of ours. And I haven't seen a single person at the reception desk. The desk isn't even staffed."

"I'm sure someone's keeping an eye on it, you can't expect too many walk-ins at a place like this. Don't worry!"

Donna traipsed off. *At least someone's enthused,* Vera considered. She knew she was overreacting; The Carriage House, after all, was a new business venture, and all new business ventures started slow. Vera was used to a big rush every night; she'd simply have to adjust.

"At least what we're getting leave good tips," Donna happily reported on her way back. "Big wheels, too. That guy at table seven is the mayor!"

Vera smiled. *Whopee,* she thought. *The mayor of Waynesville, population four thousand.* They'd also had a few town councilmen, the fire chief, and a podiatrist. Vera doubted that many more residents even existed in Waynesville who could afford to come here. What, tractor repairmen? Farmers?

And what of Feldspar? This was opening night, and he wasn't to be found. In fact, she'd scarcely seen him at all during the past two weeks. "He's busy with client promotion and the room reservations," Kyle had told her, implying that the restaurant wasn't important enough to warrant Feldspar's time. *Up yours,* she'd gestured in thought. She hadn't seen much of Kyle, either, so at least she had something to be grateful for.

Or so she thought.

She remembered her first night here, and Kyle's overt sexual moves. Initially, she'd scoffed, had even been repelled by these presumptions. She'd expected him to persist.

But he hadn't.

She knew she didn't like Kyle, but for some reason that didn't matter. Kyle had laid off, and as illogical as it seemed, this fact left her feeling flustered and even insulted. *What's the matter, Kyle. I'm not good enough for you to lust after anymore? Asshole.* Not that she'd ever let him lay a hand on her, she felt irked that he was playing hard to get. She could think of no other reason for his lack of persistence. But, *Grow up, Vera,* she thought now. Women were notorious for double standards, but she tried not to follow suit. *Yeah, Kyle, you're*

135

an asshole for putting the make on me, and now you're an asshole for not keeping it up. It made sense to her.

She was also, to herself, embarrassed, but not for any reason that anyone could know.

The hands, she thought now. Suddenly the dining room blurred in her yes. Yes, the hands, the fantasy. *I must be more sex-starved than I think.* Every night was the same. After work, she'd retire to her room, have a short Grand Marnier or two, take a hot bubble bath, and go to bed. And in bed, as sleep encroached, the fantasy would return. In her mind, the hands would lay her out, on her belly, and begin their slow, meticulous caress. Eventually, the image would wind her up so intensely that she'd further the fantasy in her mind, to intercourse with Kyle, on her hands and knees. It infuriated her. Vera wasn't a dreamer, she was a realist. She had no use for fantasies, especially masturbatory ones. Yet the more determined she became to resist it, the fantasy also came to her. Hot, tactile, erotic. Every night.

And every night, afterward, she fell into a sated sleep and she dreamed. . . .

Goddamn! What is wrong with you! She gritted her teeth and blinked hard; the recollections vanished. *I'm standing at the hostess section of my restaurant, on opening night, and all I can think about are dirty dreams.*

And dirty they were, like none she'd ever had in her life. She blushed just thinking about them—she felt tingly and hot, even now. Her panties dampened.

"I'd just like to say," a voice asserted, "we think your restaurant is outstanding."

Vera snapped out of the lewd daze. It was the mayor who was passing the hostess station—a corpulent, red-nosed man in a disheveled suit—and his wife. He complimented further, "I can't remember the last time we've dined so well. Give our compliments to the chef. Lobster cakes! What a simply ingenious idea!"

"Thank you for the kind words," Vera replied.

"It's about time someone opened a *good* restaurant in our town," the over-made-up wife contributed. "I can't wait to tell all my friends."

Oh, please, Vera thought. *Tell them all. Even tell people who aren't your friends. We need some receipts!* "It's been a pleasure being able to serve you. Please come again soon."

She received several more such compliments as some of the other diners left. At eight-thirty three more couples came in, but that was it for the night. Vera meandered back into the kitchen. Lee and Dan B. were playing blackjack on the butcher block. "Hey, Dan B.," Vera motioned. "You Lobster Cakes in Lemon Butter are a big hit."

Dan B.'s face screwed up over his hand. "A big hit? I've only done one order all night. We prepped enough for a dozen."

"*I* prepped enough for a dozen," Lee corrected, "while you read the funny papers in the can."

"Yeah, the funny papers, your last report card from high school."

"I never had time to study—I was too busy shagging your mom," Lee said. "She pays."

"No, you pay, porkface." Dan B. laid down his hand. "Twenty-one. Blow me." Then he looked up. "Hey, Vera, you wanna know the real kick in the tail? Go listen." He pointed down the line.

"What?"

"Just go listen."

Vera walked to the end of the washline. She pressed her ear to the door which led to the room-service kitchen. And flinched.

"Jesus," she muttered. "They're slammed in there."

What she heard was an absolute cacophony. It was a familiar sound, from the old days. The sound of a very busy kitchen.

137

It infuriated her.

"Your man Kyle says all of his rooms are full for the whole weekend. He must not be lying," Dan B. mentioned.

"I've got to check this out," Vera said. "I'm going over there."

"Good luck," Lee said.

"God*damn!*" she nearly shouted when she tried he door. It was locked.

"There's no reason for this door to be locked," she exclaimed. "What is that guy's problem?"

"His problem? He's an asshole."

You got that right. Vera left the kitchen, recrossed the dining room, and entered the atrium, which stood vacant. It was dead quiet, and the reception desk remained untended. She went in through the back way, down the cramped corridor, passing several maids pushing carts. None of them spoke to her. The first thing she saw when she entered the room-service kitchen was the same pasty, stooped woman she'd seen her first day on the job, who was wheeling a full twenty-shelf Metro transport cabinet into the room-service elevator. The door slid shut in Vera's face. Beyond, the RS kitchen extended as a warren of hustling figures which weaved this way and that, loading dirty plates into the dish-racks, or covering the orders to go up. They were all more staff Vera had never seen before; none acknowledged her.

"Hi, Vera," a voice called out.

Kyle stood before a long Wolf Range grill, tunicked, with spatula in hand, tending to a half-dozen ribeyes. The steaks sizzled.

"How come you locked the door between the kitchens?" she immediately asked, glaring at him.

Kyle shrugged. "No reason for it to be unlocked."

"No reason?" Vera rolled her eyes. "What if the restaurant needs something over here?"

Kyle gave a hearty laugh. "Looks to me like the only thing the restaurant needs that we got is business. What did you pull tonight, about five dinners?"

"No, Kyle, we did fifteen—"

"Hey, fifteen, that's really socking them in."

You DICK! She wanted to kick him. "And that's not the point, Kyle. You might need something from us, too—"

"Not likely, and what the point really is, Vera," he said, "is I'm in charge over here, you're in charge over there. There shouldn't be any cross-mingling of staff."

Vera stood hand on hips, tapping her foot. "Why?"

"Ever heard of pilfering? Ever heard of theft?"

"What, you think my people are going to sneak over here to steal your ribeyes?" she close to yelled. "Which, by the way, you're overcooking."

Kyle flipped a few steaks with his spatula. "As managers, it's our responsibility to keep our own areas secure. Room service is separate from the restaurant. It's supposed to be. How do you know one of my people won't go over to your end and pinch something? You don't even lock your walk-ins during the day."

"Nobody ever gave me any locks, but I couldn't help but notice that *you* have all you need."

"If you need locks, go get some. You're on the account. You need somebody to tell you everything?"

Vera was getting pissed in increments. *You got balls,* was all she could think, *saying something like that to me.* The kitchen clamor shredded her nerves, along with Kyle's subdued-egomanic, self-centered grin. "But you can send the fat kid over here if you want," he next had the gall to suggest. "Seeing how we're so slammed over here, my dishwasher could use a hand . . ."

"Sorry, Kyle. No cross-mingling of staff, remember?"

Kyle chuckled as he flipped the top row of steaks.

"Jealousy isn't what I'd call the sign of a good restaurant manager."

"What do I have to be jealous of?" she objected.

"I mean, look at you, you're *pissed*. It's not my fault your restaurant only does fifteen dinners all night while I do fifteen per half-hour."

Vera stormed out. Kyle even had the further audacity to laugh after her. She wanted to shriek.

"What's the matter?" Dan B. asked when she came back to her own kitchen.

"Nothing," she snapped. Her heels clicked hotly straight to the service bar, where she poured herself a shot of Crown Royal. She could barely hold the little glass steady enough to pour the liquor. Donna stared at her, setting down a bus bin. One thing Vera never did was drink during hours.

"Listen, Vera," Dan B. offered. "It's only our first night. We can't expect to do business like The Emerald Room right off. Gotta give people time to find out about us."

Vera knew this, she even anticipated it. So why was she shaking?

"Business'll pick up," Donna added.

Vera leaned back and sighed. "Sorry, gang," she apologized. She'd felt close to bugging out; it didn't make sense. A slow night was nothing to get bent about, nor was the scrap with Kyle. Competition between managers was a reality in this business, and one she'd dealt with often. Her sudden fervor had nothing to do with any of that. So what was it? For a moment, she felt like she was going to fall to pieces. And how would that look in front of her staff? Vera was their boss, their leader. She was the one who'd convinced them to come here in the first place.

Look at me now, she reflected.

Donna put her arm around her, steered her away.

140

"Why don't you just go upstairs and get to bed? You need some rest, that's all."

"Yeah, Vera," Dan B. said. "Hit the sack. We'll finish up down here. Don't worry about a thing."

"Okay," Vera said. She *was* tired, as a matter of fact. Maybe it was all just too much commotion, fretting over every little detail before the opening. "I'll see you all in the morning."

Vera could imagine the looks they exchanged as she left. One thing she couldn't afford was to lose the confidence of her employees. They'd been such a great team together at The Emerald Room; if they thought she was flipping out, they'd fall apart. *Get your shit together, girl,* she thought, and crossed the atrium for the stairs. She frowned yet again at the untenanted reception desk. She doubted that she'd seen a single guest sign in today, yet all the suites were booked. *Select clientele,* she remembered both Feldspar and Kyle saying. Then it dawned on her. The VIP entrance behind the east wing—that's where the guests were coming in from. It seemed almost as though Feldspar was ashamed of the atrium, that he was deliberately keeping this "select clientele" of his from seeing it. But the atrium was beautiful, as was the rest of The Inn. Why hide it?

She could hear the room-service elevators running full tilt behind the walls. She trudged up the stairs, toward her bedroom, taking each step as if in dread. And it was dread. Though she could admit that to no one else, she easily admitted it to herself.

It was sleep that she dreaded.

She closed her door, poured herself a Grand Marnier, and ran a bubble bath—her nightly ritual. A glance in the mirror affirmed Donna's observation. Vera was run down, tired out. She assessed her reflection as she took off her clothes. The dark circles under her eyes told all.

Not enough sleep. And it was more than just worrying over the opening, she knew.

It was the dreams.

The lewd dreams seated in her inexplicable sexual fantasy. *The hands,* she thought, and hung up her tulip wrap-dress. The hands slowly caressing her into a frenzy. The fantasy lover was Kyle, or at least she guessed it was, and that made even less sense. *Why fantasize about someone you can't stand?* she wondered. Perhaps it was all Freudian. Nevertheless, each night the fantasy seduced her to the point of touching herself. Then she'd fall asleep, and the dreams would begin. . . .

She slipped out of her panties, unclasped her bra. Her amethyst necklace sparkled against her bosom. She lay it on the marble counter and eased into the warm tub.

She dreaded the dreams because they made her feel ashamed, and she felt ashamed because . . . she enjoyed them. They reduced her to a slut. *Maybe I'm a slut and don't know it,* she attempted to make a joke of it. She could not believe the things that happened in the nightly dream. She couldn't even believe how her subconscious could conjure such things. . . .

The dream was always the same, just blurred in certain details. The hands, somehow, were the catalyst. They'd repeat their ministration of the fantasy, goading her, setting her off. Then they'd urge her to her hands and knees. *Doggie style,* she thought now. She'd never even liked it that way. It seemed insincere, whory, indulgent. When she made love for real, she liked to be face to face with her lover, not just a back and buttocks. It turned lovemaking into a faceless antic, a joining of bodies with no identities. Was the dream orchestrating her aversions, playing out acts she didn't consciously condone? If so, why? Why was her mind not only including a person she didn't like but also a sexual position she didn't enjoy?

She enjoyed it in the dream, however. It brought tumultuous orgasms, and sensations so erotic it dizzied her to think of them now. It seemed to go on all night. Her sex would be plumbed from behind, while the hands reached around and plied her clitoris. The penis felt huge; she could scarcely take it all. Eventually it would withdraw and release its ejaculation onto her back. The dream-lover would then push her back down onto her belly, straddle her, and massage her back and shoulders as though the long gouts of seed were body lotion. And next, the hands would urge her up, gently position her to sit at the edge of the bed. No words were spoken, none needed to be. The figure would merely stand before, with hands on hips as if in wait. What it awaited was clear. Without reservation, Vera would eagerly lean forward to admit the massive organ into her mouth.

And that was only the beginning. . . .

I should see a shrink, she considered now. *My mind has become a garbage can.* She lay inert in the tub, staring up not so much at the ceiling as at the confusing images of herself that had never presented themselves until now.

Why? she thought. Her toes diddled with drips from the faucet. *And why now? How come I'm not sleeping well? How come I feel like I'm falling apart? And why the hell am I all of a sudden having these gross dreams?*

She had no idea.

Nor did she have any idea whatsoever that all of these things had one very specific common denominator:

The Inn.

Lee popped the Gun Club tape into his boom box and boogied. He always worked better with good music. The Gun Club was kick-out-the-jambs rock. He also worked better with a beer. He'd conned Donna into copping him a few bottles of EKU Maibock before she'd locked the service cage for the night. What was the big deal anyway? A few beers, aw so what? Dishwasher was always the last man out and it was the groatiest job, so why shouldn't he be allowed to toss a few while wrapping the kitchen up?

He jammed to the tunes, a song about Elvis from hell, as he off-loaded the last rack of plates from the Hobart. Dishwasher was an erroneous job title—you didn't just wash dishes, you cleaned *everything* in the kitchen so it was spic 'n span for tomorrow. Of course, he wasn't exactly busting his ass tonight. A kitchen didn't get that dirty after only serving fifteen dinners. All he had left was the floor to mop, and he could call it a night.

Lee was enthused; he was making righteous money now, and he wasn't discouraged by opening night's low draw. Things would pick up, he was sure. With Dan B. at the range and Vera running the show, word would get around fast that the best place in town to eat was The Carriage House. He didn't understand why Vera was so bent out of shape tonight, though. She knew these things. In fact, she'd been acting funny for a while. Frazzled, off-the-mark, and a little bitchy. That made sense though, what with Paul Whatshisface cheating on her. What a scumbag. Vera was a nice lady, she didn't deserve to be duped like that. For all that time she'd had her hopes up for marrying the guy, and then the guy puts her through the wringer. *I wish he was here right now,* Lee thought and polished off the first Maibock. *I'd run his dog ass through the Hobart a few times, see if that doesn't clean up his act a bit.* Poor Vera. No wonder she hadn't been herself lately.

That and that Kyle motherfucker giving her the extra headache. That's the last thing she needed on top of the shit she had to take from Paul. One thing Lee knew from the word go: that Kyle motherfucker was bad news. He'd been on all their asses.

Speaking of motherfuckers. . . .

Suddenly the door to the room-service kitchen was unlocked and open. Standing within, and sneering big-time, was Kyle. "Hey, fatboy," he said.

Lee shot the dude a scowl. "You talkin' to me?"

"No, I'm talking to the ten other fat shits standing behind you. Who do you think I'm talking to?"

"What do you want, man?"

"I want you to get your fat can over here and finish up the RS dishes. We got slammed tonight, and my dishman's ragged out."

Lee, at once, was tempted to suggest that Kyle dine on his Fruit of the Looms. Instead, he said, "I don't take orders from you. Vera's my boss."

"Bullshit. We're both your bosses, and right now I'm telling you to do something, so how come you're not doing it, fatboy?"

Lee sputtered. Sure, he knew he was fat, but he didn't need to be reminded of that fact, especially from a cocksure, snide motherfucker like Kyle. This was a tough call. Kyle, after all, was staff management. Lee didn't revel in the idea of cleaning up room service's mess. But there was another thing he didn't revel in the idea of: a reprimand.

"What's that there?" Now Kyle was squinting, his grin sharpening. "Is that beer you're drinking?"

Fuck! Lee thought. The second bottle of Maibock was sitting there big as day next to the dressing mixer. "Uh, yeah," he answered up. What could he say? *No, it's milk, it just looks like beer.*

"Drinkin' on the job'll get you fired around here, fatboy. Dump it out."

"Aw, come on, man. It's just a beer, it's not a federal fucking offense."

145

Kyle cocked his head. "You got a hearing problem to go along with the weight problem, fatboy? I said dump it out. Pick up the fuckin' bottle in your fat little hand, walk over to the sink, and dump it the fuck out. That, or you can pack your bags and head back to Fatboy City right this second."

Lee dumped the beer out, his lips pursed as the precious pale liquid bubbled down the drain.

"Good, fatboy, good. You're learning. Now, finish up whatever fucking around you've got in there, and then waddle your fat ass over to my dishwasher and get on the stick. If you're too fat to squeeze through the door, let me know. I'll run a buscart into your fat ass and pop you in."

I don't have to take this shit from him, do I? Lee asked himself, then paused. *Yeah, I guess I do. He's a manager, and he just caught me drinking on duty. I didn't come all this way to get canned on my first night on the job.* "I'll be over in ten," he said.

"Make it five," Kyle corrected. "And turn off that redneck boom box unless you want me to bust it over your fat head."

Lee didn't know how much more of this guy he could take. Kyle retreated back into the RS kitchen. When Lee turned off the boom box, he could hear Kyle yelling at someone back there. "You fuckin' groaty bitch, what the fuck you doin' in there!" Lee just shook his head and got to mopping behind the hotline. *Boy, I just love working with nice guys like him,* he thought.

Then he thought, *you've got to be shitting me!* when he went through the door into the room-service kitchen. He didn't see Kyle, but he did see one holy hell of a mess. *Dishes stacked up till next Easter! I'll be here all night!* And that line Kyle had given him about his dishman being ragged out? What a load of shit. There'd been no dishman on duty over here at all; the machine wasn't

146

even turned on; the temp gauge read 50 degrees. They'd done a whole night's worth of room service orders and hadn't cleaned a fucking thing!

Boy, am I getting screwed, Lee thought, and lit the Hobart's pilot. *If he thinks I'm gonna clean* his *dishes every goddamn night, he's got another thing coming.* This was an outrage. There was junk all over the floor, broken plates, food, trash. And if the mountain of dirty plates wasn't enough, the entire cold line counter was stacked with racks of dirty glasses. "Hey, Kyle!" Lee called out. "I'm not a goddamn machine! What are you trying to pull?"

No response. *Where the hell did he go?* Lee cranked the heat knob on the Hobart to HIGH, then looked around. Along the aisle wall to the room-service elevators stood the tall steel doors to Kyle's walk-ins and pantries. There were all locked.

Except for one.

Lee pushed his long hair back off his brow and approached the one door that stood partway open. As he neared, he heard something, a fierce slapping sound.

Slapping?

He peeked in. Stared.

It was a storage room. Another door at the end was closed. And the sound he heard was slapping, all right. Lee couldn't believe what he was looking at.

One of the room-service staff—the short, fat, doughy woman Lee had seen around—was hunkered down in the corner against several one-hundred-pound sacks of rice. One quarter of a club sandwich lay in pieces on the floor. And towering above was Kyle, his hand a hot blur. He was slapping the living shit out of the woman. . . .

"Fuckin' fat retard bitch," Kyle murmured, slapping away at the woman's face. "How many times I gotta tell you dolts to stay the fuck outa here, huh?" *Slap-slap-*

147

slap! "Next time I catch you in here I'm gonna bust you up good." *Slap-slap-slap!*

Lee was too shocked at first to even react. Tears streaked the woman's wide, reddened face. Kyle laid his open palm twice more across the side of her head, and she recoiled, whining. "Gonna fuck with me, huh?" Kyle remarked. He roughly grabbed her by the ear, hauled her up, and drew back his fist—

"Cut it out, man!" Lee yelled.

Kyle's fist froze. He glanced over his shoulder. In the pause, the woman, sobbing, crawled out of the corner and scurried away.

"What the hell are you doing?" Lee demanded.

Kyle turned, glaring. "None of your fuckin' business, fatboy. I thought I told you to get this joint cleaned up."

"You can't be treating people like that, man. You've got to be out of your mind."

"She's a fuckin' thief," Kyle countered, "just like all the dolts around here. You don't slap 'em around every now and then and they'll steal you blind. I caught the pig ripping off food."

Lee went agape, pointing to the bits of club sandwich. "You're beating the shit out of her for stealing toast points? All she's gotta do is file a complaint with the labor board and your ass is grass, man."

Kyle ushered him out of the pantry, closed the door, and put a padlock on it. "She won't say shit, fatboy. Wanna know why? 'Cause she's illegal. She says anything to anyone, and she gets deported."

"Yeah?" Lee gestured. "Well you can't deport me."

Kyle leaned against a trans cart and chuckled. "Who're you kidding? I been working with guys like you for ten years, and you're all the same. You got no life except for this. Shit, fatboy, this is the most money

148

you'll ever make, and you know it. You fuck with me, and I'll fire your ass faster than it takes me to shake the piss off my dick, and then you'll have nothing. You wanna go back to the city where you'll have to pay rent on half the money you make with Feldspar?''

Lee didn't answer.

''I thought so. Learn quick, fatboy. Around here you don't fuck with the system''—then Kyle pointed—''and you don't fuck with me. And anytime you see me wailing on these pig-ugly dolts, you keep your mouth shut, otherwise you don't get that raise.''

''What raise?''

''The raise I'm putting you in for tonight, for 'exceptional performance and high attitudinal standards.' Get it?''

I get it, all right, Lee thought. *You're greasing me.*

Kyle grinned around the RS kitchen. ''Yeah, looks to me like if you bust that wide-load tail of yours you might be out of here by six in the morning. Me, I think I'll go viddie some tit flicks and have a few beers. Better get on the stick, huh?''

''Yeah,'' Lee replied, but many other, better replies came to mind just then. Kyle swaggered off, leaving Lee to the landslide of dirty dishes and chock-full garbage cans. *Good Christ,* he thought.

''Hey, fatboy,'' Kyle called out from his service cage. ''Catch.''

Lee flinched and caught the bottle of EKU Maibock that Kyle tossed him. ''You're real generous, man,'' he said.

Kyle laughed out loud. ''Damn right, and if this floor ain't clean enough for me to eat off of by morning, I'll shove the empty bottle up your fat ass. Have a good one, buddy!''

Kyle's laughter disappeared when he went up the

149

room-service elevator. All Lee could think was *you motherless motherfucker* as he turned on the Hobart's chain motor and began spraying off the first rack of food-smudged dishes, the first of many.

Chapter Fourteen

Donna supposed they must seem the oddest couple. Dan B. was big, brusk, brazen-mouthed—he sometimes took things too seriously—while Donna cast an opposite appearance: fawnish, sometimes flighty. Perhaps it was this very contrast that held them so securely together. Donna didn't really care about the whys and wherefores. All that mattered was that they loved each other.

Making it hadn't been easy for the two of them—they had their dreams much as any couple did. But it was difficult to pursue a dream beyond life's often brutal realities. She'd done a lot of low things in her life, back in the Bad Old Days, many of which she'd never even told Dan B. How could she? What man would want her? She hadn't had a drink in over six months; the most she'd ever gone before that was six days. It was Dan B. who had pulled her out. He never gave up on her, where most guys gave up the first week, or night. Yet Dan B. was the only one who'd cared enough about her to keep her from faltering. Many of the men before him actually encouraged her to drink. *It made me an easy fuck,* she realized now, in the tense dark. Sometimes she cried just thinking about it, and about how ugly the world could be.

She'd boozed herself right out of college. *Ten years*

151

ago? she wondered. *Twelve?* She'd spent the next decade throwing darts at a map of the country. Each new city, and its promise of a new start, spat her back out like used gum. How many towns had she been run out of? How many times had she made her name mud? *Oh, God.* From Akron to Tucson, Seattle to Baltimore, the one thing she could never escape was herself. She'd been fired from so many jobs that soon she'd run out of cities. Dark days. Each night after work she spent all her tips in the bars, and when she spent all her tips . . .

The memory made her sick. Alcoholism stripped her of her humanity. It was a common occurrence to flirt for drinks, but quite a few guys out there knew that scene. Often she'd do more than flirt. One night she tallied up a fifty-dollar tab in Fells Point, and she was broke. She wound up blowing a guy in the toilet stall to cover it. Another time, in Massachusetts, she'd been thrown out of some gin joint for coming on to customers. Trudging home, she passed out on the street. When she woke up she was in the back seat of a Delta 88 being gang-raped by three chuckling men. It went on for hours and she scarcely even knew it, she was so drunk. Later, they kicked her out of the car, half-naked, bleeding, with semen in her hair, and all she could think to say before they drove off was "Give me some money for a bottle and you can do it again." The driver got out, kicked her in the head, and pissed on her. . . .

Yeah, she thought now. *The Bad Old Days.* How much worse could they have been? She was barely holding down a barmaid job at The Rocks when she met Dan B. He'd just come up from Charleston after the four-star restaurant he was chefing at folded from financial problems, and now he was working at The Emerald Room. He didn't have to date her long to realize she had a problem; he was carrying her out of bars right and left, but the thing that didn't jibe was he kept coming back.

That had never happened before—it almost shocked her. "You're a sucker to want to have anything to do with me," she told him one night after tying on a giant one at Middleton's Tavern. "I'm an alcoholic."

"If that's what you think," he shouted in her face, "then that's all you'll ever be!"

She got fired from The Rocks for being drunk on duty. When she told Dan B., she expected him to dump her. Instead, he stuffed her in the car and took her to an AA meeting. Three times a week he took her. When she pitched a fit, he made her go anyway, often forcing her into the car. "I don't want to go!" she'd yell. "I don't give a shit what you want!" he'd yell back. "I'm not going to sit around and watch you kill yourself! Either you go on your own, or I drag you in and handcuff you to the fucking chair!"

Why did he put up with her? He even dropped a shift to take her to the meetings. Sometimes she'd actually hide, but he'd find her anyway. Once she'd skipped out to the City Dock, was about to walk into O'Brien's for a gin and tonic, when Dan B.'s dusty station wagon pulled up at the corner. "It's time for your AA, Donna," he said through the window. "Get in the car."

The meetings depressed her—that's why she initially didn't like to go. A room full of people just like her, all telling the same grim stories. But eventually it sank in. It reassured her to know that she was not the only person in the world who'd done desperate things for a drink. Alcoholism, she learned, was a genetically founded disease, not just a failure of willpower. Some people could drink with no problem, others could have just one and that was their ruin. Dan B. sat through the meetings with her, which must have been particularly grueling, for he barely drank at all. Two beers was it for him. Yet he insisted on being there with her every time. One night she'd asked him. "Why do you do all this for me?"

"Because I love you," he said. "Why do you think?"

It was an alien word to her, and one that had never been spoken to her by any man. Love—*real* love—was not something that happened to drunks. Then one day it dawned on her that she'd not had a drink in almost a month. . . .

Dan B. had given her back what a horrible circumstance had stolen from her: her life.

A month later they got married.

Which left them to their dreams. But what were they? Donna had gotten more out of the deal than she'd ever imagined; she'd gotten the chance to live again. She could scarcely think beyond that. But what of Dan B.? He'd been saving for years, in hopes to one day own his own place. The money he could bank from The Inn could make his dream real, yet he'd been reluctant to move. "If we move, you won't be able to go to your AA meetings anymore," he'd revealed his only worry. Again, it was her, it was Donna that was his only concern. "You're all the AA I need now," she'd assured him. She'd been the one to insist they take the new positions that Vera had arranged, not that she was too keen on living in the sticks, but because it provided her the opportunity, finally, do give something back to Dan B., to do something for *him.* The extra money they both made would give Dan B. his own restaurant that much sooner.

He slept beside her now, snoring softly in the big, plush bed. Donna felt blissful, sedate; they'd made slow love earlier. His semen still trickled in her; it reminded her of a gift, or a verifier of sorts. One day, when their other dreams came true, she'd give him a baby. . . .

Suddenly, she shuddered beneath the covers, like a jag of vertigo. She groaned. A bad memory swung before her mind, an unwelcome image from the Bad Old Days. It was an anonymous poem: *The past is as present as the truth is a lie, all this time you think you're living, then one day you wake up and die.* What an awful poem, and an awful recollection. The poem had always stuck in her head for some reason, perhaps to remind her to never take things for granted. It was from years ago. Donna had been blowing some cowboy in the men's room of a bar in San Angelo, Texas. He'd left her sitting there with a twenty-dollar bill in her hand. She'd spat his sperm into the toilet, and then she looked up and seen the poem amid phone numbers and expletives. It had been written on the stall door in magic marker.

Why should such a memory resurface now? Things were good now, and the Bad Old Days were in the past. *The past is as present,* she thought, *as the truth is a lie. . . .* What did it mean?

Suddenly the bedroom's warm and cozy dark felt full of unseen ghosts. A tear drooled out of her eye, and she turned to hug Dan B. *Ghosts,* she thought. The memory was one of her past's many demons, coming back for a little haunt. . . .

Donna could live with that, she'd have to. *Forget it,* she thought. Goddamn the poet, though, and that funk-crotch cowboy slime who'd known just the right way to take advantage of her. "Say, honey, you say you're twenty short on your tab? Well, I can think of way to clear that up a might fast." *Fuck you.* He was probably in the same bar right now, pulling that same ploy. *Yeah,* she considered now. *I guess everybody's got their ghosts. . . .*

Ghosts.

The thought transgressed. It reminded her of the book she'd picked up at the mall a few days before they left town. When The Inn had been a sanitarium, the doctors and staff had taken some grim liberties with the patients.

After the investigation in the late thirties, hundreds of charges had been filed by the state: rape and sexual abuse, torture, murder. It had gone on for years. Donna couldn't imagine the sheer horror that had occurred within these same walls. Hence The Inn's reputation for being haunted, a reputation so notorious that local residents had set fire to the building. Many claimed they'd seen ghosts.

Ghosts, she thought.

Vera dismissed the book's revelations as fantasy, but Donna, of late, wasn't so sure. She hadn't been sleeping well recently. Often she'd wake at night convinced someone was in the room, or standing just outside the door. Into the wee hours, she could hear the doors of the room-service elevators opening and closing downstairs, but it was strange that she'd never hear the elevators themselves traveling up and down from the RS kitchen to the upper suites. There were other sounds too, more distant sounds, like footsteps, faraway muttering, and something that sounded like a shriek. And tonight, when The Carriage House had closed, she came upstairs to shower before bed and had been absolutely irked by the impression that someone was watching her.

But what bothered her most of all was the dream.

It made little sense, and wasn't particularly harrowing. Yet she'd had it every night now since they'd moved to The Inn.

She'd dream of herself walking dim, dank corridors, dressed only in her sheerest lingerie. She felt intoxicated and aroused, as if in a trance. As if someone were summoning her.

Someone, or something.

156

Chapter Fifteen

Vera descended the stairs the next morning at ten, wearing a lightly flowered chartruese jacket and white chiffon skirt. A bleached stone statue of Edward the Confessor smirked at her on the landing when she evened the jacket's low-cut brim.

She'd slept in snatches, dragged in and out of sleep. The dream of The Hands had mauled her all night, plied her, twisted her into the lewdest positions. She'd waked just before dawn in a gloss of perspiration, having kicked off the bedcovers in her sleep. One pillowcase was torn, she'd noticed, by her teeth. *I'm so horny I'm having sex-fits,* she'd thought. Her sweat dampened the sheets beneath her. Hard as she tried, she couldn't return to sleep, tossing and turning instead.

More and more now, The Inn's resistance to light occurred to her. Little sunlight fell into the atrium this morning, leaving only quiet gloom. She went behind the reception desk and down the left hall, to the front office. Feldspar looked up from his desk and semismiled when she entered.

"Good morning, Ms. Abbot."

"Hi, Mr. Feldspar," she replied. "You're a pretty hard guy to track down."

"Indeed." He set his Mont Blanc down on the blotter

157

and stiffly rose. "I apologize for not being present for your opening night—I was horribly detained writing promotional copy for our new membership brochures. I understand your first night went well."

No one had to go to the hospital with food poisoning, she thought, *if that's what you mean by well.* "We only did fifteen dinners."

"Ah, and you're disappointed by that." This was an observation, not a question.

"Well, I'm not jumping up and down with joy. I still think if we'd run some ads . . ."

Feldspar smiled more broadly this time. He idly stroked his goatee, looking at her. "You expected a deluge of business on opening night? Surely not. What you must understand, Ms. Abbot, is the real function of The Carriage House."

"What do you mean?"

"It's a sideline, a subordination. I don't expect the restaurant, on its own, to ever operate in the black."

This frustrated, even astonished, her. *Then why the hell are you paying us all this money?* she wanted to shout. *Why do you have a restaurant at all if you don't expect it to make a profit?*

"Our priority is The Inn," he stated. "Our business profits come from guest reservations. I thought I'd made that clear."

"Well, you did," she admitted, "sort of." Then she decided to voice her query, even though it countered her best interests. "So why even have the restaurant at all? The food inventories, the payroll, and its construction costs must come to a tremendous sum."

"The building cost of The Carriage House," Feldspar finally revealed "totaled out at just under a million, and I'm figuring half a million per year for stock, salaries, and utilities, based on the restaurants from Magwyth Enterprises' other inns."

158

"What are your average gross receipts from the same restaurants?" she now felt obliged to ask.

Feldspar shrugged. "About a hundred thousand, a little more sometimes."

Four hundred grand in the hole every year? she calculated.

"And you're thinking it's an affront to business logic to maintain a quality restaurant that will never show profits."

"Yes," Vera said. "That's exactly what I'm thinking."

"Quality," Feldspar replied, "is the key word in the theorem. And long-term overall profit projections. Why does any hotel spend fifteen thousand dollars for a painting that few patrons even look at? Why does a broker spend more on office furniture than the average person earns in several years? La Belle Dame, in southern France, recently purchased a bottle of Medoc to display in their dining room. It cost one hundred twenty thousand dollars. Certainly no one's going to order it with dinner."

"So it's all a show, in other words?" Vera reasoned.

"Yes, or in better words, it's all a verification of impeccable quality standards. In our business, we amass such standards to a single, focused effect. Our select clientele want proof of such standards. They pay for it."

The Carriage House is an expensive chair that nobody's even supposed to sit in, Vera thought. *Just a pretty thing for patrons to notice out of the corner of their eye when they're walking up to their high-priced suites. We're just scenery.*

"That's why I hired you," Feldspar continued. "That's why I pay you a considerable salary. I don't care if you only serve one dinner per night, Ms. Abbot. As long as you maintain a preeminent standard of quality at The Carriage House, you're doing your job. And if you do your job, you'll be rewarded. You can manage

The Carriage House for as long as you like, or you can even transfer to one of our other inns abroad. Thus far, I couldn't be more pleased with your efforts."

It's your ball game, she thought. Why argue with him, or with the money he was paying? Vera knew that with time, and with some promotion, she could make the restaurant work on its own. But Feldspar didn't even seem to want it to.

He stepped toward a dark teak cabinet, with his slight limp, and uncorked a bottle of Château de Pommard. "Volnay is my favorite vineyard," he remarked. "Would you care for some?"

It's a little early to be drinking expensive wine, she thought, *but what the hell?* "Sure," she said. He passed her a glass, which she sniffed. A good bouquet. Its taste had an after-dazzle, a beautiful, bright dry edge.

Feldspar chugged his. *What a bohemian,* Vera thought.

"As the French say, *boire un petit coup c'est agré-able.*"

"What's that mean?"

"A little drink is good." He poured himself another glass and awkwardly retook his seat. He looked casual today, in that he wasn't wearing a suit. Instead he wore suede J.P. Tod loafers, dark slacks, and a Yohji black silk sports jacket that must have cost a thousand dollars. His hair was pulled back in its usual short tail, and the rings glittered on his wide hands. Vera remembered the gun in his desk, and the unlocked cash box, but skipped mentioning it. Admitting that you'd been snooping in the boss's desk drawer probably wouldn't win her any stars. Instead, she said, "I'm out of company checks. I've got two suppliers coming in tomorrow, so I'll need more."

"Order them from the bank in town," he dismissed.

"Well, I can't. I don't have an account ID. Kyle said

160

you'd give me an account card." She didn't want to sound like she was complaining, but she didn't have an account number for her own personal account, into which her salary checks were direct-deposited. "I could also use my own account number."

Feldspar glanced up, flabbergasted. "What a blunder, I do apologize. I've been so busy I'd forgotten about it." He quickly milled around the top desk drawer and gave her both account cards. "And don't bother showing me your inventory lists. Use your own judgment—that's what I hired you for."

Vera nodded. He was pretty much giving her a free rein on her stock orders, but that didn't really surprise her. By now, she was getting to know this odd man, and how he delegated authority. She wondered if Kyle had the same monetary freedom with room service. *Probably more,* she thought. *The prick.*

Now that she had her account numbers, she needed a way to get into town, another point she wasn't quite sure how to bring up. *He's paying me a hundred and fifteen grand, I can't very well whine about my wheels.*

But Feldspar brought it up for her. "And you're too polite," he commented, finishing off his Pommard. "As you know, I'm quite a busy man, not that that serves as an excuse. I forget minor details rather often. Please don't feel reserved to remind me of things." Again, he was digging in the desk drawer. "After all, part of your employment contract entitles you to a company car. I regret that it took so long, but I thought you'd like something nice, so I put in a special order with our headquarters. An overstock." A set of keys dangled from his fingers, which he raised to her. "I do hope you like blue."

"Blue's just fine," she said. All she cared about this moment was wheels, not colors. "And thank you. What kind of car is it?"

161

"Go and see. It was delivered this morning. Around back."

Oh, goodie, she thought. She'd only been off the premises once, in Dan B.'s dented station wagon. "I'll also be picking up some locks for my walk-ins," she added. "Kyle said—or at least he implied—that there's a pilfering problem. Is that true?"

"Oh, I'm sure it goes on. Who knows what else goes on behind management's back?"

Dolts, Vera remembered Kyle's reference to the staff. *What a malicious shithead. One day I'll dolt him.*

"It's not that I don't trust the help," Feldspar said, "but you can't trust everyone. A fair rule of thumb in this business is to put a lock on everything."

Then try locking your office door for starters, she felt inclined to advise, but let it go. Instead, she thanked him again and left.

She went up for her coat and purse, not admitting a childish excitement. *It's probably a '65 Corvair,* she thought. *It's probably a motor scooter.* "Let's go for a ride," she invited, when Donna stepped out of her own bedroom. "Feldspar finally got me my company car, and I need to stop by the bank."

Dan B. could be heard snoring in the background. "I could use a shopping spree," Donna said, whisking on her coat.

"Don't count on much of a shopping spree in Waynesville," Vera reminded. "What've they got? A Dart Drug and a Save-On?"

"And a Sinclair station! Dan B. needs some brake fluid, I can hardly wait to get out of here." They went downstairs, passing the plump, pasty maid dusting on the landing. The woman averted her eyes when Vera said hello, and made no reply.

"What is with these people?" Donna remarked. "They won't even look at us."

"I've already gotten used to that," Vera said as they crossed the atrium. "I guess there's no law that says people have to be friendly."

Outside was still and cold. The grounds looked good in spite of the drab winter; the heated fountain gushed. "So what kind of car did the boss get you?" Donna asked as they followed the long path around the side of The Inn.

But before Vera could even answer, she was staring, voiceless, into the parking lot. *I do hope you like blue,* she remembered him saying. "You've got to be kidding me!" Donna squealed. "Feldspar gave you *that?*"

Parked right alongside of Feldspar's glossy red Lamborghini Diablo was an identical one, in jet-lacquered deep blue.

"I cannot believe this," Donna said.

"Neither can I." Vera's grin felt like a net spread across her face. The blue Lamborghini seemed to soar on air when she turned out of the hotel entrance onto Route 154. Plush ribbed leather and the ergonomic interior enveloped them; it felt like sitting in a space capsule. The suspension laid a cushion over the pocked and broken route to town.

"Make it go," Donna bid.

Vera was almost afraid to. Her foot barely touched the gas, yet they were doing fifty already. She eased it down a little more, and the sleek car leapt ahead, eating up road. Another moment and they were doing seventy-five. Vera didn't even want to think about what would happen if she pushed the accelerator all the way to the floor.

Donna grinned ahead, as the open field blurred by. "When he said he was going to give you a car, he wasn't fooling around."

"Well, he didn't *give* it to me," Vera corrected. "It belongs to the company. I get to use it."

"I'll bet this thing cost more to insure than three normal cars. It's incredible."

You better keep the speed down, Vera, she warned herself. *The cops probably wouldn't appreciate an out-of-towner using a public highway for your own personal autobahn.* She eased off the gas, and let the car wend through the next bends. "Plus, you can borrow it anytime you want," she added.

"I'm a station wagon kind of gal, Vera," Donna replied. "I can't even relate to this. It looks like something in a science fiction book."

"Speaking of books," Vera reminded herself, "loan me that book you have about haunted mansions. I could use a laugh."

Donna, suddenly, seemed to flinch. "The Wroxton Hall part is pretty scary. And gross."

Vera laughed. "Come on, it's bunk, Donna."

"If it's bunk, why do you want to read it?"

"For my amusement, that's all. You should've heard Kyle, the prick. He tried to freak me out, saying The Inn's haunted."

"He wants to freak you out, all right. Out of your clothes. What did he say?"

"Just the same silly crap about The Inn being haunted. Then the asshole actually had the nerve to try and con me into going skinny dipping. Started taking his shirt off right in front of me. I guess he thought I'd swoon once I saw his chest."

"Well, he is good-looking."

Vera winced. "I don't care if he looks like Hulk Hogan, he's still an asshole."

"Be honest now, Vera. You're attracted to him aren't you?" Donna smiled coyly. "You fantasize about him, don't you?"

164

Vera's amusement over the topic quickly crashed. *Fantasize,* she thought. What of her fantasy of The Hands, and the lewd dream that always followed? Was she really fantasizing about Kyle? Then Donna said, "But you know, getting back to the story about The Inn being haunted . . ."

"What?" Vera asked, frowning.

"Well, I've been hearing weird things at night, like footsteps out in the hall, and strange noises from downstairs. A lot of times I'll wake up and feel like someone's in the bedroom. And then there's that damn racket from the room-service elevators, the doors opening and closing all night, but the funny thing is that's all I hear, just the doors opening and closing. I never seem to hear the elevators coming up."

Vera had heard the doors too, many times. "It's just some soundproofing fluke. Big deal? And of course you're going to hear footsteps and other noises at night. It's Kyle's room-service crew cleaning up."

"Yeah? I guess you're right." But Donna seemed reluctant. "And I've also been having some pretty freaky dreams."

Vera glanced at her. "What kind of dreams?"

"Nothing specific. I'm walking around somewhere, long dark halls, past rooms I've never seen."

"So? You're dreaming about a new place, an uncertain experience," Vera tried to psychologize. "What's freaky about that?"

"It's just the way I feel in the dream. I feel almost drunk, entranced. It's like I'm being summoned somewhere, and it seems really sexual, 'cause all I'm wearing is lingerie."

"And you're smoking a cigar too, right?" Vera attempted some levity, "an obvious Freudian symbol. Or maybe it's not a dream at all. Maybe it's one of the ghosts calling you, one that likes lingerie." But then it occurred to her that she needn't joke about it, for her own dreams too were undisputably sexual, and arousing to the point of disturbing her sleep. It proposed an aggravating contrast: the dreams distressed her, but at the same time she actually looked forward to them. Perhaps it was part of her subconscious that longed for what she'd been raised to believe was immoral—*having sex with a person I don't even like is definitely immoral,* she reasoned—and the part of herself that was now sexually unfulfilled. Suddenly, the image returned: herself naked on her belly, panting as The Hands worked up the backs of her legs, raising her buttocks. . . .

"What did Mr. Feldspar say about our huge turnout?" Donna asked next.

Vera was grateful for the distraction as she steered the sleek Lamborghini through another series of winding, wooded bends. "He doesn't seem to care," she answered. "The Carriage House is just a sideline; he doesn't even care if it makes a profit. He's counting on room service and accommodations to put him in the black. It's crazy, if you ask me, but he must know what he's doing. All of Magwyth Enterprises' other inns are in the black. Long as we do our job we got nothing to worry about."

Minutes later they pulled into town. MAIN STREET, the central drag was originally dubbed. The town seemed repressed by the cold; only sparse traffic could be seen, and few pedestrians. An ancient barber pole twirled lazily along a row of little shops: a general store called HULL'S, a tavern called THE WATERIN' HOLE, and a farm supply store. When Vera parked, she noticed faces squinting from windows. An old man stopped in the middle of the crosswalk and stared. No doubt they'd noticed the two hundred thousand dollar set of wheels that just pulled into their one-horse burg. A sudden frigid wind bit into them when they got out of the car. Vera rushed into a hardware store, while

166

Donna scurried into the SAVE-ON clothing store. Vera purchased several big Master padlocks. "That's some car ya got there, ma'am," a tired old man remarked at the register. "It's not mine, it's the company's," she offered. "And what company might that be, if ya don't mind my inquirin'?" "I work at The Inn," she said. "I manage the restaurant there, The Carriage House. You should try us out." "The Inn, you say?" he questioned. "Don't believe I've ever heard of it." "The old Wroxton Estate," she assisted. "It's a country-style inn now." With that, the old man made no further comment and rather hastily bagged her locks.

All right, don't try us out, she thought. *See if I care.* She found Donna raptly inspecting a small lingerie rack at the SAVE-ON. "Not exactly Fredrick's of Hollywood," Vera observed.

"Oh, but the prices are *great,*" Donna enthused, holding up a pink-lace bra that was only straps. "Three bucks!"

Vera had to frown. "There's nothing to it, Donna. A bra with no cups?"

"Oh, Vera, where's your sense of adventure? Men love this kind of stuff. Oh, I've got to get this!" Now she held up a pair of panties that looked more like a frilly g-string. "And it's only three-fifty!"

"Yeah, and a postage stamp is only twenty-nine cents, and it would cover you more." Vera failed to see the fascination. *Maybe if I'd worn silly stuff like that, Paul wouldn't have cheated on me,* she reflected. But that was a bad subject. "I can see you're going to be a while. I'll meet you back here when I'm done at the bank."

"Okay." Now Donna inspected another bra that had holes for the nipples. "Dan B.'s gonna love this!"

I'm sure he will. Vera left and strolled down the row of shops. Now several jean-jacketed men had emerged from the tavern to look at the Lamborghini. *I'll tell them*

I'm a movie star, she considered. *They'd probably believe me.* The Farmer's National Bank sat at the end of the row, one old-fashioned teller window with bars in front of it instead of bullet-proof glass. A slim, elderly woman put down a copy of *The Globe* when she entered. PEKING WOMAN GIVES BIRTH TO GORILLA! boasted the headline. And: PREHISTORIC BIRDNEST FOUND IN ROBERT CULP'S ATTIC!

Vera took care of her bank business, then withdrew some walking around money from her personal account. The teller was friendly and efficient; she seemed even pleased to wait on a new face.

"Is that your fancy car out there?" she asked.

"Yes," Vera said, pocketing her withdrawal slip. *Should I say I'm a movie star?* she wondered.

"Then you must be up at the old Wroxton place," the woman said. She glanced up over her bifocals.

"That's right. I'm the restaurant manager. How did you know?"

"On account of that Feldspar man. He drove one just like it, only it was red. Now don't get me wrong, miss, we're quite grateful to him, what with all the money he put in our branch. But I'll tell you the same thing I told him."

"Let me see if I can guess," Vera ventured. "Wroxton Hall is haunted."

"That's right, miss, and don't you laugh. There's still some folks in this town that remember. Weird goin's on up there."

"Well, we've already had the ghostbusters go through the place. It's clean."

The woman smirked. "Go ahead and laugh, miss. You'll be sorry. Lotta folks 'round here're still sorry they ever heard of that godawful place." She propped her glasses back up on her deeply lined face. "Now, is there anything else I can do for you?"

"Actually, yes," Vera said. It was none of her business per se, but, after all, she was management, and she did have authorized access to the account Feldspar had opened for the restaurant. It was a legitimate curiosity, wasn't it?

Vera held up the Magwyth Enterprises account card. "I'd like to know how much is in this account."

The old woman inspected the card again, then double-checked Vera's driver's license to make sure that the names matched. Then she pointed over the counter and said, "Just punch up the account number in the jahoozie box there."

The bank, spare as it was, did not fully lack modern conveniences. On the counter was a small keypad and LED screen, so customers could check their accounts themselves.

"Then press send," the old woman added.

Vera punched in the account number and her access code. Then she pressed SEND. *Working,* the screen read. *Please wait.*

Vera tapped her foot, waiting.

Then the screen rolled on: *Magwyth Enterprises, Ltd. Auxilliary Account: Carriage House, Access Vera Abbot ID Code 003. Please wait.*

Then Vera gasped.

Your account total is $1,000,000.00.

Chapter Sixteen

"Hey, loverboy. Rise and shine, will ya?"

Lee opened one eye amid the crush of bedcovers, at first believing it must be a bad dream that stood beyond the gloom of his room. But it was only Dan B., whose chubby face intruded through the gapped door.

"Haven't you ever heard of knocking?" Lee objected.

"Knocking? I've been knocking. You got potatoes in your ears? And how come you're sleeping so late? You on another all-night hump with the mattress?"

"I was humping your sister," Lee countered. "The girl just can't get enough."

"Idiot, get some glasses. That was *your* sister. Last night when I was done putting the blocks to her with her feet pinned back behind her ears, I slipped her an extra five-spot to come and do you. Figured it was the only way you'd ever get laid."

Lee was used to this kind of abuse; he and Dan B. were friends so it was all in fun. But it reminded him of the abuse he'd taken last night from that snide motherfucker Kyle. . . .

"What time is it?" Lee groggily inquired.

"Time for you to get your hand out of your boxers

and shag ass." Dan B. shot his watch. "It's two in the afternoon."

Two in the . . . Then Lee remembered the rest of it. He'd been up till seven in the morning cleaning up Kyle's room-service kitchen. And he didn't dare tell anyone, that and his catching Kyle beating up on that fat maid. *I squeal on him, and he squeals on me for drinking on the job. Who'll Feldspar believe?*

"We gotta start prepping for dinner in an hour," Dan B. ranted on. "So get the lead out."

"I'll be down," Lee groaned. "Where's Donna and Vera?"

Dan B. laughed. "Shopping, where else? Isn't that just like a couple of women? We're not even open two days, and they're out shopping. Looks like us guys gotta do everything."

"Yeah, but I'm the one who's gotta do your mom. And let me tell you, that's some *real* work."

"Idiot, get some glasses. That was *your* mom."

Dan B. closed the door. Lee rarely got in the last word, which was just as well. Trying to out-do Dan B. with the gross jokes was like trying to drive nails with a french bread. It didn't matter how hard you hit 'em, they wouldn't go in. Lee climbed out of bed, still muttering less than complimentary remarks under his breath, re: Kyle. He punched on his boom box, cranked up a little Pontiac Brothers, and went to the shower.

It was a nice pad they'd given him here, one door down from Dan B. and Donna's room, and Lee couldn't beat the price. Shit, a room half this size would run him seven hundred a month back in the city. They'd filled it with a lot of old-fashioned furniture and dark rugs that reminded him of his grandmother's antique shop when he was little, that and the big, high bed with carved-wood posts. The free room and board, plus the generous wage, would enable Lee to sock away some real scratch, get himself a car, get back to school. Dishman was honest work, but he didn't want to be doing it the rest of his life. Let somebody else take a turn washing grub off rich people's dinner plates.

Lee stepped on the scale in the bathroom. 217. *Fuck it,* he thought. It didn't bother him much that he had a gut on him like a feedbag. He was fat, and he was proud. He could do without that Kyle motherfucker calling him fatboy, though. Lee'd tried all the diets: Dr. Atkins, Dr. Tarnower, Dr. Bullshit, The Rice Diet, The Zero Protein Diet, The Zero Carbo Diet. He fasted once for six days, thinking he'd slim down for Ocean City, and had blacked out watching Hogan's Heroes—the last thing he remembered hearing was: "Klink . . . shut up," and next thing he knew he was in the hospital. The Tomato Juice and Sardine Diet hadn't worked much better. That had been pollen season, and everytime he sneezed, he'd rip a mean Hershey squirt in his drawers. He didn't lose much weight, but he sure lost a lot of underwear. No, Lee reasoned that life was too short and beer was too good. He could be honest with himself. One thing he positively couldn't stand was fellow comrades in tonnage making excuses for their waistlines. *Oh, but I've got a metabolism problem* or *I've got a glandular problem.* Bullshit! Lee would say. What you've got is a food to mouth problem, like me, so be real and admit it!

Yeah, fat is where it's at, he thought, quoting Root Boy Slim as he toweled himself dry after the shower. He didn't mind Dan B.'s ribbing over the lack of success in his sex life. Actually Lee wasn't the twenty-year-old virgin that Dan B.'s jokes implied; he'd gotten it on with plenty of girls in his time—well, two, really, but that was plenty to him. Lee had sold ice cream his first summer out of high school; that's where he'd met Belinda, the Good Humor girl. Blonde, flighty, cool, and cute as all. Lee didn't understand how she could be so adorably

172

slim driving an ice cream truck; hell, Lee himself probably ate a quarter of his inventory every day. They'd gotten together one hot July evening after their routes, and after a few T.J. Swans, one thing led to another. "The thing with girls is," his buddy Dave Kahill told him, "you gotta show 'em you're sincere, and not just out for a nut. You gotta go down on 'em." *I'll show her I'm sincere,* Lee remembered the words in his first and only clinch with her, in the woods behind Allan's Pond. What Lee didn't take into account, however, were certain consequences relative to personal hygiene. See, Belinda had been selling ice cream under the July sun for the last twelve hours, and Lee only realized the full, uh, impact of this once he got down to taking Dave Kahill's advice—a bite-your-face-off stench like that of a fish market dumpster in high summer. It killed his sex-drive for about a year. That's when he met Liddy, a busgirl at The Emerald Room. She was even cuter than the Good Humor girl, and she washed. "Liddy with Big Titty," Dave Kahill called her. "She's a hot number, man, and she likes *you.*" *Me?* Lee thought. And, by golly, it was true. Liddy hauled Lee's ashes all summer, but what Lee didn't know was that she'd been hauling the ashes of every other guy in town too, at the same time. Fortunately Lee had had the foresight to purchase condoms before every date. Too bad rubbers didn't protect you from crabs.

You live and you learn, he rationalized. *And I've learned.* He strolled naked back out to the bedroom; it wasn't like anyone was around to see him, was it? Then he stopped cold, his eyes bugging, and yelled, "Jesus!"

A woman sat on the edge of the bed, with her hands in her broad lap. She was looking at him.

Fat, naked, and jiggling, Lee froze in his impulse to dash. Where could he dash to? "Goddamn it! Doesn't *anybody* knock around here! What, you just walk in?"

173

The woman made no reply. She just sat there, looking at him. Lee recognized her now, of course. It was the maid, the short, rather corpulent woman with frizzy bunned hair and pale eyes. Her bosom jutted, nearly laying in her lap.

Lee grabbed the Heineken beach towel he used for a bath towel and quickly draped it around his girthy waist. *What the hell is she doing here, anyway?* She was just sitting there. "What, you here to clean my room or something?" he guessed. "Well, don't worry about it, I can take care of my own place."

Still no reply.

"How about leaving?" he said. "You know, go away. I gotta get ready for work."

But she wasn't leaving, and clearly had no intention of doing so. Instead, she stood up. She gave him a paper bag, then turned around, unbuttoning the top of her housemaid's dress and lowering it to her waist. She lay face-down on the bed, reached behind, and unhooked her bra.

Then it hit him. She wasn't here to clean his room, she was here to thank him for getting Kyle off her last night in the room-service pantry. This was her way of expressing gratitude. But—*what the hell?* he thought. *What's she doing?* She was just lying there with her back exposed.

Then, peering closer, he thought: *Holy shit . . .*

Her entire back was a mat of coarse, crisscrossing scar tissue. *Someone's been whipping the shit out of her, and for a long time,* he couldn't help but conclude. A shiver ran through him, next, when he reached into the paper bag and withdrew its slack contents:

A black rawhide whip.

"Look, lady," he said. "I'm not into kinky stuff like this."

Eventually she turned and sat up, her forearm holding

174

the large cups of the bra to her bosom. She seemed confused for a moment, as though it were a shock that he didn't want to whip her. But then the confusion in her eyes paled to a look of resigned despair. She reached into her apron pocket, withdrew a small black-plastic pouch and gave it to him, then lay back on the bed.

Lee almost puked when he opened the pouch. At first he thought it was a sewing kit, but then he remembered. He'd seen stuff like this once, on a high school field trip to New York City to see some Egyptian museum exhibit. He and Dave Kahill had slipped out to an adult bookstore on Forty-second Street, and he'd seen things identical to what he now held in his hand. Needles of various lengths, leather lashes, clip-pins and nipple-screws. This was no sewing kit—it was hardcore S&M gear.

Lee put the pouch down. Just holding it made him feel sick. "You want me to stick *needles* in you? No way. I already told you, lady, I'm not into it. It's not my scene."

Judging from the web of scars on her back, she was well-used to shit like this. Lee realized no pleasure in pain, giving or receiving. It was sick. How could anyone get a charge out of whipping a woman, or sticking pins in her? *Sick motherfuckers like Kyle,* Lee thought. *He's probably been doing shit like that for years.*

The woman sat up again. She seemed frustrated now, desperate to please him but not knowing how. She reclasped her bra, and slid back up to the edge of the bed.

Some weird expression of relief came over the pale, doughy face. She looked up at him. She smiled.

Then she got down on her knees and began to unwrap his towel.

Chapter Seventeen

Business didn't pick up much over the next week. One night The Carriage House did seven dinners; Vera could have keeled over. Another night they did thirty-seven—a record—but still nothing compared to the hundred-plus they'd done on weeknights at The Emerald Room.

Vera, generally the most stable of the bunch, had become suddenly the least tolerant of the start-up drag. Dan B., Donna, and Lee, took it all in stride. Why couldn't she? The others actually were taking to The Carriage House quite well. Dan B. whipped up specials of unheard of standards, multistage souffles, intricate flaming beef entrees, and many other dishes that The Emerald Room's big crowds never gave him time to attempt. And since Donna was the only waitress, her tips were good most nights. Even Lee, paid the least of all, seemed more content here than Vera had ever seen him back in the city.

She'd felt distracted throughout the entire week. Her very libidinous dreams had not abated; instead, they'd intensified, leaving her to wonder further about herself. She slept in fits. Feldspar was scarcely seen at all; the few times she'd gone looking for him, she instead found Kyle, who persistently made snide comments about The Carriage House's trickling turn-out. ''Yeah, we're slammed every night over at room service," he'd say. Then he'd grin. "How about you?" *Asshole,* she'd always answer in thought. Then he'd always ask, "When are you and me going to go for a dip? Oh, that's right, I keep forgetting, you don't have a swimsuit." *That's right, Kyle, and I'll never have one as long as you're around.*

Their second weekend, Vera was surprised to book a few guests into the small wing of second-floor rooms that she'd been put in charge of. The mayor had some relatives in town, and there were a few others. Vera made sure that their rooms were in pristine shape, and that anything they'd order from upstairs was of the highest quality. It infuriated her, though, to discover that Kyle's room-service elevators bypassed the second floor, which meant that her food orders had to be carried through the atrium and up the stairs. Afterward, she'd received some odd comments, however. "I hope you enjoyed your stay," she remarked to one couple. "Oh, your accommodations are superb," the wife had replied, "but it's a bit loud, isn't it?" *Loud?* Vera thought. "We kept hearing this thunking noise—" *The doors on the room-service elevators,* Vera suspected; she'd heard them too, opening and closing. "We had a very nice time," another couple cited to her, "but your housemaids aren't very friendly." *Shit!* Vera thought. Yet another couple had actually submitted a complaint card about similar noises and smirking housemaids. She felt it her responsibility to report the complaints, but when she mentioned them to Feldspar, he didn't seem to care at all. Instead, as usual, he commended her on the job she was doing, and claimed that the upper suites were booked solid. "Business couldn't be better," he'd said, and then invited her to sample a glass of Montrachet '83.

She'd hotly wanted to point out to him the foolishness of maintaining such a large inventory account for the restaurant. *A million dollars?* It was ludicrous. Less than a hundred thousand would be more then ample; the rest could be put into a higher-yield CD and at least be earning interest for the company till. But she never brought it up, far too used now to the man's lackadaisical attitude toward financial management.

And all the while, her distraction deepened. *Paul,* she thought. That final night, and its obscene imagery, had never ceased to churn through her memory. She hoped she never saw him again, but that was a false hope. Sooner or later, she'd *have* to see him. There were still a few things back at the apartment that she needed to retrieve.

Sooner or later, she knew, she'd have to go back to the city. She'd have to face him one last time.

Dinner wound down. The third night of their second week. *Twenty-two dinners tonight,* she thought. *Not bad.* Breaking twenty dinners per night was their new goal, akin to breaking one hundred in golf. Not too good, but better than shooting sevens on every hole.

The last of the diners complimented her as they left. "A simply *lovely* meal," an elderly, perfumed woman gushed, donning a mink stole. "I'm glad you liked it," Vera replied. "Please come again." "We will," promised the younger man with her. He looked like Dapper on *The Three Stooges.* While the rest cleaned up, Vera meandered to her office in the west wing. She cashed out, wrote up the night's receipts, and logged in the payroll hours. All the while, though, her mind wandered, never stopping on a single thought, image, or notion. *Paul. Feldspar. The Carriage House. Paul.* She poured herself a cordial of DeKuyper Cinnamon Schnapps and felt even more remote. *Paul. Sleep. The dream. Feldspar. Kyle . . . sex.*

178

"There I go again," she muttered to herself, and locked up her files. *Poor little oversexed Vera.*

The Inn was quiet; her office felt unoccupied even with her sitting in it. Then she noticed the package.

What is this?

It looked like a present, a thin wide box in white gift-wrap. A cryptic notecard unfolded to read, simply, MID-NIGHT in tight felt-tip. *Midnight?* she wondered. She opened the package.

You dick, she thought.

It was beautiful, a Bill Blass corselet-tank swimsuit, in a gorgeous bright-fuchsia. A half-front lace up. Her size, too: 7. Her lips drew to a tight, exasperated seam. *I am not going to go swimming with that presumptuous prick,* she told herself. *But it can't hurt to try it on.*

Suddenly she felt giddily enthused and could name no reason. Was she so bored that trying on a swimsuit, which she had no intention of swimming in, seemed like a paramount event? *Yes,* she answered herself, quickly locked the office, and scurried up the stairs.

Minutes later she was stepping into the swimsuit before the mirrored bathroom wall. She laced up the front in a big, pretty bow. Her amethyst flashed. She turned in the reflection. *This looks great,* she assayed, turning again for a side view. *Too bad I'm not going to . . .*

She strayed to the bedroom. The mantel clock ticked, luring her eyes. It was midnight.

No, she thought. *You're not.*

She poured herself a dab of Grand Marnier, thought about it. *You're a big girl, Vera. Why should you not do something you want to do because of some guy?* It was a flawed rationalization—never mind that Kyle had invited her, and had given her the swimsuit—but Vera let that pass. *What the hell,* she dismissed. She put on her robe, grabbed a big terry towel, and went downstairs.

She peeked around the bottom of the landing. What

179

if someone saw her? What if *Feldspar* saw her? The atrium stood empty, dimly lit by the chandelier and embers in the great stone fireplace. She could hear the clean-up clatter from the restaurant, but no one could be seen in the dining room. She whisked around the reception desk, slipped through the door, and traipsed down the dark hall to the pool.

This is a mistake, she told herself when she entered. A kaleidoscope of multicolored light floated amid the pool's long column. The top of its T remained dark, and all the skirting lights were out. But there was no sign of Kyle. *Good,* she thought. But was that how she really felt? The silence sounded hollow, like an empty auditorium. Falteringly, she folded her robe and towel over the first of a row of strapped chaise longues. She stood still a moment, biting her lower lip. *Part of me wishes he was here,* it occurred to her. But why? Perhaps those two drinks had hit her harder than usual.

She dipped the tip of her foot into the languid water. It felt deliciously warm. Then she dove in.

This is nice, came the slow, lulling thought. The warm water caressed her as she glided out. It was like rolling through a pleasant, idle dream. She slowly backstroked further across the pool. Gradually the warm water erased out some of the day's aches and knots. Worst thing about her job was being on her feet most of the shift, then hunching over her desk with the nightly paperwork mess. Back in the city, Paul would give her fabulous back rubs when she got home, kneading all the stress out of her at once. *I could sure use one of those right now,* she dreamily thought, floating toward the dark end.

From below, the hand grabbed her ankle—

Vera screamed.

—and jerked her down. She flailed beneath the surface, bubbles erupting with her terror. She madly kicked away, gasping as she resurfaced.

Kyle was leaning against the pool edge, laughing.

"You are such an *asshole*, Kyle!" Vera yelled.

He continued to chuckle, slicking back his long wet hair. "Asshole? Me?" His laughter echoed. "That sure got a charge out of you. You think I was the creature of the black lagoon?"

"You're a creature, all right," Vera replied, and let her heart resume a normal beat. She lay her arms along the ledge, paddling her feet. *He better be wearing trunks,* she thought and tried not to be obvious about squinting. The low merging lights made it impossible to tell.

Kyle treaded water toward the deep end. "I don't know about you, but room service was slammed tonight."

Vera minutely smirked, still rowing her feet.

"Well, come on. How many dinners you do?"

"We did all right, Kyle. You don't need to concern yourself with the restaurant."

Kyle's grin flared. "I get the message—you didn't do squat for dinners tonight. Don't worry, business'll pick up for you." He laughed again, harder. "Hey, maybe the ghost is scaring your customers away."

She watched him cockily levitate himself in the water. *Horse's ass,* she thought. "Okay, Kyle, tell me about the ghost. You've been dying to for weeks."

Kyle was a snide talking head atop the water. "The Inn's got a bad history. Used to be a—"

"I know what it used to be, Kyle. Don't bother trying to freak me out. Just tell me—have you ever seen it?"

"Sure," he said. "The night before you and your gang arrived."

Bullshit. "Okay, Kyle. What did it look like?"

"Just a big pale shape. Kind of hunched over, naked. Could hear its feet thumping as it walked. I only saw it for a second, stuck my head out the door, saw it moving down the second-floor hall toward the stairs."

Now Vera laughed. "It was probably one of your maids going downstairs to snitch booze."

"That's what I thought," Kyle said. "So I called out to it."

"And?"

Kyle's brash grin faded. "It turned around and looked at me." Suddenly he seemed restrained, even distressed. "Looked like it . . . well, its face . . ."

Vera smiled, nodding. "Yeah? What about its face?"

"I don't wanna talk about it," he said. "You wouldn't believe me anyway."

"Kyle, it's not that I wouldn't believe you. I already *don't* believe you."

"That's cool." He treaded closer, his head bobbing. "Just ask Mr. Feldspar about the wall contractors."

"The what?"

"Three, four months ago, construction was getting a little behind, so we hired an extra contractor to hang all the Sheetrock and paneling. Had 'em work at night, to save time."

"So what."

Kyle's brow rose. "Couldn't find a crew that'd stay more than a week. They all quit. Said there was . . . something here."

"Oh, Kyle, I'm shaking with fright." She expected more from him, more than trifling attempts to scare her. He quickly changed topics. "This is great, though, ain't it?"

"What?"

"Relaxing in the pool after a long shift?"

"It is nice," she admitted. Now her head tilted back, her eyes closed. The warm water line roved at her breasts. "I hate being on my feet all day, it wears me out." It had been a long time since she'd felt so relaxed, so dreamy. The drinks, on top of her fatigue, unwound

182

all her springs at once. Then Kyle was saying, "I know what you need."

Vera opened her eyes, startled. Kyle quickly climbed out of the pool next to her. She half-gasped, as first thinking he was naked, but then she noted that he wore tan trunks. "What are you doing?" she said, looking at him upside-down.

"Come on." He leaned over, extending his hand. "Out. What you need is one of Dr. Kyle's famous back rubs."

This age-old con did not surprise her. It did seem odd, though, that she'd been thinking of back rubs just minutes ago. "No way, Kyle. That's the oldest guy's trick in the book."

His hand remained extended. "Come on, don't you trust me?"

"No, Kyle, I don't trust you for a minute. You're looking for an excuse—"

"What, you think I'm gonna try to diddle you?"

Vera laughed. He was so crude. "Kyle, I wouldn't put anything past you."

"Come on," he insisted. "Out. Try trusting a guy for a change."

This comment left her distantly pissed. What did he mean? That she didn't trust men? *Don't do it, Vera,* she warned herself. Nevertheless, she eased her back off the ledge, paused, and turned. *Don't* . . . Next, she thrust her hand out. *Don't* . . .

Kyle grabbed her hand. His muscles flexed in the wavering, floating light. Effortlessly, she was lifted out of the warm water onto the skid-proof skirting. She stood for a moment, unsure, reluctant. She was dripping. . . .

"Over here," he said.

His big hands gently touched her shoulders. The contact stunned her. It was the first time she'd been touched by a man in what seemed ages, and it felt weird, shivery.

His hands urged her down the deck, into grainy darkness and half-formed shapes of lounge chairs and tables. "Boy, that's one cute swimsuit," he remarked. "Musta been a guy with some real good taste who bought it for ya."

"Thank you for the swimsuit, Kyle," she said, leaving a trail of drips as her bare feet carried her forward.

Then: "Here," he said. "Lie down right here."

What are you getting yourself into? she asked, not expecting an answer. She had a pretty good idea by now. He lowered the back of a lounge chair to a flat position; Vera lay down on it, on her stomach, thinking, *I cannot believe I'm doing this.*

Kyle straddled her at once, plopping his rump down right on hers. The sudden wet weight on her hips felt . . . lewd. Every muscle in her body stiffened. Then his hands splayed on her back.

"If you don't mind me saying so, Vera," he began—

"I probably will."

"—you're a pretty hot-lookin' babe." Then he laughed.

Hot-looking babe. Jesus. "Thank you, Kyle. I've never been complimented with such sophistication."

His hands pushed slow hard circles down over her shoulder blades. "Could use some sun, though. You're kinda white."

"It's the middle of winter, Kyle. What am I supposed to do? Lie out on the back deck in this? I'd be a Bill Blass fuchsia popsicle in about two minutes."

Now his thumbs teased along her ribs. "I mean the tanning booths. You ought to try 'em out. Get some color." His thumbs rubbed into the pause. "You really are a beautiful woman."

Vera tried to frown. Did he think he need only toss a few compliments to have his way? It sounded sincere, though. It sounded nice, simply the way he'd said that. *You really are a beautiful woman. . . .*

Am I? she thought.

His hands continued in their preliminaries, slowly breaking out her stiffness. The muscles in her back felt constricted, twisted up in their fatigue. But it wasn't only fatigue; some of it was nervousness. *Of course I'm nervous,* she realized. *There's a guy I barely know sitting on my ass.*

Yes, Vera felt very nervous.

"Relax," he whispered.

His fingers gently dug into her shoulders and neck, tensing in and out. She stared ahead, her chin propped under her hands. All she could see was darkness. Kyle's fingers briskly kneaded her, loosening the stiff muscles.

"You're all knotted up." His fingers worked lower. "Is that better?"

"Yes," she murmured.

It felt gorgeous, luxurious. Each probing touch unwound another knot. In moments she felt like warm putty stretched out across the slatted chair.

His voice was so quiet, a distant whisper. "Does that feel better?"

"Yes," she sighed again.

His long wet hair dripped water onto her back. His fingers kneaded her tense flesh all the way down her spine. Then his palms pushed all the way up in a sensation that seemed to squeeze her remaining tensions out of her like paste from a tube. *This is a mistake,* she thought. She'd let herself walk right into his trap. A few more minutes of this and he'd be making his move, and right now—relaxed, stretched out, and warmly aroused— she knew she would not resist. She knew she would let him have sex with her.

The swimsuit had no back. Now his fingers worked expertly into the flesh just above her rump.

"See, Dr. Kyle always comes prepared," he was saying next. "Every convenience for his patients."

From somewhere he produced a bottle of massage lotion. Vera felt the drops slide down her back. His hands continued then, rubbing the slick oil into her skin. The oil felt warm at first, then hot. Then he hitched down.

The weight rose. She wanted to protest. He was kneeling now at the base of the chair, between her feet. He dribbled a line of the lotion down each of her legs.

This is too good, she thought. *This is getting me too hot.*

It was just like the fantasy, and the dream. The Hands . . .

The hands rubbed the oil up and down her legs, drawing stunning heat into her skin. First, he massaged each of her feet, flexing the toes back and forth. Then each hand slowly squeezed up her calves. The oil made her feel deliciously inflamed, and there was no denying her arousal now. Her loins wanted to fidget against the slow succor of his fingers. *Thank God it's dark,* was all she could think. The dampness between her legs would surely be soaking through the swimsuit by now.

"Is that good?" the ever-soft voice inquired. "Do you like that?"

"Yes," she breathed.

She opened her eyes again, peering into the dark. The dark, like the warm, silent dark of the dream. The dream of The Hands—

She gave in then. She let herself fall into the scape of the fantasy. . . .

The Hands raised her leg. The Fingers of one kneaded her calf. The Mouth sucked her toes, nibbled them. Then the process was repeated on the other foot.

Vera was moaning, not for real but in the fantasy.

186

This was only a fantasy she was playing out in her mind. Fantasizing was healthy, normal. . . .

The fantasy drew on, The Hands inching now up her thighs, then plying her buttocks. The Fingers slipped underneath the suit.

She was cringing, she was squirming now. She felt primordial and horny. She looked at herself in the fantasy. She saw herself slip out of her shoulder straps, then she saw The Hands peel the damp suit off of her, leaving it to dangle limp off one of her feet. She saw more drops of the lotion dribble onto her buttocks, The Hands sliding up. The oil ran down the cleft, drawing its delicious heat over her rectum and then collecting into the bottom of her sex.

The Hands were rubbing tight circles now. Her own hand slipped down, touching herself, urging the approach of her orgasm. The Hands, next, embraced her, encircling her belly. The Mouth of the fantasy, then, descended. . . .

Warm tremors threatened to burst as The Mouth sucked her lower back. This sucking sensation alone made her want to come. The Mouth lovingly devoured her. She whined in the next moment, when The Mouth slid brazenly down the cleft of her rump, lingered over the button of her anus, then licked lower, lower. . . .

She needed more. She needed to be filled. Almost panting, she rose to her hands and knees atop the chair. *Do it to me now,* she pleaded in the fantasy, reaching back with a desperate hand. She felt it, closed her fingers around its warm, turgid girth. It's swollen tip teased her, bulging the wet entry of her sex. Her mind felt divided and subdivided, each piece separately transfixed on the gush of desires and smoldering sensation. She thrust her hips back in one fast, unhesitant motion, and was penetrated. . . .

"Vera?" A nudge. "Vera?"

187

The voice seemed to pull her out of a well. Her eyes eased open. *My God,* she thought.

"You fell asleep." Kyle climbed off her. She turned groggily onto her side. No, none of it had really happened, none of it was real. Kyle grinned down at her, still in his tan cut-offs, and Vera still in the bright fuchsia swimsuit.

"I . . . fell asleep?"

"You sure did. Out like a light." He casually grabbed his towel and slung it across his shoulder. Vera, still prone, paused to look at him, the pool lights shifting on his skin: the long, damp swept-back hair; the sculptured muscles of his chest, shoulders, arms; the tapered frame. *What am I thinking?* she thought.

"It's late," he said. "I'm turning in."

Vera bottled up the slow burn of angst. After all the accusations she'd made to herself, all the times she'd condemned him as a conman and womanizer, here was the truth. He'd had every opportunity to seduce her, yet he hadn't.

And, Vera, as a result, was now disappointed, irritated.

"So how do I rate as a back-rubber?" he inquired, grinning.

"I believe the word is masseur, Kyle, and I'll give you a high rating."

"Just a *high* rating? Not the highest?"

Vera reflected, still lounging on her side. It had been good, hadn't it? No, it had been better than good. "Now that I think of it, Kyle, yes, you get the highest rating. Five stars."

"I thought so. And seeing how all's fair, maybe next time I'll get to rate you."

"Possibly," Vera said.

"See you tomorrow."

Kyle turned and strode off. Vera watched after him.

These notions weren't like her at all, these desires. *I wanted him to do it.* Indeed. For the first time in her life, she'd wanted no-strings, fast-and-furious, rough-and-tumble . . . sex.

She slowly rose, still aroused by the fantasy. Her nipples poked against the suit's bright cups, the contact of the wet fabric titillating her. Diffuse chunks of light wobbled on the ceiling. She grabbed her towel, picked up the bottle of lotion Kyle had forgotten, and walked out.

Notions seemed to lag behind her down the hall. The Mouth nibbling her toes. The Hands kneading her ass. The images boggled her. *It's just stress,* she convinced herself. *New job, new place, new people.* And: *no sex life anymore.* They'd added up, that was all. The frustrations would abate once she had time to get used to things.

She stepped into the darkened atrium, then instantly stepped back. A figure had turned around the corner, as if walking from the fireplace. *The fireplace?* Vera wondered.

The fire had died to ash. It must have been one of the maids or maintenance people checking on it. But—*this late?* It just didn't feel right, though Vera couldn't name a reason. She didn't dare call out. What if it was Feldspar? He might be a bit curious as to why his restaurant manager, whom he was paying a hundred and fifteen thousand dollars a year, was traipsing about The Inn going on two in the morning, clad only in a damp swimsuit.

Still, she waited a moment, peeking back and forth. When she felt certain the figure was gone, she skipped out across the plush wool carpets to the fireplace. Only a trace warmth lingered. Its fieldstone maw was nearly large enough to stand in. Chopped logs filled a black-iron rack to the left. She peered down, noticing something else, the vaguest scent. . . .

Ah, ha. The glint caught her eye. On its side behind the stacked logs lay a bottle. *Scotch,* she noted. *A rail brand.* That explained it. One of the maintenance staff was snitching a nip. She supposed it was her duty as a manager to report it, or to at least confiscate the bottle, but she let it go.

Something else was on her mind.

She scurried up the stairs as fast as her bare feet would carry her. Down the hall. To her bedroom.

Where the fantasy of The Hands awaited her.

Chapter Eighteen

Ah, Christ, Paul thought. *What's her name?*

The hostess looked up, lissome and trim in the tight pink-sequined dress. Paul knew he'd met her—he'd met all of Vera's friends and employees at one time—but for the life of him he couldn't remember her name. *Cementhead!*

"Hi, you may remember me. I'm—"

Her expression hardened very quickly, the pretty face going cold. "Paul," she acknowledged. "I know you."

The look said it all. *My name's not Paul,* Paul realized. *It's mud.*

"You don't have a reservation," the hostess curtly pointed out. "So why don't you just leave?"

"Look," Paul said, and stepped forward. "I need help."

"You sure do. You need to have your head examined. How could you do something like that to Vera?"

"I—" But what could he say? Should he lie? Deny it? That would be useless. Women could always tell when a guy was lying about something like that. "There are always things you don't understand," he said instead. "I just want to know where she is. Please, give me her address, her new number, anything."

"I hope you're happy. Vera's a great girl, and you

really hurt her. And this restaurant's gone downhill since she left. Last week two waitresses were laid off, and I'm getting my hours cut back. Thanks. Now why don't you get out of here before I call the police."

Paul felt forged in flint. He groped for something to say. "It's a misunderstanding. I just need to talk to her, to clear things up. Look—" He reached into his pocket, withdrew a one hundred dollar bill. "I'll pay you to tell me where she is."

"I don't know where she is," the hostess said.

"All right, then. Tell me who does."

She contemplated this, her big bright blue eyes fluttering. She picked up the phone, turned her back to him, and began whispering. Paul couldn't quite make out what she was saying. Then she hung up, refaced him, and snapped the bill out of his hand.

Money always talks, Paul thought, relieved. *Women are so corruptible.*

"Go back into the kitchen," she said, not even looking at him. "Ask for Georgie. He'll tell you where Vera is."

"Thank you," Paul said.

"And don't ever come back here again."

Don't worry, I won't. Paul skirted the reservation desk. A quick glance at the book showed him it was barely a third full. Then another glance around the subdued dining room showed only a trickle of the turnout The Emerald Room was used to. Had Vera's mystic departure crimped business this bad?

He pushed through the swingdoors to the kitchen, into blazing fluorescent light. Dead silence greeted him, not the usual busy kitchen clamor. A lone guy with a bad complexion tended to a single order of Veal Chesapeake at the range. He wore not a chef's cap but an old-fashioned black derby.

"You Georgie?" Paul inquired.

192

The guy turned, grinning. "That's right. And you must be Paul, the scumbag motherfucker who shit all over Vera." Georgie walked around the hot line. "And she was so upset, you know what she did, brother? She just up and left town, and she took the chef with her, and our best waitress and dishman. You got any idea how bad business crashed? You got any idea how hard it is to find a restaurant manager on no notice?"

"Uh, well, no," Paul answered.

"We're down thirty percent on our dinners, thanks to you."

"Look, it's not my fault that—"

"Hey, Dim," Georgie called out behind him. "He's here."

A shadow emerged from beyond the cold line, a great big blushy fat guy with long greasy hair and a mole on his face. His grin looked pressed into his lips.

"Welly welly welly well," this Dim fellow said, and stepped up to Paul's side, mixing a bucket of whiskey cream sauce. "How goes, lover?"

Lover? Paul nodded. He didn't like the look of this.

Georgie went on, "See, me and Dim here gotta practically run the whole kitchen ourselves now, on account of poor business since Vera left. It's part of the new way. How would you like to have to do twice as much work for less money?"

"Look," Paul said. "The girl out front said you'd tell me where Vera is."

"Oh, right, brother, and I will. You wanna know where Vera is?"

"Yes," Paul said.

"Well, we'll tell you where Vera is, right, Dim?"

"Righty right," Dim exclaimed.

"Not here," Georgie said. "That's where she is. Not here."

Paul should have known. Before he could even flinch,

193

the bucket of whiskey cream was deftly plopped onto his head by this Dim fellow. Then somebody punched the bucket, amid a flutter of chuckles. Paul felt his head snap back. A second fist sent the bucket flying, leaving Paul's head ladeled in cream. Georgie, huffing laughter, put Paul in a full nelson, propping him up. "Let 'er rip, Dim!"

Paul could only half-see through the sheen of cream. Dim stepped up, brandishing fists that were the size of croquet balls, and probably as hard. And it was these fists that were next soundly rocketed, time and time again, into Paul's rather soft journalist's abdominal wall.

Each blow—and there were many—knocked the wind out of him and bulged his eyes, as whiskey cream flew in darts off his head.

"Evening is the great time, eh, brother?" Georgie inquested, still pinning Paul up like a moth on a board. "Had enough, have you?"

"Yes!" Paul wheezed.

"Give him one in the balls, if he's got any balls."

Dim's big combat-booted foot socked up surely as a punter's, and caught Paul between the legs. Paul collapsed.

Chuckles fluttered overhead, like bats. Paul's pain drew him into a fetal position. He couldn't move. But it was only a moment longer before Dim's big hands grasped him by the back of the collar and the back of the belt. Paul had a pretty good idea that he was going to be escorted out.

"What luck, huh Dim?" Georgie jested. "That our fine guest here should pay us a visit on garbage night?"

"Righty right," Dim responded. Paul was then lifted aloft and carried out to the loading dock, while Georgie held the door.

"See you next time, brother. And have a good evening!"

Paul was heaved, turning in the fetid air. He landed in a great BFI dumpster half full of slimy refuse.

The back door slammed shut.

Paul lay atop the garbage for a time, reflecting that he'd had better nights. When the crushing pain in his groin became managable, he crawled out of the dumpster. He stumbled back out to West Street, shaking himself off as best he could. It was so cold out, the whiskey cream turned to frost on his face. He passed the closed office of *The Voice,* the smaller city newspaper. They'd purchased his singles bar series, and the editor agreed to take him on as a contributing writer, so at least he was still writing and getting paid. Not that he felt all too ebullient at this given moment, reeking of garbage and still thrumming in the dull pain of Dim's mason-jar-sized fists. *Do I deserve this?* he asked the moon, looking up. *Do I deserve to be beaten up by rogues and thrown into a dumpster?*

Yes, the moon seemed to answer him.

It seemed like part of his brain had shut off that night. He couldn't remember much of what happened, but he remembered enough. Kaggie's, that infernal dance club. He'd been there to research his singles bar piece. He'd gotten drunk. He'd picked up two girls. He'd—

God almighty, he thought. He had to stop, leaning against the MOST machine at the corner of Calvert, trying to shake the awful images which rattled in his head like broken glass. There was no denying it. *I did it,* he realized. He was nearly crying. *I really did it. I cheated on Vera.*

That he had, and in grand style. The jagged memories made him sick, even sicker than the laced dope he'd taken. Insecurities were one thing, but when you were so insecure that you'd do something like that, you were in trouble. He didn't deserve Vera, he knew that. She'd actually walked in on them, hadn't she? Paul didn't even

195

want to think about how hurt she must have been. That skanky, skinny blonde had been bad enough, but the redhead . . .

Boy, Paul, when you cheat on a girl, you don't cut corners.

West Street stretched on in desolate cold and eldritch yellow light. He trod on, like a condemned man on his way to the gallows. *I might as well be,* he thought. Without Vera—and knowing now what he'd done to lose her—Paul Kirby didn't see a whole lot worth living for. Beyond the great dome of the State House, the moon seemed to scowl at him. An unmarked city police car prowled by, a featureless face behind dark glass eyeing his shambling steps. *Probably thinks I'm a bum,* Paul considered. *Shit, I am a bum.*

A couple stood arguing in front of the Undercroft, a good-looking blonde in a long brown overcoat, and some wan-faced guy wearing a blue shirt and bleached pants with a rip in the knee. Apparently the guy was getting the sack, and not taking it too well. Paul picked up fragments of their outburst: "You led me on!" "Oh, I did not!" "You said we could get back together!" "Oh, I did not!" "Why did you tell me to call?" "Just go back in the bar!" "What, I'm an asshole for—" "Yes, you're an asshole!" The blonde drove off, leaving the guy to stare off with a cigarette hanging out of his mouth.

It reminded Paul of his own plight, the end result: destruction. Love chopped up like raw meat on a butcher block. The universe was an extraordinary butcher. Why did these things happen? How could people love each other one minute and hate each other the next? Where was the line of demarcation?

The heart, Paul answered himself. *Vera gave me her heart, and I threw it back in her face.*

He went in the back way, and cleaned himself up as best he could in the john. *Not to be born is best,* someone had written on the wall. Paul washed his face off and got all the garbage off him. From the back room someone could be heard doing Dice Clay imitations: ". . . a fuckin' tree trunk!" Paul went downstairs and pulled up a stool at the bar.

Craig, the 'Croft's most infamous barkeep, was juggling shot glasses around the lit Marlboro Light in his mouth. "Long time no see, Paul. Where ya been?"

"Sick," Paul said. It was no lie. That stepped-on crap he'd snorted with those girls had rocked him pretty bad. "Newcastle. A pint."

Craig poured the beer from the line of ten taps, slid it to him. Paul and Craig were good friends, but Paul was not surprised to see the barkeep's back turn to him. "So you're giving me the cold shoulder too, huh?"

Craig shrugged, sliding clean Pilsner glasses into the rack. "I've been hearing some pretty shitty things about you. They true?"

"N—" Paul began. He stared into the depths of his beer. Then he said: "Yes. I guess they are."

"Vera really catch you in bed with two girls?"

Paul nodded. *Only one of 'em wasn't really a girl.* "She tell you that?"

"No, she disappeared. Just something I've been hearing. You know how word gets around downtown. That's not like you, man. And coke? Since when do you do drugs?"

"Never," Paul said. *Never in my life.* "I don't know what came over me. Got shitfaced, met two girls, next thing I know I'm in bed with both of them. I've never been so out of control in my life."

"I heard one of the girls was Daisy Traynor."

Paul squinted. "Never heard of her. In fact, I never seen either of these girls before."

"Daisy Traynor's a hooker. They call her 'Daisy Train,' on account of she pulls trains—you know, gang

197

bangs. You're out of your mind going anywhere near that. She's a crack addict. Every now and then she'll stumble in here real late, all fucked up on cocaine, and I'll just throw her right the fuck out. Last summer me and Luce hear about this big party going down at Cruiser's Creek, near the water off of Bestgate, so we check it out. Some party. When the kegs went dry some of the locals started passing around coke and PCP, so me and Luce leave. But before we're out of there, we see Daisy back in the woods behind some guy's house, doing a whole motorcycle gang. She's pure scum, man. Probably got every disease in the book."

Paul groaned. Once he'd gotten his shit together, he'd gone to the doctor's for blood tests. Thank God they'd been negative. "What's this Daisy look like?"

"Skinny, short blond hair, ragged-out. She's like twenty-two but looks ten years older. She's got a little cross tatooed in the pit of her throat."

"That's her," Paul lamented. He remembered that much. And the redhead, the guy/girl, must've been one of her friends. Days later, when he'd snapped out of it, he'd found his wallet cleaned out, his watch and other valuables gone. *Bitches,* he thought. *Goddamn whores.* That's how they worked. Get a guy all fucked up, and then rip him blind. *You got no one to blame but yourself, asshole,* he thought.

Craig stepped hesitantly closer when refilling Paul's glass. "No offense, man, but you kind of smell like garbage. And . . ." Craig sniffed, scrinching his nose. "Whiskey cream?"

"Don't ask," Paul said. "I gotta find Vera. You know where she is?"

"Naw, all I heard was she took some new job out of town. Bunch of people from The Emerald Room come in here after they close, and they're bitching up a storm.

198

Seems Vera took all their best people with her, and the restaurant's going downhill.''

"Couple guys named Georgie and Dim have already made me well aware of that fact," Paul said. "There's got to be someone who knows where this new job is."

"Talk to the owner, that fat guy. Wherever she went, she must've left a forwarding address for her W-2 and any vacation pay she's got coming. Ask him. Mc-Cracken, I think his name is."

McGowen, Paul thought. *I gotta talk to him.* Vera had mentioned him from time to time, said he was a fat slob who liked to put the make on the waitresses. He probably wouldn't be too keen on meeting the guy who'd caused his manager to leave town, but Paul couldn't think of any alternatives. He'd have to give it a shot.

"Haven't seen your byline in the paper lately," Craig remarked, shaking up an order of Windex shooters for some rowdies at the other end of the bar.

"And you won't, not in the *City Sun,* anyway. Tate fired me."

Craig just shook his head, pouring the shooters. "You want some friendly advice, Paul?"

"No, but I have a feeling I'm going to get it anyway."

"Get your act together, and do it fast. Look at yourself. A month ago, you had a great job, a great fiancée, and a great life. You had it all."

"I know," Paul muttered.

"When you were with Vera, you were going places." Craig looked at him, almost disgusted. "But you ain't going nowhere now but down."

Paul paid his tab and left. There were tears in his eyes. The moon's bright scowling face now seemed to smile in hilarity. *Down, down, down,* Paul thought. Craig was right. The dark streets were all he understood now, and the bracing cold and brittle light. He was alone, and he deserved to be. *I deserve nothing,* he thought.

His tears turned to ice on his face. *How could I have fucked up my life so bad?*

"When are you going to talk about it?" Donna asked, rather meekly. She dawdled about her open dresser, fishing through her lingerie.

"Talk about what?" Vera asked.

"You know. Paul."

The name caused her to fidget on the cushioned settee. After their shift, she'd come up to Donna and Dan B.'s room, to borrow the book about haunted mansions. She thumbed through it now, not even seeing its words. *Paul,* she thought.

"I don't know. I'm thinking that I should probably never talk about it. Why remind myself of something . . . like that?"

Donna continued to dawdle, inspecting the frilly garments. "Well, sometimes it's good to talk about things that hurt. If you keep them bottled up, they can explode."

This was true—sometimes, at least. But Vera felt differently in this case. Simply hearing his name gave her a flexing, negative spasm in her soul. Not only did it hurt, it embarrassed her, for it *was* embarrassing, to be with someone that long, and then to find out what kind of person he really was. It made her feel stupid, as though she possessed no manner of adult judgment at all.

Yes, the less she heard about Paul, and talked about him, the better. *I'll erase him from my memory,* she vowed. *I'll banish him from my mind. Goddamn him anyway, I'm gonna pretend that he was never even born.*

At least that's what she hoped.

"What do you think?"

Vera looked up and nearly gasped. While she'd been pondering over Paul, Donna had changed into black garters and stockings, and a see-through black camisole, which left little of Donna's bodily features to the imagination.

"Dan B.'ll have a heart attack when he sees you in that," Vera exclaimed.

"More like a *hard* attack," Donna laughed. "And that's the idea, isn't it?" She twirled around, giggling, then stood to appraise herself in a carven-framed wall mirror. "Yeah, this one's really going to set him off."

Donna's body, Vera couldn't help but notice, seemed as bright and robust as her newfound happiness. She was a little overweight, but in a healthy, attractive way, and the extra weight left her better proportioned with her five feet, three inches. Vera remembered how awful Donna had looked—how ragged, scrawny, and malnourished—back in the days of her alcoholism. Sobriety not only embellished her appearance but it also gave her life, energy, love. It was wonderful to see her so happy.

How happy am I? Vera thought in a sudden doldrum. Was she jealous? Donna had surfaced from the abyss, and now had quite a bit to show for it. Moreover, she had love, and a good man who loved her. *And a sex life,* Vera reminded herself.

Why can't I have those things?

She frowned then, at her selfishness. She was feeling sorry for herself, and that nearly disgusted her. It was weakness. Too often it was easy to want more—there was always more—but the fact remained: she was a healthy, successful woman in a free state, and she must never forget that. *Quit complaining, Vera. Most women in the world would give their right arms to have what you have. So stop being a baby.*

"Do you think he'd like this better?" Donna now

201

inquired. She held up a cupless red-leather corset lined with gold zippers and pin-stitches.

"It looks like something Marquis de Sade would want his women to wear," Vera pointed out. "Stick with the camisole. It's obscene but at least it's elegant."

"You're such a *prude,* Vera," Donna laughed. "It's the nineteen nineties, not the eighteen nineties. You really should lighten up. Cut loose a little."

"That's easy for you to say. You're married, you have someone to cut loose with."

"You don't have to be married to have a little fun. You're a free woman now, Vera. Take advantage of it." Donna adjusted the little black bow at the camisole's bosom, eyeing herself more closely in the mirror. "You're too reserved, you know that? What you ought to do, Vera, is just pick up a guy and have a down-and-dirty one night stand."

"Just pick up a guy, huh?" Vera didn't know whether to laugh or smirk. "I can see me now, driving into downtown Waynesville in a brand-new Lamborghini, then pulling up a stool at the ever-sophisticated Waterin' Hole, and putting the make on hayseeds."

"What an awful stereotype," Donna remarked. Now she was adjusting the frilled hem, which descended about two millimeters past her crotch. "There're probably some nice guys down there—so what if they're not stockbrokers? And of course"—Donna's reflection grinned back—"there's always Kyle."

Vera wanted to shout. "The other day you were telling me to stay away from him, now you're saying that I should—"

"I meant that you should be careful around him, Vera. That doesn't mean you can't have a little fun. What's the harm?"

"He's conceited, arrogant, malicious," Vera reeled off, "shifty, two-faced, self-centered—"

"And cute," Donna reminded. "Admit it, Vera. You're attracted to the guy."

"I am n—" Her next acknowledgement fell like an ax on her words. *Talk about hypocrites,* she scolded herself. *Last night I was actually hoping that he'd . . .* What? *Make love to me?* She mustn't lie to herself. *I wanted him to screw the daylights out of me.* "Well, sure, I'm attracted to him," she then admitted. She didn't dare tell Donna about late-night swim and back rub; that would only make her sound more hypocritical. "But I just can't ever picture me getting involved with someone like Kyle."

"You are so hard-headed I can't believe it," Donna nearly exclaimed. "I'm not telling you to get *involved* with him, for God's sake. But that doesn't mean you can't go a couple of rounds with him, you know."

"I'm not into sex for the sake of sex." But how honest a comment was that, considering her fantasies, her dreams, and what she'd wished had taken place last night? She'd always believed that sex was something that should only happen between two people who loved each other, or at least had feelings for each other. But now?

"Vera, Mother Nature gave you a sex drive for a reason."

"Yeah, to have babies, and I'm not ready to have babies."

"That's why Father Pharmacy invented the pill. You're *supposed* to want to have sex, it's human nature. It's unhealthy to repress your natural desires, and I certainly don't see anything wrong with a little harmless no-strings fooling around. And can I say something, as a friend?"

"Of course," Vera said.

"You're not going to get mad, right? You're not going to be offended?"

"I'm not going to be offended. What, I have bad breath?"

203

"No, but sometimes you're in a bad *mood.*"

Vera's mouth screwed up in speculation. "What do you mean?"

"What I mean is, since we've come here, you've been a little bitchy, that's all."

"Thanks," Vera said.

"See, I knew you'd be offended."

"I'm really bitchy?" Vera asked.

"Well, sometimes, and you were never that way before. I think it's probably stress-related, sexual stress."

"Come on." Well, there had been some occasions when she'd gotten down on Dan B. and Lee for horsing around with the gross jokes. And maybe once or twice she *had* been a little snippy with Donna for not memorizing the wine list and specials. But that was her job. She was their boss.

Or maybe Donna's right, she considered now. *Maybe I have been a little hard on them sometimes. Maybe I have taken some things out on them.* "In other words, you saying that I'm in a bad mood because I'm not getting laid regularly?"

"Well . . . yeah," Donna answered. "I don't know how you stand it. If I don't get it twice a night, I turn into the biggest bitch this side of the Mason-Dixon line." Now Donna was dabbing herself with perfume. "Remember when Dan B. went to that east coast chef's convention in Chicago last fall? I was climbing the walls. You should've seen how much I spent on batteries for my vibrator."

"Donna!" Vera exclaimed. "You don't have a v—"

"Sure, I do, several, as a matter of fact." Now Donna was applying some final touches, donning a thin gold waist chain and an ankle bracelet. "Boy, was this a bad subject. Look, Vera, all I'm saying is that a couple of rolls in the hay would do you good. Trust me. And Kyle seems a pretty good candidate. Who knows. Maybe he's hung."

"Donna!" Vera exclaimed again.

"Why don't you skedaddle now?" Donna requested. "Dan B.'s going to be coming up soon. I want to be ready for him." Then she turned, placing her hands on her hips as if frustrated. "And I didn't mean to offend you."

"I'm not offended, Donna," Vera said, and headed for the door. And she honestly wasn't. It was good to have a friend who'd point things out to her, especially things about herself. "And thanks for the book."

"You're not going to take my advice, are you?"

"What, hunt Kyle down and ball his brains out? No."

"Okay, then. Suit yourself. Any time you want to borrow one of my vibrators, just let me know."

"Don't be ridiculous. I would never—"

"Sure, I know. . . . Say, I hate to sound rude, but—"

"I'm going," Vera assured her, rolling her eyes. "Don't wear Dan B. out tonight. We have six reservations tomorrow."

Donna said good night and closed the door. *Yeah, she's in a hurry, all right,* Vera thought. Romantic enthusiasm was one thing, but this was romantic *fervor.*

I guess I'm just envious, Vera considered. Her own bedroom felt expanded in its plush, well-furnished emptiness. She skipped the usual nightcap or two that she'd grown accustomed to before bed, and took a quick shower instead of a bubble bath. Suddenly she felt desperate for something to divert her. She sat up in bed, turned on her reading lamp, and opened the book. . . .

The Complete Compendium of Haunted American Mansions
by
Richard Long

"I hope the author's friends don't call him Dick," she muttered. She skimmed down the table of contents. The Night Walker: The Hammond-Harwood House. Basement of Nightmares: Suit Manor. The House on the Hill: The Dipietro Manse of Screams.

Even the titles were silly. Vera didn't know how she was going to take this seriously. Then:

Torture Asylum: Wroxton Hall.

Vera began to read.

Chapter Nineteen

She came to him every night now—or, really, every morning, since that's how long it took Lee to cleanup the room-service kitchen. He was in a trick-bag and he knew it. Kyle had indeed given him that raise, and Lee knew he'd lose it if he complained about the extra work. He also knew that he'd lose more than the raise—he'd lose his job too, probably. Kyle would put the smear on him, and that would be that. *Terminated for drinking on duty.*

He'd gotten the hang of it fast enough; now he was usually finishing up at about 4 A.M., and it wasn't like he was busting his tail in The Carriage House, not when they were running less than thirty dinners per night. It was room service that did all the business. Life had its ups and downs, Lee rationalized. Being essentially blackmailed into cleaning up after the RS crew was one of the downs. Everything else, though, the money, the free room and board, the bennies, was an up.

So was the woman, the housemaid. Definitely an up.

Lee guessed she was a housemaid. She did a lot of things around The Inn: cleaning, kitchen prep, running RS orders. She was illegal, Lee knew, perhaps all of the maintenance staff was, so Kyle could pretty much work their asses off without worrying about them running to the state employment board.

Sure, it was an up, all right, but it still wasn't something Lee felt too great about. It seemed exploitative, almost like he was taking advantage of her. Granted, he'd helped her out getting Kyle off her that night in the pantry, but that didn't mean she was obliged to blow him every night in gratitude. Lee'd told her over and over that it wasn't necessary, but she wouldn't hear of it. By now, he suspected that she had a speech impediment; she seemed to understand him, but she never talked. In fact, he had yet to hear her speak one word.

Usually she brought things for him too. A couple of beers, sandwiches. Once she'd even tried to give him cash, but he stuck it back in her apron. *I should be paying you,* he thought. *Christ!* The whole thing was a crazy situation, and he often wished he was out of it. But . . .

Incompatabilities aside, Lee began to realize that he . . . well, he liked this woman. Nothing romantic or anything like that. He just liked her. Not to mention the head. He definitely liked that. What guy wouldn't?

Every night now, for weeks. She'd slip into his room several hours before dawn. She always insisted on keeping the lights out, which was fine with Lee. This woman—*shit,* he realized, *she's been giving me head for weeks and I don't even know her name!*—wasn't much of a looker; she was, what Lee's Emerald-Room pal Dave Kahill would call *Fugly*—that's *fuckin' ugly,* and Lee himself, of course, was none too eager to show off his less-than-trim abdominals and log-sized legs.

Additionally, Lee was none-too-experienced in being a recipient of the sexual colloquialism known as ''head.'' (Why did they call it head? Hadn't the Monkees made a

208

movie called *Head?* Moreover, why did they call it a blow job? They don't blow in it, they suck it.) Nevertheless, Lee couldn't imagine anything better. This woman . . . she had a technique that defied description. Liddy the busgirl had blown him a bunch of times, but that had been nothing compared to this, nothing at all. . . .

"Hi," he said from beneath the covers. A slant of dim light fell into the room, then fell out as she opened and closed his door. Moonlight tinseled her bulky, pasty features when she crossed the room's darkness, set down her bag of goodies, and crawled into bed with him. She seemed happy to be with him, he could sense her smile. He loved the feel of her hands on him, running under the covers, which she quickly skimmed off. Why didn't she ever take off her clothes? She'd always fuss with him, pushing his hands away when he attempted to disrobe her, but then that made sense. *The scars,* he recalled. He remembered the whip-weals crisscrossing her back; naturally she was self-conscious about that, and God only knew what other kinds of marks her body bore from so many years of abuse. The most he'd ever done was get her blouse partway down. Lee's member (which he nicknamed, for some reason, Uncle Charlie) responded quite quickly to her probing, inquisitive hands, and she didn't spend much time with preliminaries. *Aw, jeez,* he thought. It was in her mouth already, the slick delicious friction coursing tightly up and down as her nimble fingers massaged his testicles. He always seemed to fall into a dream, like time stood still, when she did this. Like the luscious sensations converged to a paralyzing pinpoint which left him helpless to do anything but lie there and absorb her pleasures.

And upon those pleasures, his mind sailed away. . . .

Now, Lee was not exactly Mr. Endurance. His climax began to amass from the get-go, and it wasn't more than a few minutes—a *very* few minutes—before reflex took command. (Thinking about baseball did little good. Lee's team was the Yankees, and year after year, it seemed, they did the same thing that this woman did, with equal proficiency; they sucked.) It was a bit embarrassing. What must the woman think? *Goddamn Yankees,* Lee thought, and there it went, the unretractable manumission of his orgasm. Lee thought he might actually die of pleasure, as the ever-reliable Uncle Charlie quite liberally relinquished the starchy-white product of Lee's loins.

Lee's body went lax in the silken, exultant aftermath. The woman happily lay her head atop his great belly, as if at total ease in the silent dark, and she gingerly cradled his spent genitals in her hand. Often she'd do it twice, three times, as many times as he wanted, or at least as often as Uncle Charlie would reclaim its necessary rigidity. Lee felt at ease, too, at unparalleled ease, lying here with her as the clock ticked on.

But he also felt . . . guilty.

More and more he'd felt this way of late. She came in here every night to do this for him, to make him feel good, and all she got in return for her generosity was a mouthful of his goo. Not much of a reward. He was determined to do something for her for a change. *But what?* he wondered now. She didn't seem to like to be touched at all—no surprise, really, considering the vicious extent to which she'd been touched in the past. Sometimes he tried to put his hands in her hair while she was doing it, and she'd jerk her head away. If he'd touch her shoulders, she'd flinch. But there must be something he could do for her.

"All right, no arguments this time," he said. He leaned up, put his hands on her shoulders, and pushed her back onto the bed. Instantly, she tensed up as if terrified, shuddering. "Relax," he said. "I'm not going to hurt you. Just . . . lay back. Relax."

She at least attempted to do this, continuing to shudder. Lee began kissing her; her lips remained sealed tightly as the seam between two bricks. Meanwhile he gently ran his big dishman hands over her plump body, feeling her through her housemaid uniform. *Christ, this is like pulling teeth,* Lee thought, persisting. But eventually his persistence paid off. Soon she was kissing back, lightly opening her mouth to his. Then the tips of their tongues were touching. *That's better,* he thought. Now she was getting into it. Now she was— *Hoooo!* Lee thought—practically sucking his tongue out of his mouth. Her arms wrapped around him, tightening. She made stifled moaning sounds into his throat. Soon it was not even a matter of inference. She was getting aroused.

But when he began to unbutton her starched, collared top, she went to seizing up again. *Don't freeze up on me now!* Lee thought. *I'm finally getting somewhere!* "Relax," he kept assuring her. "Relax." Her bra-cupped breasts felt huge and wobbly in his hands. He slid up and straddled her. *Careful, big boy. Your fat ass'll crush the poor girl if you're not careful.* She seemed to like it, though, his weight atop her, pinning her. But her hands kept grasping at his, as if she didn't want her breasts exposed. He realized why a moment later, when he managed to unclasp the big bra and unloose her breasts.

Jesus, he thought very slowly. *Don't freak out, Lee. You'll hurt her feelings.* Instead, he pretended not to care, not to even notice. But as he gently kneaded the big breasts in his hands he couldn't help but feel their blemishes, and, even in the dim moonlight, he could see them too. Nests of scars and healed-over punctures made a thick map of each breast, and things that

211

felt like old burn-marks. *This woman's really been through the S&M wringer,* he lamented. Still, he did not falter. This was what he could do for her in return for what she'd done for him. Not care. Not react to it. Accept her as she was, not a scarred, pasty gross foreigner, but a human being with real feelings and real desires. It was tough, though. When he began to lick her left nipple he flinched. It had been punctured with pins and needles so many times it felt like a puckered knot of leather. Her hands caressed the back of his head as he carried on, she squirmed gently beneath him.

He swallowed his shock, then, when he moved his mouth to the right nipple, which had long-since been bitten off.

It made him happy, nevertheless, that she had given in to him, that she was dismissing her inhibitions and letting him excite her.

I know, he thought next, remembering the advice of his old buddy Dave Kahill. *You gotta go down on 'em, man.* Lee decided he would—yes, by God, he'd do it. He'd make this stifled, odd woman have an orgasm if it killed him. He, of course, realized the potential consequences. First off, she was no cute pixie, that was for sure. Second, and worse, given her upbringing, her social standing, and the sad lot that life had paid her, he doubted that she was a example of high hygienic standards. Performing the act of cunnilingus on her, in other words, would probably be no picnic. But that didn't matter; Lee was forthright in his determination, and besides, she couldn't be any stinkier than the Good Humor Girl of years ago. *No, no way,* he cheerily told himself. He doubted that anything on earth could be stinkier than that.

He unbuttoned her housedress fully now, letting it fall to her sides. The tragedy of scars and sadism followed the trail of his tongue down her quivering front. He licked the inside of her navel and found it as toughened by needle insertions as her nipple. More old burn-marks became apparent when he stroked the insides of her thighs. Down, down Lee's mouth went, over the warm, excited flesh. Her legs parted to receive his attentions, her hands gently grasping his head, urging him further. His finger traced the wet entrance; she shivered in pleasure, then his mouth found its target, to which she immediately cooed and wrapped her legs around his head. Lee, of course, didn't know exactly what he was doing—Dave Kahill had been great for advice but not so great for detailed instruction. He must be doing it right, though. Judging by her reaction, in fact, he must be doing it *very* right. Her hips gyrated under him, her finger laced in his hair and her back arched. Lee was pleasantly overwhelmed. Her pubis was completely barren of hair, soft and smooth as silk. Furthermore, she tasted nice—she tasted sharp and vivid and clean, and there was not a trace of the dead-catfish-in-the-sun odor he grimly recalled from his unfortunate liaison with the Good Humor Girl. This was actually fun, and more fun still in the proof that she was enjoying it. His tongue prodded her clitoris diligently up and down, and in periodic circles for diversity, and soon she was going subtly nuts in the bed. Her big thighs clamped against his ears like a warm vice, she was panting in repressed shrieks and rocking her hips back and forth quite vigorously. *I guess she's having an orgasm,* Lee reckoned, head rolling to and fro in the clenching embrace of her legs. This went on for a considerable period, such that Lee was beginning to wonder if it would stop before his next shift. But that was fine, that was even better. The more pleasure he could give, the happier he would be. . . .

The protracted climax simmered down later, all her

213

tensions draining at once, and her heels slowly running up and down his back. Her sated smile was bright enough to light the room when she pulled him back up to her and kissed him. Lee was exhausted. *Next time bring a snorkel,* he thought. But it was fun, it was delightful. He would do this every time from now on, finally adding some mutuality to this bizarre relationship. He'd no longer have to feel guilty about taking advantage of her. Now, the pleasure she gave him he could return in spades.

Her hands were at him again, all over him in their newfound enthusiasm. Lee speculated that it had probably been a long time since anyone had treated her as anything more than an S&M pincushion and whipping post for someone else's sick fantasies. Lee was probably the first person to ever do anything solely for her. And he would do more! Why not? Her caresses enlivened him; old Uncle Charlie was raring to go again; he was *hopping.* The woman made to fellate him again, but he pulled her back. "Let's go all the way this time," he said. Oral sex was great, but there were other things too, and it was high time they'd moved on to those things.

Suddenly, she slumped in frustration, or despair.

"What's wrong now?" Lee asked. "We can do it. I even have rubbers."

She didn't tell him what was wrong; she couldn't, and perhaps this only added to her flattened frustration. She couldn't tell him—

So she showed him.

She grabbed his hand, placed it between her legs, and pushed his middle finger into her sex.

Hooooooooly shiiiiiiiit, Lee thought.

His finger was not able to penetrate her deeper than an inch. He didn't need to see, he could feel it, he could

214

easily feel with his fingertip what some sick sadistic monster had done.

A dozen stitches of heavy gauge suture had sewn her vaginal passage shut.

Chapter Twenty

"How about discount coupons in the local papers?" Vera fairly insisted. "It would up business a little at least."

"No, no," Feldspar told her in his white silk shirt and tie. Gold cuff links flashed as he raised the champagne flute to his lips, sampling a bottle of their Perrier-Jouet order. "Ah, like sipping from a glass of rainbows," he smiled. "Why stock DP at all?"

God, he's infuriating sometimes! Vera thought. "The discounts, Mr. Feldspar. How about it? We'll run a $19.95 special, choice of entree, appetizer, dessert. It worked great in the city."

"Really, Ms. Abbot. You worry too much." Next he poured a snifter of the new Remy, twirling it. "And you forget all I've informed you of regarding The Carriage House. It's only use to Magwyth Enterprises is that of a subordination."

"So you've told me." Vera slumped behind her desk. "It just doesn't make sense to me. Why lose money when you don't have to? With a little ingenuity, I could put The Carriage House in the black, or at least cut down its loss margin."

"I'll tell you why I don't want you to do that, Ms. Abbot, and I would've thought that it could have been easily deducted from all I've related to you thus far. We *don't want* The Carriage House to make a profit. For it to make a profit it would have to attract an influx of business—''

"Yes!" she wanted the shout. "And I can do that. I can get customers in here if—''

"And I reiterate," Feldspar cut her off. "That's what we don't want. I've told you time and time again, haven't I, we intend for The Inn's profits to be generated from a very exclusive and select clientele. An amplitude of outside restaurant business might only sully The Inn's overall reputation in their eyes."

Vera frowned good and hard at that one. *Select clientele*, the words drifted. What Feldspar meant was he didn't want townspeople crowding the restaurant for fear that one of his rich, hoity-toity select clientele might see them. It seemed almost a bigotry, Feldspar's refusal to allow his secretive, wealthy guests to mix company with the middle class. *This is useless,* she dismissed. *One day I'll learn not to argue with him.*

"So, how are things going otherwise?" he inquired next, running a stray, ringed finger along the dark goatee.

"Fine, I suppose. I'm still getting some funny complaints though. Unfriendly housemaids, noisy elevator doors. Some of your suite guests must be partying a little loud. I had some reservations in my rooms, and they complained about noise."

Feldspar merely shrugged. "Can't be helped. As they say, you can't please everyone." He chuckled slightly, sipping his Remy. "I'd rather your guests be the ones complaining than room service's."

This remark was very difficult not to respond to. Vera could almost feel her face pinken.

"I'm sorry," he noticed. "I've offended you. You take things too personally, Ms. Abbot. Room service's business is purely and simply more important to The Inn than the restaurant's. As an experienced businesswoman, you should have no qualms with that.''

"I don't," she said, leaning back behind her desk. "It's just frustrating sometimes. I know I could make The Carriage House tick."

"But what you must understand, Ms. Abbot, is this. You are making it tick. You've turned The Carriage House into exactly what we need, and if you are able to maintain that, the rewards will be considerable. I've told you in the past, if you can maintain the highest standards of quality at the restaurant, your future with Magwyth Enterprises is virtually limitless."

It's not hard to maintain the highest standards of quality when you've got a one million dollar business account and your boss doesn't care how you spend it. Vera wanted to laugh.

"And, as I've also told you, when your contract here expires you'll be free to transfer to any of our other exclusive inns, abroad."

So you've told me, she thought. *Over and over.*

"Well, I best be off now. A rather lofty New York brokerage is planning to have their anniversary banquet here next month. I'm expecting a call." Feldspar got up and set down his snifter. Quite abruptly, then, but just as calmly, he asked, "Would you like to go to dinner with me tonight, Ms. Abbot?"

Vera was taken aback. "I—well, yes, of course. But I have to work."

"A mere formality, since we'll be dining at *your* restaurant." He smiled at her. "Nine o'clock?"

"That would be fine. Dinner'll be winding down."

"Until then . . ." He limped out of her office, presumably back to his own. Vera's astonishment watched after him; it took a while to kick in. *My boss just asked me out, and I said yes.* But why shouldn't she? She sat with chin in hand, reflecting. *How weird,* she thought. With Kyle, for instance, her feelings—as well as her attractions—were constantly at odds. One minute she'd be condemning him as a cad, the next she'd be hoping he'd make a pass, and the next she'd be disappointed when he didn't. Feldspar was different. She could not, and never had, denied her attraction to him. It was not physical. It was purely an adult and sophisticated attraction. All along she'd wished that he'd show some interest in her, and now that he had, she felt in a heady quandry. *Don't go overboard here, Vera,* she smirked to herself. She'd be getting her hopes up, perhaps, for nothing. *What do you want? Do you want to go to bed with him?* She couldn't picture anything less conceivable. He wasn't even really taking her out; he'd simply be having dinner with her at The Carriage House. *It's business,* she suddenly felt convinced. He wanted to appraise the restaurant's cuisine for himself in Vera's presence.

That's all, she thought.

Still, her mind wandered, over other, less rational possibilities.

"Excuse me, miss. Can you help me?"

Vera glanced to her open office door. She was about to speak but any response quickly turned to mush.

A cop? she questioned.

Yes, a big hick cop, fiftyish, with a broad shiny face and a VFW haircut. He smiled rather sheepishly, a cowboy-type hat with a badge on it under his arm. He looked huge in the brown, down-filled jacket, and spoke with a slight drawl. "I'm sorry to interrupt. The name's Lawrence Mulligan, *Chief* Lawrence Mulligan. Waynesville Police Department."

"Please come in," Vera invited, but all she could

219

think was: *What the hell is the chief of police doing here?*

"Thanks kindly." He waddled in and set his hat down. A big pistol hung on his hip through a slit in the jacket. It reminded her of the gun she'd seen in Feldspar's desk, only because of its size. "Actually, I'm looking for a Mr. Feldspar. It's my understandin' that he runs the place," Mulligan said.

"Oh, well let me call him. I think he's right over—"

"He's out, Vera."

Another surprise. Suddenly Kyle was standing in the doorway, looking at her over Mulligan's giant shoulder. "He just left for the airport."

"The airport?" Vera said.

"Yeah, you remember. He had to go to that Historic Inns of America Convention in New York." And after Kyle said that, he quite deliberately winked.

Vera got the message at once, and this was too spontaneous a situation to question it, though that didn't mean a flurry of questions did not sweep through her mind. *Why's he lying?*

Kyle was gone as quickly as he'd appeared. Vera refaced the big police chief, a hand diddling at her collar. "Well, so much for that. My name's Vera, I'm the restaurant manager. Is there a problem?"

"Well, yes, er, no. Er, I should say kind of," Mulligan quite elaborately stated. "Actually, I feel sort of silly, but what ya got to understand is that in these parts, chief of police is an elected post." He paused, exhaled as if winded, and went on. "I'm a tad thirsty, miss. Might I—"

"Would you like me to order you some coffee from room service?"

"Oh, no, I wouldn't want you to go to all that trouble

220

on my account. Just anything you might happen to have on hand would be much appreciated.''

Vera smiled at the stereotype. Mulligan cast a glance to the small walnut bar behind the desk. *Country bumpkin cop, figures a little nip on duty cain't do no harm.* Vera poured him a snifter of the new Remy. "You were saying something about an elected post.''

Mulligan's brow rose at the first sip. "Ooo-eee, that's shore got a kick. . . . Er, uh, yes, Miss Vera, and what I mean is that sometimes we gotta check things out that're surely nothin', on account of that's what the folks who vote want, ya see?''

"Not really,'' Vera said.

Mulligan seemed at once uncomfortable, or maybe it was just that he hadn't taken off the winter jacket. " 'sa free country and all, sure, but it don't make a lot of common sense to build a place like this up here, in Waynesville.''

Now Vera found herself reciting Feldspar's own business sentiments, almost reflexively. "Actually, it makes quite a bit of sense if you examine our marketing designs. The Inn caters to a very select clientele. There are a lot of very rich business people in this country who enjoy coming to a remote, exclusive facility such as ours, a place where they can enjoy total privacy and serene surroundings, a place where they can get away from it all for a little while.''

Did Mulligan smirk? He didn't seem to buy this explanation. "Very rich business people, yes,'' he said. "And what sort of businesses might these very rich people be involved in?''

Vera didn't quite know how to answer the question, nor did she know how to interpret it. "Well, I'm not actually sure. Our clients' business interests are a matter of confidentiality. I don't see what difference it makes, though.''

"Let's just say it makes a whole lotta difference if your clients' business interests aren't exactly legal."

What did *that* mean? Vera peered at him.

"And did you know that Magwyth Enterprises is a holding company?" Mulligan added before she could even reply to his first implication.

Vera hesitated, thinking, then said, "So?"

"Well, I, uh, saw fit ta run a little tad of a check on this holding company of yours, and there don't seem ta be a whole lot of info on 'em. Shore, they got theirselfs a little listing in the U.S. Department of Small Enterprises Directory, but that's about all. Cain't check I.R.S. without a subpoena."

"Why on earth would you want to subpoena our tax records?"

Mulligan downed the last dram of his Remy. At seventy bucks a shot, it proved a nifty little free pick-me-up. "Well, don't you think somethin's a bit off here? And this boss of yours, this Feldspar fella. You know he wired several million dollars into that little bank of ours in town? What'cha think of that?"

Again, Vera hesitated. "Chief Mulligan, it sounds to me like you're accusing Mr. Feldspar of using The Inn to launder money and to serve as a resort for white-collar criminals."

"Oh, no, miss, not at all. I'm not accusing anyone of anything. I'm just a bit . . . mussed is all."

A bit mussed? Vera thought. *Bullshit. You came in here to plant seeds, and now that you have, you'll probably thank me for my time and leave.* This was irredeemable. What right did Mulligan have to imply such things? Moreover, what were his grounds?

Vera brought a finger to her lip. *Maybe he's got grounds that I don't know about.*

"Anyway, thanks for your time," Mulligan said and got up. "I better leave, get back to the beat. I'm shore this is all nothin', but I didn't figure there'd be any harm in me comin' up here to talk to ya. And please don't think I'm accusin' your boss of anything. Just checkin' things out, ya know."

"Of course," Vera said. "It was nice meeting you."

"And thanks fer the drink."

Vera bid the large man a cordial good day, and watched him leave. Initially she'd been offended, but only for a moment. Why would he say such things? *He must have some reason,* she realized. Now she poured herself a drink, a half-flute of the PJ. She watched it fizz. Mulligan's implications did not mix well with the fact that Kyle had lied about Feldspar's whereabouts.

And I went along with it, she thought.

Should she say anything, go to Feldspar right now and tell him the chief of police was nosing about? What would Feldspar's reaction be? Then she remembered their "date," tonight at The Carriage House.

And a better idea crossed her mind. *I'll wait, bring it up tonight. That way I can catch him off guard.*

These feelings fuddled her, though. Why, for instance, should she even want to catch Feldspar "off guard?" He was her employer. He was paying her a lot of money, and had just given her a two hundred thousand dollar automobile to use whenever she liked. *Curiosity killed the cat,* she considered in afterthought. Might it also not kill the restaurant manager's job record?

Later, she'd finished her trickle of preshift paperwork, mostly stock notices, and the food and beverage orders for next week. All at once there was nothing to do; The Carriage House wouldn't open for another few hours. She poured herself some more champagne, remembering the figure she'd seen sneaking away from the atrium the other night, and the bottle of rail-brand Scotch. She knew it must be one of Kyle's people; the liquor supply for The Carriage House was kept locked during off-hours and inventoried daily. *Who cares?* she thought, drinking herself now. Then she thought back further, to Kyle's innocent back rub and the brazen fantasies that had accosted her throughout. That had been two nights ago. Last night, however, she'd slept quite soundly. The fantasy of The Hands had eluded her, and she did not dream. Now that she thought of it, last night had been the first night since her arrival that she'd not dreamed or fantasized sexually. By now she'd grown used to the dreams—she even had to admit to herself that she often looked forward to them. The dirty dreams, and the fantasy that seemed to trigger them, felt like an escape to her, her chance to be a naughty little girl behind the curtain of her sudden celibacy. But why should she have the dreams every night but last night? What was it about last night that was different?

Or maybe the dreams are all over now, she nearly regretted. *So much for my sexual attraction to Kyle.*

Or perhaps that attraction, with time, had supplanted itself with someone more real to her.

Feldspar's image still lingered, like the scent of his Russian cigarettes and his faint cologne, and the flash of his amethyst ring.

She frowned at herself. Her office was windowless; it felt cramped with hard fluorescent light, which made the fine paneling look sticky. She'd have to change the lights, and hang some pictures. Or was it her mood that made everything look dull? *You're dull, Vera,* she came clean with herself. *You're a twenty-nine-year-old spinster, a dull old maid before her time.*

The book lay closed at the desk's veneered corner,

The Complete Compendium of American Haunted Mansions. She'd read the Wroxton Hall segment last night, and dismissed the book as a lurid sham. It hadn't even been scary, it was so ridiculous. Overwritten, sensationalized, and hackneyed. The chapter recounted the takeover of Wroxton Hall in the early nineteen hundreds as a state sanitarium. Apparently the superintendent, a man named Flues, hadn't placed much priority into the care of his patients. Most of the state funds that maintained the facility were diverted by Flues himself, to support a predilection for the finer things in life: imported gimcracks, English carriages, opium, and a conclave of young, fiscally demanding mistresses. He therefore left the entirety of the hospital's logistics and in-patient care to a cadre of ruffians and a pittance of a maintenance allowance. "A majority of the staff," the author reported, "had not been adequately screened for an aptitude in such intense hospital services. Many were exconvicts and former mental patients themselves, and some such warders demonstrated ravenous—as well as distinctly aberrant—libidos upon the more desirable female patients, schizophrenia, manic-depression, and acute catatonia notwithstanding. A staff journal, confiscated during the state inquest which would follow, detailed countless acts of unnamable sexual abuse. . . . " The author proceeded to name each unnamable act.

The frequent pregnancies, of course, were blamed on insensible male patients, and were expeditiously aborted via the crude surgical standards of the day. Things went as such for years, in complete ignorance of the authorities, and eventually warders of higher rank developed a knack for, shall we say, creative entrepreneurship. To serve the occasions when patients died, a cemetery was fashioned beyond the estate's grounds, in a secluded dell, though it was later discerned, after much digging, that not a single cubic inch of earth had ever been turned beneath the countless dozens of gravestones. The bodies, in reality, were sold to out-of-the-way medical schools, and to increase the financial gain of the warders, some of the less manageable and more obscure patients were quickened along to their eventual passings, with the thoughtful assistance of garrots, bars of soap in socks, and pharmaceutical overdoses. In the early forties, when the country's involvement in World War II became undisputable, human freight, for research purposes, became quite lucrative. A discreet lab facility at the Edgewood Arsenal, enthusiastic about germ warfare, paid top-dollar under the table for "lab specimens" of a particular nature, that nature being that they be delivered *live* to the facility. The warders of Wroxton Hall were all too eager to assist in the defense of their nation, and many times logged certain patients as "deceased" when they were in fact still among the living, only to transport them without reluctance to the open arms of the Edgewood Arsenal.

But this proved merely the icing on the cake. What went on on a daily basis at the hall was even more disturbing. Unruly patients were taken aside and disciplined by a coterie of "technicians" that would make the Inquisitors of the Holy Office look like the cast of Sesame Street. Of course, this was regarded instead as "behavioral therapy"; it was difficult to get out of line when one's orbital lobe had been thoroughly routed by knitting-needle lobotomies administered up through the anterior eye socket. (Staff members, naturally, sterilized the knitting-needles before each application.) A less sophisticated manner of taming rowdy patients involved a simple tourniquet fashioned about the throat just under the jawline, which cut off blood-flow to the brain. The tourniquet was maintained for just a period of time to effect the level of brain damage desired to take some of the zing out of said patient. The relatively unsupervised staff, too, when they weren't applying such contemporary behavioral therapies, were quite forthcoming in the application of *sexual* therapies. All manner of libidinous abuse was pursued at Wroxton Hall, no perversity ignored, and no orifice unplundered. Boys will be boys, after all. And since the induction of semen into fecund vaginal passages was known to result in pregnancies, Wroxton Hall became perhaps the most expeditious abortion clinic in history.

Certain patients however, upon expiration, and due to the extreme state of physical disrepair racked by decades of subhuman living conditions, were deemed not only sexually undesirable, but also unpurchasable by the buyers from the medical schools and the illustrious Edgewood Arsenal, but that did not mean that some profitable utility couldn't be found for them. In other words, when the state investigators came, it was more than pork that was discovered in the briny stew that served as the patients' daily food ration.

Shortly thereafter, Superintendant Flues died in prison of tertiary syphillis. Many of the hospital staff were either executed or incarcerated. Wroxton Hall was closed down, sealed shut, and gratefully forgotten.

Except by the local residents, who came to think of the hall as a curse and an embarrassment. Some residents, upon investigating the dank corridors of the hall firsthand, claimed that the edifice was abundantly haunted by the spirits of those who died there.

Not too long afterward, Wroxton Hall was anonymously set ablaze, its interior gutted, and its horrors wiped clean from memory . . .

The story seemed too trite to even consider; Vera scoffed and closed the ludricrous book. But her mind wandered to other things: questions? Why had Feldspar invited her to dinner? Did Chief Mulligan know something she didn't? Could it really be possible that Feldspar and Magwyth Enterprises were involved in some sort of criminal activity?

Vera was determined to find out.

Chapter Twenty-One

"I've got a surprise for you," Zyra panted.

Phil Brooks gave the large, hanging nipples a pinch and grinned up at her. "I'll bet ya do, baby. You been surprisin' me all night."

Zyra felt blissfully lost in herself. How many times had she come? Every so often she'd lose control, she'd do things that startled even her. It was the moment, she knew, and the spontaneity: the quick collision of passion, lust, curiosity, and a plethora of other feelings too intricate—or too dark—to even attempt to put a name to. Maybe it was love—not love for the grainy, overmuscled redneck who now lay exhausted beneath her—but love for herself, and all of the beautiful things she was capable of feeling. Feelings were truth, of a sort, an honest acknowledgement of who she really was in the scheme of things, in the blazing reality of the world. She'd bathed his entire body with her tongue, she'd drunk up his sweat. She'd sucked his testicles, nibbled his perenium, had let herself be sodomized by him, after which she'd immediately fellated him to orgasm. And this had only been the prelude to a very long and energizing evening.

I'm a pervert, she thought, and almost laughed. *A*

pervert of truth. She caressed her own breasts and sighed.

They'd met Phil Brooks and his drunk, flirtatious girlfriend at the old pool hall off Furnace Branch Road. The Factotum had left instructions for them to bring in one more girl; this would be their last abduction for some time. *Bar dogs,* Zyra had concluded when they'd first entered. Some fat girls, some worn-out older women missing teeth. *Not much to choose from.* Then Phil Brooks and the girl walked in—Ellen was her name, Zyra thought. Blond hair with black roots, a flowery bracelet tatooed around her wrist, and over-applied makeup, but she was well-breasted, shapely, and seemed to have the type of spirit they were looking for. She and Zyra had got to chatting—*Not much for brains,* Zyra concluded; all she could talk about were pickup trucks and diets. Zyra had asked her about the Middle East, and Ellen had responded, "Oh, yeah, I have some relatives in Maryland and North Carolina." Meanwhile, Lemi and Phil had taken to making wagers at the billiards table. "You win the next game," Phil challenged, "and I lay fifty on ya, and if you lose, we swap squeeze. How 'bout it, friend?" "You're on," Lemi said, and wasted no time in losing the game. They followed them back to their big SilverLine trailer, alone on its own lot back off an old logging trail. The big propane tank outside would provide a fiery finish. . . .

They'd paired off at once. Zyra turned up the heat, way up. It should be hot for this, hot and sultry and damp, to parallel her mood. She left the lights on, as she frequently did. She wanted to see him—or she *needed* to—and she needed him to see her in every detail. Their bodies blazed in sweat for hours, through every offering of flesh, every configuration she could conceive. Phil was good for several bouts, which gratified her. It made her feel humble to the lot she'd been given in life, and to the Factotum, and to her lord. Where others had faltered and failed, Zyra had been given this holy and cyclic bliss. It was wonderful.

Everything's wonderful, she thought.

In the interims of their coupling, she masturbated for him, she let him watch. All she could think, for the entire time, was: *More, more, more. I want more.* She had to be careful, though, she mustn't masturbate beyond control, not yet. Zyra was a complex woman, and a prudent one, but even she on occasion would lose the reins on herself. She mustn't spoil the moment, she mustn't spoil the surprise. Nevertheless, the fervid teasing of herself, and its wet, shiny imagery, revitalized him each and every time, lending him the ability to give her exactly what she wanted. More. More. She felt crazy in her passion, more so tonight than ever perhaps. Was it her growing maturity? Her evolution as a complete woman? Each caress, each thrust into her sex, and each release of his semen into whatever orifice he tended, made her feel more and more real, and more purposeful. But still, there was always the irrepressible desire, the unrelenting urge:

More.

"What's this?" he coyly inquired. "This right here?" His finger touched her navel, which glittered sharp, faceted purple: the amethyst she wore there.

"It's my lucky charm," she replied, still stroking herself.

"It's pretty. It's like you."

Zyra moaned. "You like it?" She slid up, over his wet chest, leaning into his face. "There. Kiss it. Lick it."

Phil Brooks obliged, squeezing her rump as he did so. She was getting too close, and in a moment she was turning him over, sculpting his slickened physique with

231

her frantic hands. *I can't kill him yet,* she thought. *No, not yet.*

She gazed down at his tapered, shining back, the muscled buttocks, the sturdy, corded legs. *Lord, my lord,* the weeping sigh of her thoughts swept through her head. Her breasts were thrumming orbs. Her finger kneaded her clitoris, chasing her ultimate release. But what would she kill him with afterward? Her bare hands? She might be strong enough to do it. Lemi had the gun, and she'd left the ice pick in the console in the van. Strangulation bored her; she'd done it too many times, and bludgeoning seemed too primitive. *Blood,* she thought. *More.* Perhaps she'd just bite out the side of his throat and suck him to death. She'd swallowed enough of his semen tonight. Why not his blood too? *Yeah,* she mused. *Oh, yeah.* Just gulp down his blood like a famished, raging animal. Swallow it till her belly was fit to burst . . .

Zyra's eyes narrowed to the thinnest of slits. Her fervid passion, merged with the panting, hot breaths, seemed to turn her words to steam.

"I have a surprise for you," she said.

"Can't have you catching cold, now can we, Ellen?" Lemi thoughtfully remarked as he wrapped the limp, naked girl up in the blankets. She hadn't been much of a tumble—she'd passed out. At least she was slender; she'd be easier to get out to the van. Carrying that tub of lard Mrs. Buluski had been like throwing three or four bags of cement over his shoulder. Lemi was a strong man, but he wasn't a forklift, for God's sake.

He set the little timer for thirty minutes and placed it on the cheap fiberboard bookcase, like the kind you buy at Dart Drug for twenty bucks and put together yourself.

Lemi figured that any five pieces of furniture at The Inn probably cost more than this whole place.

He heard the shower turn off. Zyra always took a shower after a job; she had a way of making a mess of herself. *I like to watch the blood go down the drain,* she'd told him once. *It's sort of symbolic, isn't it?* Zyra went off on these bends every once in a while—weirding out, but the way Lemi saw it, all women were weird. He couldn't figure them. You do what they tell you, and then they're pissed off that you didn't assert yourself. You assert yourself, and then they're pissed off that you're overbearing and selfish. Lemi was grateful he didn't have to worry about romance. *I'd go fucking nuts,* he concluded.

Zyra traipsed in naked, slipping into her panties. "You turn on the gas?" Lemi asked.

She only nodded. She seemed dreamy, or contemplative. Lemi squinted at her.

"What did—" He squinted harder. "How come your belly's stickin' out like that?"

And it was. Zyra was a hardbody—trim, toned, and zero body fat. But right now that lean stomach of hers protruded almost like she was four months pregnant, and wouldn't that be a kick? *Zyra the murderer mother.* The Factotum would shit right there on the chancel floor if one of his girls got knocked up.

"I drank his blood," Zyra said very softly, rubbing the tight belly. It was sticking out so tight her amethyst might pop out. "It makes me all warm inside, and full. I kind of like that idea. Even though he's dead, there's some of him still alive in me, like I've taken him into me, like he's become *part* of me. You know?"

Lemi rolled his eyes. "Quit blabbering all that philosiphal shit and get dressed. We gotta slip."

"That's *split*, Lemi. Not slip. Jesus." She pulled on her jeans, top, and coat, having to leave the jeans un-

233

buttoned against the grossly distended stomach. "What's wrong with her?" she asked, peering quizzically at Ellen.

"She passed out." Lemi chuckled. "I guess my TCL was a little too much for the gal."

"*T-L-C*, you stupe," Zyra complained yet again, regarding Lemi's continued ignorance of colloquialism. "Tender loving care. There's no such thing as TCL."

Lemi didn't care. He hoisted the reedy black-rooted blonde over his shoulder. "Let's *split*, okay?"

"Go warm up the van," Zyra suggested. "I'll get the guy."

"No need to. Just leave him. Let him burn up with the place."

"But why?" Zyra objected. "It'd be a waste."

"We don't need it." Lemi began to walk toward the door. "The Factotum says we're all full up on meat."

One step at a time, Vera thought, running her finger down the rezz list at the hostess desk. *Sixteen reservations*. And that didn't include the walk-ins. It was only seven thirty and the dining room was half-full. Things weren't great, but they were sure getting better.

Donna whizzed by with a tray of covered main courses for a four-top in the corner. When she came back, Vera asked, "What's the kitchen done so far?"

"Twenty-two, and about half of them are walk-ins," Donna responded as she automatically tabulated a check. "The grilled Louisiana *andouille* is going like mad, and so is the banana-cream pie and the Michelanglo Peppers. This isn't bad at all. I'm actually pulling some serious tips."

"Good. If this keeps up we might have to hire a part-time waitress."

"Over my dead body," Donna said. She crammed a wad of bills into the tip jar. "Did you read the book?"

"Yes," Vera close to groaned. "Ghosts from an insane asylum. The whole story was just so silly."

"Silly, huh?" Donna shot her a wicked grin, then headed back to the kitchen. Was she chuckling?

She's a trip all right. Vera just smiled. As far as she was concerned, Donna could believe in ghosts all she wanted, so long as she remained a proficient waitress.

Vera took a minute to slip to the ladies' room, ever mindful of her watch. In little more than an hour, Feldspar would be coming in for dinner. *With me,* she thought. Or would he? Suddenly she felt afret. Maybe he'd forgotten. Maybe something else came up. Then she smirked at herself. *You're worrying like a little high school girl.* And she was: inventing catastrophes. Still, she couldn't deny the subtle excitement, not just that he wanted to have dinner with her, but she couldn't wait to probe him out over today's surprise visit by the chief of police. Or perhaps she was so bored of late that she was also inventing her own intrigues. Nevertheless, another thing she couldn't deny were her own suspicions regarding The Inn's financial success—or what Kyle and Feldspar claimed was a success. Is that what they were? Suspicions? *Don't be gullible, Vera,* she reminded herself. What did she have to be suspicious of? A country bumpkin cop walks in spouting unfounded implications about money-laundering and ill-gotten gains, and now she was thinking the silliest things. Certainly a cop of Mulligan's low caliber was no reason to suspect Feldspar of improprieties.

She surveyed herself in the long mirror, checked her hair, made sure her earrings were straight. *Quit fussing! You look fine.* Actually, she looked great. She wore a flowered pink-white silk jacket, rather low cut, and a white chiffon skirt. Her amethyst necklace sparkled keenly; she always wore it now—since Feldspar had complimented her on it so many times. She easily admitted to herself that she was out to impress Feldspar—via her job performance, her insights, even her looks. But what she still had yet to discern was . . . *why? Do I want to impress him as my boss, or as something more?*

The dinner shift seemed to pass in scant minutes. Every single table complimented The Carriage House as they left. From Vera's end, everything clicked: Donna's service was outstanding, Dan B. turned out one superior entree after the next, and the place was running without a hitch. But tonight, in a sense, was the trickiest test so far. She could please customers, sure.

But can I please the boss? she wondered now.

He hadn't been in for dinner before, which seemed strange. He was a connoisseur and probably a snob. He smoked cigarettes that cost five dollars a pack and drank $300-per-bottle wine like it was Yoo-Hoo. A man like Feldspar, ultimately, was never easy to please. Now Vera began to wonder, or even fear, what his impressions would be.

"Shit!" she whispered, glaring at her watch. "I knew it. He's not going to show."

Donna laughed beside her. "Vera, it's only thirty seconds past nine. What's wrong with you?"

"I—" *I don't know,* she thought. But it was only thirty seconds more before the shadow slid across the entry.

"Good evening," Feldspar greeted. Vera noted the crisp gray suit, and black shirt with no tie—exactly what he'd worn the night she met him. He smiled at her. "I believe we have a reservation."

"Is there a particular table you'd prefer, Mr. Feldspar?" Donna inquired, assuming the role of hostess.

"The choice is Ms. Abbot's."

Vera chose the furthest four-top in the east section, well removed from the few diners who remained. It flustered her at once: Feldspar still called her *Ms. Abbot,* and of course she still called him Mr. Feldspar, as he'd yet to bid otherwise. Donna seated them, as she passed them their menus, Feldspar said, "Perrier-Jouet, the flowered bottle." He glanced to Vera. "Yes?"

"That would be perfect," Vera responded.

Feldspar immediately lit a Sobraine. "So. How are things?"

"We actually did some business tonight," Vera was happy to answer. "And we had a lot of walk-ins, which is always a good sign."

"Any complaints about the restaurant?"

"None. Lots of compliments, though."

"Good." He seemed distracted, but then he always did in a way, as though there were always something of the future on his mind. He seemed clipped, ever the businessman. *Just once I wish he'd lighten up,* Vera thought. *Be himself.* Or was he doing just that? The possibility depressed her.

"I've spoken to Kyle, regarding your room-guest complaints of last weekend," Feldspar mentioned. "I suppose it's rather embarrassing for you."

"Well, no," she said. Actually it was; it pissed her off to receive complaints about *Kyle's* room guests. "It comes with the territory. Even rich people get rowdy."

"Actually much more so than the middle class, more often than not, I'm afraid. It can cause one to wonder about civility and sophistication—that the extravagantly wealthy generally behave as ill-mannered, inconsiderate idiots."

There had, in fact, been still more complaints of late, always from room guests of the first-floor suites, Vera's rooms, and never from Kyle's guests. In fact, Vera had yet to even see any of the guests renting the second- and third-floor suites. Evidently, they were content to order all their meals from room service. Not once had any of

237

them come down to eat at The Carriage House, which only furthered Vera's irritation. But now the complaints were more descriptive. "We kept hearing this awful thunking sound all night long," came the grievance of the town's podiatrist, who'd spent several weekends at The Inn with his dowdy wife. A good-paying customer, and one Vera didn't want to lose. There'd been similar "thunking" complaints from others, too. Vera concluded that this thunking was actually the room-service elevators opening and closing, which she'd heard many times at night herself. The funny thing was she couldn't hear the elevators running, just the doors opening and closing, which made little sense. And still more complaints were made about noise in general.

"I'm still getting complaints from my room guests, though," Vera elaborated, "about loud noises at night, you know, typical party noises—loud talk, footsteps, laughter." She fingered her chin in contemplation. "The weird part is the noises don't seem to be coming from the second and third floors, but from below."

"Hmmm," Feldspar remarked without much interest. "Perhaps some of the night owls are taking their revelry into the atrium during the wee hours, or the pool."

"That probably explains it. And another strange complaint I keep getting is elevator noise."

Feldspar made a facial gesture of befuddlement. "It's true that the room-service elevators are in fairly constant use, but I've never heard them making any undue noise while running."

"Well, no one's complaining about the elevators going up and down, they're complaining about a thunking noise. I figure it's the doors opening and closing."

Feldspar nodded, still without much interest. "I'll have Kyle get a service person out here, and maybe a

238

contractor to see about some more soundproofing. It's difficult to forecast a building's acoustics."

"And one more thing," Vera began. Then she paused partly in reluctance and partly in amusement. *Mafioso,* she thought. *Drug financiers.* That's what Chief Mulligan had implied The Inn actually catered to. But how should she bring the matter up?

Fortunately, after Feldspar poured the champagne, she wouldn't have to. "And I feel absolutely dreadful about the business this morning with the police," he owned up. "Kyle reported it to me."

"It's nothing to feel dreadful about," Vera told him. "If you want to know the truth, it was kind of funny. I'm still not quite sure what the man was digging for."

Feldspar leaned forward slightly, looking at her. "What do you *suppose* he was looking for?"

Vera nearly sighed. *Go for it,* she thought. "It's my impression that Chief Mulligan is suspicious of The Inn's location and is therefore suspicious of The Inn's clientele."

She expected Feldspar to scoff, or laugh. But he didn't. He just looked at her.

"Why?" he asked.

Vera shrugged. "I'm not sure. He just thinks it's odd that a place like The Inn, very upscale, could turn a profit in an area like this."

"And what did you tell him?"

"The same thing you told me from the start. That The Inn caters to a very upscale and very private clientele."

"A select clientele."

"Yes. And I think that's why he's suspicious," Vera went on, hoping she wasn't saying too much, or exaggerating what Mulligan had seemed to imply. But Feldspar had *asked* for her opinion. *So I'm going to give it to him.* "I think he believes, in other words, that our

239

'select' clientele aren't legitimate businessmen but white-collar criminals. Mafia. Organized crime. Drug distribution. That sort of thing. He's also very suspicious that Magwyth Enterprises is a holding company. For instance, he knows that you wired several million dollars into the bank in town, and in addition to that, he wasn't able to find out anything about Magwyth Enterprises itself. It's pretty clear to me that he's challenging the legitimacy of your company. He seems to think it's a money-laundering outfit, and that you're the honcho behind it.''

"Preposterous," Feldspar said. Yet he seemed off kilter at once, even slightly perturbed, and it was obvious. *Is it my imagination,* Vera wondered, *or is he hiding something?* "Yeah, preposterous," she went along with him. "What I don't get are his motives. It's one thing to make implications like that. But what are his grounds?''

Feldspar made no immediate reply; instead he refilled their champagne flutes and set the towel-cloaked bottle back into its ice bucket. "Small town police chief, big ideas, I suspect. Who knows, really? Nevertheless, whatever his motives, I can assure you, Ms. Abbot, The Inn is quite legitimate in its services to its guests, and its guests are equally legitimate.''

"Of course," Vera said.

They dined first on an array of appetizers: Equadoran Shrimp Cocktail, Lasagnettas with Roasted Peppers, and Dan B.'s famous Minted Pea Salad in Radicchio Leaves. Vera ordered Crayfish Brittany as her main course, and Feldspar the Fillet of Charollais Beef in a truffle gravy. Even Vera was astounded by Dan B.'s skills tonight; everything was state-of-the-art, yet Feldspar scarcely made comment during the meal. Instead, he spoke off and on of business in general, some upcoming banquets, etc., nothing of note, and nothing really of himself. Vera had no choice but to deduce that her revelations regarding Chief Mulligan's visit had put him on edge. *But why?* she kept wondering. *If The Inn is legitimate, what's he so distracted about?* It was a good question, and one that continued to occur to her throughout the meal. *Select clientele, money-laundering, Mafia,* she repeatedly thought. Earlier she'd found these implications amusing. Now, though, she wasn't so sure.

And if it was so "preposterous," why did Feldspar keep bringing it up? "I suppose I should go and speak to him," he said next, quite by surprise.

"I'm sorry?" Vera said.

"This . . . policeman."

"I wouldn't worry about it," Vera said. She paused. *Careful, girl, careful.* Perhaps it was the champagne, which was gone now, unraveling her better judgment. Or perhaps it was her own suspicions. "But may I ask you something?" she said next.

"Of course," Feldspar granted, and then very inappropriately ordered a bottle of 1983 Montrachet.

Just what I need, Vera thought. *More booze. I'll wind up getting sloshed in front of my boss. I'll be asking him how he got his start washing money for drug lords.* "It just seemed a little curious," she said. "When Chief Mulligan asked to see you, Kyle said you went to the airport." She paused once more. "Why did he lie?"

Feldspar nodded, stroking his trimmed goatee. "A sound query, Ms. Abbot, and one to which you are entitled a sound answer." He sipped the Montrachet, peered at it in the fine Cristal d'Arques glass. "I have somewhat of an aversion to police. And I'm sure you've been wondering, quite understandably, if I've ever been in any trouble with the law."

"Oh, Mr. Feldspar, that's not what I was thinking at

all," Vera . . . lied. Of course she had. Deep down she knew she'd been wondering about that all day. But—

"The answer, I'm afraid, is yes."

Vera blinked. *Holy shit*, she thought. *Now I've really done it! Next time keep your big mouth SHUT!*

Feldspar didn't seem at all fazed by the alcohol—he never did. Vera didn't believe that it was the champagne and wine that had loosened his personal armor. Feldspar wasn't a man to go blabbering on drink. Vera knew that type—the typical general manager. Feldspar's high rank in the chain of command didn't allow him to confide in anyone. *So why is he confiding in me?* she wondered.

"Quite some time ago, I held a similar post for an investment company quite like Magwyth Enterprises. It was an identical operation to what we're doing here, and it was very successful. And I'm ashamed to have to admit, however, that it wasn't entirely . . . *clean*. Money corrupts, Ms. Abbot, just like power. In many ways they're very much the same."

"Mr. Feldspar, you don't have to tell me your personal b—"

"One thing led to another," he went on. "Improprieties . . . I'm not creating excuses for my conduct, mind you. What I did was wrong."

What! Vera thought with fervor. *What did you do!* She couldn't ask, of course—that would be uncouth. But—*Goddamn!*—she wanted to know.

Feldspar smiled meekly across the table. His rings glittered as he poured more wine. "You're wondering—naturally. I can tell. Who wouldn't be, under such circumstances?"

"Really, Mr. Feldspar, I don't—"

"I'm afraid I was accused of the very same offenses that our ever dutiful Chief Mulligan has accused me of now."

Vera set down her fork. She tried not to appear floored, but she was. She tried to think of something diverting to say. "I don't think Mulligan was *accusing*. Just implying."

"You're too kind." Feldspar smiled again, very faintly. "I've told you that I was accused. Aren't you going to inquire as to whether or not I was guilty?"

"No, that's your—"

"I was, quite guilty. At least in an indirect sense. However, I was never charged."

If he was never charged, why did he tell me all this? Vera now wondered. *Why practically verify to me that Mulligan's suspicions are right on the money?* This made no sense at all.

"Which is hardly an excuse," he continued. "Guilt is guilt. Guilt by association, in my case. Now, though, as I've stated, The Inn is absolutely legitimate, and I can guarantee you of the same in regard to Magwyth Enterprises, Ltd."

Some dinner, she thought. *Some date*. She couldn't imagine anything more awkward, or more difficult to maneuver through.

"I cannot prevaricate," Feldspar said then. "Not to you, at any rate."

"I don't understand," Vera told him, for lack of anything else.

"After all, you've made quite a sacrifice for me: coming here cold, running a restaurant for an enterprise you know nothing about, giving your all. It would be immoral of me to leave you uninformed. I appreciate your loyalty and discretion, and I'm grateful to you for handling this unpleasant business with the police. You know as well as I, loyalty is perhaps the most essential interpersonal element in this kind of business. Your loyalty will not go unrewarded, nor will your outstanding performance."

At first, this depressed her, because it sounded as though he were merely patronizing her, for getting Mulligan off his back. But as she watched him, and continued to assess his demeanor, and the manner with which he expressed himself, she began to doubt that patronizing her had any part in what he'd just told her. *But what is his motive then?* she wondered, sipping her Montrachet.

Perhaps there was no ulterior motive at all. Perhaps he was coming clean with her for the reasons he'd just explained.

"So much for confessions." Now Feldspar leaned back in the plush armchair, his smile going wan. He diddled with an ash in the ashtray, almost as if he felt embarrassed now. "It must not be an easy thing to reckon," he said.

"What?"

"To suddenly become aware that your employer has a bit of a checkered past."

But Vera couldn't help continuing to think: *Select clientele. Mafioso, money laundering.* "I don't guess anybody's slate is perfectly clean," she excused.

"No, perhaps not."

Another glass of the fine Montrachet. *God,* she thought. She was getting drunk. The wine left her buzzing, warm inside, but remotely unhappy. She had a parfait for dessert, while Feldspar ordered expresso and smoked. Afterward, he paid cash for the meal, which seemed odd. He *owned* The Carriage House. Why pay? Vera supposed he was just trying to seem gracious. It depressed her further, though. The meal had been outstanding, yet Feldspar made no comment whatever. At least Donna was happy. She bubbled enthusiasm in silence, upon discovering Feldspar's fifty dollar cash tip in the leather tab book.

"I'd invite you to the convention with me," Feldspar

244

said next, "but I'm afraid that would leave The Inn a bit short in the management department. Kyle's a very loyal, steadfast employee, but I wouldn't be too keen on leaving him totally in charge. A bit uncultured, if you will."

Vera had to backpedal on everything he'd said; the wine and champagne wasn't mixing well. "Convention?" she queried.

"Oh, I mustn't have mentioned it to you, sorry. I'll be gone for several days. The East Coast Hotel/Motel Association is having their annual convention tomorrow, in Maryland. I'm expected to attend, not that I really want to. At any rate, you and Kyle will be in charge."

"Okay," Vera said. But she'd barely heard the words. Now it was her own distractions that diverted her, and of course the alcohol. This whole dinner thing had been a bust; it was obvious to her now that Feldspar's only interest in her was professional. He was the boss giving the little restaurant manager a pat on the head.

"Well." Feldspar rose; his bulky shape left the table enshadowed. "Your company was a pleasure, Ms. Abbot, and the meal outstanding . . ." He squinted forward. "Are you all right?"

No, I'm drunk, she felt inclined to say. "A little tired, that's all." She rose herself, and escorted Feldspar to the entry. "Thanks for dinner. I hope you have a good time at the convention."

"Yes," he said. "Oh, and forgive me for neglecting to mention one thing."

"What's that?"

His smile seemed distant. His entire self, in fact, all evening, seemed more and more distant. "You look lovely tonight," he said.

The words were like a dull shimmer in the air. Before

245

Vera could reply, he was saying "Good night, Ms. Abbot" and leaving.

"How'd it go?" Donna came up from behind and asked.

"It didn't, not really," Vera said.

"You look bummed."

I am. "I don't know, I just thought—" What, though? *What did you expect, Vera? You expected him to wine and dine you and take you to bed? Your boss, for God's sake?* "I'm tired, I guess. I drank too much." She had to actually lean against the service bar to keep steady. "How are things going in the kitchen?"

"Lee and Dan B. are cleaning up now. They're going to check out that little bar in town if they get out early enough. If you ask me, we did pretty good tonight."

"Yeah, it's catching on." Vera handed Donna the Lamborghini keys. "Tell Dan B. he can take my car. I never have time to drive it—might as well let him have some fun with it."

"Oh, he'll love this!" Donna enthused. "I'll be sure to tell him not to wrap it around a phone pole."

"Please. Are you going with them?"

"No way. Once I get all the tables changed, I'm going straight to bed."

"That's what I'm going to do right now," Vera said. "See you tomorrow."

She trudged out into the atrium, woozy and weary. Then: "Yes. Yes sir," she heard. It was Kyle's voice. Vera glanced across the atrium and saw Kyle signing someone in at the reception desk: a man of medium height and build, dressed in a tailored crisp brown suit. "Right this way, sir," Kyle was saying, and picked up the man's suitcase. "Your suite's ready now."

Vera tried not to appear obvious; this was the first upper floor room guest she'd seen, and as she watched

246

from the corner of her eye, all she could be reminded of was what Mulligan had implied. Money laundering, mafia, drug lords? Some people had a look—you could tell, just by looking at them, what they were into, and this guest that Kyle was checking in—he had it. The man's face reflected a darkness, even an ominousness, which clashed with his fine suit. He looked like a thug.

Select clientele, huh? Vera mused, then went up the stairs to her room.

Whoever that guy is, he's bad news.

Chapter Twenty-two

Lee off-loaded the last dish-rack from the Hobart's big chain conveyor, then began to automatically stack the hot dry plates. The shift had passed like sludge in a gutter, and that was about how Lee had felt lately—sluggish in dark questions and dread.

"Get rollin', Lee," Dan B. happily remarked. He was whistling as he polished up the range and the line table. "Looks like we're going to be out of here by midnight, still plenty of time to go into town, huh?"

Lee merely nodded, carrying more plates to their metal shelving.

"And guess what, dishman? Vera's letting us take *her* car. Ain't that slick?"

"Yeah, man. Slick."

Dan B. frowned across the kitchen, his big white chef's hat jiggling. "What's the matter with you? You still want to go, don't you?"

"Sure," Lee said.

Dan B. easily sensed his friend's sullenness. "Come on, man. What's wrong? You've barely said a word all night."

"I'm fine," Lee responded. *Yeah, right, fine.* But even if he'd wanted to talk about it, what could he possibly say?

"This place looks good enough. Let's roll." Dan B. slapped Lee on the back. "Aren't we going to change?" Lee asked, indicating their sneakers and smudged kitchen tunics. "We're going to The Waterin' Hole, not the Kennedy Center. Quit stalling, let's get out of here and have a couple beers," Dan B. said.

They donned their coats and went out the side exit. Lee cast a glance over his shoulder; Kyle wouldn't like this at all—most nights, for weeks now, Lee had finished the roomservice dishes after he'd finished up at The Carriage House. He didn't much care now, though; he was too confused and depressed. *Kiss my fat ass, Kyle. Clean up your own mess.* Brisk strides took them across the darkened parking lot; the bitter cold slapped them in the face. Lee glanced up, at The Inn. He was thinking about the woman, as he did now almost constantly. Grim images weaved in and out of his mind.

"You forget your brain?" Dan B. asked. He was already in the Lamborghini, starting it up. "Get in unless you want to freeze."

Lee climbed in and idly closed the door. *Snap out of it,* he urged himself. Dan B. would be thinking he was weirding out. "Hey, Dan B., you ever seen the serial number on a rubber?"

Dan B.'s brow knit as he pulled out of the lot. "What are you talking about? Rubbers don't have serial numbers."

"Sure they do, I guess you've just never rolled one down far enough to see it."

"Funny. Put a potato in your pants and keep dreaming."

"On the way back, how about letting me drive?"

Dan B. laughed. "You? This? Shit, you probably don't even *know how* to drive."

"I admit, it's been a while since I've driven a car, but I drive your sister crazy every night."

"Yeah, crazy with laughter. Besides, you couldn't squeeze between the seat and wheel."

"Yeah, you may be right. So I guess I better just settle for squeezing between the ceiling and your mom."

"You're on a roll tonight. I was beginning to think you'd lost your terrible sense of humor."

But it was all a fake; joking around didn't help. Lee could only wonder the darkest things. The housemaid continued to come to him, every night, in her silent gratitude, in her passion—perhaps even in her love. Yet Lee wondered repeatedly: *What did they do to her? Who did all those awful things?* It could be a cold world sometimes, and an ugly one. What made it all worse was that Lee was beginning to really like her. . . .

The sleek car glided gracefully along the old, weaving roads. The cold sky beyond the ridge looked like black murk. The winter, and its bitter cold, its stillness and lifelessness, made Lee feel more isolated than ever.

Only a few other cars were parked in the drab little lot before the bar. A neon OPEN sign blinked in the window, advertising Bud. "Class joint," Dan B. whispered when they entered. Lee expected as much. He was a bit of a beer snob, and he groaned when he spotted the sign on the bar wall: DON'T ASK FOR IMPORTS, 'COS WE AIN'T GOT 'EM! *Great. I'll have to drink Carling.* Several oldtimers sat up at the bar, drinking Kessler's straight and complaining about "the goddamn recession." Some other patrons occupied several cheaply upholstered booths in back, too dark to be seen. Two women in their fifties sat closer up, smoking Salems and yakking away. One laughed drunkenly, showing bad teeth.

"Is that your mom?" Lee asked.

"No," Dan B. said, "but your dad's here." He pointed to the end of the bar, where one of the oldtimers passed out and went face down into a bowl of peanuts.

Dan B. ordered two Buds, draft. "All right, no more fooling around," he asserted. "Out with it."

"Out with what?"

"You can't bullshit Dan B.," Dan B. said. "You haven't been yourself all week. What's bugging you?"

I can't tell him, Lee reminded himself. *No way.* He'd sound absurd, he'd sound like an idiot. First off, Dan B. would go apeshit if he knew Lee was sexually involved with an employee, especially one of Kyle's employees. And what could he say that wouldn't sound absolutely demented? *Well, you see, Dan B., I've sort of become, uh, involved with that pudgy housemaid, you know, the one who never talks to anyone. She comes into my room and gives me head every night, see? And there's this slight problem, like, uh, she's got all these scars and burn-marks all over her body. Oh, and one other thing. She's got stitches in her vagina. . . .*

"I guess I just haven't been feeling too hot." But there was one thing he could mention, wasn't there? "You been hearing weird things at night? Like real late?"

Dan B. plowed half his beer in the first gulp, contemplating the question. "Come to think of it, yeah. Like people talking out in the hall and walking around. And a lot of ruckus too, but it sounds like it's coming from downstairs, not upstairs."

"Me too." Lee winced when he sipped his Bud. But he'd heard more than that, or at least he thought he had. Things thumping around, thunking, laughter. A couple of times he was sure he'd heard someone shriek. *Just dreams,* he tried to convince himself. Who

251

would be shrieking at a high-class private resort like The Inn?

"In fact," Dan B. continued, "one night last week I woke up to hang a piss, and I thought I heard someone shriek."

Lee looked at him.

"And a few nights ago I thought I heard someone walking around the hall. So I looked out, and saw someone going down the stairs, walking away from our rooms."

"Maybe it was Feldspar," Lee suggested. "Vera told me his room's on the end."

"Yeah, I know, but it's funny. I've only seen him once or twice since we got here. And that Kyle motherfucker. Where's his room?"

"I don't know. On the upper floors, I guess."

"But that doesn't make sense. The upper floors are all the higher priced suites. Why give one of those to an employee when there're still several unused rooms on our floor?"

Lee shrugged. "Who knows. Maybe it was your mom, looking for a fresh doorknob."

"No, no. *Now* I remember. It was your sister. She got lost on her way to the smokehouse."

Lee tried to think of a suitable derogatory comeback, but in the next instant, Dan B. gently poked him with his elbow and said under his breath: "Check this out. These old sticks over here are eyeballing us like we got no heads."

Lee discreetly took another wincing sip of his Bud, taking a quick glance right. It was true. The old, rustic-looking men at the other side of the bar were staring at them.

"They probably got the hots for you, buddy," Dan B. suggested and got up off his wobbly stool. "A cute gal like you, shit. Excuse me while I go contribute to the Waynesville reservoir.''

Dan B. walked off for the men's room, while Lee smirked. What he needed after a long shift was a good beer, like a Maibock or a Blue Herren Ale, not this limp, fizzy domestic swill. And one thing he definitely didn't need was being stared at by a bunch of drunk old codgers.

Then he nearly jumped off his stool at the surprise slap to his back. ''If it's not my favorite fat boy,'' greeted Kyle, who'd been sitting in the opposite corner. ''How goes it, slim? I didn't know they had an all-you-can-eat pasta bar here.''

Kiss my fat ass, Lee wished he had the gall to reply. Kyle slapped him on the back again, downed a shot of Jack, and smacked his lips. ''How come you're sittin' here bending this bar stool when you're supposed to cleaning up room service?''

''Kiss my fat ass, Kyle,'' Lee finally summoned the courage to suggest. ''I'm not doing that anymore; it's not my job. And you can go ahead and fire me if you don't like it. I don't give a shit.''

''Relax, Oprah, relax. I got my own crew squared away so I won't be needing you back there breaking the floor tile anymore.'' Kyle raised his hand. ''Hey, keep, get my buddy here a beer on my tab. A *light* beer.'' Then he laughed and went on, ''And of course I realize you're pretty busy these days after hours.''

''What are you talking about, man?''

Kyle leaned closer. ''I know you've been fucking that housekeeping dolt, tubby. She any good?''

How does he know. . . . This was a dilemma. Lee set down his beer. He struggled for a reply.

''Don't worry, man,'' Kyle assured. ''I can keep a secret, you know, like as a favor. And maybe you can do me a favor sometime.''

How could Lee deny it; Kyle obviously knew all about it, and if he knew all about it, maybe he knew . . . Lee decided to have out with it, then. What did he have to lose?

"All right, sure. I'm kind of involved with her. So what? You gonna fire me for that? I'm still the best dishman you ever seen. And since we're on the subject, I want you to tell me something."

"Sure, Winny. Anything."

Lee lowered his voice, sickened by the images that the question conjured. "What the hell happened to her?"

"What do you mean?"

"You know what I mean. You said you've been working with her for years. Somebody's done all kinds of disgusting shit to her."

Kyle ordered another Jack from the medicine-ball-bellied keep. "Oh, you mean the scars and all that."

"Yeah."

"I told you, man, we get these groaty dolts from all over the place—Mexico, the Phillipines, East Europe. They work like dogs, and for peanuts. Lot of them used to be whores and strippers and stuff like that. You ever seen the gross shit a Mexican or Phillipino hooker'll do for a buck? Just about anything. They're all like that. They've seen it all, believe me. S&M, bondage, the works."

Lee stared off. Could this be true? *A prostitute,* he thought. He didn't care—it wasn't her fault. People from third world countries were products of environment, they had to do whatever they could to survive. But the possibility only saddened him further, that some people clearly weren't as fortunate as others. . . .

"What'choo lookin' at, gramps?" Kyle exclaimed across the bar. The roughened old men looked away.

"Whole fuckin' town's like this, Ollie. It gets on my nerves."

"They've been staring at us since we walked in," Lee told him.

"Of course they have. We're the outsiders here in this pisshole of a burg. We're the people from The Inn."

"What?"

"You've heard the stories," Kyle said. "The place is supposed to be haunted. Used to be an insane asylum, and they killed the patients and sold 'em to labs and medical schools, shit like that. Up your ass, pops!" he nearly shouted again, giving one of the old men the finger.

"Pay up and get out, buddy," the big, mutton-chopped barkeep ordered. "We don't want your kind here."

"My pleasure." Kyle slapped down a twenty and put on his coat. "I'd put my foot up your big redneck ass except I'd ruin a perfectly good shoe, and the same goes for all of you backwoods fuckers."

"Get out, or I throw you out."

Kyle gave him the finger. "See ya tomorrow, Slim," he said to Lee. "You know, at the *Haunted Inn? At the insane asylum just up the road?*"

Kyle stormed out, the door banging behind him. The old men were muttering amongst themselves, glaring. The women laughed.

"Hey, I barely know the guy," Lee explained to the keep, who lumbered away with a grimace. "Your twin brother Kyle was just here," Lee told Dan B. upon the chef's return.

"That snide cocker?" Dan B. made a face. "Glad I missed him."

"He says the reason we're getting the once-over is because all these people think The Inn is some kind of haunted mansion."

255

Dan B. ordered another beer. "Not that crap again. Donna was reading about it in that kooky book of hers. These townspeople got a hard-on for The Inn—it brings back bad memories. You know, all the torture and shit that supposedly went on there, and all this shit about ghosts. These oldtimers here? They're old enough to remember. The book says it was the townspeople themselves that set fire to the place." Dan B. chuckled. "Can't say that I blame them. I wouldn't want a haunted insane asylum in my back yard either. Brings down the property values." Then he laughed.

Lee laughed too, but only half-heartedly. The old men at the end of the bar continued to stare at them. *Ghosts,* he thought, looking back into his beer. He didn't believe in them; the whole thing was silly.

But then he remembered the noises he'd been hearing at night, and he—well—

He couldn't help but wonder.

Vera couldn't help but wonder. She lay awake in bed, unable to sleep. *Too much on my mind.* But how much of it was even legitimate? Chief Mulligan's strange implications, and Feldspar's even stranger behavior at dinner. Then there was that well-dressed thuggish-looking man who Kyle was checking into a suite close to midnight. . . .

Go to sleep, for God's sake, she whined at herself. The bedroom's darkness felt thick with heat. *What the hell time does Kyle close room service?* she wondered next, noting by her alarm clock that it was now past 3 A.M. She could hear the doors of the RS elevators opening and closing. . . .

thunk-thunk . . . thunk-thunk . . . thunk-thunk—

It went on all night now, every night.

Then she heard—

What the . . . She got out of bed, exasperated. Moonlight tinted the carpet eerily across the room. She padded for the door.

Footsteps, she thought.

Yes, she felt sure this time. She'd heard footsteps out in the hall.

She clicked the bedroom door open, peeked out. . . .

All that lit the hall this late were the little marker lights by the door to each room. She couldn't see well but well enough:

That maid, she realized.

That chunky woman with bunned hair, the one who never talked. Of course, now that she reminded herself, none of the housekeeping staff ever seemed to utter a word.

Obviously the maid had been coming from the far rooms down the floor. Lee's room, and Dan B. and Donna's. Her generic white shoes carried her silently down the hall. *What's she doing up here this late?* Vera wondered. Vera's own little group of rental suites were located at the other end of the wing, and no one had been checked into any of them. Just Kyle's rooms on the upper floors. So what could this maid be doing *here?*

Then . . .

Vera squinted out. As the maid walked on, another figure appeared, just stepping onto the landing. Vera wasn't sure but—

Donna? It that . . . Donna?

The figure passed the maid without a word or so much as a glance. After another few steps, Vera knew her eyes didn't deceive her.

It is Donna, she recognized.

Another mystery. Donna had gone to bed hours ago. What was she doing coming up from downstairs at this hour? There was no reason for Donna to be downstairs now. And—

What the hell! Vera thought next.

Now she simply *couldn't* believe her eyes.

Donna was dressed in nothing but that racy lingerie she'd bought in town the other day. . . .

The darkness swarmed. Even in the feeble light, Donna's state of attire could not be dismissed as a trick of the eye. The stout breasts shone more than plain in the sheer nippleless lace bra. Even more than plain was the thick plot of pubic hair revealed by the diminutive crotchless panties. . . .

"Donna!" Vera whispered. *"Donna!"*

Her friend approached, or at least seemed to—

"Donna, what in God's name are you doing walking around The Inn dressed in—"

—and then she walked *right past* Vera without reply or even recognition. Donna's face, in the grainy dark, looked blank.

Then she went into her bedroom and closed the door quietly behind her.

This is ridiculous! Vera seethed. Sure, she was whispering, but it was a pretty fierce whisper, and there was no way Donna wouldn't have seen her standing in her own doorway.

Vera stepped out into the hall, approached Donna's door, and raised her fist to knock. . . .

But at once she felt too embarrassed. What would she say? And surely she'd wake up Dan B. *Maybe she has some sleep disorder,* she then reluctantly considered. And as her thoughts ticked, standing there before Donna's door, she . . . *smelled* something.

Oh no, she thought.

The smell, just the faintest trace, could not be mistaken, and that made her think at once of the bottle of rail liquor she'd found hidden beside the fireplace. . . .

Downstairs.

Donna, her friend, but the reformed alcoholic nonetheless.

And this was what she smelled in the air at Donna's door: Scotch.

Chapter Twenty-three

"Right in there," she heard Kyle's voice beyond her office doorway the next morning. Vera looked up from the weekly stock inventories spread across her desk. A man stood there—not *a* man, she realized at once, but *the* man she'd seen checking in last night.

The thug, she thought.

"Ms. Abbot?"

"Yes, come in. Can I help you?"

"I'm Terrence Taylor, and I represent an accounting firm," the man said. He entered casually and sat down. "We're called Morton-Gibson Ltd."

"Nice to meet you, Mr. Taylor," Vera said, slightly off guard. *An accounting firm?* This didn't sound right, not from a man whom just hours ago she suspected of being a mafioso lieutenant.

Taylor was ruggedly handsome, with dark hair combed straight back. He wore an elegant dark suit, a rich steel-blue, and he seemed fit, like a city yuppie. "Your facility is very nice," he went on, "very well appointed. And my suite on the second floor was charming."

Second floor! Vera thought. *That's not one of Kyle's suites, that's one of mine! He checked someone in and didn't even tell me!* But before Vera's mental rage could go on, Taylor added, "A bit noisy, if you don't mind an objective grievance, but still, a very nice accommodation. Anyway, we heard about your recent opening, so my bosses sent me up here to have a look around and to see if you'd be interested in our services."

Vera let her previous anger tick down. "Well, uh," she stammered, "we're not having any accounting problems to my knowledge, and even if we were, I'm afraid I wouldn't be the person to talk to about that."

"Oh, I'm sorry. I was told you were the manager."

"The restaurant manager," Vera corrected. "You'd want to talk to Mr. Feldspar." She immediately regretted saying this; Feldspar obviously wasn't interested in contracting an accounting firm. "But I'm afraid he's just left for a business convention, and he won't be in for several days."

"He's in," Kyle announced, appearing at once in her doorway. *The little creep,* Vera thought. *I'll bet he's been standing out there the whole time, eavesdropping.* Her phony smile fluttered. "Oh, well in that case, would you please take this gentleman to Mr. Feldspar's office. He's an accounting contractor."

"Sure," Kyle said. "Right this way, sir."

"Nice meeting you, Ms. Abbot," Taylor bid and got up. "Before I leave, I'll be sure to have dinner at your restaurant."

"Please do," Vera said. "Oh, and Kyle? When you're done showing Mr. Taylor to Mr. Feldspar's office, could I have a word with you, please?"

"Sure, Ver."

Sure, Ver, she mimicked. Kyle showed Taylor out, and Vera's irritation trickled further. *The little prick!* And what of this Taylor fellow? A mafia thug? He was obviously just an errand boy for an accounting firm, looking for business. *Some thug,* she thought. *Some mob boss.*

"What's up Ver?" Kyle had returned, loping back into her office. Vera immediately got up, closed the door, and yelled, "Who the hell do you think you are checking a guest into one of *my suites* without even telling me!"

Kyle stepped back, sporting an amused grin. "Simmer down, will ya? What's the big deal?"

"The big deal is that guy was one of *my* customers, and therefore it was *my* job to have him taken care of."

"Hey, my people took care of him. Relax."

"Bullshit, Kyle! The second-floor suites are mine, and you know it! Don't you ever do that to me again!"

"Jesus, Vera," Kyle said, still not wiping off his grin. "The guy checked in late, you weren't around, so I—"

"That's a bunch of shit! I was right there in the restaurant! You should have come in and gotten me!"

Kyle shrugged, but the smartass grin never waned. "I didn't want to interrupt your dinner with Mr. Feldspar."

How did he know about that? And who had told him? Was it Feldspar? And if so, what did he say? The flood of insecure questions clogged in her head all at once. She couldn't think of anything sensible to say. "And what about the convention?"

"What about it?"

"Feldspar told me last night he was going to a convention in Maryland today."

"You mean *Mr.* Feldspar," Kyle snidely corrected. "And what are you all bent out of shape about? He was going to go to the convention, and then he changed his mind. So what?"

Vera steamed. "He *changed his mind?* Without telling me?"

"Why should he tell you?" Kyle laughed. "You're just the restaurant manager."

Vera's rage swamped her. "Just . . . get out of here."

"Sure, but hey—" Kyle's grin flared over his shoulder. "How about you and me going for another swim tonight—"

"Get out!"

She heard him laughing in the hall, which made her even more angry. *Punk!* she thought. She tapped her pen on her invoices. Just as she was beginning to settle down, Dan B. walked in, his chef's apron tight around his considerable midsection. "Hey, Vera, we're about out of Frangelico, so I won't be able to run the Mushrooms Cracow with Hazelnut sauce for the special."

Vera felt weary. "Do the Morels and Pheasant Mousse then."

"Okay," he said. "And we're fresh out of avocado butter."

Fine! I'll order more goddamn avocados! she wanted to yell. "Just try to make do without for tonight. I doubt anyone'll order it anyway." *But with my luck, everyone will.* She felt frazzled, but why? *Kyle?* she wondered. She hadn't slept well, and the dreams had returned, the seamy yet titillating dreams of The Hands. . . .

And then she remembered something else.

Who she'd seen, or thought she'd seen, in the hall.

"Dan B.? Has, uh . . ."

"Has, uh, what?" Dan B. asked, looking at her a bit funny.

Vera squinted. "Has Donna been acting—you know— a little weird lately?"

"No, not at all. Why?"

Why? she asked herself. *I must have dreamed that stuff last night. What, Donna sleepwalking downstairs in crotchless panties, nipping at hidden booze?* It seemed too absurd now to even bring up. *That's it, I must've dreamed it.*

"You are, though," Dan B. volunteered.

"*I* am?"

"Acting a little weird lately."

263

Vera considered this. She guessed it was true. "Yeah, I confess. Kyle's ticking me off again."

"Still scoping your milk wagons, huh?"

Vera winced. Male lexicon seemed at no loss for sexist references to female physiology. "I thought it was rib melons, Dan B."

"Rib melons, milk wagons—same thing," Dan B. defined. "Just let me know when you want me to lock the asshole in my walk-in for a few days. See ya."

Dan B. was about to leave, then turned back. "One thing, though. Lee's been acting a little weird too."

"How so?"

"I don't know." Dan B. fingered his chin. "But I can tell something's bugging him."

"Maybe he's just homesick," Vera offered.

"Nah, no way—he hated the city. He just seems down, you know, distracted or something. And he acts even weirder whenever that maid is around. You know, the one with her hair in a bun?"

Yeah, the one I saw last night at three in the morning, walking away from—

Vera felt a little jolt.

Lee's room. . . .

"I don't know," Dan B. went on. "It's probably nothing. Anyway, I'll see you at dinner."

" 'Bye."

Vera's perplexity sat on her shoulder like a bothersome parrot; weird things seemed to be amassing, none of which she could even begin to figure. Dan B.'s departure made her feel sullen in the office, and bored now that she'd finished the daily paperwork. When the phone rang, she snapped it up, grateful for anything to get her mind off her confusion.

"Is this The Inn?" a rough, rusty voice asked.

"Yes, it is, and I'm Vera Abbot. Can I help you?"

"Yeah, ma'am, well maybe you can. This is Sergeant

Greg Valentine, Waynesville Police. Our dispatcher's 10–6 log has Chief Mulligan dropping by your inn yesterday. That true?''

"Yes," Vera said, though she had no idea what a 10–6 log could be. "It was yesterday morning; I talked to him myself."

"How long was he there, ma'am?"

"Only a short time. Twenty minutes maybe."

"Then he left?"

What an odd question. *No, you moron, he pitched a tent in the atrium. Right now he's roasting marshmellows in the fireplace.* "He left immediately after talking to me, Sergeant," she eventually answered. "Is there a problem?"

"Well . . . yeah ma'am there is." A pause wavered on the line. "No one's heard hide nor hair of Chief Mulligan since."

Such wonders, the Factotum mused.

Everything in the nave seemed to be shimmering in sizzling candlelight, even the dull rock walls. Zyra was off tending to the women, while Lemi commenced with the usual preparations.

Yes, every night a new and separate wonder!

Mosaics of light seemed to swarm atop his bald head, as dazzling as his visions and his thoughts. Could there be a greater honor than this, or a greater blessing?

Oh, my most resplendent lord, I am bound to serve you. . . .

Under his cassock, his hairless chest tingled with the beat of his heart. His blood felt hot in his veins, hot with duty, hot with joy. That's all he could remember, for as long as he'd lived: the delicious, sultry joy of giving this bounden service, this homage, this witness. . . .

Rending the fat one had been noisy; the Factotum smiled as Lemi, as always, expertly slit the bulging belly from groin to sternum. The organs within swelled forward through the crack as if by pressure. Arms red to the elbows, then, Lemi extracted the dead heart, held it high much like an offering to a god—

—then laughed and tossed it in the trash.

Sacrifice? the Factotum thought in jest. But in a way it was. Everything they did, and had always done, was in a sense a sacrifice to greater things.

"There's one dead fat cop," Lemi remarked.

"Yes, poor Chief Mulligan," the Factotum added. "He won't be bothering us anymore . . ."

And with that, Lemi raised the hatchet and cut off the police chief's head.

Chapter Twenty-four

It was Paul's good fortune that he'd never actually met McGowen, though Vera had griped about him endlessly: an obnoxious, ill-mannered slob who had a knack for sexually harassing the waitresses. McGowen, nevertheless, was The Emerald Room's general manager, and Vera's boss when she'd worked there. Vera's sudden departure had left the Emerald in managerial chaos, so it stood to reason that McGowen would be all too eager to help Paul out.

Provided he fell for the lie . . .

"Yes, Mr. McGowen, my name's Kevin Sullivan," Paul said, "and I was wondering if you could help me. I work for a collection agency. Of course I realize that you might not want to help me at all, since a general manager might feel a sense of loyalty towards an employee."

McGowen smirked, corpulent behind his cluttered office desk. Unconsciously, he picked his nose. "Which employee are we talking about?"

"A Vera Abbot."

McGowen's eyes thinned like those of a cat spying fresh prey. Then he smiled. "Well you can bet I don't have a whole lot of loyalty for Vera Abbot. The bitch quit without even putting in proper notice, and she conned three of my best employees to quit too. She left the place in a shambles, we're still recovering.''

And it's a good thing you don't know who I am, Mr. McGowen, Paul thought, *'cause I'm the reason she quit.* ''Oh, I'm sorry to hear that.''

An unnoticed booger seemed to dangle from McGowen's sandy mustache. ''Sullivan, huh? A collection agency? What, Abbot owes money?''

''Indeed she does, Mr. McGowen, quite a bit of money,'' Paul lied further. ''She owes thousands and thousands of dollars on her credit cards.''

''Anything I can do to help you burn that bitch, just ask.''

Ahhhh, Paul thought. *It worked! Finally I'm getting somewhere.* ''She's been ignoring our calls and notices for quite some time, and when I paid a visit to the address on her credit application, the landlord told me she no longer lived there. And she left no forwarding address. Did she by chance leave one with you?''

''Not a residential address. But she did leave her new employer's address with me for her tax forms and W-2. Would that help you out?''

Paul had to consciously resist shouting out with glee. ''Yes, Mr. McGowen. That would help me out more than you can imagine.''

When the night wound down, Vera retreated to her office to tabulated receipts. *Forty-seven dinners tonight!* she nearly rejoiced. *An all-time high!* At least it was something. After all, The Carriage House hadn't been open that long, and though these numbers were nothing to rave about compared to The Emerald Room's typical receipts, it was a clear indication that business was looking up. Vera even felt inclined to scoot over to room service and brag, but then she remembered that even the restaurant's all-time high would be significantly less than the nightly RS receipts. *Why give Kyle an excuse to rub my nose in poop?* she reasoned.

"Can you believe it?" Donna remarked, suddenly sauntering in. "It's the third night this week that the mayor came, and tonight he brought a bunch of town council members!"

"Tip City, huh?" Vera said.

"I did great." Donna seemed calmly elated. "Didn't I tell you things would start to get better?"

Yeah. But Vera's mood flattened, as Donna counted out her tips. *She looks fine,* Vera observed. *The same old Donna.* Vera thought again of what she'd seen last night: Donna sleepwalking past her door, reeking of alcohol. But if Donna had relapsed, wouldn't it be obvious, wouldn't the telltale signs have reemerged? The dull listlessness, the facial pallor and anguish lines, the overall crushed features of the alcoholic? Vera noticed none of that, so again she had to conclude that she must have dreamed the whole thing. It made sense, given the stress of the new job combined fitful, dream-laden sleep. . . .

"You okay?"

Vera looked up from her ponderings. "Yeah, why do you ask?"

"Well . . ." Donna hesitated. "You're acting a little weird lately, a little depressed."

Dan B. had said the same thing. "I don't know, I guess I—"

"You're still letting Paul get to you," Donna said. It wasn't even a suggestion—it was a statement. "If you want my opinion, you need to confront him. It won't be easy, but it's something you need to do. You need to go and tell him off, give him a piece of your mind, tell him to his face that he's a piece of shit for what he did to you."

Vera supposed she knew this all along but was deliberately avoiding the issue. And she *had* avoided it, hadn't she? For weeks she'd been telling herself that eventually she would return to the apartment to pick up some of her things, but she always found some excuse not to. *That's all I'm doing with my life right now—making excuses.*

"Don't make excuses," Donna said, ever the psychic. "You're pretty easy to read, Vera. Why not just get it over with?"

"I know you're right." Vera fingered a paperweight. "I'll go soon."

"No, you'll go tomorrow. There's no reason to put it off anymore. You'll feel a lot better once you get it over with, believe me. Tomorrow. No more excuses. If you run late, we can handle things in the restaurant till you get back."

Vera nodded. *She's right. It's time.* "All right, I'll go tomorrow—"

"You'll see. If you don't let it out, it'll simmer inside you forever. Go tell that scumbag off."

"I will," Vera agreed. "Tomorrow. I promise."

"And, besides, once you've got Paul out of your system, you can start thinking about getting laid again!" Donna was kind enough to add, laughing at Vera's quick smirk. "Anyway, I'm off to bed; I'm absolutely exhausted."

"Good night."

"Oh, and remember, my offer's always good. Anytime you want to borrow my doctor, just let me know."

"Your *doctor?*" Vera queried.

"Yeah . . . Doc Johnson!" Donna finished, and left the office before a trial of more laughter.

Laugh it up, Vera thought. She was weary of everyone implying she was a cranky, sex-starved bitch—

Even though it's true. . . .

It annoyed her, that her thoughts so often roved to sex. It made her feel inadequate. Whenever she saw Kyle, or even heard his name, she thought of her dream, the fantasy of The Hands, a dream she now admitted she looked forward to. And lately, she'd caught herself appraising male restaurant customers in secret—checking them out, envisioning their bodies minus clothes, wondering what they'd be like in bed.

And then there was always Feldspar. . . .

I wonder what he'd be like—

She grit her teeth, shook her head. *What is WRONG with you! You're fantasizing about sleeping with your boss!*

But the image behind the question lingered, as much as she tried to banish it.

She poured herself a little wine, to relax. She hated to think of Feldspar's reaction were he to know that such things crossed her mind. She could not deny it, though: Feldspar attracted her, in some odd, incalculable way. It was the man's mystery, she supposed.

Kyle, on the other hand, she was attracted to only in the roughest sense. *Purely physical,* she told herself. It *couldn't* be anything more than physical, she knew, because she couldn't stand him as a person. *Snide, egotistical, smartass.* But . . .

So good-looking.

She began to feel sluggishly excited. She was tired—it had been a long day—yet she knew the root of her excitement. Soon, she'd go to sleep and dream. She only wished she could exchange the sponsor of the fantasy—Kyle—with someone she liked, or just anyone, anyone other than the rude room-service manager. *Chief Mulligan?* she thought and laughed to herself. An obese redneck twenty years her senior? *No thanks.* But that reminded her of the bizarre call she'd gotten today, the police sergeant reporting that Mulligan hadn't been seen since yesterday. *Probably passed out at Elks Lodge.* And then she remembered that other man, the accounting hawk, Taylor. To think she'd actually believed he was really a mob lieutenant! *But he was definitely good-looking,* her sex-muse continued. *Handsome, fit.*

Evidently, Feldspar had sent him packing. Taylor had said he'd be dining at the restaurant, but Vera hadn't seen him all night. *What are you thinking now?* she questioned herself. *What, you were going to make a play for him? Have sex with him in his suite? For all intents, a perfect stranger?* Preposterous.

Nevertheless, she felt curious as to whether or not Taylor had had dinner at The Carriage House, as he'd said he would. Certainly, as a scout for an accounting firm, Taylor would have a company credit card for business expenses. She flipped through night's credit receipts but—

No Terrence Taylor, she discovered.

Kyle had checked Taylor into one of Vera's suites. Next, she checked her room register to see when Taylor had checked out.

That's weird . . .

According to the register, Mr. Terrence Taylor, Room 201, never checked out at all.

He'd checked *in* instead—

Good Christ . . .

—into a nightmare.

When Mr. Terrence Taylor's eyes finally opened, all he could see at first was an ill-lit wash of murk. His legs felt numb, and a headache gnawed his brain. *What the fuck happened?*

Taylor's memory struggled back . . .

That guy! What was his name? Kyle? He'd taken him to meet this Feldspar fellow, the general manager, but

272

he hadn't been in his office. "Oh, that's right, he's in the stockroom checking in a morning shipment. Follow me."

Sure, Taylor thought. *But hurry it up, will ya? Wrestling comes on in a half hour.* Kyle led him down a cramped hallway behind the front offices, which seemed an odd access to a supply room. And—*wait a minute. Why would Feldspar be tending to a supply delivery?* Taylor had been a manager himself once, at a T.G.I.F in Charlotte. Inventory and supply receipt was the service manager's job, not the *general* manager's. . . .

Along the way, they passed several housemaids who were not exactly . . . provocative in the looks department. Sullen. Pasty-faced. Fat. One, with breasts like flaccid goldfish bowls, seemed to shrink at the sight of Kyle. *If you were the last girl in town,* Taylor thought, *I'd be cutting holes in watermelons. You better forget about trying out for that Cosmo cover, baby.*

A large security door stood at the end of the hall. ROOM SERVICE STAFF ONLY, read a plaque. Kyle unlocked it, and showed Taylor in. "The first pantry," Kyle indicated.

Pantry? Taylor wondered. "I thought we were going to the supply room."

"We are. Right in here."

Taylor viewed the long kitchen, amid vague cooking smells. *Pretty complete set-up,* he appraised. Sure as hell more complete than the kitchen at T.G.I.F. Everything looked brand new. Along the back wall behind the prep line stood three heavily padlocked pantry doors, the first of which Kyle unlocked. *They're awfully security conscious around here,* Taylor concluded.

"Mr. Feldspar's right in here," Kyle said.

It never occurred to Taylor (not the most deductive of men) to wonder why the general manager of The Inn would be behind a *padlocked* door. He was too worried

273

about making his pitch. He straightened his tie and lapels, then his hair, then checked to make sure his phony Rolex was still ticking. Yeah, it would be great to sell this Feldspar guy a bookkeeping contract. The company needed more business, and Taylor sure could use a contract himself since he worked on commission. At least at T.G.I.F. he'd gotten a salary.

Then:

What the hell is this? he thought when he entered the pantry.

The pantry was smaller than a trailer bedroom. And it was—

Empty, Taylor realized.

Nothing on the shelves because there *were* no shelves. No foodstocks, no supplies—

"What gives?" Taylor began to turn. "This is no pantry—"

And before he could finish turning, Kyle had the garrot around his neck nice and tight. Taylor tried to yell but no sound came out. His fingers tried to dig in under the garrot. His heart beat to explode. . . .

Kyle was chuckling from behind, tightening the cord. The buttons on Taylor's suit jacket flew off as he struggled. Next, he was powered to the floor, his Florsheim's thunking the walls. The cord around his throat tightening in increments; Taylor felt his face swell up. He was a strong man, more than a match for this psycho Kyle, yet every expenditure of his energy proved a waste. Not much more than shock and pure, primitive terror coursed through his brain. Beyond that, however distantly, he somehow sensed that he was . . . descending.

Kyle's knee pressed against Taylor's neck; the garrot continued to tighten. And next:

A gush of air. A block of bright light.

Feet thumping, his eyes fit to launch from his skull, Taylor was dragged out by the throat. "Right this way,

Mr. Taylor,'' Kyle mocked, his face huge in Taylor's warped vision. "Mr. Feldspar seems to be detained for the moment, but I'm sure that *we* can take care of you."

"Oh, we'll take care of him, all right," another voice issued. It was clearly a woman's voice, rough and densely sultry. Two more hands were on him now. His brain starved of blood, Taylor could think now only in snatches and obscure chunks of terror. As he felt himself being lifted up onto some sort of table, his consciousness began to dim out. . . .

"Aw, shit!" complained the woman's voice. "He's dead already. Why'd you kill him so fast? We could've had some fun first."

Kyle's hands came away. The garrot lost its tension. "Well, what difference does it make if he's dead?"

"Yeah, I guess you're right." The woman laughed. "We can still have a little fun at that."

Blood swam back into Taylor's brain—

They think I'm dead, he thought.

Unseen hands next were pulling off his slacks.

"Oooo! Red undies!" exclaimed the woman. "How sexy. I just hate plain old white shorts on a man."

Don't move! Taylor thought beyond the madness of what was being done to him. *Play dead! Let them think you're dead!*

Not an easy task, considering what happened next. His fancy red undershorts were skimmed off, and, very quickly—

"Holy shit!" Taylor yelled, lurching on the table.

"How do you like that? He's not dead after all—"

A bottle cracked Taylor in the head, then shattered. His brain bounced within his skull.

"Yeah, that ought to calm him down a little."

Only then did Mr. Terrence Taylor pass out for real. But just before that final spark of his consciousness faded away, he did indeed realize what exactly what was being done to him:

He was being very enthusiastically sodomized.

Eventually it all came back. No details, just the barren facts. *The fuckers tried to kill me. . . .* His vision, and consciousness, returned to him in little drips. Pain roared in his skull.

Where am I now? he struggled to wonder.

He lay flat on his back, elevated. *A table,* he thought. It felt cold beneath him. His eyes roved behind slitted lids, against cold white light, but his vision remained too blurred to make out any features of the place; beyond just a few feet, objects turned to blobs.

Then he heard . . . whistling.

Very slowly, Taylor turned his head to the right. Just a yard off a figure stood with his back to him. *It's that Kyle psycho*, Taylor realized. *The fucker that tried to strangle me, the fucker that—*

Well, Taylor didn't finish *that* thought. He squinted on. Kyle was whistling as he tended to some unseen task at what appeared to be a long stainless-steel table.

Like the prep tables he'd seen earlier, and the ones he remembered when he'd worked at T.G.I.F. A kitchen. A restaurant kitchen. Was that where he was?

Taylor strained his eyes. The effort steepened the throbbing pain in his head, but soon his vision began to clear.

He craned his neck off the table, staring. Then his thoughts ground to a halt. . . .

Kyle was fileting strips of meat off a long bone, and placing each strip in a pan. Yes, it was meat, all right—

Human meat.

For what Taylor made out next, as his vision continued to focus, were the two bare human legs lain out across the table before Kyle.

What in God's name . . . is this place?

This was a reasonable question, but by now the answer scarcely mattered, at least not to Mr. Terrence Taylor. Because in the next moment he became aware of an even more atrocious fact:

He managed to rise up on his elbows.

He looked down.

Oh my God no holy Jesus—

It was'nt enough that the legs on Kyle's cutting table were human. When Taylor looked down—

—holy Jesus holy Jesus to God . . .

—he realized, upon the sight of his own short-stumped hips, that the legs Kyle was so calmly fileting were his own.

"Well would you look at this!" Kyle had turned, noticing Taylor over his shoulder. "You're *still* alive? I'm impressed, Mr. Taylor. Not many guys could go through what you been through and still be kicking." Kyle smiled, picking something up. "But I think we can fix that real quick."

Taylor shuddered as if encased in ice. He tried to get up but, of course, that prospect wasn't very good since his fucking legs were no longer connected to his body.

Kyle, still whistling, inserted the long, thin Sheffield fileting knife directly into Terrence Taylor's right eye. When the tip of the blade met the back of the eye socket, Kyle smacked the butt with his palm, driving the blade deep into the brain.

Terrence Taylor croaked aloud. He should have stayed at T.G.I.F.

"I'll bet you're dead now," Kyle remarked.

For good measure, he gave the knife a couple of quick, hard jiggles. Then he withdrew it and went back to fileting the legs on the opposing prep table. He was whistling "Sweetest Legs I Ever Did See" by Robert Johnson.

Chapter Twenty-five

He's here, Vera thought.

Or at least his car was. At once, butterflies careened in her stomach. *In less than a minute, I'll be talking to him. I'll be standing right in front of him. Paul.*

This realization caused a surge of the most unpleasant dread. A thousand excuses came to mind, to get out of it, but then she remembered what Donna had advised. Until she gave herself the chance to have her final word, she'd never be at peace, she'd never get the memory fully out of her psyche. As unnerved as she was, Vera knew there was no other way.

She parked the Lamborghini in the apartment lot, sat a moment, then got out. The cold chafed her, wisping down her chest through her collar despite her efforts to keep it clasped shut. She looked up at the apartment, and felt hollow. . . .

Don't think about it. Don't think about anything, she insisted to herself. *Just go up there, get your stuff, tell him he's an asshole, and leave.*

The long drive from Waynesville back to the city had been neutral and numb, despite the initial scenery and open, winding roads. What would her reaction be, seeing Paul again for the first time in months, for the first time since . . .

The hideous *ménage à trois* played in her mind, and the look in Paul's eyes when he'd glanced up from the bed. An expression empty of recognition, empty of any sort of care whatsoever.

She seemed to be shoving against a great, invisible weight when she walked up the steps. Full minutes passed while she stood at the front door, staring at it. Should she knock? She should let herself in with her key? Maybe Paul wasn't alone—

Maybe he's in there right now with one of his drug-head perverted little girlfriends, she considered.

God. That was one scenario she didn't even want to think about much less see again.

Then her mind strayed. *Maybe I should forget about this. I'll just tell Donna that I told him off. What good will any of this really do? It's not necessary. It's stupid.*

But then another, more sensible voice screamed at her. *Bullshit, Vera! You're going to go in there! Right now! You're not going to chicken out!*

All right, all right, she agreed with herself. She withdrew her key, took a deep breath, and opened the door.

She expected a mess, and contrived den of drugs and iniquity, but when she stepped into the living room, it looked exactly as she remembered it: neat and tidy, everything in its place. *What do I do now?* she wondered. She felt imbecilic standing there. *Just walk down the hall, go into the bedroom, and get it over with.*

She turned, took one step into the hall—

Paul nearly walked into her.

"Dammit, Paul!" Vera yelled. "You scared the shit out of me!"

Paul had turned out of the hall just as she had turned into it. The moment held him in a mute shock. He blinked hard and stared—then rejoiced: "Vera! You're back!"

"Yeah, I'm back to get my things," she said, and

brushing by him. "And that's it." She stormed into the bedroom, expecting to see evidence of Paul's decadent secret life, but the bedroom, like the rest of the apartment, was clean and orderly. Come to think of it, Paul himself looked . . . *normal,* she considered. Dressed in jeans and the typical flannel shirt he wore when he wrote. He looked like the Paul she'd always known, not a sadomasochistic drug denizen she'd seen the last time she was in this room.

Paul jabbered as he scampered behind her. "Vera, Vera! I've been looking all over for you! We really need to talk!"

"No, Paul. *We* don't need to talk, *I* need to talk." She traipsed about the room, but, now that she was here, she really couldn't think of anything she wanted. *So just say what you came here to say,* she resolved.

"You're a deceitful, cheating scumbag, Paul," she said, staring him down. "I can't believe what you did to me, and by now I don't even care—"

"But—but—" Paul stammered.

"And that's really all I came here to say Paul. You're a—"

"But Vera!"

"—lecherous, disgraceful—"

"Please, listen to me!"

"—disgusting—"

"Vera! No!"

"—piece of shit."

They faced each other then, in thickening silence. *That should shut him up,* Vera thought. *Watch. Next I'll bet he'll say something really original, like 'You don't understand' or 'Let me explain.' What a pathetic schmuck.*

"I know what you must think, and I know how you feel," he began.

"No, you don't!" she spat back. She rummaged

through the closet, then the dresser. All her old things refaced her now, but they seemed tainted, poisoned. She didn't even want them anymore. "You don't know how I feel, and you don't give a shit anyway," she finished.

Paul tremored in place. "Vera, at least let me explain."

Vera laughed. Yes, so predictable. "What's to *explain*, Paul?" Then she marched out of the bedroom and back down the hall. "But since you're so talkative, tell me this? How long were you cheating on me?"

He followed her, frantic. "Vera, I *never* cheated on you! I swear it!"

She had to look at him in the utmost incredulity. His audacity astounded her. "Oh, and you were just playing hopscotch with those two girls I caught you with . . . Well, one of them was a girl. I don't know *what* the other one was."

Paul's face appeared corrugated as he groped for words. "Please, Vera, listen to me, I'm *begging* you. I don't remember much about what happened that night but—"

"Um-hum, and let me guess. You smoke marijuana too, but you never inhale."

"I know what I did was wrong, but, really, Vera, it wasn't my fault."

"Oh, so whose fault was it then? The girls? They put a gun to your head and forced you to have sex with them? They *made* you snort cocaine? Is that it?"

"I don't even think it was cocaine, I don't know what it was. I was sick for days afterwards," Paul yammered. "But at least hear me out, Vera. Please—"

Vera crossed her arms, smirking. "All right, Paul. I'll give you one minute."

Paul sat down on the couch, pushed his hair off his brow. "That night, you remember—I went to Kaggies to do my piece on the downtown singles scene. Those two girls showed up, and I *swear* I never saw them before, and, yes, I started talking to them. But I never had any intention of . . . you know—"

"Of fucking them," Vera assisted. "While I was at work."

"It's not like that at all," he pleaded. "All I did was have a drink with them. I wanted to talk with them, I wanted to hear their perceptions about singles bars and stuff. Next thing I know we're back here, and all kinds of weird stuff is happening. I didn't know what I was doing, I wasn't myself at all. I think—I think they must've put something in my drink."

Vera's eyes turned in her head. "Paul, that is the lamest bunch of crap I've ever heard anyone say. You've got to be out of your gourd if you expect me to believe that cock and bull."

"Vera, I swear, it's true, they put some drug in my beer that made me nuts. I didn't even know who I was. I was unconscious for two days. I missed my deadline. I lost my job . . ."

"Good," Vera told him. "You deserve to lose your job for talking such ridiculous shit."

Paul's face fell into his hands. Suddenly he was sobbing. "Aw, God, Vera, please believe me. And please, please forgive me . . ."

"Forgive you? What, and then we'll just pick up where we left off? Just forget it ever happened, and everything'll be peachy? Is that what you want?"

Even he must realize how foolish he sounded. His face was wet now when he looked up at her. "We had so many plans, didn't we? We had a life together. You want to throw that all away?"

For a fraction of a second, Vera paused. It was true. They did have plans, wonderful plans. They did have a life together; what they had together, in fact, was what she wanted more than anything in the world. They'd had it all—

And he destroyed it all, she thought.

"I'm leaving now, Paul—

"No, please!"

"—and I hope I never see you again."

Now Paul sobbed outright. It was so pathetic to see him cry; it was also *very* satisfying. His words hitched out of his throat like a ratchet: "I'm begging you, Vera, please forgive me. Please don't go . . . I love you, Vera."

Vera had her hand on the doorknob; again, she paused. *I love you,* he'd just said. How many other men had said that to her in her life, with any degree of genuineness? *None,* she knew.

Her pause at the door wavered. . . .

Don't fall for it, Vera, that other voice crept back into her head.

"I love you, Vera."

Don't be a sucker!

No, no, she wouldn't be. She wouldn't let him do this to her. Hadn't he done enough already?

"Your love is like the rest of you, Paul. It's fake. It's a lie. It's pure grade-A shit."

Then she walked out and very quietly closed the door behind her.

She cruised downtown in the Lamborghini, sorting her thoughts. At first she felt very confused; she ran two red lights on Church Circle and nearly drove the wrong way down Main Street. *Get hold of yourself, you airhead!* She doubted that Feldspar would be pleased were she to bring the 'ghini back to The Inn with a bashed-in front end. She parked at the City Dock, buttoned up her coat, and got out to walk in the cold.

Full winter made the city look flattened and drab. Most of the boat slips were vacant; the few that weren't berthed tarp-covered bulks. Her heels ticked on the cement as she wandered about the city's deserted nub. Frigid wind clawed at her like a molestor's frantic hands.

Was she having second thoughts? How *could* she, after what she'd seen that night? *They put drugs in his beer,* she remembered. He could at least manufacture a better lie than that! Suddenly it didn't matter that he regretted what he'd done; it didn't even matter that he claimed to still love her. She knew she could never see him again, never even consider him. Vera had always tried never to hold a person's past against him (wasn't Donna, a former alcoholic, a perfect example?), but this was sorely different. Drugs, bondage, group sex? She'd be out of her mind. . . .

You did the right thing, Vera. You'd never be able to trust him again.

Yes, she felt sure of that, and all at once she felt a lot better. Donna had been right all along: once she confronted him, once she told him off for good, she'd feel like a new person. All her stresses and uncertainties fled from her, right there on the cold, cobblestoned incline of Main Street.

She felt cleansed, exorcised. The drab city seemed brighter now, and clean, as if she'd just stepped into a different, better world.

Now I can really get on with my life!

Before she returned to the parking lot, she stepped into the Main Street Crown, to browse. She hadn't read a book in months, save for that ludicrous tome about haunted mansions. A good romance would be nice, something hot. She picked several titles off the rack, and smiled when she turned and noticed the occult/new age

285

section right behind her. *The Complete Compendium of Demons,* the title of the big glossy-black hardcover jumped out at her. *By Richard Long!* she noted, *the same guy who wrote the haunted mansion book!* Vera couldn't resist. *I simply must buy this for Donna,* she decided. *She'll definitely get a kick out of it.*

After she bought the books, she considered stopping into The Undercroft for lunch, but then thought better of it. No doubt she'd run into people she knew, who would all ask questions about where she'd gone, and why. That part of her life was over, so why bother? *I live somewhere else now,* she thought, and got back into the car. *My life is somewhere else. . . .*

Goodbye, city.

She drove back up Main, to catch Route 50 off the Circle. She slowed but wasn't quite sure why. The streets were relatively empty, rows of shops shunned by the cold. A thin woman rushed across the street at the light, dressed in old jeans and a shale-colored overcoat. A stiff wind disheveled her short blond hair. Then, at the opposing sidewalk, she turned, obviously taking note of Vera's shiny Lamborghini.

Then she walked on.

Vera stared dumbly ahead; at first she couldn't imagine why. But when her subconscious finally clicked, she stomped the gas.

The blond woman was just turning at the Circle. Vera idled past the Old Post Office, lowering the power passenger window.

Don't make an idiot of yourself, she fretted. *Are you sure it's who you think it is?*

She was definitely sure when the blond woman, no doubt noticing that she was being followed by a brand-new two hundred thousand dollar car, stopped at the next corner and leaned over to look.

It's her!

However faint, Vera recognized the telltale tattoo: the creepy green southern cross needled into the hollow of the blond woman's throat. This was one of the women Paul was with that night.

"Excuse me," Vera raised her voice. "I'd like to talk to you."

The woman's eyes thinned, and she smiled just as thinly. She got into the car, and seemed awed when the door lowered by itself.

"What a great ride," she commented, then, oddly, she asked, "Are you a cop?"

Vera winced. "Of course not. I don't know many cops who drive Lamborghinis."

"Yeah, I guess you're right," the woman chuckled. She pushed her hair out of her eyes and briskly rubbed her hands together. "So, I guess you know the score. Guys, girls, it don't matter to me as long as the money's right."

"What?" Vera asked before really thinking.

The blonde lit a cigarette, spewing smoke as she continued. "You want to get it on, right? Fifty bucks for a half-hour, a hundred for an hour and a half. And I'll do anything you want. But you also gotta spring for the room, unless you want me to do you in the car." She chuckled again. "I've never eaten pussy in a Lamborghini. That might be kinda neat."

Oh my God, Vera finally realized. *She thinks I want to . . .* "No, no, you don't understand. I just want to talk."

The blonde shrugged. "I'll talk as dirty as you want, I'll make you soak right through to the seat, but I have to see some green first."

Vera was mortified. "I just want to talk to you, you know, just *talk*. Don't you remember me? A couple of months ago? Paul Foster? Westwind Apartments? You and some redhead—"

287

"Oooooh, yeah," the blonde slowly acknowledged with a nod. "You're the chick who walked in on us. What, you're his girlfriend?"

I thought you were his girlfriend now, Vera thought, puzzled. "I *was* his fiancé, until you and your redhaired friend got hold of him."

"Oh, now I get it. Well, don't think about starting any shit with me. None of that was my doing."

Vera's scowl felt hot. "Whatever it was you *weren't* doing, you sure as hell seemed to be enjoying it at the time."

"Look, honey, a trick's a trick. I don't ask questions when the money's on the table."

This was even worse than what she'd always thought. "You mean Paul *paid* you for sex?" The idea crushed her, it made her feel suddenly more inadequate than she'd ever felt in her life. *Was I that bad? Was I so lousy a lover that he had to go out and solicit prostitutes?*

"Not the guy," the blonde said. "The trannie."

"The *what?*"

The blonde's chuckle darkened. "The redhead. You know, the girl with the cock."

The transexual. Vera began to understand less and less with this conversation; she pulled in front of the first available meter on West Street and parked, her sensibilities in knots. "I still don't understand. You mean—"

"Hang on, all right?" insisted the blonde. She scratched absently at the cross tattoo. "A person like me, you know, whether I'm fucking or eating pussy or just talking, it's all the same. It's *time*. And you know what they say about time, don't you?"

Yeah, time is money. What a bitch! Vera passed the woman a couple of twenties. "Now, explain to me. You're saying it wasn't Paul who paid you, but the redhead?"

288

"That's right," answered the blonde, who quickly slipped the cash into a pocket. "I was trying to hustle down off Clay Street and she walks up. She said she wanted me to help her with something, and right off the bat she offers me a grand."

"A *thousand dollars!*" Vera outraged. "For what?"

"She told me there was some newspaper writer named Paul she wanted to fuck with."

"But why?"

The blonde shrugged. "I don't know, and I didn't ask. When someone drops a grand in your lap, you don't ask questions."

Vera's mind swam in all this confusion. "Well let me ask you something. Is Paul still seeing this—" Vera gulped. "—this trannie?"

"I don't know, but I doubt it. She didn't seem interested in him at all once we were done. I figured it was just some guy she wanted to fuck over for some reason."

But what was the reason? Vera wondered.

"This is how it went," the blonde went on. "She gives me a grand to play along. Wants to put the make on this writer guy who's gonna be at the bar that night. Just wants me to pretend I've heard of him and act interested. She also says there'll be plenty of free blow."

"Cocaine," Vera muttered to herself.

"Naw, this stuff wasn't coke, but whatever it was it was really top. One line and I was flying, and the stuff made me hornier than all of the Kennedys wrapped up into one. I'm telling you, just one toot and I didn't give a shit about anything except getting it on. I didn't even know who I was while I was on the shit."

Vera paused. Paul had said essentially the same thing.

"It was probably some new designer dope, wish I could get my hands on more," the blonde said. "Anyway, back to the story. Me and the redhead go to the bar and sure enough, there's this Paul guy sitting there by himself. So we start talking, drinking, and all that, and after a while we put the make on him.''

The knots of Vera's confusion tightened maddeningly. *All right, the girls put the make on him,* she thought. But that was still no excuse, was it? ''And he obviously went along with it.''

The blonde lit another cigarette, glancing at her watch. ''No, actually he didn't. I mean, me and the trannie were working this guy over pretty good, but he wasn't biting. Said he was engaged, he just wanted to talk to people, wasn't interested in any partying.''

This, too, made even less sense. It infuriated Vera. ''Yeah, well he must've changed his mind real fast, because what I saw going on on the bed looked like one hell of a party.''

''You got that right. But let me tell you how it happened. It was the trannie. This guy Paul wasn't going for it, says he wants to be faithful to his fiancé or some shit. So the guy gets up to take a piss, and the trannie says to me 'After I hit him with some of this, he'll forget all about his fucking fiancé.' ''

Vera felt numb. ''I still don't understand,'' she croaked, but part of her thought she was beginning to.

''The trannie spiked his drink,'' the blonde said.

''You mean—''

''That's right. While he was taking a piss, she put some of that blow into his beer, and after that he did anything we told him to do.''

290

Chapter Twenty-six

"Vera, you're being ridiculous," Donna attested.

Vera sat nervously on the edge of Donna's bed; she was biting her nails. "It's *not* ridiculous," she insisted between bites. "My God, I think I've made a terrible mistake."

Donna fussed with her hair in the mirror as she continued to tear Vera's fears apart. "You're too impressionable. It's too far-fetched to even consider, and you know it."

"Donna, everything Paul said was verified by the blonde. *Every last detail!* Sure, I thought it was bullshit too when Paul said it, but the blonde?"

Donna's reflection frowned back. "Listen to what you're saying, Vera. Just because Paul and some street junkie had the same story doesn't mean it's true. Look at the sources, for God's sake. Paul obviously *instructed* the blonde to tell you the same shit he told you at the apartment."

"Oh, that's impossible. How could Paul have known I'd see the blonde on the street? He didn't know I was going downtown after I left."

"Vera, you're being so naive I can't believe it. Paul and the hooker probably followed you, then he dropped

291

her off at a corner he knew you'd have to pass to leave town. He knew you'd see her, he knew you'd remember her, and he knew you'd stop and ask her about what happened that night. Then she took if from there. You're letting these people make a fool of you. Christ, you were supposed to tell Paul off to get him out of your system, and now look what's happened. You're worse off than before you went.'' Donna, next, began to change lace bras in the mirror, appraising each one. What she wore down below were scarlet panties of the edible variety. "Look, I know how things can be sometimes. When you're with someone for two years, it's hard to let go. But you're believing what you *want* to believe, Vera. That's not going to do you any good at all. Paul *cheated* on you with a couple of dope-addict whores.''

Vera meandered forward, as if to make an enfeebled plea. "But he wasn't really himself,'' she attempted without much conviction. "The blonde verified it—they *coerced* him. They put—''

Donna sighed heavily. "The big bad prostitutes put evil drugs in poor little innocent Paulie's beer, and the drugs just made him so confused that he couldn't be responsible for his actions.'' Donna tapped her foot, a hand on her hip. "If you believe a load of crap like that, you're the most gullible person to ever live.''

Vera sat back down, eyes locked to the floor. "Well, I guess it is a little far-fetched.''

"A little far-fetched? Don't make me laugh. It's bigtime primo garbage, Vera. Paul's so full of shit he probably uses a toilet brush to clean his ears.''

Donna refaced the dressing mirror to effect some lastminute adjustments to her attire. The scarlet edible panties made for a unique clash with the black four-inch high heels and black garters, while the fishnet stockings matched perfectly with the fishnet brassiere she finally decided on. Then she pinned her hair tightly behind her head.

"Getting ready for Dan B., huh?" Vera presumed.

"Yes, and don't change the subject. You need to get over him, Vera, and you need to do it soon. You're letting him and his bullshit get under your skin; you're playing right into his hands. You have to forget about him, you have to write him off. I mean, look at how he treated you. This guy's got you so confused you're actually thinking about forgiving him, aren't you?"

Vera felt cornered. Was it true? "Well—"

"Well forget it," Donna stated, misting herself with Red Door. "Is that the kind of guy you want? Someone you can never trust?"

"No," Vera admitted.

"You deserve a lot better."

Vera thought about that. *Do I?* she asked herself in remorse. *Maybe I don't deserve anything.*

"All good things take time," Donna tritely offered. "That's cold comfort but it's the truth. Give yourself a chance, girl; don't mope over that dickbrain Paul. Be patient and eventually you'll find the kind of man you really want."

Everything Donna said, of course, made perfect sense. *So what's wrong?* she wondered. *Why am I so bent out of shape?*

It was probably a combination of things: moving to a new place, working for a new boss, new responsibilities. *Not to mention that I'm almost thirty and I haven't had sex in months.* Yes, that might have something to do with her shuffled conceptions. But had she really been thinking about giving Paul another chance? Was she that foolish to consider his story? *It does sound ridiculous now,* she agreed. *Donna's right. I was believing what I wanted to believe.*

"And since we're sort of on the topic of good things that take time, Dan B.'ll be off shift in a few minutes," Donna politely urged the point. "So would you like, you know—"

"I'm leaving," Vera said. "Have fun, but remember, don't wear your husband out. We have twenty-five reservations tomorrow night."

Donna grinned. "Well, in that case, I guess I can take it easy on him."

"See you tomorrow."

"Good night. Oh, and Vera, anytime you want to talk, I'm here."

"Thanks, Donna."

It was past midnight. Vera headed toward her suite, so weary her head felt light. The Inn seemed draped in silence and cozy, muffled warmth. It isolated her. . . .

In her room, she poured herself a drink, took a long bath, and hoped that relaxing would sort out her feelings. Then, in bed, she opened one of the romance novels, but just couldn't get into it. *I'm bored shitless,* she glumly realized. She turned out the light. *I'm over the hill, unfulfilled, insecure, confused. I've got nothing going on in my life, and I'm so bored I could scream!*

It was an interesting outburst of self-disclosure. She curled up beneath the plush down comforter. She longed for sleep but she knew it wasn't just her fatigue. When she was asleep, she dreamed, and lately it was beginning to seem that dreams were her only real excitement. When she dreamed, there were no confusions, no stress, no Paul, no contemplations. There was only her fantasy, and the heady bliss that always followed.

294

Minutes later she was asleep.
Dreaming.

Dreaming, Donna assured herself.

She must be. She didn't know where she was, but she knew what she was doing.

She was drinking.

Yes, it's just a dream. There was no way she'd ever go back to the bottle; those days would always be the ugliest bruise on her spirit. The Scotch tasted exquisite. *Just like the old days,* she thought in the dream, because it was a dream.

She knew it was.

It had to be.

Yes. Just a dream . . .

Bladelike heat fluttered in her belly; the loveliest sensations rose gently to her head. She took another sip, carrying the bottle along with her. *But where am I going?* The dreams were always like this, as cryptic as they were dark. Equally, she never cared. She felt *safe* in the dreams. So she'd merely walk on, sipping the aromatic liquor, and let the dream take her away. . . .

She felt grateful for the dream; Dan B. hadn't proved of any use at all tonight. "Aw, honey, I'm really not in the mood right now, you know?" he mumbled in bed. "We got slammed tonight, wound up doing twenty dinners after nine." Then he'd rolled over and gone to sleep.

This hurt. Donna went to serious efforts to turn him on, to make him happy. But this seemed to be happening almost every night now: she'd dress up for him in the sexy garments, and he scarcely even noticed. So, frustrated, annoyed, she'd go to sleep herself.

And dream.

She never remembered at first. Soon, though, as the

dream-Scotch rushed to her head, she'd think: *Yes, here it is. I remember this place, from all the other dreams.*

Suddenly she knew where the dream was taking her.

Her buzz deepened; the dream became a cloud which muddled her perceptions but one: arousal. She was *hot.* Something was summoning her excitement, beseeching her with vaguely remembered promises of pleasure. The corridor wound down.

A figure was approaching just ahead of her. Another figure came up from behind and urged her away. Donna never remembered entering a room. Was she at The Inn? Had they taken her into one of the upper suites? More candlelight flickered as the two figures lowered her onto what seemed a bed of fragrant pillows. Gentle heat stirred in the air, like the heat in her belly, her head, and her sex. . . .

She could barely see. The candles backlit the figures to crisp silhouettes. One figure was a woman—Donna could tell by the contour of hips and breasts—and the other was a man. But as her eyes tried to focus up she noticed one more thing. These two figures, these dream-escorts, were—

They're . . . bald.

She could tell by the silhouette-shapes of their heads that both of them—the women included—were bald.

And a third bald figure seemed to be standing aside.

Who are all these bald people? Donna thought.

A moment later, though, she didn't care.

It didn't matter.

Her senses slipped into a chaotic swirl. Hands prodded at her, removing her fishnet bra and stockings, snapping off the scarlet panties. The three bald dream-chaperones stepped back, yet other figures continued to probe her. Another woman slithered forward, breasts rubbing, and in her sloppy kisses, Donna dully noted that the woman had no teeth. Then yet another woman, a brunette, lowered her face to Donna's sex. . . .

Before her stupor finally claimed her, Donna managed to lean up. She'd never seen these two women who tended to her. They seemed sluggish, woozy. One mouth alternately sucked her nipples, while the other quite pointedly sucked her sex. Beyond this, however, and past the three bald silhouettes, she thought she could see even more figures, many more.

Watching.

And there were sounds. Glasses clinking. Silverware ticking against plates. Soft, unintelligible chatter. Was she dreaming of some outré dinner party? And what of these two sluggish women in bed with her? *Am I a latent lesbian?* came Donna's muted thought. *Why am I dreaming about women?*

She'd never been with a woman before, so perhaps the dream was telling her something about herself. Soon, in the dream, she was coming. The brunette's mouth expertly plied her sex, a finger slipping in at prime moments, which caused her loins to jettison blade-sharp pulses of bliss. Her pleasure seemed to *gush.* . . .

And her stupor deepened. Soon, the figures more distant became impatient with mere watching. They approached the bed, perhaps a half-dozen of them. Donna, through her strange haze, couldn't really see them, and she didn't need to. She didn't care. The candlelight dimmed; each orgasm that claimed her only left her in want of more. Soon the bed was acrawl with figures, and things were being done to her that she had never even thought of.

And as the night lolled on, Donna began doing things in return, which beggared description, reveling in her infidelity and newfound decadence.

But none of that bothered her.

Because it was only a dream.

It's only a dream, she assured herself, as she admitted yet another stout, musky penis into her mouth.

Chapter Twenty-seven

Vera wandered through the main dining room, checking the place setting and flower arrangements. Lately it seemed she had nothing to do before opening but that: wander. The early afternoon light looked drab in the gaps between the heavy gray draperies. In the far wing, one of the housekeeping staff seemed to grimace whilst laying out more place settings and teepeed linen napkins.

A solitude, drab as the winter light, fell down on her: The Carriage House felt dead. What was wrong now? She couldn't stop calling up the memory of her encounter with the blond prostitute, and how so much of what she'd said corroborated Paul's explanation. And the business with Chief Mulligan disappearing—she knew it had nothing to do with her, or The Inn, but it still seemed so strange. Earlier, in her office, she'd gotten a call from Morton-Gibson Ltd., someone inquiring as to the whereabouts of one Mr. Terrence Taylor. Vera told him all she knew, that Mr. Taylor had checked in but had forgotten to check out. This, too, seemed strange. But that wasn't all that bothered her—

"You look bothered," the soft but solid voice drifted out. Feldspar stood by the hostess station, eying her. He wore fine black slacks and a loose gray-silk shirt, diamond cuff links winking. *Bothered?* Vera thought. *Me?* What could she tell him? Nothing, really, so she lied, "I'm fine, Mr. Feldspar."

He unlocked the glass cognac case and poured himself a shot of Louis XIII. Vera winced when he threw it back neat. *That stuff's a hundred years old and cost five hundred fifty dollars a bottle,* Vera wished she could scold. *You don't throw it back like it's Old Grand Dad.* Of course, it was his; he could do what he wanted with it. He could wash his hands with it if he so desired. "You're fine, you say?" he seemed to challenge. "Frankly, I've never seen you appear so . . . disconsolate."

Well, I think someone was in my room last night. Is that something worth being disconsolate about?

No, it wouldn't work. What could she possibly tell him? Last night, her dream had returned, her fantasy of The Hands. The Hands had caressed her into ecstacy, after which their phantom possessor had made love to her in the graven dark. Well, no, not *love*—she'd been *fucked*, roughly and primitively, her face shoved down into the pillows so intently she thought she'd smother, her buttocks slapped till it stung, her hair yanked like a bell cord on an ice cream truck. Yet in spite of the dream's flagrant violence, she'd enjoyed every minute of it.

And when she'd awakened . . .

She swore she'd heard a click.

As if her bedroom door had just clicked shut.

Suddenly it hadn't felt like a dream at all. Her sex ached, and her buttocks seemed—yes—it seemed to *sting*. And hadn't Donna reported having bizarre dreams too, undeniably *sexual* dreams?

Laved in sweat, she'd lurched from bed, donned her robe, and stepped quickly into the hall. No, this hadn't seemed like a dream at all. It had seemed real in some hazy unsorted way. She even harbored the consideration that maybe, just maybe, someone *had* been coming into her room all these nights. Molesting her. Raping her.

In the dim hallway she'd seen the figure, its back to her as it walked away. "Who are you?" she called dizzily out. She'd always believed the dream-lover was Kyle, but this figure didn't look like him at all. "Who are you!" she called out again.

When the figure turned at her call she saw at once that it wasn't Kyle.

And she *knew* that it must be a dream.

No, the figure wasn't Kyle. It wasn't even human.

The memory snapped like a thin bone, bringing her back to Feldspar, the dining room, reality. "I just haven't been sleeping well," she said. "Bad dreams."

"I'm sorry," Feldspar offered. "I suppose we all have them from time to time. They say that dreams, particularly nightmares, represent abstract depictions of our darkest desires."

If that's true, I need to be locked up, Vera thought. She remembered the dream-figure's face, once it had turned: pallid, malformed, hideous. Rheumy, urine-colored eyes peered back at her with irregular irises. A cluster of pale slimy tentacles emerged from a mouth like a knife-slit in meat. . . .

When you have a nightmare, Vera, you don't fool around. But what in her subconscious could be so demented that her mind would produce such awful images in her dreams? *Am I that screwed up?* she wondered.

Feldspar obliquely smiled, something he rarely did. "I'm very enthused, Ms. Abbot. Things are just going so well."

"I'm glad to hear it," Vera said, though she still had yet to see any evidence of The Inn's success. Evidently, room service was still blowing the restaurant away. "Oh,

I meant to mention something to you. Remember Chief Mulligan? He seems to have disappeared."

Feldspar's eyes narrowed quizzically. He ran an unconscious finger across his bright amethyst ring. "I don't understand."

"One of his deputies called me, said he never returned to the station after he dropped by here."

"How queer," Feldspar remarked. "I suppose they believe he was abducted by one of The Inn's evil ghosts." Then Feldspar chuckled.

Even Vera shared the laugh, but then she kept thinking: *Mulligan.* And his fairly direct implications. Feldspar had admitted to a checkered past, though she hadn't asked him to elaborate. And what she asked next went against all good judgment.

"May I ask you something? Personal?"

"Of course," Feldspar invited. "Personal questions are always the most enlivening."

"Well . . ." Vera hesitated. "The other day, when I was telling you about Chief Mulligan's visit—"

"And his suggestion that we might be involved in some sort of corruption," Feldspar added for her.

"Yes, and all that. You said that you had been in trouble with the authorities once in the past."

Feldspar nodded. He poured himself another shot.

"I realize it's none of my business," Vera tacked on, "but I can't help but be curious . . ."

"Ah, you want to know exactly what happened. Well, as you know, I've always been in this business in one way or another. My employer always had great faith in me—"

"Magwyth Enterprises, you mean."

"Correct. I've managed resorts similar to The Inn, all over the world, the very best inns, facilities that make our inn here pale in comparison. Well, it was at one such inn that I gave my associates a bit too much leeway in the way things were to be run. I'm afraid some improprieties occurred, and my associates, unbeknownst to me, took it onto themselves to engage in some rather unusual management practices.''

Vera's brow twitched.

''Yes, Ms. Abbot. Crimes were committed. Nothing serious, mind you, but crimes no less. Several of our best-heeled clients took exception to this, and since my associates were under my supervision, I was quite justifiably held responsible. But I assure you that none of these misgivings were anything remotely similar to the good Chief Mulligan's accusations. They weren't so much crimes as they were unauthorized liberties.''

Vera pondered this. Certainly many liberties were taken in the hotel and restaurant business: pilfering, misuse of funds by mid- and upper management, fraudulent business deductions and record-keeping. These must be examples of what he meant.

''At any rate, my employer was not pleased. I was demoted back to the field, so to speak, to manage a new facility and re-prove my worth. It's a bit like penance.''

Some penance. It sounded more like a slap on the wrist to Vera. Sending Feldspar to the cost-no-object Inn as a demotion was like putting a fat person on a 5,000-calorie-a-day diet. *If this is how Magwyth Enterprises punishes its managers for screwing up, I'd hate to think what their idea of a promotion is.*

But Feldspar, next, even answered the joke, by repeating something he'd already mentioned many times. ''If The Inn continues to succeed—and I suspect it will— then I'll be back in the good graces of my employer, back to running our very best inns.''

Feldspar made The Inn seem like a highway motor lodge. Vera found it hard to imagine that the company's other inns could be significantly superior to this one. He

303

must be talking about places in Europe or the Middle East, which catered exclusively to royalty and billionaires.

And Feldspar went on, "In which case I'll need a preeminent restaurant manager to take with me, Ms. Abbot."

Another implication he'd been making since she started up here. Part of her felt like a dog being tempted by a distant bone, yet another part of her felt quite flattered. "Well, Mr. Feldspar, I don't like to count my chickens before they hatch. We haven't even been open long enough for a full quarterly report. It's probably not a great idea for either of us to be worrying about promotions until we see exactly how well we're doing here after the initial numbers are in."

Feldspar lit a Turkish cigarette with a jeweled lighter. "Ah, so businesslike, a natural predilection toward pessimism. My hunches, however, almost always come true. I hope that you will keep any potential possibility in mind."

He's such an odd man, she thought. Was that why she admired him? Was that why she *liked* him? "Don't worry. I will."

Again, he smiled, the fetid smoke blurring his face. "Indeed, Ms. Abbot, I believe with the utmost certainty that you and I will both enjoy a considerable success in the very near future."

What could Lee say? He didn't even know her name. *Excuse me, but have you seen . . . well, you know, the pudgy housemaid who never talks? That's right, the one who gives me head every night, and who can't have sex because some S&M pervert sewed her vagina shut? The one who's got burn marks and scars all over her body?*

Lee was worried.

She hadn't come to his room in the last three nights. Nor had he seen her working about The Inn. The other housemaids—the ones who seemed equally distant and nontalkative—sure.

But not . . . *her.*

Lee didn't know what he was getting into; he didn't even know how he *felt.* He knew one thing though:

Something's fucked up around here.

They seemed to be running a fair amount of dinners that night—not exactly in the weeds, but they were busy. There was no time to take a quick break and skip over to room service to ask Kyle if he'd seen her. And he couldn't really ask anyone else because they'd want to know why.

"Hey, Lee, what's the matter? Your Jack-'o-matic break down?" Dan B. called out from behind the range. "How come you're acting weird these days?"

"Weird? Me?" Lee tried to joke back. *I think I'm in love with a fat woman who never talks.* "Your mom dumped me for Cujo. I'm depressed."

"Aw, that's a shame. But look at the bright side, you've still got your sister, that is if you don't mind the sloppy seconds after me. One thing I can't figure out is that parking-garage-sized cooze on her. What've you been doing, sticking your whole head in?"

"Why don't *you* stick *your* head into that pot of creek water you call Le Chabichou Sturgeon Soup? And take a deep breath."

"I took a deep breath last night when I was going down on your grandma. About died, but fifty bucks is fifty bucks."

Lee slid another tray of glasses into the Hobart. No point in trying to out-do Dan B. with the gross jokes. He sipped a Maibock he'd hidden behind the big dishwasher, and let his thoughts flee.

They didn't flee far.

He couldn't stop thinking about the housemaid.

He couldn't stop thinking that something bad had happened.

Chapter Twenty-eight

The food was exquisite: rich, savory, remarkable.

As remarkable as this heady reprieve. They sat and watched, stuffing their gullets on steaming ambrosia and delectible wines. A taste of the cursed world! This blasted scape of insult!

The women were splayed naked before them, dumbly following their own initial instincts. Lapping at one another upon fragrant beds of feathers as countless candles sizzled. Holy preludes drenched with ungodly designs! The acolytes stood aside in wait of their wishes: more rich foodstuffs, wines, fellatio . . .

Eventually they rose, their lips glossed by succulent greases, and approached the beds. A male acolyte produced wondrous little blades, while the female shrieked in cosmic enthusiasm, a most diverting creature. Her pleasure was obvious.

One blonde's throat was delicately slit, and the warm blood allowed to sheen the soft flesh of the others, which several reveled to lave off with their tongues. Several more pried apart the blonde's brittle skull, to feast upon the still-warm brains. . . .

Stout members turned rigid. They each waited patiently to take their turn.

* * *

Lee woke up past three A.M. For the third night in a
row now, his lover had not shown herself. *I guess she's
sick of me,* his male paranoia presented. *Probably in bed
with Kyle right now. Or that weird fucker Feldspar.*

He couldn't sleep. The room's dark unnerved him,
aggravated him like an incessant, yapping poodle. Subtle noises cloyed at him further; he knew he must be
imagining them.

Whispers, shrieks, remote thunkings . . .

Fuck this, he thought. *I need a beer.*

He hauled on old clothes, taking care to leave the
suite as quietly as possible. The hall to the stairs seemed
cramped, unearthly in silence. A barely noticeable heat
wafted against him as he crossed the atrium, from the
fireplace.

The kitchen sparkled back at him when he eased
through the double doors. The service bar was unlocked.

Where are you? he wondered, strangely close to
tears. Did he love her? What was going on? *You fat,
silly fool. You've fallen in love with a whore.* That's
what Kyle implied she'd been in her past life. Scarred
by the dementias of others, probably insensible by the
way the world worked. *Doesn't care, doesn't know
how to.*

The Maibock tasted great. Lee leaned against the big
Hobart dishwasher, savoring each sip. He finished one
bottle, and opened another. . . .

Next, he felt walking through a dream, yet he knew
it couldn't be a dream. *I'm awake,* he assured himself.
But it beats the shit out of me where I am. Strange warrens led him to stranger ones, he felt immersed in rock
and moist air. The walls now seemed *carved,* like a
catacomb. Smoky torches lit the way.

Then he knew he must be wrong; he knew he *must* be dreaming. Rock-arched entryways showed him flagrant horrors. The warrens were lined with ill-lit rooms, and in each room some new, hideous atrocity unfolded. Things he could never have imagined. Women fettered to beds by leather straps so tight their hands and feet glowed blue. Gorged nipples pierced by needles, tips of clitori snipped with shears and lapped of their blood by greedy tongues. In another room, a misshapen man penetrated a woman with a penis that looked large as a summer squash; the woman vomited, somehow, in ecstasy. In a third room a woman fellated a man who didn't even look human. A gray corrugated face grinned down; the eyes looked blood-red. Weirdly jointed hands grabbed shanks of dirty hair, guiding the woman's mouth over the worm-veined shaft. . . .

An in yet another grottolike room, a bald man molested a squirming woman chained to a bed. Beyond a sheen of smoke, other men watched intently. The woman seemed fat, anguished; she squirmed against metal shackles while the bald man snipped off a nipple-end with scissors. He squeezed the breasts hard, blood jetting from the insult into some gaping mouth which yawned in the smoky dark.

Lee winced, disbelieving these mad bits of vision. *Did I drop acid and not remember?* he asked himself. This was the sickest nightmare he'd ever had. Then something jarred him, as solidly as a hammer to the bridge of his nose:

The bald man, muscles shining in sweat, paused as he drew a thin needle through the fat woman's other nipple.

"Hey, fat boy, ever wondered why this ugly piece of cooze never talks?"

Lee squinted hard. The bald man's features eventually jelled—the brazen grin, the fucked-up glint in his eyes.

The bald man was Kyle.

And the woman he was so nonchalantly torturing was—

Holy shit no! Lee's thoughts screamed.

The silent housemaid. His lover.

"We cut all their vocal cords so they don't get noisy. Sometimes the guys don't like to hear a ruckus."

"Stop that!" Lee screamed as the fat woman lurched at yet another needle piercing. Some thing that only vaguely resembled a man crawled forward to tongue the reddened sex.

Kyle chuckled, his bald head aswarm with tails of candlelight. "And we sew the dolts' pussies shut every now and then for kicks. The fellas get off on watching shit like that."

Then Kyle, quite calmly, went back to his needle torture.

Yeah, this is a dream, Lee thought. *So I can do anything I want, can't I?*

Of course he could.

He rushed forward, and cracked the Maibock bottle over Kyle's shining, bald head. The glass shattered; Kyle howled and rolled off the pillowed bed. "How do you like that, *dick?*" Lee asked. "And don't call me fatboy anymore—I'm getting a little tired of it."

Lee, then, jammed the broken bottleneck into the base of Kyle's spine. Ground it in deep.

Kyle collapsed, convulsing.

God, that was fun, Lee thought. It really was. Next, he contemplated a way to free the housemaid from her shackles. It shouldn't be too difficult; this was only a dream. "Take it easy," he assured the housemaid, who flinched naked against her restraints. But as he turned to find something to break them with, he—

BAM-BAM!

—fell to the dirt floor as if swiped at the knees by a scythe. At first, his shock left him shakily numb, then the pain exploded with his scream when he saw the two ragged, gristled knobs that had previously been his knees.

"You were in the wrong place at the wrong time, fatboy." Kyle stood above him, a huge smoking revolver in his hand. "It's too bad. I was beginning to like you."

Lee shuddered as blood oozed from his burst knees. Above, he noticed queer, shadowed figures converging on the bed. They seemed in glee as they inserted long needles into the housemaid's flesh: her nipples, her navel, her clitoris. She jerked dumbly. Then more needles slipped into her nostrils, her ears, her eyes. . . .

Kyle grinned. "She was getting pretty beat so we decided to check her out. But unfortunately, fatboy, you've seen too much. We gotta check you out too."

Kyle set the pistol down and picked up something in its place.

God Almighty, Lee's thoughts groaned.

The gutting knife slid serenely across Lee's beer belly, parting fat in a neat divide. Lee felt electrocuted. A deeper slice, next, opened the abdominal vault, the lightning bolt of pain bloating Lee's face like an angel food cake in a hot oven.

And from the sooty darkness, several more misshapen, hallucinatory figures approached. Twisted faces hovered in wait. Strips of sight showed Lee rows of glossy teeth, propped-open bulging eyes, and tongues skimming inflamed lips.

"Sushi, fatboy. You're it."

Lee's only consolation was the thought which repeated in the fashion of a carousel: *It's only a dream only a dream only a dream only a dream—*

—as he had the rare and unique experience of watching as the choicest of his organs were extracted from his gut and eaten raw.

Chapter twenty-nine

Vera's head felt as though something were pounding inside of it to get out. The more she slept, the less rested she felt. When she opened her eyes, recollection of her dreams closed them again, and the pounding continued.

The door.

Someone was pounding at her bedroom door. . . .

Christ, I feel like shit, she thought. She felt slimy with sweat in her nakedness, pulling on her robe as she swung out of bed. Twice she nearly stumbled. When she opened her door, Dan B.'s concerned face peered through the gap.

"Look, Vera, I'm sorry to wake you up, but it's getting late, and—"

"Well, what time is it?"

Dan B. tried hard not restrain his frown. "It's, like, close to four."

He must mean four in the morning, but then the sunlight in the rive of her curtains showed her sunlight. *Four in the afternoon?* She couldn't believe it; nevertheless, when she looked at her clock she knew it was true. "I guess I've got the flu," she lied as an excuse. "Haven't been feeling too good this week. I'll be down in a minute."

"I need to talk to you now." Dan B. and his bulk

shouldered into the room. He appeared nervous, on edge. Vera felt tempted to object until he blurted out: "Feldspar closed The Inn. When I asked him why, he walked away."

Vera winced to gather her thoughts. "He *closed* The Inn?"

"That's right. And he wouldn't tell me for how long."

Vera's adrenalin rushed. "We've got reservations for tonight! He can't close The Inn!"

"Well, he did. You better find out what's going on."

Oh, don't worry, I will! she thought. "I talked to him last night, for God's sake. He didn't say anything about closing."

"Look, Vera, I'm just the chef, I don't know anything about what's going on. All I know is there're a lot of fucked up things happening, and I can't figure out any of them. For one, Donna's acting really weird lately."

Vera didn't know how to react to this. In the dream she'd had the other night, she'd seen Donna, but then she still didn't feel secure that it was a dream. . . .

"And Lee's gone," Dan B. said.

She squinted forward. "What do you mean he's gone."

Dan B. held up his hands. "He's gone. He left. He didn't show up for prep so I checked his room. All his stuff's out. The room's empty. I can't find him anywhere."

Lee's gone, the thought finally hit her. "I'll be down in a minute," she said. "I'll find out what's going on."

Dan B. backed out of the room; he looked suspicious. Vera showered quickly, tripped over the pile of books she'd bought the other day, and dressed. She about stormed downstairs, turned into the front office, and cursed when she found Feldspar's office door locked. Then she stormed into Kyle's office. The door was unlocked, but there was no sign of Kyle.

"God*damn* it!" She went to his desk, dialed Room Service, and cursed once more when no one answered. *Someone should be there!* she thought. There were room guests who'd be ordering dinner! At once the sheer frustration flattened her.

Then she noted Kyle's top desk drawer slightly open.

Some impulse—she didn't know what—impelled her to open it further. And when she did so, she noticed the strangest thing.

The gun.

The gun she'd seen in Feldspar's desk some time ago now sat plainly in Kyle's drawer. She knew it was the same one; it looked large and clunky, unusual, like an antique.

"Hey, Vera, if you want to go through my drawers, that's okay by me."

Vera looked up, outraged. Kyle entered the office with a loping, arrogant stride, grinning at the fact he'd caught her invading his managerial privacy, which she easily ignored given comment regarding his "drawers."

"Why do you have a gun?" she demanded.

Kyle shrugged, along with his pectorals. "In case we get robbed. Hotels do get robbed every so often."

Fine! What could she say? That she'd seen the same gun in Feldspar's desk? Then some weird mental fog cleared in her head. *The dream,* she thought. Despite the usual demented sex, hadn't she dreamed of hearing gunshots?

She'd sound ridiculous voicing it. So she voiced the next outrage. "Dan B. told me Lee's gone."

Kyle nodded, arms crossed. "Yeah?"

"*Yeah?*" Vera nearly spat.

"If you were anything close to a decent personnel manager, you'd know what's going on with *your* personnel."

315

She wished she could kick him, or slap him, or—something. "What's that supposed to mean?"

"Lee got fired. Drinking on duty. Shit, Vera, I gave the guy as many breaks as I could but never got it in his head. Last night the guy was blotto cleaning up. I had to fire him. He packed his bags this morning, got a cab to the bus station in Waynesville."

Bullshit! she felt inclined to say, but then she had to admit that Lee had been known to drink a few beers while working the dishwasher. She'd never known him, however, to be drunk. "Lee was *my* employee. How come I wasn't consulted about the decision to fire him?"

Kyle, again, shrugged. "You were asleep. I guess you gals need your beauty sleep." Then he offered the faintest chuckle. "You knew the guy was tipping the bottle on duty, don't tell me you didn't. If you cared more about your employees than your sleeptime, then this might never have happened."

What could she say to *that?* Vera felt a pang of guilt, but her anger still fumed. Lee was a lot of things, but impulsive wasn't one of them. *Would he really leave without even telling me?* She just couldn't accept that. "And what's this crap about The Inn being closed?"

"The Inn's closed," Kyle responded in his usual smart-ass manner. "What am I? An information desk? The Inn's closed for the rest of the week."

"Why?"

"Plumbing problem. One of the domestic waterlines broke, I think."

"What do you mean, you *think?*" Vera seethed. "When did this happen?"

"Last night, while you were beddy-bye. A main froze up and broke, so the out-water line backed up."

This sounded as fishy as the business about Lee leaving. "If the main ruptured, how come my shower worked this morning?"

316

"We have more than one main, Vera. Listen, I've got work to do, and no time to take a ration of shit from you. You got anymore questions, go ask Mr. Feldspar." And with that, Kyle walked out.

He is such a prick! Vera thought. *Yeah, right, go ask Feldspar. I would, you schmuck, if you could friggin' find him!* Vera left the office herself, then slipped into the lobby ladies' room. She was not surprised to find that all the faucets worked when she turned them on. Then she scurried to the restaurant kitchen—all the water worked there too. *Broken water main, my ass.* This was outrageous! And when she went to check the water in the room-service kitchen, she—

Shit!

—cursed heartily aloud.

The door to room service, as always, was locked.

You can't just close The Inn, the irate thoughts followed her up the stairs. *The kitchen water if fine—I've got reservations!*

She had no choice. Feldspar was clearly a private person, not one to appreciate being bothered in his room. But as a manager, Vera felt it her right to know what was going on, and she deserved a better explanation than Kyle's cock and bull. She marched briskly down the second-floor hall, passed her own suite, to the suite at the very end. Centered on the door shined a tiny brass plaque which read: FELDSPAR, DO NOT DISTURB.

Well, sorry, boss, but I'm going to disturb you. Vera stood a moment to compose herself, then firmly rapped on the ornate door.

The door not only was unlocked, it was ajar.

It swung open.

"Mr. Feldspar, I'm sorry to disturb you," she apologized, "but—"

Vera stared, vexed.

She knew in a glance that Feldspar was not in the

317

suite. In fact, there was *nothing* in the suite. No drapes, no carpet, no wallpaper.

No furniture. No bed.

Just four bare walls and a bare floor.

And a lot of cobwebs.

"Things are going well. It's a *wonder,* is it not?"

The Factotum's voice loomed, his satisfaction akin to the most gentle halo in the turbid, hot dark. "My servants, soon we'll be one as was my promise. Have faith. We *must* have faith."

Zyra and Lemi nodded. The sweat of their labors slickened their young sheens of skin. *So beautiful,* the Factotum mused. *So young and full of voracity . . .*

"Nor must we allow *our* servants to get out of hand," he added then, and led them away in his frock to the next vault. Horrors prevailed, such wondrous deeds. A nude woman, chained to the floor, squealed in bliss as both orifices were penetrated simultaneously. They'd been feeding her; her mouth bulged with remnants of Lemi's delights. "We must never forget what happened last time," the Factotum finished on a portentous note which hung in the air.

Yes, things had definitely gotten out of hand that time. Desire was often hard to reign; they'd been too free with the liberties they'd overlooked. Some hierarchs had been slighted, even abused in the zeal of certain less-comprehending electees. *Such things will happen,* he supposed. Now, though, he hoped to earn back his fortune. He grew so weary of this pale and flavorless place. *Back to my richest heaven,* he thought. *Soon, I pray.*

All of eternity is a trial. . . .

In the next grotto, several electees fed ravenously, while a third cawed, serving mammoth gentials to a blonde's oral cavity. *Yes, even infinity must have its graces.*

He turned his smile to his underlings. "Tonight, we will begin our preparations. The indoctrination . . ."

Talk about the boondocks, Paul dumbly thought.

The blue Pinto's heater had all but crapped out; Paul drove with gloves on, and his heaviest winter jacket. To make matters worse, the roads were icing up. He'd bought a map of north county back at the QUIK-STOP before he'd left town, hoping to use it in conjunction with McGowen's address for Vera's new place of employment, The Inn at Wroxton Hall. *Not,* he thought. The map proved all but useless; most secondary roads were either too small to read, or had been left off altogether. A minuscule perimeter of red dots outlined Wroxton Estates, but that was it.

Happy hunting, Paul.

State Route 154 unwound for what seemed forever, winding past outskirts of forest and infinite cornfields scratched barren save for the cut stems of last fall's harvest. Paul had never seen such drab countryside. Even the sky seemed drab as mourning, leading him up toward the northern ridge of the county. *Just northwest of Waynesville,* he remembered from the map. He'd never heard of Waynesville, and he hadn't noticed a single roadside indicating he was anywhere near it. *This is the pits! I'm never gonna get there, and I don't even know where I'm going!*

Just as he began to fear he'd passed Waynesville, he found himself idling through some little corncob of a town. One main drag, a bar, a general store, a discount clothing shop, and a bank that looked smaller than most broom closets. No road signs had announced the little town's title which, by now, Paul was not surprised by.

But at the next four-way stop (evidently stoplights were not deemed necessary here), Paul thought: *finally!* The last store in this one-hundred-yard berg sported a clipped sign reading: WAYNESVILLE FARM SUPPLY. *At least I know I'm there.* Paul felt grateful.

There came no confusion in getting back onto Route 154; the town offered no exits. Paul accelerated, the Pinto's big 2.0 engine shuddering. The state route wound around a vast forest belt that looked like myraid skeletal extremities. If he'd been driving faster he'd have missed it, the puny wooden sign barely visible in the encroaching winter dusk:

THE INN

I'm here, he realized, nearly not believing it after the grueling journey.

Paul turned up the narrow, newly paved access, and wondered just what he was going to do once he got to The Inn.

Chapter Thirty

Vera napped in annoying snatches. With The Inn closed, she decided it might be a good idea to catch up on her sleep, for certainly she'd gotten very little in the past months—at least not good sleep, *sound* sleep. The effort proved futile. Each time she lay down, she'd waken moments later pestered by lewd dreams. *Par for the course,* she thought. The fantasy of The Hands was always there, bristling, hot, erotic. Even after she'd awakened, she swore she could still feel their afterimage: roughly investigating her sex, kneading her breasts as if to squeeze out milk, fingers invading her rectum. Once she'd wakened to find herself masturbating so frantically, she'd rubbed her sex sore. Another time she'd alighted from her slumber to find herself sopped with a sheen of what she first thought was semen. But that was ridiculous. It must only be sweat. She'd been sweating a lot lately.

Upon each waking she sipped a shot of Grand Marnier, hoping the heavy alcohol content would soon drag her to full sleep. Twice she showered, to blast off the sticky sweat, but on both occasions she found that, as her hands coursed soap suds about her body, she'd wind up touching herself. She felt in a trance. Without even knowing it at first, her fingers teased her to paltry yet preposterously successive orgasms. Each climax felt like the next pearl on the string being extracted from her sex. The sensation seemed to never end, yet it never left her satisfied. It always left her longing for something more, something succulent and sating.

Goddamn, Vera. You're becoming a compulsive masturbator! In the past she'd hardly ever masturbated at all. Paul, whether with his penis or his tongue, had always slaked her needs. But that brought up another dim thought. *Paul.*

She felt so confused about everything in her life now she wanted to scream. The only love she'd ever had in her life was him. Was she being gullible and stupid, as Donna had implied? Or was there something to his *story?*

When she looked at the clock, she saw it was past midnight, which came as a sharp shock. Had she really slept the entire day away? Had she become so maladjusted that she'd forget her responsibilities? Not that she had many right now. The Inn was closed. She still felt infuriated that she'd never been able to find Feldspar. And why would he tell her that he was using the last suite in the hall when the last suite in the hall clearly had never been occupied? So many things seemed to be adding up to a false figure.

She took a bath, sipped more GM, and slept again. Snow pelted silently against the panes of her window; the heat in the room felt smothering, and the vents ticked. Half drifting off, she could swear she heard the now-familiar thunking of the room-service elevators, but that couldn't be.

The Inn was closed.

That's what she'd been told. That's what Kyle had told her, and Dan B. too. She'd even, earlier, looked out on the front door and read the apologetic sign: *The Inn is closed due to unanticipated repairs. We regret any inconvenience.*

Still . . . her dream.

When she plummeted to full sleep, The Hands were on her at once. They flipped her onto her back in the dark, one hand pinching a nipple as the other plied her buttocks. Simultaneously, a tongue which felt huge attentively laved her from anus to navel, then plodded into her sex. Her fluids seemed to gush. As turned on as she was, she felt an accommodating shame: The Hands roused to abuse her, pinching her nipples till she yelped, slapping her face. Then the large, warm body slid atop her. The tongue licked her open eyes while The Hands alternately girded her throat and yanked her hair. Her dream-suitor's genitals sunk so deeply into her sex that she stiffened as if gored; its sheer size stole her breath. But at least now her satisfaction was at hand—the veined shaft pummeled her, each stroke finishing to nudge the bulb of her cervix. The mouth sucked her lips as if to eat them as handfuls of hair were seized and pulled. Vera came in a series of detonations, and when she could come no more, The Hands rearranged her and coaxed the stiffened genitals to her lips. She chuckled in her throat, delighted at the flavor of her own musk as she intently sucked upon a penis that felt almost too large to admit into her mouth. One hand stroked the unseen buttocks while her other cradled testicles that seemed like twin tomatoes on a vine. When the saline gobs emptied into her throat, she swallowed them greedily and without a flinch. . . .

And when she awoke . . .

Was that the door she heard clicking closed in the dark?

No. It was just the heater.

Winter twilight shone mutely in her window. Flakes of snow burst to melt upon each impact to the panes.

323

Again, she'd kicked all the bedcovers off and found herself naked and shiny in her own sweat, and the faintest irritation pawed at her stomach.

When she touched her sex, she knew she'd really come; the telltale sensitivity snapped her legs closed like a trap. She leaned up in the dark, feeling plundered, squashed by all the desires that had been so expertly milked from her.

Sleeping again seemed impossible. Would the dream-figure reappear? The idea titillated her, yet at the same time felt terrifying. Surely she couldn't go through that again; though her desire lately never seemed to abate, there was nothing left now for it to give up. *Empty gas tank,* she thought, and slid her hand off the damp mount of her pubis.

She flicked on the bedside lamp, looked around. On the antique night table lay the stack of paperback romances by bestselling Melinda Pryce. Vera'd barely cracked them, not because they weren't well-written, but because they reminded her of all the things she didn't have in her own life. Beneath them, though, lay the hardback tome. *The Complete Compendium of Demons* by Richard Long. She'd bought it for Donna but had forgotten to give it to her. Vera slid the book out, flipped idly through it. It was like a dictionary of demonic entities, none of which she'd heard save for Baalzephon, which she remembered from some distant mythology class. And the Ardat-Lil, a ghostly female sex addict from pre-Druidic lore, said to become incarnate by the ritual sacrifice and feasting upon of male genitalia. Names, lithographs, medieval sketches, etc. mystified her as she turned more glossy-stock pages. . . .

Then her eyes snagged upon a single entry.

Her disbelief bloomed.

The entry, in the M's, read as such:

MAGWYTH.

"Come on," Donna whispered. "Like that."

Her request resulted in a sensation akin to being gently gutted. *Oh, God, that feels good*, she thought in excruciating slowness. She didn't even know exactly what was being done, and she didn't care. Each night her dreams entreated her to the most robust pleasures, attentions she had never imagined, climaxes the likes of which she had never even conceived. *It's just a dream*, she thought. So why should she feel guilty? How could she be cheating on Dan B.? It was just her subconscious. Just dreams.

"It's just a dream," she muttered.

She looked down, and to her astonishment, a mouth peeled her lace panties off her groin, then chewed them, then swallowed them. Another, hotter mouth sucked her toes. Next, she was sucking something herself: a penis with a drape of foreskin so abundant it hung off the glans like a long snout. Two more women lay to either side, moaning bliss as they were penetrated by hideous dream-shapes. That's why Donna knew this was a dream. Instances such as this couldn't possibly happen in reality, nor could such figures exist. The darkness, conjoined with her drunken haze, obscured the details. But she could make out enough: the figures were only caricatures of men, with every extremity distorted to extremes. Probing fingers seemed a foot long, and so did darkened faces. Not to mention the penises—so many of them!—thrust before her eager mouth. Finally she squinted down and realized the harbinger of her bliss: one figure gently turned an entire fist back and forth in the vault of her sex, whilst tending her clitoris with a tongue like a wet flap of steak.

A bald woman grinned down at her. "Join in!" Donna pleaded as yet another orgasm quaked. Her hand reached out.

325

"Can't," the woman regretted. Her breasts jutted firmly as melons, with dark-pink nipples. Her pubis shined hairless in the crackling candlelight. Then a man, equally hairless, joined the woman's side and put an comradly arm about the woman's shoulder. . . .

It was Kyle!

His grin radiated like a knife-flash. Erect genitals bobbed as he leaned further to explain: "We'd love to join in, Donna, but we can't."

"We're busy," added the grinning bald woman.

And Kyle: "We've got to get dinner ready."

What they said made no sense. Donna, though, didn't care. She felt inclined to concentrate on her lust. Huge penises worked in and out of both of her lower entries, while a third plowed so far down her throat she thought sure it was in her belly. The exploding flood of warmth made her think further, then the slackening member was extracted only to be replaced by another.

In the distance, she noted more figures—inhumanly large eyes widened upon the spectacle of the low bed. They were . . .

Eating, Donna realized.

The bald man and woman parted, bringing in trays of steaming kabobs, chunky soups, filets of seasoned meats. Seductive aromas wafted in the air. Rich sauces steamed above garnished, silver-plattered helpings.

Yet the *main* helping seemed to be Donna.

It's only a dream, she consoled herself.

Next, a penis large as a typewriter platen eased into her sex; a greased fist popped into her rectum. Donna's orgasms began to beat her to a pulp. Two long fingers stretched her mouth wide as yet another penis dropped strings of semen down her outstretched tongue.

Stringent liquor was poured next into her throat. Her desires rekindled; her breasts swelled in the same way ripe fruits burst to release their gush of seeds. More mouths, a veritable succession of them, lined up to suck her toes, her nipples and navel, her clitoris which ached as though it had been squeezed by a pair of pliers. . . .

"It's just a dream," she whispered aloud.

Kyle's bald head returned to Donna's field of vision. An amethyst jewel hung from a silver chain about his neck, and when the bald woman joined Kyle, a similar stone glittered like a purple eye sunk into her navel.

"It's just a dream!" Donna shrieked in unison with the next string of climaxes.

Kyle grinned above her.

"Hey, baby," he said, "I hate to tell you this, but this ain't no dream."

Chapter Thirty-one

MAGWYTH: A unique and immortal factotum, also known as The Servant of Demons. A second-generational demon himself, Magwyth is reported to be the chief purveyor of pleasures for the better-regarded occupants of the abyss. Though God rules in heaven, certainly Satan rules in hell, and his favorites he allows, whenever possible, the utmost liberties. Magwyth, in other words, has been trusted since time immemorial to serve his master's favorites with whatever pleasures they desire, and at the expense, of course, of the less smiled-upon tenants of the netherworld—a luciferic pimp, in other words.

Vera squinted at the words, faintly amused. Naturally the name Magwyth had flagged her attention. *A luciferic pimp,* she repeated. The whole thing was just a coincidence. . . .

Magwyth's appearance is not known, though it is known that he works with underlings, two vassals who assist him with his eternal duties: the Zyramon—the hermaphroditic offspring of the notorious owl-like demon Amon. The Zyramon is known to be quite sexual in her antics, reputed to resemble a beautiful woman, but surprising unsuspecting men with her auxilliary equipment—male genitalia, in other words, which emerge from her feminine recesses at will. Though very passionate, the Zyramon is cunning, brutal, and merciless in her resolve. So, too, is Magwyth's second underling, the less-resourceful twin brother of the Zyramon: Kyl-Lemi, distinctly male, yet equally murderous. A handsome male figure in human form, Kyl-Lemi's chief role is to provide Satan's hirelings with the most exotic culinary delights—hell's chef!

At this Vera blinked; the coincidence seemed to warp in her mind. *Magwyth?* she thought. The name of the company Feldspar worked for? And now this satanic chef?
Kyl-Lemi?
Kyle?
A handsome male figure in human form?
She read on:

Magwyth and his pair of helpers are all fully hairless, it is said, since all inhabitants of hell come in such extreme proximity to fire. Long ago, when Magwyth served directly in hell, the zeal of his co-attendants, it is cited, flew off the proverbial handle; it seems that several of Satan's personal favorite demons were mistaken for pleasure-fodder, and were heinously abused as a result. For this injustice, Satan was infuriated and he banished Magwyth and his two underlings from hell for an indeterminate time—to the earth. Here was Magwyth's penance for his blunders as overseer: to live in the world, and his job then was to provide Satan's friends with the pleasures of that same world. Incarnations were allowed for short periods of time, whereupon certain demons were permitted to come into Magwyth's domains on earth and partake in earthly gluttonies. . . .

Earthly gluttonies? Vera thought.

And more thoughts backtracked. Hadn't Feldspar said he was on a *penance?* Hadn't the implication been that his penance had come about for something akin to *blunders as overseer?* And hadn't he told her that Magwyth Enterprises existed to cater to a "select clientele," and that in the past he'd been reprimanded for getting into trouble with the "authorities?"

Though even in his punishment upon the earth, Magwyth has retained certain privileges—financial security, for one. His lord Satan promised to always provided untold riches for Magwyth's use—

Another queer snag. Vera couldn't help but be reminded of the amount of money which no doubt had been sunk into The Inn's refurbishments, nor could she forget the inexplicably large sum of capital that Magwyth Enterprises had deposited into Waynesville's local bank. . . .

Then:

Magwyth, in other words, has been condemned to provide for Satan's favorites until he is back into the good graces of the Prince of Darkness. . . .

Still one more snag. Wasn't it coincidental that Feldspar himself had used essentially the same terminology: that he'd be transferred to a better inn once he got back into this employer's—

Good graces? Vera recalled.

She read on.

Magwyth and his two acolytes are, to no surprise, cannibals, and so, too, do the tenants of the
abyss enjoy the flavor of human flesh. And in more
ways than one—it is Magwyth's job to provide not
only satisfaction for his clients' bellies but also for
their libidos. To put it more bluntly, Magwyth's
duties, during his indeterminate penance, is to also
provide Lucifer's favorites with other manners of
earthly delight—not only the taste of human flesh
but the sexual satisfaction thereof. The abduction
of female humankind is a chief task of Magwyth,
to offer to hell's underlings the opportunity to enjoy
the pleasures of fornication. . . .

Vera blinked hard, shook her head. This was some of
the worst writing she'd ever read, yet somehow she remained enthralled.

Then she read more slowly, and intently. She made
herself read the next passage several times.

Yet Magwyth, in his time on earth, must remain
in league with the powers of his acursed lord. The
notoriously occult semiprecious gemstone amethyst serves as Satan's total empowerment to Magwyth. The stone of passion, the gem of surfeit.
Magwyth and his pair of acolytes always wear an
amethyst to keep them aligned unto the powers of
Lucifer. . . .

Vera nearly gagged now. *Amethyst,* she baldly
thought. Feldspar always wore a big amethyst pinky ring.
And there could be no mistake: Kyle, too, wore an amethyst. Vera clearly remembered the bright purple stone
hung about the man's neck the night he'd invited her to
the pool. And one more thing—

She also remembered the large, finely cut amethyst

set into the stone transom above The Inn's front door. . . .

And the last passage:

Little is actually known on Magwyth, save for the minuscule registry left by certain pre-Druidic settlements. It is known, though, that Magwyth is the offspring of the first earthly generation of the pre-Adamics, or the initial foundry of Satan's failed attempt to rule the physical world. The original Magwyth, according to the early Britonic archives, was originally imprisoned for heinous misdeeds, sentenced, and executed by knife upon an altar of the then-abundant sedimentary rock: feldspar.

Chapter Thirty-two

Paul parked off a little layby in the woods rather than The Inn's parking lot; he wanted to be discreet. He crunched up through the winter thicket. It was starting to snow. When he made it to the elaborate, paved cul-de-sac, he stood gazing up in awe.

The Inn was immense, grandly refurbished, eloquently lit by spotlights planted in the outer yard. *It's a palace,* he thought, then noted with some astonishment that the resort's parking lot was empty save for a beat-up Plymouth station wagon and two Lamborghinis. He traipsed to the huge stone-framed front door, passing granite verandas before high windows. But a sign on the door indicated that The Inn was closed for repairs.

All this money for this big place, and they're closed? Paul wondered. Was Vera inside now? If so, what was she doing?

An oddity caught his eye: the large, finely cut gem-stone set into the door's granite transom. Its darkness flashed in the strangest way. Midnight-purple razor-sharp facets. *Amethyst,* he realized. But the largest amethyst he could ever imagine.

He pulled away, skirted around the front facade. In the center of the cul-de-sac, a heated fountain gurgled, whose splattery noise seemed to follow him along the building's left wing. He wasn't even quite sure what he was doing; bitter cold air and some vague impulse propelled him around the corner of the building and down a steep slope. Several times he almost fell, and he had the sensation of submerging into dark. When he came around the bend, though, more floodlights lit the back of The Inn. And behind that, there was only dense woods.

Except . . .

He peered down, shivering. Through branches of winter-starved trees he spied what seemed a curving sweep.

It was the snow, he realized. Glittering on . . . *pavement.*

He followed the incline down farther, then pushed into the woods. *Something* was there, he just didn't know what. Was it some kind of hiker's trail? *A service road,* he realized once he'd trundled through the net of trees and vines. The light snow sparkled like halite on fresh, new asphalt. He followed the road around the bend.

Deeper, he discovered an embankment, a man-made one judging by the way it was cut against the declivity of the landscape. What he was looking at now appeared to be a loading dock, which made sense in a way, because all hotels had loading accesses. What didn't make sense, though, was the distance. *Why put the loading dock here?* Paul at once questioned. It was a good hundred yards from The Inn. Almost as if the building's designers had—

Hidden it, Paul realized.

Why hide a supply access?

Then he saw the stranger part.

Obscured amongst leaveless tree branches was the mouth of a great sewer pipe. *A sewer pipe at a loading dock?* It didn't fit. A shiny white van had been parked next to the pipe's exit, and that was the part that seemed even stranger. It wasn't really an exit drain for a sewer pipe. There was no receptacle, no means for waste waters to exit. Then he thought:

If it's not an exit . . . maybe it's an entrance. . . .

It made as much sense as anything could at this moment, before this bizarre sewer pipe in freezing cold. Paul walked toward the cement mouth of the pipe, then stopped—

Shit!

—then ducked back around the side of the embankment.

A sound had issued from the pipe, he felt sure of it. *Footsteps.*

And a moment later, he knew he hadn't been hearing things. He hunkered down, one eye peeking beyond his cover. . . .

A figure emerged from the exit or entrance or whatever it was.

Bags of some sort seemed slung across the figure's back. The figure was bald, Paul saw in the dim light, though he appeared youthful, strong, a spring in the step. But what struck Paul even more immediately was that the figure wore only a pair of jeans. No shoes and no shirt, though, in this killer cold. Paul watched, deflecting his breath. . . .

The man disappeared down a thin divide in the trees, then reemerged a minute later, minus the bags he'd been toting. He was whistling. He paused a moment on the pavement, and in that moment Paul noticed something else:

A sparse pendant about the man's neck, and at its end, laying between well-developed pectorals, hung a shiny, dark-purple gemstone.

Amethyst, Paul suspected, remembering the transom.

Then the shirtless figure reentered the sewer pipe and disappeared.

Who the fuck was that? Paul thought the logical question. Was he The Inn's garbage man? And why dump garbage back here? There'd be a dumpster, wouldn't there?

See for yourself.

Paul stepped into the narrow divide between the trees.

A scratch of a trail descended; leafless branches threatened to claw Paul's face. The footpath wound down further, then opened into a large dell encloaked by trees. aul noticed steam. . . .

He couldn't see much, but he could see enough. A faint stench drifted up in the biting cold air. *Bags,* he realized.

A pit had been dug out of the dell, and the pit was full of large, stuffed, plastic garbage bags. And the two bags nearest the top . . . wafted steam.

Paul climbed down.

His fingers, like cold prongs of stone, tore open the uppermost bag.

Paul gazed down.

Focused.

Then gasped.

His feet took him briskly back up the narrow, tree-lined trail. His heart raced, and his eyes, even if he closed them, refused to release the image. . . .

The bag he'd torn open had been full of steaming human body parts.

GOING ... down ...

Chapter Thirty-three

Reality check, Vera, she implored herself.

After reading the occult text, she stood in check.

What was she thinking *now?* What could she possibly be considering? *Coincidence,* she determined at first. What else could it be?

All the things mentioned in the book she just read, certainly, were seriously coincidental. But . . .

Consciously, at least, she didn't think for a minute that any of it could be true.

Demons?

Satanic servitude?

Amethyst, the source of their power?

The only one that really bothered her was the reference to Magwyth, in ancient times, being executed upon a slab of—

Feldspar, she remembered.

Don't be ridiculous, Vera!

But the dreams she was having, every night nearly, somehow beckoned her.

She could not describe the impulse just then, nor any motivation she could fathom.

Nevertheless, her mind still ticking against her will, she pulled on her robe, paused another stifled moment, then . . .

She walked out of her bedroom.

* * *

Skinned skulls. Long arms and legbones clipped at the tendons of their muscle meat. Emptied ribcages and plundered abdominal vaults . . .

These were the steaming things Paul had glimpsed within the black-green plastic garbage bag.

Back up at the loading dock—or whatever it really was—he prepared to flee but then something flagged him. *What?* he thought. Initial impulse told him to get the fuck out of there, sprint back to the car, head on down the highway, and find the nearest state police barracks. After all, he knew what he saw.

Or did he?

Shock, sometimes, proved very elusive. He got to thinking. *Maybe it wasn't what it looked like,* he suggested to himself. *Come on—human body parts?* That seemed a bit far-fetched. The eyes were known to play tricks sometimes. *It must've been a trick,* he thought. Suddenly he felt convinced of this.

Or . . . did he?

The round maw of the sewer pipe seemed to call to him. The shirtless bald man, he remembered, had disappeared into it.

Where'd he go? Paul wondered.

Then a more stolid thought flashed in his head.

Vera's in there. Somewhere.

Vera . . .

I still love her, he realized.

And then, with no hesitation whatsoever, Paul Foster did the least logical thing he could do under the circumstances:

He entered the great pipe's entry and began to follow its dark, damp course up into the ridge, toward The Inn.

Instantly he felt drowning in moist darkness; the con-

340

course of the sewer pipe seemed like a spectral esophagus into which he was being swallowed. Just as he thought he could walk no more, due to the cloying dark, gobbets of light rasped his eye. He knew he was walking upward into the ridge. Eventually he detected the most diminutive illumination. *Light,* he thought. Yes, it was definitely light. . . .

Paul followed the light.

After what seemed a hundred yards through the bowels of the ridge, the round, cement concourse left him standing in a warm, wanly lit corridor. He heard the faintest humming, like machines far away.

He walked on, eyes flicking back and forth. *What if I get caught in here?* he wondered. *What will they do? Process trespassing charges?* He didn't much care, though. Some unbidden curiosity urged him on. Some query, some dementia.

He wasn't sure what it could be.

The corridor turned. Doors lined it, on either side. He peeked into one and saw something that looked almost like a cave: rough rock walls lit only by sputtering torches set into sconces. A large bed of pillows lay in the center of the cave-room.

But the room, other than that, was empty.

A dream, he thought when he looked into the next room.

Not men but *things* fornicating frenetically with two listless women tied down to a similar bed of pillows. Others stood round watching, an eager glint in impossibly huge eyes. A few of these watchers masturbated erections the size of rolling pins. . . .

Yes. It must be a dream.

It *had* to be.

In the next room a similar scene ensued, only some of the queer-looking spectators seemed to be engrossed with plates of food. Women, however, moaned in unison as still more figures with strangely warped heads steadily performed cunnilnigus. Inordinately large tongues, like pink snakes, delved without reluctance into the spread, moist fissures. One figure admitted an entire hand, while its glaze-eyed recipient tossed and turned in heady bliss. . . .

A dream, he thought a second time.

In the next room, a bald woman seemed to be cleaning up, placing large, smudged platters into a plastic bustray. Her pubis was as bald as her head, and large, pert breasts seemed erected on her chest.

There was something—

Something, he slowly thought.

—that seemed uneasily familiar.

Then she turned and looked at him. Recognition widened her eyes.

"Paul!" she acknowledged.

Paul's sight seemed to droop like warm putty.

"You," he croaked, and in the same instant of grim recognition he was grabbed from behind, by the throat.

The Inn felt dead, its long halls muted, vacant, and quiet as a crypt. Vera couldn't quite calculate what impression coaxed her on. It seemed to be a cluster of thoughts so swarmed together that none of them could be singularly deciphered. Down in the atrium the great fireplace exhaled dying heat from its pile of embers.

Her nightgown and robe shifting, she traipsed around the front reception desk. To her surprise, behind the back hall, one of the room-service elevator's yawned open when she pressed the UP button. Generally they were locked. She got in and went up.

Feldspar said The Inn was closed, she remembered, so she needn't worry about any guests popping up to spy the restaurant manager wandering about in her

342

nightgown. She got off on the third floor and found it immediately cold.

No, *very* cold.

What the goddamn hell? she wondered.

She peeked into each suite on the floor and discovered them to be not only empty but *barren*. No furniture, no carpet, no fixtures. And each suite felt as cold as the walk-in freezers downstairs.

Same thing on the fourth floor. Each suite empty, unfurnished, obviously never occupied.

Just like Feldspar's suite, she recalled.

Feldspar certainly had some explaining to do. What could he possibly say. Why were all the suites empty?

One thing was clear: despite The Inn's being open now for months, *no one* had ever rented these suites.

So where did the guests stay?

The elevator took her back down to the atrium.

She cut through the darkened restaurant to the kitchen, flicked on the overhead lights. The kitchen's long rows of stainless steel sparkled cleanly. Then, in another unbidden impulse, Vera approached the inner door to the room-service kitchen. *What are you doing, you idiot?* she asked herself. *That door's always locked—*

click

Vera's hand froze when she pulled back on the handle. The door was not locked.

How do you like that? Look's like Kyle's getting careless.

The room-service kitchen sparkled back similarly, a carbon copy of her own kitchen for The Carriage House, if not slightly larger and better equipped.

What am I doing here?

She had to admit, she had no idea. And just as she prepared to leave, she heard—

A distant, long drone, which seemed to be moving closer. And then—

A *thunk.*

Indeed, a familiar thunk, like the strange thunking she'd been hearing every night.

The room-service elevator, she realized.

But it couldn't be. For she was standing beside the room-service elevator right now.

It was dead silent, obviously not in use.

Then where'd that thunking come from?

Not the pantry—that would be impossible. Nonetheless, she pulled on the door's metal latch—

And found it locked.

Another impossibility. The hasp on the door hung open. No padlock. Which could only mean—

Locked from the inside?

There could be no other answer, which made no sense at all. How on earth could anyone get into the pantry if it was locked from the inside? And who could possibly unlock it?

Unless . . .

Shit! her thoughts shrieked. She heard a quick rattling now—from *behind* the pantry door. *This is crazy!* she thought, ducking madly behind the service line.

Someone was *in* the pantry. . . .

Squatting, she peeked over the stacks of gray bustrays beneath the cold line. Sure enough, the pantry door opened. Someone walked out, whistling some twangy C&W tune. Vera spied jean-clad legs and typical slip-resistant workboots. But from her low vantage point, she couldn't see who it was.

"Goddamn it," a voice muttered. "What a fuckin' mess."

Vera recognized the voice at once:

Kyle.

Next she heard a quick clang, as though Kyle were rummaging for a steel mixing bowl or carry-platter. Then the booted feet tracked back to the pantry. Vera

344

risked giving herself away when she raised her eyes over the top of the cold line and peered across the walkway. It was only a glimpse: Kyle carrying some pan-pots back into the pantry cove. Yes, it was definitely Kyle, all right.

With just one incongruety—

He's . . . bald, Vera dumbly realized.

Had he shaved his head? Had he been wearing a wig all this time? One or the other *had* to be true. But—*why?* Vera wondered.

And as he disappeared back into the pantry, he pulled the door to it behind him. Vera, finally, was in luck.

When the door closed, it didn't catch.

Wait, wait, she ordered herself from her squat. *Don't move. Don't get up yet. Wait and see if you hear the—*

th-thunk

Then: the motor drone.

She knew now before she even entered the pantry herself. There was an elevator in there—*another* elevator that no one knew about. She couldn't imagine a reason for this, but now she felt determined to find out.

She skirted in. As expected, at the end of the pantry stood a closed elevator door. Along the walls were shelves full of marinade buckets. A reach-in fridge lined the other wall, and through its glass doors she saw typical dinner preps in trays, kabobs, meat rolls, and lots of steaks, though she didn't recognize the cuts. She hadn't even been aware of this particular refrigerator, nor could she guess why it had been hidden in the pantry.

None of that, however, was the point. Right now only one thing interested her:

The elevator.

Vera, dressed only in a sheer nightgown and robe, approached the end of the pantry. The elevator's brushed-steel face returned a vague reflection. This was the elevator, she knew now, that she'd been hearing all along, running into the wee hours.

And whatever the reason, she was about to discover it.

Vera pushed the button.

The doors *thunked* open.

Then she got in and began to go . . . down.

The revel reared. Mist seemed to seep from the rock walls, shiny condensation trickled. A melee of aromas rose: spiced candlewax, musk, cooking smells . . .

Paul regained consciousness to discover a hideous woman sitting on his groin, fornicating with him. Her strange hand clamped just under his jaw, and Paul felt himself oozing in and out of sentience. Because of this semiconsciousness, he knew that his eyes deceived him, for the woman sitting on him scarcely even appeared human.

Gray, taut skin flecked with crust. Only patchy ribbons of frizzy black hair. Her sex, which now fully engulfed his erection, felt like a gnawing mouth, and her avid eyes looked huge and faintly yellowish. And her breasts . . .

Her breasts, though high and large and firm, shone gray beneath the sheen of musky sweat. Paul tried to focus up, to glean the details, but he couldn't quite believe it.

Blurred vision, he thought.

The woman's breasts sported multiple nipples. More nipples, puckered and blood-red, ran down her sides to her thighs. Eventually she leaned over, offering a breast to his mouth. Despite Paul's disgust, his lips sucked in the clustered nipple, and he could swear it voided milk, however foul. And when he could look up again, as the hideous woman stepped up her shrieking intercourse, he noticed one more thing—

What are . . . those things . . . on her head?

Even in the shifting dark he could make them out. The strange light made a silhouette of her large, runneled forehead. *My God,* Paul thought, *I'm gonna be sick—*

Small, rounded nubs seemed to jut from the forehead. Small, rounded nubs . . . like horns.

Vera's descent in the pantry elevator seemed greviously long, and the motor's hum was hypnotic. *Is it ever going to open?* she couldn't help but wonder. Down, down, down, it went. . . .

Then it jerked to a stop.

And, at last, opened.

Heat blew in. Vera looked forward and saw a rough stone wall. When she peered out she saw what looked to be a long aisle through a cave. *This is no basement,* she realized. She took a left and walked down, the hot air making her sweat. Crude doors had been fashioned along the corridor. And under their gaps, light flickered.

Vera stopped. She faced one wood-plank door.

She turned the brass knob and pushed it open. . . .

Candlelight danced in her eyes. She froze. What she saw she could not comprehend:

Monstrous figures copulating with several naked women tied down to a strange bed. Squirms, squeals, and shrieks roved the air.

More figures seemed to encircle the spectacle. Some were watching, some even masturbating. Others seemed to be . . .

Eating.

Vera backed out of the entry.

I'm dreaming again, she convinced herself. *It's just another nightmare, like all the others.*

Many more such doors lined the strange hallway. Would she find a similar scene behind these other doors? From the low chorus of shrieks and moans, Vera imagined so. She looked back into the first mist-filled den. A croaking sound augmented the roving moans, and a dark, clicking chuckle. The nude women writhed enfrenzied as their hideous suitors stepped up the pitch of fornication. Discolored, bony hips pummeled splayed white thighs. Maws like gouges in dark meat drooled copiously into the woman's open mouths.

"Hey, Vera! Come on in!"

Her eyes dared up. Through shifting, hot mist another figure turned from what appeared to be a sconce cut into the earthen wall. A male figure different from the others. Naked. Bald. And *human.*

Kyle.

"We knew it was only a matter of time before you found out," he commented, grinning. The amethyst pendant glittered in candlelight. The cocky grin widened. "But that's the way he wanted it. He likes you, Vera. He needs you."

He, she thought numbly. And at once the dreams came back, The Hands, the brutal sex, and the ecstacy.

The hideous face seen departing down the hall.

A face, she realized now, so similar to these.

"See anyone you recognize?"

Vera couldn't move. Instead she remained where she stood, gazing into the carnal den, one cheek pressed against the edge of the doorway. She felt helpless.

And, indeed, there was someone here she recognized. . . .

One of the women on the bed, who now locked her ankles behind her grotesque lover's back, heaved shrieks in response to her obvious climax.

Vera felt her heart shrink very quickly.

The woman was Donna.

Her mate grunted in its knobby throat, eventually withdrawing a penis that looked like a mold-ridden log and discharged streams of semen onto Donna's breasts. But at the same time, the thing—and that's all Vera could think of it as: not a man but *a thing*—strangled Donna with a leather strap. Donna, still in the throes of orgasm, convulsed wildly, her tongue bulging between her lips. The thing chortled, its hideous penis drooped. Donna's swollen face turned red, then blue. Then she died.

Kyle slapped his bare thigh, laughing. "Now that's what I call coming and going!"

Vera stared at him through the rank mist. This wasn't a dream, she knew that now. This—however mad, however impossible—was real.

Kyle turned back to his hidden task at the sconce. "Yeah, they're party animals, all right. Sometimes they get a little carried away. But that doesn't matter; we're here to serve them—"

Serve them, Vera thought, remembering the book.

"—and if they snuff a chick every now and then, well . . . shit happens, you know? We can always get plenty of girls. Me and Zy have been snatching them for months."

The other woman next to Donna looked unconscious or dead. Her breasts joggled frenetically as a similar consort copulated. And beyond the bed she still could see the band of primeval spectators, gorging themselves on mysterious food as their intent eyes watched on. Their faces looked like noxious masks of pulpy gray paraffin, sinuous muscles and tendons flexing beneath tight clay-colored skin. Their jaws worked obviously, munching hunks of food. Some of them sported preposterously large erections with veins stout as bloodsuckers. And some of them had what could only be horns jutting from their malformed foreheads.

One of them stood up as the thing that strangled Donna retreated.

They're . . . taking turns, Vera deduced.

"Come on in, Vera," Kyle repeated the offer. "We've got lots of great grub here, stuff like you've never seen or tasted. They're delicacies, Vera. Ambrosia. You can probably guess where the recipes come from."

Vera felt as though every joint and every muscle in her body had melted together, akin to welded metal.

"We've got a great steamed tripe—you know, chopped bowel, served with a wonderful remoulade sauce. Fantastic belly filets baked with my famous cashew crust and basil cream." Kyle, seriously enthusiastic, turned with a silver service tray in hand. "And if all that's a bit too rich for ya, try our crispy spring rolls. Of course, we don't wrap them in rice paper, we wrap them in skin. You'll also want to try our special of the day . . ." Another silver plate was offered. "Kyle's famous cherry-pepper and sesame brain purée. Great on baked toast points brushed with duck fat."

It was a kaleidoscopic madness that churned in Vera's head. She thought she might collapse, or throw up, or simply die.

Kyle chuckled, and ate one of the topped toast points. It crunched in his mouth. "Bet you can't guess where we get the brains."

The hellish paralysis broke. Vera moved away from the entry, prepared to turn, to leave, to run away as fast as she could—

"Hey, Vera! See anyone you recognize?"

Indeed she did, in that final glimpse. Kyle had raised two objects in the feeble light—

Two heads.

And despite the missing skullcaps, through which the

brains had obviously been evacuated, Vera easily recognized the *faces* on the severed heads. The accountant, Mr. Terrence Taylor. And Lawrence Mulligan, chief of the Waynesville Police Department.

Vera ran back down the hall, her cheeks bloated from disgust. And Kyle's raucous voice followed after her like a trailing banner:

"You're wasting your time, Vera! You'll never get out of here! You'll never get away . . ."

I'll get away, you asshole, Vera determined. The elevator opened immediately. She jumped in, punched the UP button, and the doors quickly thunked closed. At once she was rising. *Come on, come on!* The lift felt so slow now. All she had to do was get to the atrium and she could flee. She'd run down to the main road, and she'd keep running till she could flag a motorist. She wouldn't waste time going back to her room for her shoes or car keys. It wouldn't take the elevator long to go back down to that hellhole, admit Kyle, and bring him up after her—

Seconds seemed like grueling minutes.

Her heart was racing.

Then:

thunk!

The doors opened. She dashed out, scrambled through the pantry, then skidded on her bare feet around the corner of the service line. *I made it!* she celebrated. *Another ten seconds and I'm out!*

Kyle stood in the room-service entrance, arms crossed. He grinned. He'd redonned his jeans, one foot proverbially tapping as he waited for her. He began to whistle some truck-stop tune.

"How the *FUCK!*" Vera screamed.

351

Kyle shrugged. "There's another elevator at the other end of the hall."

"You *motherFUCKER!*"

"Hey, women have called me worse things, that's for sure."

Vera backed up inadvertantly, nudging the pantry door.

The door locked behind her.

Now there was only one way out: *through* Kyle.

"They're devils, Vera," Kyle said, and took a step. "They're demons. They're our brethern of our lord's earth—"

More bits and pieces of the book reassembled in her mind. But all she could think about actively was one thing: getting past Kyle. And there was only one feasible way to do that.

I'll have to kill him.

It was with a surprising confidence that the thought occurred to her. She scampered down along the aluminum-topped service line, past the ovens, ranges, and fryers, and stopped at the cutlery rack.

By now, Kyle's chuckle was all too familiar. "You can't kill me, Vera. Not like that. I'm not quite like you, you know? I'm not from around here." Then he laughed again, as if amused at her antics. His bald head shined like a chrome trailer hitch in the harsh fluorescent glare. *Hairless,* she thought, scrabbling toward the knives. *The book said Magwyth and his acolytes were hairless.* At the same time her hand slid a Sheffield #11 fileting knife out of its rack holder. She turned quickly. The exquisitely sharp knifepoint flashed like a finely cut diamond.

Kyle took a few more steps toward her, unafraid. "Don't do this, Vera," he pleaded. "I mean, I know we never really got along, but I always did like you. I'd hate to see something shitty happen."

"Fuck you, you evil, bald motherfucker!"

"Talk about a woman's wrath, moly holy—" Kyle paused, squinting, then shook his head. "Or is it holy moly? Shit, you'd think after all this time, I'd get my quips right."

Spittle flew as Vera screamed, "If you take just one more step so help me I'm gonna cut your bald head right off I swear to God!"

"Not much point in swearing to God here," Kyle suggested. Then he took another step. "It's funny how women always blow their lids, or flip their tops . . . or is it flip their lids? Whatever. But why don't you listen to reason before you going running around like a head without its chicken? Why don't you join us? You'll live forever, like me, like all of us. And let me tell you something—it is a *trip* to live forever."

Live forever, huh? Vera thought. *You're not gonna live another five seconds, you pompous dickbrain.*

And with that conclusion, Vera lunged forward, both hands firm about the Sheffield's polished wood handle. The 440 carbon-steel blade sunk at once into the pit of Kyle's sternum, and the sick grisly sound was music to Vera's ears.

She stepped back. The knife was sunk to its hilt.

Then Kyle smiled. He withdrew the knife from the bloodless wound and tossed it to the floor.

"No more Mr. Nice Guy," he said. "It looks like what you need is a serious adjustment in attitude, Vera. And I know just the ticket."

Kyle came forward, unbuckling his jeans. . . .

Paul was scrabbling, screaming—all to no use. *She's so strong!* he couldn't help but think during his struggle. He'd punched her in the face as hard as he could, kicked her, choked her, yet she didn't seem to notice at all. Instead, she tossed him around like a fluffy toy, dragged him about the strange cavelike room by his hair, and twice slapped him in the face so hard he vaulted through the air. *I am in some serious shit,* he groggily realized.

"It was all a setup, Paul," she said, now vising her hand under his throat and carrying him to the other side of the room. "But I guess you didn't know that, did you? No, of course not. He wanted your girlfriend, so that's why he sent me."

Stars burst before Paul's eyes. He didn't know what she was talking about, and really was in no shape to give it much thought.

"You shouldn't have come here," the bald woman said.

She dropped him onto the tuft of pillows.

"But I'm glad you did because I really liked fucking you that time in your apartment. What do you say we do it again?"

"Not tonight," Paul gasped. "I—I've got a headache . . ."

Yes, this was her, all right, this was the redhead who'd drugged him, seduced him, and ruined him. Minus the red hair, of course, which he now logically assumed was a wig, though he couldn't fathom why. In fact, he couldn't fathom much of anything just then, not while he was getting his ass royally *kicked* by this woman.

She crawled right up on top of him, her downcast grin like an evil beacon. Her flawless body slithered in its perfection; she was like a cat: nimble, quick, deliberate. A moment later, she was sitting right on his face.

"I'm the Zyramon," she said, "Zyra for short. And you really were a great lay, probably the best hum-job I've had in a couple of hundred years. And you're gonna do it again, Paul. I gotta have it."

Paul's stomach churned with his terror. She'd planted her bald pubis directly against his mouth, the large clitoris protruding like a teat. And that gave Paul an idea. . . .

Bite it! he thought. *Bite it right off!*

"And don't get any ideas about biting me, Paul," she said a split second later. Then she placed her thumb over his left eyeball. " 'Cos if you do, if you bite me, I will sink my thumb right through your eye into your brain. You wouldn't want me to do that, would you?"

"Uh . . . no," Paul mumbled. "No, I would not."

"Excellent. So just be a good little boy now. And suck."

Paul sucked. What else could he do? He'd already experienced the woman's extraordinary strength, and her thumb against his eye remained a convincing reminder of what would happen to him if he resisted. Paul's unwilling tongue roved; she tasted like sharp brine, she tasted like a real woman, and this he could see too, with his other eye: the sleek, curvaceous shape, the hourglass middle, the large high-riding breasts centered with big dark distended nipples. Yes, she was all woman. . . .

But—

Paul remembered something else, vaguely in the most distant recess of his brain, from that night. . . .

"Oh, Paul, that's *so* good," she slurred. "I-I-I think I'm gonna have to . . ."

She slid her sex off his lips. Her right thumb stayed pressed against his eye, while she rubbed the large pink bud of her clitoris with her left index finger. Her body tremored in waves.

"Do you remember, Paul?" she whispered. "Sure you do. I'm the Zyramon, I'm one of his most special concubines . . . I'm synoecious, Paul. Do you know what that means?"

Paul gasped in a musky breath.

"I'm an hermaphrodite, and I have a big surprise for you . . ."

Paul watched in his daze, her soft milk-white thighs still clamping his cheeks. Her finger continued to tend to her clitoris, and soon she herself began to gasp. And then—

You've gotta be shitting me. . . .

Something began to emerge from the fissure of her vagina. Very slowly yet very clearly, he realized what was coming out of the place of her womanhood:

An erect penis.

And a very large one at that.

"Okay, Paul. You've already sucked my pussy, now you're going to suck my cock." She added a bit of pressure to her thumb over his eye. Then she inserted the tumescent penis into his mouth.

Paul began to fellate her. *I'm sucking a woman's dick,* came the insane awareness. He tried to do the best he could but . . . he couldn't help but shudder. . . .

"Goddamn it!" she yelled above him. "You're not doing it right! Do it *right!*"

Paul gave it the All-American try but this was no easy thing, since he'd never sucked cock before, much less a woman's. He gagged repeatedly as the swollen glans slid against the back of his throat. One thing he noticed, though, with his free eye, was the sharp purple glint. . . .

What is that?

A well-cut purple stone had been sunk into her navel. *An amethyst,* he realized.

And then he remembered the much larger amethyst he'd seen mounted in the transom of The Inn's front door. . . .

"You little peon piece of shit!" she yelled. "Can't even suck cock, I should've known." She withdrew her penis, then pinched his lips together hard. "What's the matter, is little Paulie nervous, hmm?" she suggested

356

in a chastising tone. "Little Paulie too scared to suck a good dick like a good little boy?"

Paul exhaled long and hard when she got off him. Into the dim candlelight, she was walking away. *Keep walking,* he thought, traumatized, exhausted. But he wouldn't be so lucky. Before he could even try to muster the energy to rise, the bald woman returned, bearing a bottle of wine. "Remember that blow, Paulie?" she said, standing with one beautiful hip cocked. Of course, the image of that hip lost some of its beauty considering the nearly foot-long erect penis which bobbed betwixt her legs. "You know, the blow? Shit, you probably snorted a pound of it that night—"

The cocaine, he remembered. Or whatever it was . . .

"Well, let's just say that it comes from a very special place, and we use it a lot around here. We spike all our booze with it. It makes people a little more willing to—you know—*do things.*"

That shit I was snorting, he remembered, the strange brownish-white powder that made him crazy. The stuff she'd no doubt also put in his beer.

"You're gonna drink this, Paulie," she told him. "It'll make you lighten up. Then you'll give me a *good* blow job before I fuck you in the ass."

This was not good news. Paul moaned as she approached the bed and uncorked the bottle. Her erection bobbed along with her breasts. Then she leaned over and prepared to dump the wine into his mouth.

Paul lurched forward, more unconsciously than anything else. He didn't even know what he was going to do, but one thing he knew he *wasn't* going to do was give this woman any more head.

He collided into her abdomen, surprising her enough to actually jar the bottle from her hand, which hit the earthen floor and broke. Paul's face bulled into her belly,

357

his mouth opened, and he bit down hard on whatever was there—

The woman screamed.

When she fell away, Paul discovered that he'd bitten out the oval of soft flesh around her navel. And with it . . . the amethyst.

Paul spat the stone, and the little ring of flesh, out onto the floor.

Then the woman did the strangest thing.

Instead of coming for Paul, she dove howling for the amethyst. This Paul didn't know what to make of. She'd already easily demonstrated her superior strength, yet without the amethyst in her navel, she seemed desperate with fear. She began to crawl across the floor, toward the lightless corner where he'd spit the stone. And as she did so . . .

What the fuck is happening now? he thought in dismay.

She began to change. . . .

As she crawled forward, her sleek body darkened, shuddering. Her joints seemed to expand, and so did her head and hands and feet. Hip bones and shoulder blades protruded, the skin between her ribs turned gray and sucked in. Her terrified howls turned inhuman, and Paul could see why.

Because she *wasn't* human, not anymore.

Taloned, long-fingered hands padded at the dark corner, searching hungrily for the amethyst that Paul's teeth had divorced her from. By now her skull looked warped, with a long fissured forehead. And horns.

Strike when the iron's hot, he reasoned.

Beside the bed lay a tray of sadomasochistic instruments: knives, thumbscrews and nipple-clamps, and long, long needles. Paul stuck one of the needles into the thing's back, about where the kidneys might be. She screamed like a machine, faltering. Then he inserted

358

several more needles in a random pattern about her back. She convulsed, wailing like an animal on fire, and collapsed onto her belly.

Hmmm, Paul thought. *This looks like it has some possibilities.*

Then he picked up the heavy stone tray on which the torture instruments had been lain. He hefted it in his hand, raised it up—

"Here's some head for ya," he remarked.

—and brought it down on top of her head. The head burst, splattering a plume of black brain mush across the earthen floor.

"There. Blow *yourself.*"

The corpse began to fizz, as if effervescent. In only moments it seemed to dissolve to a crackling discolored fluid which, in turn, was then absorbed into the floor.

And in one more moment:

Gone, he observed.

Nothing at all remained of her. Nothing.

He was not sorry to see her go. So much amassed in his mind, however, that he couldn't even contemplate what he was in the midst of. *I'm crazy, that's all,* he thought. *I've gone insane.* That was some consolation, at least.

At the far end of the hallway, he found an elevator which took him up to a normal, paneled hallway. Around the corner, he found himself standing in a spectacular hotel atrium. *This is it. This is The Inn.* But where was Vera? He didn't even know where to begin looking, but given the hour, he suspected she'd be asleep. A banistered staircase swept up to the next floor; Paul noted a tiny plaque: EMPLOYEE SUITES. *If she's here, this is where she must be.* But a glance down the wing showed him a dozen doors. Which one was hers? He couldn't very well just barge into each room and wake people up, could he? Then he laughed at the absurd reservation.

Why should I give a shit if I wake people up? I can do anything I want—I'm insane. Jesus Christ, I just killed a female demon with a penis and I'm worrying about being polite? It made sense. Each suite he stepped into, however, was untenanted. He peered through closets and bathrooms, hoping to recognize something of Vera's. And in one of the suites farther down—*Eureka!* he thought—he spotted her purse, and her name and face on the enclosed driver's license verified what he needed to know. *She's here, but . . . where?*

The big four-poster bed lay unmade, yet all else appeared in order. Why would she have gotten up this late? Where could she have gone? It was going on four in the morning.

Then he noticed the book.

It lay opened amid rumpled covers.

Holy shit, he thought when he began reading the text.

"Yeah. Attitude adjustment. That's just what little, pretty Vera needs, I'd say."

Kyle, then, quickly grabbed a shock of her hair and dragged her to the rubber-matted kitchen floor. He'd lowered his jeans, and though flaccid for the moment, his penis hung at his groin like a slack summer sausage. Vera squealed at his fist's grip on her hair hauled her immediately to the floor. Tears blurred her eyes. He slapped her once so hard in the face, her consciousness reeled.

"You're such a bad little *bitch,*" he whispered to her, lowering his jeans further. "I could get in trouble for doing this, but . . . but . . ."

His open palm cracked her across the face again—

"—but I think I really do love you. And now I'm going to show you, Vera." He jerked up her robe and nightgown, baring her raw hips. "If you think Feldspar

360

was good, well . . . you don't know what good is till you've had a good, hard fucking from me.''

In her terror, though, Vera managed to ponder, *Feldspar?*

Kyle, now grotesquely erect, pried apart her thighs. The glans looked as large as a billiard ball, throbbing on the end of a veined shaft more stout than a stair prop.

If he sticks that thing in me, Vera thought, *I'll throw up and just die. . . .*

"It's only because I love you," he whispered some more. "You'll understand. We'll keep it a secret, okay?''

Vera's face felt pinched shut.

Kyle's open palm cracked her against the other cheek. *"Okay?''* he whispered.

She'd never felt so helpless. She felt a thousand times worse than every other woman in history who'd been raped, because she was about to be raped by something far different from a man. . . .

"I'm gonna come in you, Vera. I'm gonna make a baby in you . . .''

Just let me die. . . .

And if she had the means to kill herself, she knew she would. She'd lay open her throat without hesitance. She'd jump from a one-hundred-story window. She'd gulp down gasoline. Anything—

Anything to prevent this.

Kyle's impressive pectorals flexed above her. The amethyst pendant swayed. He slapped her once more in the face, this time so hard she blacked out for a moment.

"Baby? Baby? I know you like it, that's the only reason I do it. I'm gonna make love to you now. I'm gonna make you come—''

At the same moment, though, he . . . shrieked. High and hard like he'd just been gelded. A stubby hand reached around and snapped off the amethyst pendant. Two stubby fingers sunk into Kyle's eyes, like fingers

361

sinking into bowling-ball holes—and then Kyle's shriek hitched up to a full, chest-heaving scream. He was lifted off her. One stout hand bent his head back while another hand stuck the end of the big, antique pistol into Kyle's ear, and—

Ba-BAM!

The pistol-shot's concussion made Vera's ears ring. At once she was speckled by dots of black ichor. Kyle's body collapsed to the matted floor. More black gruel slid out of the ruptured skull.

"The amethyst," she was told by a high, articulate voice. "It's a gift from our lord, our safeguard. And it protects the underlings from all physical harm. But without it . . ." A leather-thonged foot kicked Kyle's broken pendant across the floor. "They are as mortal as you are."

Vera feebly tried to wipe Kyle's strange blood off her face. Her saviour, whose own face she still could not see from the harsh backlight of the overhead fluorescents, continued in something of a remorseful tone: "The Kyl-Lemi served well, but he was becoming unreliable. He's back now, from whence he came."

A sizzling, like bacon frying in a pan way too hot, crackled in Vera's ears. What had been Kyle's corpse only a moment ago was quickly reverting to bubbling black slime before her eyes. Soon it evaporated altogether.

"Questions now? Of course. I will answer them all."

Vera slid up to her feet against the service line. She could see now, the features of the man who'd saved her from Kyle. The short figure wore not the typical fine, custom-made garments but a mere sackcloth frock. He was completely bald and bereft now of the neatly trimmed goatee she'd always known him to wear. Yet despite all this, his identity was undisputable.

"Feldspar," Vera whispered.

His words seemed to nod in the air. "Yes. But you may call me by my real name. You may call me Prince Magwyth."

Chapter Thirty-four

"It's all relative, Ms. Abbot. It's all the same in a way, isn't it? Think about that."

Flecks of gore began to dry on Vera's face as she numbly stared back at Feldspar.

"We're all servants, are we not?" he suggested. "You are, I am, only to different degrees. All of life is experience, as they say. The same applies to infinity."

In silence, Vera's eyes darted about for a weapon. Feldspar had set the big revolver beside one of the Jenn-Air ranges, far out of her reach, and just as out of reach now as the cutlery rack. But what could she be thinking of anyway? She'd seen how useless the knife had been on Kyle; certainly it would be even less effective on Feldspar, who was obviously the core of power in this place.

Unless—

His amethyst, she reckoned.

She remembered what she'd read in the book, that amethyst was their protection. And Kyle had been destroyed only *after* Feldspar had removed the amethyst pendant. And . . .

Feldspar wears one too. In fact he always had, since the first night she'd seen him.

And that same amethyst sparkled at her now from the ornate pinky ring on Feldspar's hand. . . .

"Kyle said I was set up," she told him. She needed to divert him, she needed to keep him talking and distracted. "How?"

"I should think it would be obvious to you by this point," Feldspar replied. "I *needed* someone very badly to run the restaurant, and when I found out about you, I knew that you were the one. I also knew you'd be reluctant to leave your fiancé, so I simply made certain arrangements."

Vera's eyes thinned. "What kind of . . . arrangements?"

Feldspar smiled, as if at a naive toddler. "I instructed the Zyramon, via her own sense of creativity, to effect a situation that would *induce* you to leave your lover."

"The Zyramon," Vera repeated dreamily. She'd read about this person in the book. "It said she was a—"

"She's a synoec, a hermaphrodite. The beautiful woman with red hair? Surely you've not forgotten your encounter with *her*. I believe she engaged the services of a particularly seamy prostitute to lend assistance. They drugged your beloved fiancé, seduced him, and made sure that you would have the opportunity to bear witness."

Vera's mind seemed to swim suddenly in obscure, dark clouds. *Paul wasn't lying. It was all true. . . .*

"A fine ploy that proved to be quite effective, wouldn't you say, Ms. Abbot? But I had no choice. You were the one, and I was determined to have you regardless of the means." Feldspar's brazen bald head shined like a shellacked orb. "And as for the matter of finances, I should also think that that, too, would by now be more than apparent. Our—shall we say—enterprise has access to unlimited financial resources. And I suspect you can guess from whence these resources originate."

Vera felt sick, her mind still aswarm in the tarn of confusions and impossibilities. . . .

"And we have access to far more resources than mere financial ones," Feldspar went on, unconsciously eyeing his amethyst ring. "Power, protection, knowledge. And an array of intricacies."

"Intricacies?"

"Coercions, instigations, influences," he defined. "Your dreams provide a sound example."

Merely the word—*dream*—set her mind off yet again. What would Feldspar know of her dreams, her fantasies? *The Hands,* she grimly remembered. And the lewd nightmare that always followed. The faceless night-suitor violating her in ways she'd never imagined. . . .

"It was me," Feldspar said.

Her glare turned to stone.

"I'm very . . . fond of you, Ms. Abbot," he confessed. "I've always been. Our lord purveys certain provisions—certain elixers, emulsions, and ointments—which serve our needs well, which make people exceedingly desirous. We enhance things with it, our liquor, our food, massage oils, etc."

This revelation unreeled in her head like a roll of ribbon tossed off a precipice. *Drugs,* she realized. Like the drugs that hideous redhead had spiked Paul's drinks with. *Feldspar put the same drugs in my drinks.* Drugs which made her confuse reality with fantasy, which made her *want* things she'd never really wanted: rape, sadism, masochism. And when she thought back further, it made even more sense. The only nights she hadn't had the fantasy of The Hands were nights she hadn't drunk any of the Grand Marnier Feldspar had given her, or taken a bath with the lavish bath oils. And the night Kyle had given her the back rub at the pool—*He used massage oil.* . . .

So they'd drugged her, to be more responsive. None of it had been a dream at all. Every night Feldspar had been secreting into her room, to rape her. . . .

"And I know what you may be thinking," the squat, frocked man went on. "But it was all bound to one very important consideration."

"What!" she spat.

"I love you."

Her rage roiled, but she knew she mustn't show it. She must not let herself break. She needed to think, didn't she? She needed to calculate—

The sick motherfucker . . .

—a way to destroy him.

And the cutlery rack wasn't *that* far away.

She knew what she must do. . . .

Keep talking, keep distracting him.

"And The Inn itself," she said. "I don't understand. None of it makes sense. All the money you pumped into the place and it seemed from the start that you *wanted* it to fail."

"Of course I did," he answered. "We needed a sufficient cover."

"A *cover?* What are you talking about?"

"We needed camouflage. A fine restaurant backed by a lucrative holding company provided that. But we couldn't have it become too successful, could we? We couldn't have too many people coming here. After all, they might take note of our *real* services. You do know, Ms. Abbot, why we're really here, don't you?"

Again she remembered the book. Magwyth. Servant of Demons. Banished to earth as penance, to provide gluttonies for Satan's hirelings.

"Yes," she said. "I do."

"Then likewise you can see our need to do things the way we did. The Inn needed to provide a legitimate, expensive restaurant. Yet on the other hand it *had* to fail, to keep out an influx of local residents. No one makes queries when the bills are paid and the books are in order, Ms. Abbot. We chose The Inn's remote location

367

deliberately, for the same reason. And as for The Inn's checkered past, the same reason too."

Now Vera understood. "And you chose *me,* a legitimate restaurant manager, to cover for you without even knowing it."

"That's . . . correct, Ms. Abbot," Feldspar admitted. "And I hope you will forgive me. In time, I'm *sure* that you will, when you fully realize what I can offer you ultimately."

Vera sneered. "And what's that?"

"Eons, Ms. Abbot. I can offer you eons. We're both alike, you and I. We are both servants, in a sense." His eyes pricked into her. "Love me, Vera, and serve with me. And I will give you anything you've ever wanted and a million times more. Forever."

She knew what he was implying, the same thing he'd so discreetly implied all along. She knew there was only one way out:

"All right," she said.

The shiny face peered back at her, skeptically hopeful. Was he actually shaking, he was so nervous?

"Do you think—" he faltered. "Do you think you could love me?"

"Yes," she said.

He expression blanked. "Then prove it."

Vera approached him, willingly, and with desire. She didn't flinch at all when she noted a white marinade bucket on the cold line—a marinate bucket containing Dan B.'s head.

"Make me immortal and I'll love you forever," she whispered, and with that confession she wrapped her arms around Feldspar and kissed him on the mouth—an *eternal* mouth, a mouth which had reveled in the utterance of blasphemies for a thousand years. She *kissed* that mouth with all the voracity and passion that she'd ever kissed anyone in her life. . . .

368

Feldspar returned the kiss. He began to weep.

"Make love to me," she whispered. "Just like you did all those other nights. Here. Right here."

Vera sat upon the service line, and with no hesitation whatever she pulled up her nightgown to bare her sex.

"Now," she breathed.

Feldspar, teary-eyed and in bliss, stepped up between her spread thighs. He placed one hand down, and with the other began to unsash his frock. Between the sackcloth divide, his erection sprouted: a pale and hideous tuber with dark blue veins, pulsing upward.

Vera spread her legs further, to offer herself as fully as any woman could. . . .

"My love," he whispered and closed his eyes.

Instantaneously her hand snapped up, plucked the shiny rib cleaver from the cutlery rack and brought it down on Feldspar's hand, which remained opened on the wood butcher block beside the range—

chunk!

His scream sounded disappointingly *human,* and when he raised his hand, backing away, Vera saw with great satisfaction that three of his fingers remained on the butcher block, his ring finger among them, the finger that sported the big, faceted amethyst. . . .

She swung the cleaver in a lateral arc. It's bright blade sunk inches into Feldspar's stout neck, releasing a spray of brackish, black blood. He howled further, shuddering.

And with all her might, Vera brought the cleaver down with both hands—

swack!

—into the center of his bald forehead.

He teetered back, arms reeling. The cleaver's formidable blade had bitten into Feldspar's brain no less than three inches, the great cranial fissure oozing the midnight blood.

Then he collapsed.

Vera squealed. *I did it! I did it! I—*

Then her squeals of victory corroded.

Feldspar got up.

The look on his halved face was not one of rage or betrayal or anger. It was a look of wounding, or heartfelt *hurt.*

He removed the cleaver from his head and tossed it aside. Then, his other hand—the hand whose fingers Vera had so expertly chopped off—he turned over and looked at.

She'd separated him from his power, from the amethyst, and had buried a Sheffield meat cleaver into his head to boot, but he didn't even seem to care.

"Kyle was just an acolyte, a weakling," Feldspar said with a vast sadness in his voice. "My power here—my fortitude—comes from a far greater source."

Vera screamed, a reasonable thing to do under these newfound circumstances. Feldspar's good hand snapped to her throat. He raised her up fully off her feet, then threw her down. Her head smacked the tile floor, her vision churned, then darkened. She knew she was passing out.

And she also knew what was going to happen next.

Just . . . let me . . . die first. . . .

He hauled up her gown, spat on her sex. His hand clamped again to her throat as he bared himself. "I'm afraid I'm going to have to kill you now, Ms. Abbot. But first . . ."

The bulbed, nearly white end of the thing nudged her sex, began to enter. . . .

"NOOOOOOOOOOOOOOOOOO!" he bellowed.

Perhaps Vera really was dying, or maybe she was hallucinating. But in the furthest recess of what remained of her consciousness, she thought she heard something.

It reminded her of a dream-sound, a reverberation from a nightmare:

chink! chink! chink!

What was it?

Feldspar struggled shambling to his feet, his eyes for some reason so large that they appeared to be on the brink of launching from their sockets. His face contorted, and his ears—

Vera, in her daze, squinted.

There's blood coming out of his ears. . . .

chink! chink! chink!

With each *chink!* Feldspar seemed to buckle. Still issuing the maleficent howl, he staggered out of the kitchen. . . .

To the atrium, Vera deduced.

She crawled at first, then managed to rise to her bare feet. She blundered out of the kitchen, into the black restaurant, each succeeding *chink!* goading her on.

When he made it to the atrium, she knew she'd been right.

The Inn's grand front doors stood open.

chink! chink! chink!

Vera eventually made it to the floodlit front cul-de-sac. And what she saw was this:

Feldspar shuddering, on his knees . . .

And a silhouetted figure wielding what appeared to be a sledgehammer up at the front door's transom . . .

Vera felt drunk, insane, and unreal all at the same time.

She recognized the hammer-wielding figure. . . .

"Paul!" she shrieked.

chink! chink! chink!

"NOOOOOOOOOOOOOOOOOOOOOOOOOOO!"

Feldspar screamed louder.

And Vera screamed again herself: "Paul!"

He held the sledge at its downswing, sweating, maniacal, ugly. His hair was sticking up, and he grimaced at her, then shouted in reply: "Get out of here!"

"But—Paul! I—"

"GET THE FUCK OUT, GODDAMN IT! GET *OUT!*"

Tears flowed, her throat swelled shut—

chink! chink! chink!

Vera gulped, swallowed tears—

"GET THE GODDAMN FUCKING HELL OUT OF HERE, GODDAMN YOU!" Paul shouted one last time. Then:

chink! chink! chink!

Vera turned around, went back into The Inn, and began to run. . . .

Chapter Thirty-five

chink! chink! chink!

"How do you like that shit, you bald fuck!"

Paul felt high he was so charged up. Who knew what would happen, but what did that matter? At least he'd get his digs in. . . .

He swung the long, hickory-handled sledgehammer ever upward at The Inn's ornate granite transom—

chink! chink! chink!

—bringing its butt, steel face as hard as he could against the inordinately large amethyst set into the stone mount.

Feldspar remained whimpering on his knees at the entry.

Then, finally:

chink! chink! chink-CLACK!

The amethyst popped out of the transom mount and clacked to the second step of The Inn's front stairs.

"Magwyth, huh?" Paul cackled. He raised the sledge high. "Well you can stick your bald head between your legs and kiss your ass good-bye—"

"Don't . . . be . . . hasty, Paul . . ."

"Why?" Paul snapped. "I know all about you now, and all I gotta do is bust this big rock and you're out of here."

Feldspar composed himself, managed to rise to his feet. He donned the sackcloth hood, and spoke like an incantation. "Why not, first, consider your options? If you destroy the fount of my protection, I'll still kill you. Or . . . you can desist. And join me."

"Fuck you," Paul replied.

"You can join me forever, Paul." Feldspar's eyes seemed to widen in circumference, something beneath them reaching out. . . . "Forever, Paul. Some of us are born to serve—"

Magwyth, Paul remembered from the book. *Servant of Demons.*

"—and those who *I* serve are immortal." The stolid stare focused, sharpening to an awl-like glint.

Paul felt adrift.

"Be immortal with me, Paul. I will show you *wonders.*"

Paul froze, the sledgehammer poised. At his feet lay the amethyst, large as a goose egg, its purple facets sparkling. All he need do—

Immortality, came an intruding thought.

All he need do—

Live . . . a voice seemed to whisper . . . *forever* . . .

Paul blinked. "I said it before and I'll say it again. FUCK YOU!"

Feldspar howled.

Paul brought the sledgehammer down so hard he nearly came off his feet.

The amethyst shattered. . . .

Feldspar fell to hands and knees, roaring. He seemed to be convulsing within the muck-brown frock, while his endless bellow buffeted high into the night.

Finish him off! Paul's instincts shouted back.

He dashed up the steps, took a deep breath, and again raised the heavy sledge. Then he brought it *down*—

From somewhere a hideous chuckle rumbled. Feldspar's hand snapped up, caught the sledgehammer just under its head . . .

Then he rose back to his feet.

The sledge was jerked away and flung into the trees. The awful, black chuckling rose.

And Paul was left to stand staring into the face of the *real* Feldspar.

The *real* Magwyth, Servant of Demons . . .

All the accesses, she knew, were barred now. Vera scrambled across the silent atrium, then back into the kitchen. *The elevator!* she remembered. *In the pantry!*

From the basement she knew she could escape out the back, through the long bogus sewer pipe that emptied out behind The Inn.

Her heart beat insanely fast. She sprinted back through the RS kitchen, barged into the pantry, and pressed the DOWN button on the elevator plate.

Then she heard the screams.

God Almighty . . .

They were human screams, she realized. They were—

The elevator doors thunked open.

—Paul's screams . . .

It was as if she suddenly had fallen into a trance. Vera backed away from the elevator; the doors reclosed without her. She turned and, almost calmly, went back into the kitchen.

She stood a moment, looking around amid the harsh overhead light. *There it is,* she thought, and then she leaned over to—

Paul's horror locked him down in rigor. The thing that Magwyth had turned into seemed to unhinge its jaw. Breath like corpse-pit gas gusted from the stretched maw

375

lined with rows of needle teeth. A slick, sinewy hand clamped his throat, as the maw stretched open further to admit the entirety of Paul's face. . . .

—pick up the big revolver Feldspar had killed Kyle with. The old gun felt heavy as a brick in Vera's hand, and it was still warm. From outside, Paul's screams rose to a fever-pitch.

Vera hefted the revolver. Then she—

Its eyes had transformed into huge spherical nuggets the color of sick urine. Its nostrils were but rimmed pits. And as the abysmal maw descended, eddying chuckles, Paul could see the nublike horns protruding from the twisted, grayish forehead. . . .

—sprinted through the restaurant, crossed the atrium, and strode to the foyer. She gazed out onto the front stoop before the floodlit courtyard. Saw the big amethyst crushed to dust. And saw—

I'm dead, Paul thought stoically. If the taloned hand's grip on his throat didn't kill him, certainly the jagged maw's saw-rows of teeth would. It's going to bite my face off. But first, and worse, was the thing's tongue, which then reeled from the trapdoor mouth. Not a tongue but a cluster of fleshy, wet tendrils, akin to tentacles, each blood-red tip moving independently to lick his face, squirm under his lips, and shudder down his throat. . . .

* * *

—not Feldspar but some demented *thing* straddling Paul. *It's going to kill him,* she thought very methodically, *and then me.*

Unless—

Then the tongues rejoined, a mass of convulsing flesh, and shot fully down his throat. They were so long . . . Paul could feel them writhing now in the pit of his stomach. . . .

—what she'd read in the book was all true. They were immortal, they could not be killed unless the energy of their protection—the amethyst—was diffused. Kyle had died at the hands of Feldspar, but only *after* his pendant had been stripped of him. But did the same vulnerability apply to Feldspar himself?

She raised the gun.

"Paul!" she shouted—

"Paul!" came the shout. The thing's spread mouth backed away just as it was about to close to slough all the flesh off Paul's face, much like eating the icing off the top of a cupcake. The taloned hand lifted off his throat, and the primeval face then turned to look back at the source of the shout. . . .

—and then nearly fainted at the sight of the face which turned to look at her . . .

The face of Magwyth . . .

The angled, pointed cheekbones, the huge yellow eyes, and the sprout of tentacles roving enfrenzied from the slitlike lips.

The face in her dreams . . .

Vera squeezed her eyes shut as she squeezed the revolver's cold, clunky trigger—

Ba-BAM!

Paul's eyes locked open. A mammoth sound cracked in his ears, then a CRACK!, then a titanic wet SPLAT! The thing's warped head exploded.

The heavy pistol fell from Vera's hand. Hot and sooty smoke stung her eyes. Her ears rang.

A plume of vomit-colored slush vaulted out of the thing's head. Some of the pulp shot so far it landed in the heated fountain in the center of the cul-de-sac.

The figure shuddered. . . .

Then it fell over limp to Paul's side.

And dissolved to nothingness.

Epilogue

Her head lay in his lap as he drove.

The Lamborghini's gears screamed, its engine revving at alternate pitches. The tires hypnotically hummed.

As the sleek car sucked down into each drastic veer and turn, she could feel her innards shift against the inertia.

Neither of them would speak for days, and why should they? What good were words? What on earth could they say?

A gibbous moon broke through the low clouds. Its yellow face followed them out and away. . . .

As he drove, Paul slipped his right hand between her breasts, to feel her there, to feel her heart beating.

Feel the Seduction of
Pinnacle Horror

HORROR FROM PINNACLE . . .